The Weekenders

Mary Kay Andrews

St. Martin's Griffin
New York

This is a work of fiction. All of the characters, organizations, and events portrayed in this novel are either products of the author's imagination or are used fictitiously.

www.stmartins.com

The Library of Congress has cataloged the hardcover edition as follows:

Names: Andrews, Mary Kay, 1954– author.
Title: The weekenders / Mary Kay Andrews.
Description: First edition. | New York, N.Y. : St. Martin's Press, 2016.
Identifiers: LCCN 2016009101| ISBN 9781250065940 (hardcover) |
ISBN 9781250109729 (Canadian edition) | ISBN 9781250107060 (signed edition) |
ISBN 9781466872929 (e-book)
Subjects: | BISAC: FICTION / Contemporary Women.
Classification: LCC PS3570.R587 W44 2016b | DDC 813/.54—dc23
LC record available at https://lccn.loc.gov/2016009101

ISBN 978-1-250-06596-4 (trade paperback)

First St. Martin's Griffin Edition: May 2017

10 9 8 7 6 5 4 3 2 1

Praise for *The Weekenders*

"Andrews's novels, such as *Save the Date* and *Beach Town,* are the epitome of relaxing yet involving summer reads, and her latest is no exception.... Andrews blends romance, intrigue, and soap-opera-like twists in this entertaining novel about a gossipy beach town." —*Booklist*

"As her fans can already attest, Andrews has this 'perfect beach read' label down pat—and then some. *The Weekenders* is not just good, it is beyond good.... Summer doesn't truly begin without a Mary Kay Andrews book in your beach bag." —*RT Book Reviews* (Top Pick, 4½ stars)

"One of the many books you'll want to keep in your beach bag this season."
—*POPSUGAR*

"Atlanta's prolific chick-lit queen returns to her roots as a mystery author with this frothy tale of divorce, shady real-estate deals, and murder.... Venturing into plots a tad darker than usual, Andrews still finds room for humor, romance, and zany characters worth spending a weekend with."
—*The Atlanta Journal-Constitution*

"The bestselling author, who has been called the 'Beach Read Queen,' marks summer's start with a mystery set on quaint Belle Isle, North Carolina."
—*Star-Telegram* (Fort Worth)

"Fun and frothy... Think sun, sand, romance, drama, and a fine sheen of witty commentary." —AARP.org

"Fast-forward to summer with this breezy mystery." —RealSimple.com

"This book has all the makings of a beach read.... The perfect blend of drama, humor, intrigue, and just a touch of murder." —*Bustle*

"There is no doubt that this will be the hit of summer 2016 as Mary Kay Andrews has outdone herself once again and produced her best novel to date... a wonderful mix of drama, mystery, Southern life, rich characters, and love—a page-turner that won't last a long weekend!"
—*The Book Report Network*

ALSO BY MARY KAY ANDREWS

The Beach House Cookbook

Beach Town

Save the Date

Christmas Bliss

Ladies' Night

Spring Fever

Summer Rental

The Fixer Upper

Deep Dish

Savannah Breeze

Blue Christmas

Hissy Fit

Little Bitty Lies

Savannah Blues

For Beth Fleishman,
with a heart full of love and gratitude

Acknowledgments

Writing a novel can truly be a long day's journey into night, but the following folks lit up my days and illuminated the path by sharing their knowledge, wisdom, talents, and in some cases, their homes, with me.

To Dick and Jane Hansen of Atlanta, many thanks for allowing me to spend time in their beautiful home on Baldhead Island, North Carolina. Baldhead is NOT Belle Isle, but my fictional Belle Isle was certainly inspired by the beauty of Baldhead.

To Beth Fleishman, my sister from another mister, I must offer hugs and thanks for becoming both navigator, copilot, and all-around font of information yet again. Thanks, too, to Beth's husband, Richard Boyette, for additional help with legal research, and to Sharon Stokes for more of the same.

To Billy Howard and Laurie Shook, who allowed me invaluable writing sanctuary at their Sky High Cottage in the mountains near Highlands, North Carolina, thanks.

Kay Flowers Johnson gave me insight into the world of broadcast journalism. Anne Ksionzyk told me about parenting a child (or two!) with juvenile diabetes. The Rev. Patricia Templeton of St. Barnabas Episcopal Church in Atlanta advised on funeral protocol and scripture.

It's been fifteen years since I last committed (fictional) homicide, so when it came time to return to my mysterious roots, my Weymouth Seven sisters were invaluable in helping me get away with murder. As always, thanks to Margaret Maron, Bren Witchger, Alex Sokoloff, Diane Chamberlain, Sarah Shaber, and Katy Munger for their friendship, advice, and support.

Speaking of support, the talented, meticulous, and yes, paranoid-but-in-a-good-way Susan Goggins of Atlanta came to my rescue (again) to help with brainstorming and copy editing, and I will be forever in her debt.

I've been so blessed in my career to work with such an amazing team of publishing professionals. Stuart Krichevsky proved, once again, to be the best damn agent in the world, and the folks at SKLA, including Ross Harris, and David Gore always have my back. Thanks, guys!

I can't remember NOT having the always awesome Meghan Walker of Tandem Literary (aka Jersey Meg) on Team MKA. Here's hoping for many more launch day spray tans and massages.

And oh, the St. Martin's Press team at the Flatiron Building, how grateful I am for all you do for me and my books! Thank you, Sally Richardson. Thankyouthankyouthankyou, Jennifer Enderlin, for never giving up on me and always making my books better than I believed they could be. Thank you, Mike Storrings, for another enticing book jacket (and a new author photo that doesn't make me look like a real estate agent). Thank you, Tracy Guest, for giving me Jessica Lawrence, a dream of a publicist. Thank you, Brant Janeway and Karen Masnica, Jeff Dodes, Anne-Marie Talberg, Caitlin Dareff, and everybody at Macmillan Audio and Macmillan Library.

I owe my many loyal long-time readers a huge debt—for allowing me to pursue my lifelong dream of writing for a living. I promise, I never take you for granted. Thanks, y'all.

I may thank my family last, but I hope they know they always come first in my heart. Especially my starter husband, Tom Trocheck, who became first reader, sous chef, fire-maker, furniture builder, and research assistant this time—literally with one arm tied behind his back. Thanks, too, to the very able Katie Trocheck Abel and her crew, along with Andy Trocheck. I am nothing without my family's unending love and support.

The Weekenders

1

Wendell Griggs was big on promises. Always had been. On their first date, he'd promised Riley Nolan she'd never want to date anybody else. When he'd presented her with her engagement ring—a three-carat diamond bigger than any of her girlfriends had—he'd promised it was the start of a life that would be big and rich and exciting. No doubt about it, her husband was a dreamer. And a schemer.

But lately, Wendell's promises meant nothing. Just talk. Hollow words meant to placate or stall. Nothing more. What was it her grandfather used to say?

"All hat, no cattle."

Like today. Wendell had promised—sworn—he'd meet them at the ferry dock at Southpoint in time to make the last boat over to Belle Isle.

It was Memorial Day weekend, a tradition they'd established even before they'd gotten married, kicking off the season on the island where Riley's family had summered for the past hundred years.

And yet, here she stood. She brushed a stray lock of dark brown hair from her eyes and squinted down at the screen of her smartphone. Still nothing.

Her fingertips raced over the keys.

WHERE R U?

All caps. It was the texting equivalent of screaming. And that's how she felt, like screaming.

The late afternoon sun shimmered off the water's surface, and the light breeze whipping the surface of the river carried the faint scent of honeysuckle. It was the prettiest day in weeks, but Riley Nolan Griggs was oblivious to all of that.

She glanced again in the direction of the parking lot, willing his car to appear. The black Jeep CJ. *What a stupid car for a grown man.* Vehicles were streaming into the lot now, station wagons, big SUVs, all of them carrying people intent on making the last ferry of the day. All of them with the distinctive oval BI sticker connoting membership in the tribe of Belle Isle. Vehicles pulled to the curb in front of the ferry terminal to unload everything needed for another summer on the island. Passengers spilled from the cars, lugging coolers, wheeled suitcases, bicycles, leashed dogs, and fishing gear. Deckhands, most of them deeply tanned college boys in navy blue BI-logo golf shirts and baggy cargo shorts, scurried around the baggage area, loading all the freight into aluminum carts that would be rolled onto the ferry.

Women greeted each other with that peculiar high-pitched Southern squeal of delight. "Heeeeyyy!" *What did Wendell call it? Oh, yes.* "The mating call of the ivory-breasted Tri-Delt."

It was six thirty. The boat would leave at seven on the dot. He knew that, knew how crazy it made her when he cut things this close. But there was no sign of the black Jeep. She checked to make sure she hadn't missed a call, and checked her e-mail too, but there was still no word from him.

Selfish bastard. He was doing this to torture her, she was sure. Waiting until the last possible minute to make an appearance. She could already picture the moment. He'd stroll across the pavement, just as the *Carolina Queen* was blasting the "last call" horn, maybe make a quick dash before the deckhands pulled up the metal gangplank.

Her face reddened, her stomach twisted, and she felt the familiar acid taste in her mouth.

He'd promised. Sworn to her he would make the last ferry today, no matter what. Most importantly, he'd sworn it to Maggy. Even with things as crappy as they were between them, he didn't usually break a promise to their daughter.

"Heeeeyyyy, Riley!"

She turned. The woman was bearing down on her with laser-like intensity. She wore a pink-and-lime-green cotton Lilly Pulitzer shift and pink Jack Rogers sandals. Riley, trapped, managed a weak greeting in return.

"Oh, hey, Andrea."

"It's so great to see you!" Andrea Payne gushed. "You look terrific. I swear, I wish I had your metabolism. Have you lost a ton of weight over the winter?"

Without waiting for a reply, Andrea wrapped her slender arms around Riley's neck and hugged her close. Too close. Riley was already tense and overheated, and the last thing she needed right now was a volley of nosy questions.

Riley managed to subtly loosen herself from Andrea's grasp. She took a step backward.

Andrea turned to her companion. "Melody, doesn't Riley look fantastic?"

Andrea's friend Melody Zimmerman dutifully nodded her head in agreement. "Fantastic." She gestured at the handbag slung casually across Riley's shoulder. "Is that a Michael Kors? OMG, I love it so much."

"Um, maybe," Riley said, glancing at her bag. It was an oversize leather number in trendy turquoise, with a large, dangling gold-monogram charm that Riley secretly found just the tiniest bit gaudy. But she knew the gift had been expensive, and besides, it did hold a lot of stuff. "I mean, I'm not sure. Wendell gave it to me for my birthday last year."

"It's adorbs!" Andrea pronounced. "Are y'all going to the full-moon party tonight? Is Maggy here, or did she decide to do summer camp this year? Where's Wendell?"

Riley deliberately sidestepped the issue of Wendell's whereabouts. "I haven't really been dieting. Maybe just eating healthy. And yes, Maggy's here. For now, anyway." She looked around for an escape route and conveniently spotted her daughter weighted down with tote bags and a backpack, struggling to keep Mr. Banks, their unruly pug puppy, under control.

"Maggy, hold on. I'm coming!" Riley called out. "We'll catch up later, ladies."

"You and Wendell *have* to come over for drinks, before the party," Andrea burbled. "Right, Melody?"

"Absolutely!" Melody agreed, bobbing her head.

"I can't wait for you to see my new kitchen tonight," Andrea said.

"OMG—she got an eight-burner Wolf range," Melody said. "And a Sub-Zero fridge. It's my dream kitchen!"

"Oh geez," Riley said, looking in the direction of the parking lot. "Sounds great. But I really need to go give Maggy a hand with that crazy dog of hers."

Andrea tapped Riley's arm. "So, I won't take no for an answer. You're coming for drinks. Right?"

"We'd love to."

"Said nobody, ever," Riley muttered under her breath. She hurried away from the ferry dock, the soles of her rubber flip-flops slapping against the furnace-hot asphalt.

"Maggy!"

Her daughter had come to a dead stop in the middle of the parking lot and was tapping furiously on her cell phone, oblivious to the oncoming stream of cars, her mother, and Banks, who was squatting down on one of the carefully manicured landscape islands, amidst the grass and pink Knock Out roses, doing what puppies liked to do.

"Maggy! Don't let him . . ."

But it was too late. Banks finished his toilette and came scampering toward his mistress, his plump little body wriggling with happiness and relief.

Now Maggy looked up. "Huh?"

Riley picked up the pair of overstuffed totes and nudged her daughter out of the path of a looming white Mercedes SUV. "Sweetie, pay attention! While you were busy Snapchatting with your girlfriends just now, you nearly got run down. And Banks managed to drop a deuce on those rosebushes over there." Riley rummaged around among the groceries in the tote bag until she found a roll of paper towels. She tore off a sheet and handed it to her twelve-year-old daughter.

Maggy recoiled. "Gross. No way."

Riley took her daughter's hand, deftly removed the phone, and replaced it with a paper towel. "Way. He's your dog. Your responsibility. Your poop. Now go clean it up before somebody rats us out and we get issued a littering citation."

Maggy rolled her eyes but handed the dog's leash to her mother before stomping off in the direction of the landscaped island.

Riley was struck by how much her daughter had grown over the past year. Micro short shorts showed off Maggy's long, tanned legs, and the tank top that left bare a two-inch strip of her abdomen also revealed a modestly developing bustline. She'd let her taffy-colored hair grow out over the spring, and although she wore it now in carelessly fashioned pigtails, Maggy was already starting to raid Riley's bathroom for her expensive salon shampoo, conditioner, and styling products.

No more sweet-smelling baby shampoo for Maggy. No more baby anything, for that matter, Riley thought ruefully. In October, Maggy would officially be a teenager.

Despite the heat, a shiver ran down Riley's spine. Banks pressed his muzzle between Riley's sweaty calves. She absentmindedly scratched the dog's ears and glanced down at her daughter's phone.

It was the latest model iPhone, of course, ensconced in a neon purple case with a florid monogram on the back, and the screen was littered with a dizzying array of unfamiliar app icons. Riley's own phone was at least two years old. She'd told Wendell it was ridiculous to buy such an expensive cell for a kid who'd already managed to lose two phones in one year, but Wendell, being Wendell, had overruled Riley's objections.

"I want her to have a good phone. What if her blood sugar gets low? Or she needs to get in contact with me?"

Maggy's diagnosis earlier in the year with juvenile onset type 1 diabetes had thrown them both for a loop.

Riley remembered that particular "discussion" with crystal clarity. She'd stared back at Wendell, startled by what she was suddenly seeing.

Her husband had changed in the past two years. His thick black hair was streaked with silver. He'd started wearing it longer, letting it brush his shirt collar. He'd stopped wearing the business suits she'd always enjoyed picking out for him, instead buying his own skinny designer jeans and Armani designer shirts. His blue eyes, made brighter by new contact lenses, narrowed.

"What if *I* need to get in contact with you?" Riley asked.

"What's that supposed to mean?" Wendell demanded. "Are you going to start in on this again? I call you every night. I talk to Maggy every morning. I'm working, Riley. I'm trying to save Belle Isle. Trying to make a living for my family. For *us.* You think I want to work all these crazy hours? Think I don't miss spending time with my kid?"

Snippets of those tense conversations over the past year played in an endless loop in Riley's mind.

Maggy was back. "Hey! No snooping." She snatched the phone out of Riley's hand.

"I wasn't snooping," Riley said. "Who were you Snapchatting with?"

"Nobody."

Riley raised one eyebrow.

"Okay," she relented. "I was texting Daddy, letting him know we're here at the ferry dock."

"Did he text you back?"

"Not yet," Maggy admitted. "But the ferry doesn't leave for another twenty minutes. He'll be here."

Riley squeezed her daughter's narrow shoulder. "I wouldn't get your hopes up. You know how busy he's been. He'll probably have to catch the morning boat."

"He's coming tonight," Maggy insisted. "He promised. For the full moon party."

"I just don't want you to be disappointed if he doesn't make it. . . ."

But Maggy wasn't listening. "Parrish!"

The leggy redhead in a white tank top and black capri pants darted across the parking lot toward them, teetering dangerously atop stylish, red, alligator-skin, three-inch, cork-soled, platform sandals.

Maggy flung herself into Parrish's outstretched arms. "You dyed your hair! I love, love, love it!"

"Thank Gawd somebody does," Parrish drawled. "Your uncle Ed detests it. He says I look like a hoochie mama."

She grinned at her best friend over the top of the child's head. "What's your verdict?"

Riley lifted a lock of hair and considered. "It's different."

"Always the diplomat," Parrish said, laughing. "Tell the truth. You hate it, too."

They started to make their way back toward the ferry dock, arm in arm, with Maggy and Banks bringing up the rear.

"No, really. It's cute. You just took me by surprise, that's all," Riley said. "This is definitely not a hoochie-mama shade. I think it suits you. What made you decide to go red?"

"No special reason. I was bored with being blond."

"You're the only woman I know who could get tired of being a blond bombshell."

"More like a cherry bomb than a bombshell," Parrish corrected. "Hey. I spotted you chatting with Belle Isle Barbie when I pulled into the lot. What did your new best friend want?"

Riley didn't want her daughter to overhear the two of them dishing up a serving of snark on Andrea Payne.

"Mags, it's too hot out here on the asphalt for Mr. Banks. Why don't you take him over to the shade of the loading area and pour some cool water into his bowl? It's in that tote with the blue handles."

"Okay."

Parrish watched the girl and her dog lope toward the dock. "My Lord. She's grown another inch just since I saw her at Grayton on Easter. And did she just now sprout boobs, or is that my imagination?"

"She's growing like a weed and already wearing an A-cup bra, although she'd kill me if she knew I'd told you that. She's so self-conscious about her body right now. I think she's going to take after Wendell's side of the family."

"Let's hope she's not a hundred-percent Griggs," Parrish said, rolling her eyes. "How's that going, by the way? Is Wendell coming, or do you think he'll be a total no-show?"

"He promised both me and his daughter that he'd be on the ferry with us this afternoon. But so far, no sign of him. He hasn't returned any of our calls or texts or e-mails. Not even Maggy's, which isn't like him."

"He'd never break a promise to Maggy," Parrish agreed. "But to his wife? Different story. Right?"

Riley wiped a bead of sweat from her brow. "All too true."

"Typical passive-aggressive bullshit. He doesn't want to be the one to break his kid's heart."

2

"Shitheel," Parrish said. She shook her head. "I know. You don't have to remind me. It's all my fault, right?"

Riley shrugged. "If you hadn't made me go to that stupid barbecue . . ."

It was the summer of '97. Riley was working as a reporter for the local CBS affiliate in Raleigh, living in a tiny, bug-infested garage apartment in Cameron Park, while Parrish had gotten a job clerking at a local law firm.

After a messy breakup with her senior-year boyfriend and a series of laughable one-night stands and blind dates, Riley had sworn off men—at least for the summer. But Parrish had insisted on dragging Riley to a law-firm party at the managing partner's country house.

At first, Riley had flatly refused to go. "No way," she'd told Parrish. "No offense, but your work friends are either boring, stuck-up, or ancient. I'd rather stay home and give myself a facial."

"This party is different," Parrish said. "It's a pig-picking, and it's at Boomer Grayson's farm. He's having a bluegrass band play, and besides, it definitely won't be all lawyers. Boomer's son, Bryan, played shortstop at Wake Forest and he even played a season in the minor leagues for the Boston Red Sox farm team until he hurt his throwing arm. He's moved back home and is in his third year of med school at Duke. So there'll be plenty of hunky baseball players and hot doctor types. You gotta come!"

"Why do you need me?" Riley had asked, her suspicions aroused by Parrish's insistence. "Why not save all the hunky medics and jocks for yourself?"

"Okay, well, I might have a little crush on Bryan. But I don't want to go to the farm for the weekend by myself, because that would look too obvious."

"So I'm your wingwoman?" asked Riley.

"You got it."

"I'll go. But you're driving, and if you take off with this guy to go play doctor and leave me alone with a bunch of boring lawyers, I'll never speak to you again."

Despite Riley's threats, Parrish had totally snuck off with the jock-doc almost the moment they'd arrived at the pig-picking.

But the band was great and, left to her own devices, Riley found herself drawn into a circle of partygoers clustered around the fire, tapping her toes to "Little Liza Jane."

He'd materialized by her side, seemingly from nowhere. Tall, preppy looking, singing along to all the verses. He was sunburnt, which made his blue eyes look bluer, sipping on a red Solo cup of what he swore was moonshine.

"I say we name our first kid Little Liza Jane. That okay with you?"

She'd turned to this brash stranger and frowned. "What if it's a boy?"

He had an easy answer, of course. "Liza James?"

His breath on her cheek was warm and boozy.

"Do I know you?" she'd asked, amused.

"Not yet. My name's Wendell Griggs, but I already know yours," he confided, leaning in. "You're Riley Nolan."

"And how do you know me?" Riley asked.

"I see you every night on channel nine," he replied. "You're the girl who did all the stories about that puppy mill over in Kinston, right?"

"Well, I'm not on every night. More like once or twice a week. But, yeah, I did the puppy mill stories."

"I actually went over to the Humane Society and tried to adopt one of those beagle puppies, but the shelter wouldn't approve me because I live in a condo without a yard."

"Those little guys were soooo cute. I just wanted to scoop one up and run away with him," Riley confided. "But, let me tell you, beagle puppies are *loud*! And my landlady doesn't allow pets. Anyway, I'm gone all day, so I guess it doesn't make sense for me to have a dog right now. But someday . . ."

"I know, right? We always had black Labs growing up. I can't wait to get a real house with a yard so I can get another Lab."

A little while later, after some more pleasant chatter—and a lot more moonshine—Wendell had a sheepish look on his face. "We have something else besides puppies in common," he admitted. "I actually work for your dad."

"No! You work for Belle Isle Enterprises? How come we've never met?"

"I just started working as a leasing agent for the new retail shopping village a couple of weeks ago. I'm mostly working in the Wilmington office right now."

Wendell had been so easy to talk to in the beginning, so charming. So much fun. He'd been interested in everything. They'd stayed talking by the bonfire that night until finally Parrish had emerged from the shadows, hand in hand with Bryan Grayson, her hair mussed and her clothes askew, sometime around 3 a.m.

Early Saturday morning, Riley had gotten called back to the station to fill in for an ailing reporter, but somehow, Wendell had finagled her phone number from Parrish, who'd stayed over for the rest of the weekend.

He'd called that Monday, and she hadn't bothered to call back. Then he called again the next day, and the day after that, had a huge bouquet of sunflowers delivered to her at the station, with a note that read, *You Are the Sunshine of My Life.*

Tamika, the noon anchor, had read the note over Riley's shoulder and given her nod of approval. "A dude who sends something besides roses? And quotes Stevie Wonder? That's a dude worth keeping."

It didn't take long for Wendell's charm—and persistence—to erode Riley's resolve to take a hiatus from dating.

But it had been her father who'd swayed her opinion on the matter.

Although her parents always spent the summers on Belle Isle, her father had made a special trip to Raleigh on a weekday, called her ahead of time, and invited her to lunch at the Carolina Country Club, an unusual move for him.

"I understand Wendell Griggs has been trying to wangle a date with you," her father had said, sipping on his usual pre-lunch scotch and water. "He claims you've shut him down every time."

"He told you that?" Riley blushed.

"He casually mentioned that you'd met at a party, and that he was very taken with you," W.R. said. "I guess he was just trying to figure out why you won't go out with him."

"Casually. Right," Riley said, her voice dripping with sarcasm. "Okay, I'll tell you what I told him. I'm not dating anybody right now. I'm concentrating on my career."

"Your career," W.R. scoffed, putting the phrase in finger quotes. "Covering the Miss Carolina tobacco pageant and cow-milking contests."

"I'm the newbie at the station right now. They always give rookies the crap assignments," Riley said. "But that story I did on the puppy mills got picked up by *The News and Observer* and by the wire service. And I'm working on a piece about the county foster-care system."

"Good for you," W.R. said, nodding his head. "But I still don't see why you shouldn't have a little fun on your own time. Wendell Griggs is a nice guy. A real go-getter. Your mother likes him, too."

"What is this?" Riley asked, half-amused and half-annoyed. "You and Mom are now taking votes on who I should date?"

W.R. tipped his glass and emptied it. "And why not? Who knows you better than your own parents?"

"Forget it," Riley said flatly. "Sorry, Daddy, but I am not currently in the market for a boyfriend. And when I am in the market, I doubt I'd choose a guy like Wendell Griggs."

W.R. had sighed and shook his head, then signaled the waiter for the lunch ticket, which he'd signed with a flourish. "That's what your mother said you'd say. But I had to try."

The next time Wendell Griggs called, for reasons she still couldn't remember, Riley had finally said yes.

He took her to dinner at the most expensive restaurant in Raleigh, insisted on ordering champagne, and afterward, as he walked her to the door of her garage apartment, he'd given her a chaste kiss on the cheek.

Which had come as a surprise to Riley, considering how hotly he'd pursued her.

She'd been intrigued, enough to say yes when he'd called the next night to ask her out for the coming weekend.

Things were not nearly as innocent that night. And the following week, he'd insisted she move out of what he referred to as her "roach motel" and in with him. Two months later, he'd surprised her with the most magnificent diamond she'd ever seen. A diamond so big it took Riley's breath away.

Wendell Griggs, Riley quickly learned, was all about the grand gesture.

It took several years before she realized that her husband wasn't quite as attentive when it came to the nagging little details of daily life.

3

"So, what's happening between you two now?" Parrish asked as they walked toward the dock.

She'd known for months and months that things weren't good between her best friend and husband, and Wendell's conspicuous absence during their traditional spring break trip to the Florida panhandle had only confirmed her suspicions that the marriage was doomed. But up until now Riley had been typically tight-lipped about her marital status, saying only that they'd been going to couples therapy.

She'd known something was off the minute she'd set eyes on her. Riley had lost weight—at least twenty pounds. Riley was still beautiful—she had the kind of effortless good looks that money couldn't buy—but today her jaw was set in a rigid line, and fine new worry lines radiated from her eyes and chin.

"Separation. And a divorce, I guess," Riley said, keeping her voice low as they approached the throng of people gathered near the departure ramp. The ferry was tied alongside the dock now, its big diesel engines thrumming.

"Oh, God," Parrish moaned. "I had a feeling, but still. Things are really that bad, huh?"

Riley nodded, then glanced down at her watch and frowned. Ten minutes until boarding time.

She looked around to be sure they wouldn't be overheard.

"I put the house on the market two weeks ago. And it's under contract."

Parrish's eyes widened. "Riles! You always loved that house! What does Wendell have to say about that?"

"What can he say? He's been trying to keep up this crazy façade, but despite what he says, I know things aren't going well with the business. I think he's overextended but, of course, he denies that. Anyway, it's ridiculous for us to live in an eight-thousand-square-foot house, even if we aren't splitting up."

"That's a pretty drastic change. How is Maggy handling everything?"

"She's sad about it, naturally. She grew up in that house. I've told her we're moving to be closer to her new school, which is true, partly. I've found a new place, with a yard for the puppy."

"And the puppy was a consolation prize, for having to give up her house—and her dad?"

Riley's smile was tight. "Yes, that's about the size of it."

"And Maggy has no idea—about the divorce?"

"If she knows, she's keeping up a good front. Wendell's clothes and things are still at the house, but he's almost never there. Typical of him, he doesn't want to be the bad guy, doesn't want to break his daughter's heart by just admitting that the marriage is over. The plan was that we'd tell Maggy *together*—this weekend. And you see how that's working out. No sign of him. He just assumes I'll do all the dirty work by myself."

"Forgive me for pointing out the obvious, but he's such a selfish douche-canoe," Parrish said. "I know how hard you tried to make it work, but sometimes, it's just time to admit you're licked. Have you talked to a lawyer?"

Riley sighed. "Not yet, and that's another thing I'm dreading. The property settlement process is going to be brutal. Belle Isle Enterprises is *my* family's business, of course, but Dad himself anointed Wendell as CEO. . . ."

"And, knowing you, there's no prenup, right?"

Riley gave a rueful smile. "Right."

"You're right. It will be a nightmare. But Ed will know who you should call. There's a woman who does divorce law whom I like a lot... Susan, something. I can't remember her name. She's got the face of an angel and the soul of a pit bull–piranha hybrid."

"She sounds terrifying."

"That's the general idea, dear. You want a divorce lawyer who'll make the other side's testicles shrink just at the mention of her name. I just remembered her last name. Simpson. Sue Simpson."

"Speaking of Ed, he's coming this weekend, right?"

"Yoo-hoo! Parrish!" Andrea Payne had spotted the two women and was waving her arms frantically to draw their attention.

"Oh God," Parrish said under her breath. "Belle Isle Barbie. Hide me."

"Too late. Houdini couldn't hide from that woman."

"What's she want? Besides my soul, I mean?"

"She wants to invite you over for drinks before the full moon party tonight. And to see her new kitchen. Now, what about Ed? Don't tell me he's a no-show, too."

"He took the first ferry over yesterday so he could start opening up the house for the season."

"Ed's such a love," Riley said. "We've been summering on Belle Isle for nearly twenty years together, but do you think it ever occurred to Wendell Griggs to help me get the house opened up? Never! He's just like my dad that way. He thinks magic elves show up to take down the storm shutters, sweep up all the dead bugs, air out the house, drag the lawn chairs out of storage, and get the golf cart batteries charged up."

"Ed's just feeling guilty. He didn't help close the house down at all in November and, except for spring break when we were with you at Grayton Beach, he's been mostly AWOL for the past six months.

"Lots of trials?"

Parrish nodded. "That big plane crash in the Alps, plus there was a corporate jet that went down in the Maldives last year that got hardly any press. People die in a plane, Ed Godchaux is the man to call."

Riley gave Parrish a sideways glance. There was a bitter undertone to her best friend's glib patter that hadn't been there before.

Parrish spied her next-door neighbor across the deck. "I'll be right back," she said, and hustled off in that direction.

The ferry's horn sounded—loud and low. It was the five-minute warning. The metal gangplank clanged against the concrete dock, and arriving passengers began trickling off the boat while the crowd of departures edged closer. Memorial Day was about to start.

"Mom!" Maggy appeared at her side, her face reddened and tearstained.

Riley looked backward over her shoulder. No black Jeep. No Wendell. Another broken promise.

Before Riley could find words to comfort her daughter, Maggy was suddenly lifted into the air by a pair of hairy, tanned arms encircling her waist.

"Saggy, baggy, Maggy, why you lookin' kinda draggy?" he sang—in perfect pitch.

The girl's tears were instantly forgotten.

"Bebo!" She thumped her uncle's chest.

"Magpie! Why the tears?"

Banks sat on his haunches and gave a bark of happiness at the sight of the newcomer.

Billy Nolan had that effect on people. He'd been an irresistible imp as a child, and had grown into an adorable adult. He was irresponsible, drank too much, and played too hard. He was a wildly talented and totally unmotivated jazz pianist who worked only when it suited him, which was rarely.

And Riley Nolan Griggs doted on her baby brother, her only brother.

She hugged Billy now and whispered in his ear. "Wendell's a no-show, and Maggy's heartbroken."

"I'll kill the bastard if you want me to," Billy whispered back.

"Deal," Riley agreed.

"How shall I do it?"

Riley watched while the ferry's motors churned the surface of the river as it backed away from the dock. There was still no sign of the black Jeep. "I don't care, as long as it's slow and painful."

They stood against the railing on the lower deck, watching as the mainland retreated. Billy had one arm loosely draped around his sister's shoulder and the other around his niece.

"What are you now, fifteen, sixteen?" he asked, tapping the top of Maggy's head. "All of a sudden, you're three inches taller than me."

"I'm almost thirteen, as if you didn't know it. And, no offense, but everybody's taller than you, Bebo," Maggy retorted.

"True that," Billy agreed. "I'm that tragic cliché—a short, sassy, gay man. Doomed to spend my life shopping in the boys' department at J. Crew."

"How come you're so tan?" Riley asked, studying her brother's face. His dark hair was close-cropped, and his hazel eyes looked almost green against his deeply bronzed skin. He wore a blue-and-white-striped boat-necked T-shirt tucked into white jeans with rolled-up cuffs and immaculate white espadrilles. "Has it been that nice in New York?"

"I wouldn't know," Billy said. "I got summoned down here by Mama two weeks ago and I've been at her beck and call ever since."

"You two are speaking again?" Riley lifted an eyebrow in surprise.

"Oh, sure. She sent out all the living room furniture to get recovered and refinished back in the fall, and she needed a stooge to pick it up and haul it back over to the island and rearrange it at Shutters. So all is forgiven. Until next time. I take it she's not currently on speaking terms with you?"

"Nope," Riley said. She cut her eyes meaningfully in Maggy's direction, a clear sister signal that she did not want to discuss family drama in front of her daughter.

"Count your blessings," Billy said. "Hey, Saggy Maggy. Does your forehand still suck, or did you get some coaching since I played you last?"

Maggy shrugged. "I'm not so into tennis. It's boring."

"Tennis is boring? Since when?"

"I've started running. I want to try out for the cross-country team, but Mom doesn't want me to." Maggy stuck her tongue out at her mother.

"I'm worried that her blood sugar could get low on one of those long runs and something . . . could happen," Riley said.

Billy ruffled Maggy's hair. "Boring or not, you'll still be my mixed-doubles partner this summer, right? Remember how we killed 'em in the round-robin last Memorial Day weekend?"

"I left my racquet at home," Maggy said, her face still sullen.

"I packed both our racquets," Riley said.

Riley and Billy made their way up to the ferry's observation deck, stopping to greet and chat with island neighbors they hadn't seen in months. Finally they reached their destination.

Riley leaned against the railing and inhaled deeply—this, she thought, might be her favorite summer perfume—diesel fumes mixed with salt spray with top notes of sunscreen and popcorn. Seagulls wheeled and cried overhead in the dusk and, on the horizon, a line of pelicans flying in V-formation raced westward.

As the ferry dock and the mainland slipped away, she felt the anxiety and frustrations of the past few months doing the same. Her shoulders loosened, her face relaxed, her heart rate slowed. She closed her eyes, tilted her head back, and let the dying sunshine wash over her face, the way she'd always done since she was a little girl.

One way or another, this weekend, she would have to find a way to tell Maggy about the impending divorce. If she had to do it solo, so be it. Things were about to get really, really ugly. But for right now, she promised herself, she would live in this moment.

Besides, being on the island, her island, her special place, would make things better. She and Maggy would burrow in here for the summer, weather the storm of divorce, and when the season ended, they would be healed.

Riley found herself crossing and uncrossing her fingers, praying it would be so.

"Where's Scott?" Riley asked finally, opening her eyes after she was sure the last speck of land had disappeared.

"Who knows? Atlanta? Vegas? One of those television chefs is opening three new restaurants this summer, and he's been driving Scott crazy. One day he hates the dining room chandeliers in Atlanta, the next day he wants Scott to rip up the brand-new carpet in the Vegas dining room. The money's fabulous, but the travel is killing him."

Riley nodded sympathetically. Billy's partner, Scott Moriatakis, was a much-in-demand restaurant designer whose work took him around the world. They'd met years earlier, when Scott was called in to redecorate the dining room of an Art Deco hotel in South Beach, Miami, where Billy was the lounge act.

Billy loved to tell people, "Scott pitched out everything in the joint. But he kept me."

"But he's coming this weekend, right?"

"Maybe. Did you know he's been talking to Wendell's hotel people about Pirate's Point? They flew him down here in the corporate jet the first week in April so he could walk the property with the architect."

Riley felt her jaw clench. "Wendell told me the deal was dead."

"Whoops. Maybe I got it wrong."

"No," she said, shaking her head. "Wendell knows I'm dead set against anybody putting anything on that land. This is just his latest stunt."

"Here comes Parrish," Billy said, looking over Riley's shoulder. "With red hair, yet. Yikes!"

"Billy the Kid!" Parrish cried, embracing him warmly. "What's with the George Hamilton tan? Don't tell me. I'll bet you and Scott have been cavorting in the Hamptons."

Parrish looked around the deck. "Where did Maggy get to?"

"She was going to the snack bar for a drink, but that was twenty minutes ago," Riley said, standing. "I'm just gonna go check to make sure she's okay."

"Hellooo, helicopter mom! You're hovering again," Parrish said in a singsong voice.

Riley shot her a dirty look over her shoulder and made her way down the stairs to the concession stand on the main deck.

The ferry's main cabin was a simple affair. A large room with wooden benches lining the outer walls, and rows of booths lining the middle of the cabin. A concession stand on one wall sold coffee, soft drinks, sandwiches, snacks and, in the summertime, beer and wine.

Every bench and booth was full, and the space buzzed with excited conversation from weekenders catching up after a winter away.

She spotted Maggy sitting in a booth with a group of kids, preteens all, whom she recognized from previous summers. A smartphone sat in the center of the table blaring loud, raunchy rap lyrics.

As Riley watched, an older man approached the table, tapped the tallest boy on the shoulder, and then pointed at the phone—signaling that the boy should turn down the volume. He did so.

"Thanks," the man said. "Some of us don't enjoy that kind of music."

But as soon as he stepped away, the tall kid smirked and returned the volume to its previous level, provoking a round of giggles from his admiring circle of friends. As though sensing her mother's presence in the vicinity, Maggy glanced over her shoulder, saw Riley, then quickly looked away.

"Hey!" the older man called angrily from his table, about to stand up.

The kid turned down the music, to another chorus of giggles. The other passengers watched, shaking their collective heads in disapproval of this blatant infraction of unspoken ferry etiquette. Riley moved toward the table, intent on extricating her child from the midst of the troublemakers.

Now the music was blaring again, and the lyrics were so obscene, Riley could feel the heat gathering in her cheeks.

As she approached the table, a younger man strode across the cabin. In three long steps he was there. His hand darted out and plucked the phone from the table. A second later, all was quiet again.

"What the hell?" The kid's voice was sharp. "That's my phone, man."

"Was your phone."

"No, man, it's mine. Give it back." The kid stood and stuck out his hand, expectantly. Now that he stood, Riley recognized him. Shane Billingsley was beanpole skinny, and the early stages of teenaged acne had ravaged his cheeks and chin. He was two years older than Maggy, and the oldest of Craig and Gynn Billingsley's five kids.

Riley didn't recognize the man who'd confiscated the phone because the bill of his baseball cap obscured his face, but she felt like applauding him.

Now he put the phone in the pocket of his shorts and addressed its owner in a low, terse voice that Riley couldn't quite make out. Whatever he said to Shane Billingsley shut him up fast. He slumped back down onto the bench alongside his friends, and his assailant melted back into the crowd of holidaymakers.

The cabin was eerily quiet for a moment or two, and then the passengers resumed their previous conversations.

Riley was torn. Should she march over to the table and retrieve her daughter? Thus removing her from the bad influence of Shane Billingsley and company—and in the process humiliating her already ticked-off daughter? Or should she settle for a stern discussion with Maggy later—on the finer points of respect and courtesy?

Maggy looked backward at her again, her face anxious, pleading even.

The message was clear although unspoken. *Do not act like a mom right now.*

Riley took a deep breath. And then another. Now was not the time.

What it was time for was a glass of wine. She'd had a long, hot drive down from Raleigh earlier in the day. While she waited in line at the snack bar she searched in her pocketbook for cash, inching forward without really looking up. The concession stand didn't take credit cards, and she'd left Raleigh in such a hurry, she hadn't stopped at the bank for cash.

She was still patting down the pockets of her shorts, inching toward the front of the line, when the person in front of her stepped aside and she found herself standing at the snack bar. "A glass of white wine, please," she said, finally grasping a wad of bills at the bottom of her back pocket. "Pinot grigio if you've got it."

"Riley?"

She looked up. The snack bar attendant wasn't the usual college kid. This was a man. In fact, it was the same man who'd just snatched the cell phone away from Shane Billingsley.

His green eyes were quizzical, but familiar. He was medium tall, though not as tall as Wendell Griggs, with a scruffy blondish beard, and a baseball cap that obscured much of his face. For a moment she was confused. She knew him, but she didn't know how she knew him.

"It's me," the stranger said. He laughed. "Nate. I can't believe you're still drinking pinot grigio after all these years."

"Nate?" She felt dumb and tongue-tied. Surely not . . .

"Nate Milas," he said, sweeping off his baseball cap. Dark blond hair spilled over his forehead and ears. Laugh lines radiated out from the corners of his eyes. He reached across the battered bar top, clutched her hand in both of his, and shook it vigorously.

"Great to see you. God, it's been forever."

Nate Milas? Forever, Riley thought, was not long enough.

"You look terrific," Nate was saying. "Really great.

"Wow," he said, running a hand through his messy hair. "I can't even remember the last time we saw each other."

Riley could remember precisely the last time she'd seen Nate Milas. It was a moment indelibly etched on her brainpan. Still, Evelyn Nolan hadn't raised her to be rude. Not even to him.

"It's good to see you again," she said coolly. "What brings you back to Belle Isle?"

"Oh, uh, just some family stuff," he said. "I'm, uh, helping my mom out now that the season's getting started."

Nate Milas's father was Captain Joe, who ran the ferry. His mother, Annie, ran the Island Mercantile. The Milases had been running the Belle Isle ferry for as long as anybody on the island could remember.

"How nice for your mother," Riley said, the essence of civility. "Could I have that wine, please?"

He hadn't missed the ice in her voice.

"Sure thing," he said, turning to grab a bottle. He poured the wine into a plastic cup and handed it across to her.

"So how are you? How's uh, Wesley?"

"It's Wendell," Riley said crisply, pushing the money across the counter toward him. "He's super. Supergreat."

She took a step backward. "Good to see you again, Nate."

She sped away from the snack bar and Nate Milas and all the horrible memories of that horrible December night in 1992, as fast as her flip-flops would carry her.

And Nate Milas stood, staring down at the three crumpled dollar bills she'd paid him for a five-dollar glass of wine.

4

You look like you've seen a ghost," Parrish said as Riley rejoined the others on the top deck. They'd moved to a bench near the bow, and Riley was careful to wipe the salt spray from the seat before she sat down.

"Not a ghost. Worse. Nate Milas."

"Belle Isle Nate Milas?" Billy asked.

"Yes." Riley left it at that.

But Parrish couldn't. "For reals?" She craned her neck and surveyed the deck. "Where?"

"Downstairs in the snack bar. He's like, working as a soda jerk. And now that I think of it, I'm pretty certain I shorted him a couple of bucks for my wine."

"Serves him right," Parrish said, laughing.

"I remember Nate Milas," Billy said. "He was a decent guy. What's he ever done to you, sis?"

"Only shattered her heart," Parrish said.

"Ancient history," Riley replied airily. "I didn't even recognize him until he introduced himself. I wonder what he's doing these days? Besides running the snack bar for his parents."

"Are you kidding?" Parrish said. "What kind of journalist are you?"

"Retired."

"Still. Have you been living in a cave? Nate Milas is a dot-com boy wonder. After college he ended up bumming around in California, and then he and one of his fraternity brothers started Cribb."

"Which is?"

"Even I've heard of Cribb," Billy volunteered. "It's a real-estate-listing app. Right, Parrish?"

"Which they just sold to Google for about a bajillion dollars. He and the other two partners were on the cover of *Fortune* magazine a month or so ago."

"So what's he doing back here slinging wine on the ferry?" Riley asked. "Not that I care. Because I don't."

"His dad died recently, you know."

"Captain Joe? Oh, that's so sad. I hadn't heard. That's a shame. He was a lovely man. Unlike his prick of a son."

Billy blinked. "Not Captain Joe? Shit! I loved that old guy. He used to let me come up to the wheelhouse and pretend to drive the ferry."

Riley felt her face turning crimson with embarrassment. "Now I feel like an idiot. When I saw Nate downstairs, I just assumed he was here working for his dad."

"More like he's probably here helping his mother deal with estate stuff," Parrish said. "From what I read in that article, Nate Milas could buy and sell this ferry. Hell, he could probably buy and sell Belle Isle, and everybody on it, ten times over."

"Hmm," Billy said thoughtfully. "A real-life tycoon in our midst. I wonder if he's straight?"

"Ask your sister," Parrish said, waggling her eyebrows for effect.

"Can we please drop this?" Riley begged. "I was nineteen, okay? It was a long, long time ago."

"She can't drop it until you tell me why you hate this guy so much," Billy declared. He squeezed his sister's arm. "Come on. Tell BeBo."

"It's really not that fascinating a story," Riley protested.

"Why don't you let me be the judge of that? Now, tell."

"Parrish can tell you the whole sordid tale, since she seems so fascinated with it," Riley said.

"They started dating the summer before our freshman year, and from the beginning, it was a story of forbidden love," Parrish began in a stage whisper.

"Oh, for God's sake, it was not forbidden. Daddy really liked Captain Joe, and Nate."

"But Evelyn did not approve. At all," Parrish said.

"As far as Mama was concerned Nate was not 'our kind,'" Riley agreed, making air quotes with her fingertips. "She considered him the help, which made him seem that much more attractive to me."

"Nate Milas wasn't just attractive, he was H.O.T.," Parrish said. "Anyway, in the fall, we both went off to Carolina, and he went back to Wake Forest."

"And I went back to Ravenscroft, a lonely little queen in the Waspiest wasps' nest of a prep school in the South," Billy said wistfully.

"You guys kinda drifted apart once classes started back, right?" Parrish asked, consulting Riley.

"He dropped me because I wouldn't put out," Riley said.

"And right away you started dating that obnoxious S.A.E. from Greensboro . . . what was his name?" Parrish asked, snapping her fingers to summon the information. "Jason . . . something?"

"Rohrbaugh," Riley said reluctantly. "Mama loved him. She'd been in Junior League with his mother."

"The question is, did you put out for Jason Rohrbaugh?" Billy asked, poking his sister in the ribs, already enjoying her discomfort.

"She totally did," Parrish volunteered. "I came home early from a date one Saturday night and caught them in the sack together."

Riley fixed her best friend and former roommate with a steely glare. "Do we want to start dredging up all the times I caught you in bed with various guys—including our English 201 teaching assistant?"

"So I was a little bit of a ho back then. It was called youthful experimentation."

"She was a big ol' ho," Riley told her brother. "She put out more than the Tab machine in the Tri-Delta house."

"Yes, yes, that's all fascinating stuff, but could we get back to why you still despise Nate Milas? It can't be just because he dropped you all those years ago," Billy said.

"Oh no, it gets much worse," Parrish said. "She eventually broke up with Jason. . . ."

"Because he was screwing every girl on campus, including my Tri-Delt big sister," Riley said.

Parrish picked up the narrative. "So the next summer, before our sophomore year, Evelyn decides Riley has to be a debutante, which means nonstop parties all summer long. And Nate shows up at some of those parties, looking all dreamy and buff, and how could she resist? So they hooked up again."

"We did not 'hook up,'" Riley protested. "We went to a couple of parties together. I'd asked Jason to be my junior marshal, but then we broke up, and Nate was available, so I asked and he said yes. It was mostly a matter of convenience."

"You were crazy about him," Parrish insisted. "Totally gaga for the guy."

"I mostly asked him to piss off Mama," Riley said. "Anyway, the night of the ball, I'm standing around the ballroom of Carolina Country Club in Raleigh, wearing my fluffy white dress and elbow-length gloves. . . ."

"I remember those gloves. And that dress," Billy said dreamily. "I might have borrowed them for my first drag performance my junior year at UVA."

Riley stared at her brother. "You wore my deb dress to a drag show? Really?"

"I had my very own coming-out party! But I did have to cut it down a little," Billy admitted. "Lucky for me you were always kind of, um, flat-chested."

"I bet Evelyn doesn't have a silver-framed photo of *that* on the baby grand at Shutters," Parrish said. She waved at Riley. "Continue, please."

"There's not much more to tell. Nate pulled the classic show-up-and-throw-up stunt. There we were, all lined up, ready to take our bows, and I kept looking for him, but nothing. I was so upset, and Daddy felt so bad, he shared his flask of Maker's Mark with me. When Nate finally did get there, he was falling-down drunk. The first dance, he took me in his arms—and blew chow all over my white dress."

"I took her in the bathroom and managed to mop most of it up," Parrish said, "but Evelyn went all to pieces and ordered him to leave."

"All the other girls felt sorry for me, and they made their junior marshals ask me to dance, which was even more humiliating, so I spent most of the night in the ladies' lounge, doing Jäger shots with Sarah Catherine Coomer."

Despite her glib exterior, Riley suddenly felt hot pinpricks of tears at the memory of the long-ago disastrous evening. She looked out at the water, rapidly blinking them away.

"Dateless at the deb ball," Billy said. "Kinda sounds like a Neil Sedaka song. But I don't remember any of this. Was I even there?"

"I've managed to block the entire night—the most humiliating in my life—from my memory—right up until now," Riley said. "You would have been fifteen then, right? Oh, wait. Was that the year they sent you to that 'alternative school' in Arizona?"

"Yup. It was billed as a drug rehab, but I think Daddy really thought they'd cure me of being queer. Poor Daddy. Little did he know that my cabin counselor was a major chicken hawk."

The three of them sighed simultaneously.

"Anyway," Riley said. "Who cares about all that ancient history?" She held up her empty wine cup. "I think I need a refill."

"Wait!" Billy protested. "What happened to Nate? Did you ever speak to him again?"

"He called me about a dozen times the next day."

"But she wouldn't come to the phone," Parrish said. "He wrote her letters."

"Which I tore up."

"He even sent roses."

"Which I threw in the Dumpster."

Just as Riley stood up, Maggy and her friends came flying up the stairs. The five kids raced to the bow and hung over the side. "Look! Right there! See it? See it?" shouted one of the boys, a redhead who Riley recognized as yet another of the Billingsley clan.

"I see it, I see it," Maggy cried, leaning so far over the rail that Riley automatically stepped forward, intending to grab her daughter and haul her to safety. Until Parrish yanked her backward.

"Don't." Parrish mouthed the word.

"What are you kids looking at?" Parrish asked casually.

"It's a shark!" the Billingsley kid said, pointing down at the surface of the bay.

"Two sharks!" another redhead added.

"I'll bet it's a hammerhead," a tall blond girl said, standing a little back, but still craning her neck to see.

"No, stupid, look how big they are. That's a great white," the Billingsley kid corrected.

Riley and Parrish leaned over the rail to take a look.

Sure enough, they spotted two side-by-side dorsal fins cutting through the anemic waves. And then a third, smaller fin joined the first two. And then a sheen of curved dark gray backs as the creatures dipped and resurfaced.

"Sorry, guys," Parrish said. "Those are dolphins."

"Whaaat?" the Billingsley kid said, turning a disbelieving eye to the adult.

"Dolphins. A whole pod of 'em," Parrish repeated.

"You don't know nuthin' about sharks," the kid muttered under his breath.

Parrish regarded the boy silently for a moment. "What's your name?"

The kid smirked. "Dylan. What's yours?"

"I think you mean, 'what's yours, ma'am,' right, Dylan?"

"Whatever."

"Well, Dylan. It happens that I do know how to tell the difference between a shark and a dolphin. For one thing, that fin you see, sticking up above the water? That's a dorsal fin. Now, a dolphin's dorsal fin is curved, backward, while a shark's dorsal fin sticks straight up. Wait just a minute, and tell me what you see the next time that dolphin surfaces."

Six pairs of eyes were trained on the water. Nine, if you counted the adults.

"It's curved!" one of the younger redheads said, pointing.

"That's because that's a dolphin," Parrish said. "I'll tell you something else, too. Dolphins and sharks both have second, smaller sets of dorsal fins, but the dolphin's is usually not visible above the waterline, while a shark's is. You know what you do if you're in the water and you see two sets of fins coming at you?"

"Kiss your sweet ass good-bye," Billy whispered.

"Stab it in the eye with your knife!" Dylan Billingsley said.

Parrish shook her head. "I give up."

"I know what you're supposed to do," Maggy said. "I saw it on the History Channel. You stay really still, because you don't want the shark to think you're bait."

"Very good, Maggy," Parrish said approvingly.

"Who's the smart-ass ginger?" Parrish asked, after the youngsters drifted to the other side of the deck in search of another shark sighting.

"Yet another of the Billingsley clan. The parents have that huge house on Driftwood Lane, the one with all the golf carts. I think they live in Charlotte and he's something big with Wells Fargo. They have five kids, including two sets of twins," Riley said. "The oldest one is a juvenile delinquent in the making."

Parrish winced. "Poor woman."

More and more passengers were making their way to the top deck. Riley glanced at her watch and called to Maggy, who'd drifted away from her friends.

"Honey, we should be docking pretty soon. Wonder who'll see Big Belle first?"

Maggy rolled her eyes. "I can't believe you expect me to play that stupid game."

Billy swatted at his niece, but she danced out of distance. "Hey! I'll have you know I invented that game when your mama and I were younger than you. And it's not stupid. It's genius."

"What's the game?" Parrish asked. "I'll play."

"Oh yeah, duh, it's a really tough game," Maggy said.

"It's called 'I Spy,'" Billy said, ignoring the girl. "It's elegant in its simplicity. The first one to spot the Belle Isle lighthouse wins the game."

"I'm in. What's the prize? A case of Moët & Chandon?"

"Two scoops of ice cream at the Mercantile," Maggy said. "But they always let me win."

"Not this year," Riley said sharply. "Not since you got too big for your britches."

"Fine." Maggy took a few steps away and made a show of turning her back to the horizon—and the looming appearance of Big Belle.

"It's gonna be a looong summer," Riley murmured. "And she's not even a teenager—until October."

"I love that child, but it does make me glad that I had a son—and that he's already nineteen and out of my house," Parrish said.

A few minutes passed. And then Big Belle's black-, green-, and white-striped column loomed on the horizon.

"I see it! I see it. I win, I win, I win!" Parrish chanted.

Maggy edged over to her mother and gave her a discreet nudge. "Um, Mom? Speaking of I Spy? That lady over there has totally been staring at you for the last ten minutes. Don't look!"

Which prompted all three of them to turn in the direction in which Maggy had nodded.

A middle-aged woman in ill-fitting khaki slacks and a navy-blue windbreaker stood by the railing. She had a frizzy blond perm and wore mirrored sunglasses and ugly black lace-up shoes.

"I was just thinking the same thing," Parrish whispered. "She hasn't even looked at the water. She just stares at Riley whenever she thinks we're not watching."

"Probably a fan," Riley said. "It's been six months, but people are still pissed at me for quitting the show."

"Still?" Parrish asked. "It was just a cheesy morning TV magazine show. No offense," she added.

"You don't even know," Maggy said. "Some crazy woman cornered her in the bathroom at the Cracker Barrel on the way down from Raleigh today.

Mom was trying to pee and this lady was all, like, how Mom ruined her mornings because *Wake Up, Carolina* isn't on WRAL anymore."

"People hate change," Riley said. She gave Parrish a rueful smile. "Some people actually like a dose of cheese with their morning coffee."

As they watched, the woman began making a determined march in their direction, a piece of paper clutched in her hand.

"Ohmygod. She's coming over here," Maggy said. "I bet she's, like, some crazy stalker fangirl that followed us down here."

"Oooh. Like in *Misery*! Maybe she plans to abduct you and tie you to a bed until you agree to go back on the air and do rescue puppy adoption features and interview third-rate sitcom actresses," Parrish said, getting into the moment.

"No, no, no," Billy said. "She's a big-deal New York talent agent, sis, and she wants to hire you to take over Katie Couric's slot on the *Today* show."

Before Riley had time to fill her brother in on current events, she felt a tenuous tap on her shoulder. She turned around to find Nate Milas, holding out a single-serving bottle of pinot grigio, with an upturned plastic cup on top.

"Um, Riley?"

Billy and Parrish leaned in to eavesdrop.

Riley looked up into Nate's face. It was flushed with embarrassment. And he'd tucked his baseball hat into the pocket of his shorts. It struck Riley, reminded her, actually, that Nate's face was an honest face.

Back in the day when she'd been a real reporter, she'd learned a little about reading people's expressions and body language. Politicians blinked a lot, looked away, dissembled. Criminals, real criminals, were much harder to read. So many were sociopaths who felt no remorse for doing whatever they thought necessary to further their agenda. But Nate's face was open, guileless, and obviously guilt-stricken.

"Look, it's been a long time, but I still feel bad about, you know, that deb thing. I know you hate me, and you have every right to hate me, but I just wanted to tell you . . . I mean, it's not an excuse. It's not because I wasn't into you. I was into you. But . . ."

"Excuse me!"

The stalker woman's voice was shrill and loud. Very loud. She was standing directly beside Riley, brandishing the piece of paper, actually shaking it at her. Now that she was close, Riley could see she had a laminated ID tag with some sort of gold shield worn on a lanyard around her neck.

Every head on the top deck of the *Carolina Queen* seemed to swivel in their direction.

"Hi," Riley said, trying to be kind. She'd always been kind to fans, appreciated them, since, after all, they were the reason she'd had such a long television career, such as it was. But there had to be boundaries.

"I'll be with you in a minute," Riley said quietly. "But I'm with my family and friends right now. Private time, you understand? I don't usually sign autographs like this."

The woman was not to be deterred. She thrust the paper into Riley's hands, closed both Riley's own hands over it.

"I don't want an autograph. I just need to serve you with this document. So consider yourself served."

5

For a moment, things went perfectly silent. Riley couldn't hear the ferry's diesel engines, the cries of seagulls, the excited voices of the other passengers anticipating landing at the dock on Belle Isle.

What she did hear was the thudding of her heart in her chest. She felt every set of eyes on the upper deck of the *Carolina Queen* glued to her face.

Riley stared down at the paper in her hands. The print was fuzzy. It was a legal document of some kind. Her mind froze for a second, and then the awful, inescapable truth dawned.

She felt boiling blood rush to her face and spill out through her mouth.

Wendell. This was all Wendell. He hadn't made the ferry today because he'd never intended to make it. Every promise he'd made her, every tearful declaration of his love for his family—all lies. He'd taken the coward's way out, and now he was having her served with divorce papers—in front of their daughter, her closest friends, that fucking busybody Andrea Payne, and half the residents of Belle Isle. Even the last man who'd broken her heart got to be a witness to this fresh humiliation.

"No!" Riley cried in a hoarse whisper. "Oh no, you don't get to serve me divorce papers."

The woman blinked but didn't move. She'd been at this job a long time.

Parrish tugged at her friend's arm. "Come on, Riley. Let it go. We'll figure it out. Just let it go." She looked up at the sheriff's deputy. "Never mind, Officer. Er, Deputy."

Riley glanced over at her daughter. Maggy stood, frozen in place, with one hand on the deck rail. Her mouth was open, her eyes wide, her cheeks stained red. A second later, she dashed down the stairs.

"I'll go see about her," Billy said quietly, following behind.

In the midst of the commotion from Riley's outburst, Nate Milas beat a swift retreat to the pilothouse on the upper deck. The ferry captain gave him a quizzical glance as he stepped inside.

"Everything okay?" Wayne Gates asked.

"All good," Nate assured him. "I just felt like getting away from the crowd down there."

Wayne nodded his understanding. "Lots of folks still want to talk about the old man passing."

Nate didn't bother to tell him the real reason he'd needed to escape.

He stared moodily out at the approaching shoreline. Just like the old days, his timing with Riley Nolan was impeccable in its flat-footedness. What a jerk he'd been. Then and now.

From his perch in the second-floor manager's office he'd spotted Riley and her daughter as soon as they'd arrived at the ferry dock. He'd known they'd be on the boat, because he'd made it a habit, since arriving back at Southpoint for the old man's funeral, to check each day's manifest.

Zero chance he'd overlook the name Riley Nolan. Or Riley Griggs, her married name. He'd noticed Wendell's name too, of course. Interesting that Wendell had been a no-show. He wondered whether Riley had any idea of the financial hole her husband had dug—for himself and their family. Not really his business, except, of course, he'd already started to make it his business. And why had Riley assumed the sheriff's deputy was serving her with divorce papers? Obviously, all was not well.

What the hell made him think he could ever make things right with Riley? And of all the stupid times to attempt an apology, this had to be the worst.

How many years had he been brooding over that goddamned debutante ball?

According to Cassie, he'd never stopped brooding about it, never stopped thinking about his first disastrous romance. But then, according to Cassie, he was a world-class brooder. It was on her top-ten list of Nate Milas's fatal personality flaws.

Belle Isle locals assumed he'd stayed on after his father's funeral to help his mother settle Joe's estate, but the truth was that Annie Milas was more than competent to take care of her own affairs. His mother had always been a full partner in all her husband's business dealings. All those years she'd taught school at the tiny elementary school on the mainland, she'd also kept the books for the ferry as well as running the Mercantile.

The ugly truth of the matter was that he had no compelling reason to return to California. He'd lost the battle for control of Cribb, lost Cassie, his longtime girlfriend, and lost his best friend and former fraternity brother, Matt, who, it turned out, had been carrying on a long-term clandestine affair with Cassie.

With all that, who could blame him for brooding?

His mother, for one.

The week after the funeral, she'd rousted him out of a sound sleep in his old bedroom in their wood-frame family home that overlooked the marina.

"You do know it's after eleven, right?" she'd said, staring down at him.

"So?"

"So I think it's time you quit moping around my house and get on with your life."

He leaned on one elbow and stared at her in surprise. His mother's round, unlined face was etched now with concern.

"What makes you think I'm moping?"

"You're my son. I know how you do. You hardly eat anything, stay up half the night on that computer of yours, and then sleep past noon. You look like a hobo with that long hair and beard. And you haven't called any of your old friends since you've been home. In fact, you've hardly left the house."

"Maybe I don't have any old friends left around here."

"What about Michael and Andrew and Kevin—all those guys who came to the funeral. Kevin brought his mother's kolache back to the house afterward."

"They were just being polite. Doing the right thing."

"No," Annie shot back. "They were doing what friends do. And if you could stop wallowing in your own self-pity for more than five minutes, you'd realize how lucky you are to still have friends here. Or family."

"Ow." Nate blinked and rubbed a hand through the week's worth of stubble on his cheeks.

She gave him an exasperated smile. "This is for your own good, Nate. I'm sorry about what happened with Cassie and Matt. They did you all kinds of dirty, that's for sure. And God knows, I'm sorry about your dad. He was my best friend too, you know. For more than forty years. But what's done is done. You need to get on with your life now, son."

"Are you kicking me out of the house?"

She picked up the pair of jeans he'd left on the floor and tossed them onto the bed. "That's one way to look at it."

He got up and headed for the bathroom.

"I put a new razor in there for you," Annie called after him. "I know I'm biased since I'm your mom, but that face is much too handsome to hide behind some scruffy beard."

6

Maggy sat alone on a bench at the Belle Isle ferry landing, cradling a squirming Banks in her arms, while Riley, operating on autopilot, supervised the deckhands unloading the Rubbermaid tubs containing all the supplies and luggage she'd brought down for the summer. She glanced over at the shuttle, which was a series of connected carts for passengers and baggage, pulled by a tractor-type conveyance.

The only motorized vehicles allowed on Belle Isle were emergency or service conveyances. Everybody else got around on golf carts.

Since the family's golf cart was still in the garage at the house on the south end of the island, she'd booked a shuttle ticket, but now Riley dreaded the thought of crowding into the tram car with the prying eyes of weekenders who'd just seen her at her very worst.

"Come on," Parrish said, nodding at the six-seater golf cart that had just pulled up to the passenger loading area. "Ed brought over most of our stuff earlier. We'll give you guys a lift."

Riley watched while Parrish gave Ed Godchaux a hushed, condensed version of the events that had just occurred. Ed jumped out of the cart and, within five minutes, he and Billy managed to load everything into the golf cart.

Billy hugged Riley tightly and whispered in her ear. "Now I really will kill him for you. But first I'll get Mama's groceries and crap unloaded over at Shutters, and then I'll come over and help you get settled in at your place. Okay?"

"Thanks," Riley said wearily. "Don't tell Mama, okay?"

"Never!"

Maggy sat, stone-faced and teary-eyed on the rear-facing last seat on the cart, as far away from her mother as she could get. Banks sat on the seat beside her, tethered by his leash. Maggy still hadn't uttered a single word.

Billy approached the golf cart and tapped his niece on the arm. "Be nice to your mom, okay? Remember, she's on your side." He ruffled the girl's hair and sighed. "Hell of a way to start the summer."

As the golf cart bumped over the crushed-shell path leading away from the landing, Riley held on to the back of her seat and watched the passing landscape with mild disinterest. She'd been here a month earlier, but for less than twenty-four hours. It was as though the entire island was exploding with lush, green, summer growth. Confederate jasmine with creamy, star-shaped blossoms climbed the trunks of the bent and gnarled pin oaks, dwarf myrtle scented the air, and tiny yellow wildflowers bloomed along the road's shoulder.

The temperature had dropped just in the half hour since they'd docked, and shafts of dark golden sunshine pierced the tree canopy.

Parrish turned around in the seat to face Riley. "I can't believe Wendell would pull a stunt like that. Having you served with papers in front of Maggy and everybody." She tapped Ed's shoulder. "As soon as we get back to the house, Ed's going to call Sue Simpson. Doesn't she have a house down here somewhere, honey?"

"At Wrightsville Beach." He turned halfway around in the seat, and his craggy face signaled his concern. "She's the best at what she does, Riley. That's who I'd hire if I were you."

"Okay," Riley said. She glanced at the back of Maggy's head. "Let's talk about it later, okay? I don't want her any more upset than she needs to be."

Other golf carts passed them on the road. Ed and Parrish waved and nodded; Riley kept her eyes downcast. By now, the whole island would know what had happened. Andrea Payne would see to that.

The ride to Sand Dollar Lane and their dream house took fifteen minutes.

For the first few years of their marriage, when her father was still grooming Wendell to take over Belle Isle Enterprises, they'd always stayed at the Shutters during vacations and summers on the island.

But as big and gracious-looking as her parents' home seemed, the old house had only three bathrooms, all of them fitted out with charming but undersize claw-foot bathtubs, and the only shower was the outside cold-water shower. Her parents saw no need to modernize, a fact that infuriated Wendell Griggs.

"Jesus! It's not like they don't have the money," he'd griped to Riley. "I bet they could completely redo all those bathrooms plus the kitchen for around fifty thousand dollars."

"But you know Mama. She wants everything at the Shutters left just like it was when her grandfather built the place."

"It's like living in the Dark Ages here," Wendell complained.

When they were ready for a house of their own, Riley wanted to buy one of the original houses on the bluff that her great-grandfather had built, one that was half a mile away from Shutters, which had been the first house built on the island.

Like the other homes of that 1920s era, the house she'd lusted after had been built in the twenties with weather-beaten gray cedar shingle siding, wide, gracious porches, sweeping views of the sound, and yes, miniscule bathrooms and a kitchen a quarter the size of the one in their house back in the Hayes-Barton neighborhood in Raleigh.

Wendell was having none of it. "I can build us a house on one of the new oceanfront lots that'll be ten times better than those old dumps," he'd said. "It would take at least a hundred thousand dollars in improvements to make one of those places comparable to a new house. Anyway, how's it going to look if the CEO of Belle Isle Enterprises doesn't buy into our new development?"

He'd had a point, of course. The old houses on the bluff were beautiful but wildly impractical. The one Riley liked best had no insulation, windows that rattled in the wind, a sagging roof, outdated plumbing, and original knob-and-tube wiring. The cedar-shake siding needed replacing and leaked in places. And Maggy had been only two years old, and a fussy toddler, and Riley hadn't had the energy to fight him on the issue.

Which was how Wendell came to build a contemporary six-thousand-square-foot, five-bedroom, four-bathroom home for a family of three.

He'd seen a house like it on the cover of a magazine in an airport newsstand in L.A. and, by the time Riley picked him up at RDU, he'd sketched out the entire house on the back of the paper place mat they used for first-class meal service.

"This is going to be a statement house," he'd told Riley excitedly. "The cantilevered roofline, the skylights, the masses of poured concrete and the urban silo observation tower? Crazy good, right? Steel frame windows that can withstand hurricane-force winds, and the concrete will never need paint. You'll have the best kitchen on the island—a master bath with all Carrara marble and a soaker tub like the ones in your decorating magazines. And I'll have a man cave in the silo with a flat-screen television."

He'd picked the best lot in the new development for their house, and when it turned out that a large sand dune obscured the view of the ocean from the open-plan living room with one whole wall of windows and doors, he'd waited until January, when Belle Isle was largely deserted, and simply bulldozed the dune, and the sea oats and beach rosemary, along with Riley's protestations, into oblivion.

As the sun retreated, Riley felt chilled. "You okay back there, Mags?" Riley asked, tapping her daughter's arm. "Warm enough? I've got a windbreaker in my bag if you need it."

"I'm fine," Maggy said. She clutched Banks so tightly the dog yipped in protest.

"Almost there," Riley said, trying to sound cheerful. Ed whipped the golf cart off Sand Dollar Lane and onto the narrow drive that led to the house. Palmetto fronds and wax myrtle branches slapped against the sides of the cart.

Riley dug in her tote for her phone. Wendell loved gadgets, and he'd had everything in the house wired so it could be remotely controlled with a tap on their smartphones.

Normally she would have turned down the air-conditioning from the ferry, but due to circumstances beyond her control, the thought hadn't occurred to her.

All the lights were on timers, and as the drive curved around, the gleaming white mass of house emerged from the dusk. Tree-mounted spotlights threw washes of yellow light on the monolithic entryway, and pale blue light shone through the tall, narrow front windows.

"Here we are," Riley said, trying for cheery and failing.

Ed pulled the cart up in front of the garage. "I'll go ahead and get your golf cart charged if you'll open the doors," he offered.

"That would be great," Riley said. She tapped the Unlock icon on the phone, and then the icon for the garage and front door. She tapped the Open icon and waited for the garage doors to slide noiselessly upward.

"Banks needs to pee, and so do I," Maggy announced as she climbed out of the cart. The dog scampered over to a clump of oleanders, and Maggy held on to the leash. "Hurry up, Banks," she ordered. "I gotta go, too."

The garage doors didn't move. Riley tapped again.

"What's wrong?" Parrish asked, as she climbed out and grabbed one of the suitcases.

"I don't know. Maybe the battery's dead on the opener."

"Open the front door, Mom," Maggy called, pulling Banks away from the trees.

Riley tapped the icon and got out of the cart, shouldering one of the L.L. Bean canvas tote bags. "I hope the damned computer thingy isn't on the fritz. I don't know why we can't just have a lock and key like normal people."

"Hey, Mom!" Maggy called.

"Honey, I'm coming! Just give me a minute, will you? You're not the only one who needs a bathroom."

"There's some kind of sign on the door," Maggy called.

Riley dropped the bags and hurried toward the doorway, where her daughter stood bathed in a pool of light.

Taped to the door was an official-looking plastic-coated poster.

NOTICE OF FORECLOSURE.

"Oh my God," Riley whispered.

"What's it mean?" Maggy asked, dancing from one foot to another. "Why can't we get in the house?"

"Oh my God," Riley repeated. She took out the document she'd been served on the ferry and actually read it this time, her eyes glazing over all the legalese. But there were two words she understood: default and foreclosure.

"Ed," she called, holding up the document.

"Right here," he said, setting down the tub of groceries. He took a pair of reading glasses from his breast pocket and stared at the notice for a moment. "Ah shit," he said under his breath.

"What the hell?" Parrish said, joining them. "Is this somebody's idea of a joke?"

"It's no joke," Ed said. He handed his phone to his wife. "Parrish, see if you can get the sheriff's office on the line."

"Mom!" Maggy cried. "I've got to go. Don't you have a key? Or something?"

"Let's go around to the back of the house," Riley said. "Your dad was the last one here, and sometimes he forgets and leaves a door unlocked."

"Ohmygod, I'm gonna wet my pants," Maggy said, following Riley along the flagstone path toward the rear of the house. "I can't hold it."

Riley pointed toward a clump of shoulder-high azaleas. "Just go over there and wilder-pee like you used to do when you were a Girl Scout."

"Gross!" Maggy protested, but she hurried over to the shrubbery and a moment later rejoined her mother on the path. "Ugh. There were tree frogs over there. And a lizard."

"You used to adore tree frogs and lizards," Riley reminded her. "Come on, let's see if we can get in the house."

The light was a dusky purple now. Cicadas thrummed from the tall grass, and an owl hooted from a nearby tree. She glanced up at the sky, and was somewhat reassured by the ever-present blanket of stars. It was the one constant on Belle Isle. Oh yes, and there was a full moon tonight, too.

As they walked, Riley composed a mental to-do list. Call sheriff's office. Get house unlocked. Have old–fashioned locks installed. Charge up golf cart. Get grass cut and shrubs trimmed. Track down Wendell Griggs and divorce his ass.

"Come on, let's try the kitchen," Riley told her daughter. They crossed the dense green lawn, their ankles damp with evening dew. She tried the kitchen door, but it too, was locked.

Now Maggy pressed herself up beside her mother. "Mom? Can we get in? What's going on?"

Riley curled an arm around Maggy's shoulder. "I don't know, honey. Dad must have changed the locks for some reason. Um, let's go back to the front of the house where Ed and Parrish are."

She willed herself not to break into a run, or burst into hysterics, or do anything to alarm her daughter.

"This has to be a mistake," she said to herself.

They heard the putt-putting of the golf cart before Billy pulled up alongside Ed's cart.

Ed held his cell phone to one ear while Parrish sat in the cart and fumed. "What's going on?" Billy asked. "Where are the girls?"

"Right here," Riley called, as she and Maggy rejoined the others.

Ed held his phone away from his ear. "I'm on hold with the sheriff's office. What did you see around back?"

"Nothing. Everything is locked up tight, and I can't even see inside."

"Is there any way to jimmy one of the doors open?" Parrish asked.

Ed frowned. "Not until we know what's going on."

"I don't get it," Billy said, looking from Ed to Riley and back to Ed again.

"There's a foreclosure notice posted on the front door, and the locks have apparently all been changed," Parrish said bitterly. "And that document your sister was served on the ferry—that was a foreclosure notice."

Billy's jaw dropped. "You can't be serious."

"Dead serious," Riley said.

"Can they do that?" Parrish asked her husband. "I mean, is that even legal? Riley, you didn't get any kind of notices or anything in the mail, right?"

"No!" Riley said sharply. "Don't you think I would have paid attention to something like a foreclosure notice?"

"That can't be legal, right?" Billy said, turning again to Ed.

"Hang on, somebody's coming on the line," Ed said.

He held the phone to his ear again. "Hi. Yes, this is Ed Godchaux. I'm an attorney for Riley Griggs, who owns the property at 555 Sand Dollar Lane over on Belle Isle. There's a foreclosure notice posted on her front door, and the locks have been changed. All of this has occurred without any prior notification to her. I need to speak to somebody to get this straightened out."

He listened, shaking his head in frustration.

"That's the best you can do? Yes, I realize *you* probably don't consider it an emergency, but I can assure you, my client and her daughter who have been locked out of their home consider it very much of an emergency."

Ed removed his glasses, polished the lenses on the hem of his shirt, then put them on again.

"Well, who can answer my questions? Let me give you my cell number and my client's. Okay? Can you have somebody call me?"

He glanced over at Riley and she gave him her cell number. He repeated both numbers to the dispatcher. "Can you have the sheriff call one of us back?"

Ed rolled his eyes in frustration. "Not until Tuesday? You're kidding me."

"That's right. I'm well aware that it's Memorial Day weekend. So you're saying nobody can tell me anything, or unlock my client's house . . . or do ONE GODDAMN THING TO HELP HER OUT until Tuesday?

"I'm sorry, ma'am, but I tend to take that tone, and the Lord's name in vain, when I'm faced with blatant disregard for . . . Hello?"

Ed tapped the disconnect button. "She hung up."

"Can they just do that?" Billy repeated.

"I don't know. Maybe. You gotta understand it's been thirty years since I had a class in real estate law. And I went to law school in Massachusetts. Every state has different statutes when it comes to foreclosures. I really have no idea how things work in North Carolina."

"So much for a Harvard law degree," Parrish said. "Look, we obviously can't get anything done standing around here in the dark. We're all hot and tired and hungry. At least, I am. Riley, you guys can just come back to our house. I'll fix us some dinner. . . ."

"Riley, have you talked to Wendell?" Billy asked abruptly.

"No," Riley said, her lips compressed. "I've tried calling and texting. All day. His phone goes right to voice mail."

"It's not his fault," Maggy said shrilly. "Daddy wouldn't do this. My parents are not getting a divorce. Somebody screwed up, that's all." She raised her voice, shouting now, the words echoing in the darkened treetops, alive now with blinking fireflies. "So everybody stop acting like this is all my dad's fault!"

Riley tried hugging her child, but Maggy pulled away. "Leave me alone."

"Okay, Mags," Parrish said, her voice soft, soothing. "Nobody's saying it's your dad's fault. You're right. It's just some big screwup. We'll get it straightened out in the morning. Now, can we go get some pizza? Or Rice Krispies? Or something?"

"Parrish is right," Riley said. "You haven't eaten in hours. We need to check your sugar and get some food in you."

Maggy put her hand out. "I'm fine. Just give me a protein bar and one of your stupid juice boxes. Okay? And stop looking at me like I'm gonna pass out or die. How many times do I have to tell you? I. Am. Okay."

Riley handed her the bar and the juice without comment. Maggy tore off the wrapper and deliberately tossed it to the ground and took a savage, defiant bite of chocolate and oatmeal.

"It's settled then," Parrish said. "You'll spend the night at our place, right? We can stash your stuff in the garage until this is all worked out."

"What about your cats?" Maggy said, chewing with her mouth open. "Thelma and Louise will beat the crap out of Banksy." She turned suddenly pleading eyes toward her mother. "Why can't we just stay at Mimi's house? I could sleep in my old room, and you could have your old room, and Banks can play with Ollie."

"Who's Ollie?" Ed asked.

"Mimi's dog Ollie is Banksy's sister," Maggy said. "Please, Mom?"

This was a moment Riley had been dreading, ever since seeing the black-and-white notice tacked to her front door. She thought of herself as a strong, competent, modern woman. She was a hard-hitting journalist. Well, formerly hard-hitting, former journalist. She'd faced down cops, politicians, crooks, Hollywood publicists, even deranged fans who'd started an online petition two years ago after she'd changed her hair color. But tonight, after everything that had happened, she just didn't know if she had the energy to deal with her mother.

"Oh, I don't know that we need to inconvenience Mimi tonight," Riley said uneasily.

"Pleaaaase?" Maggy picked up Banks and held her out to her mother. "Banks wants to go to Mimi's."

Billy stepped in to assist, sensing Riley's reluctance. "Mama was already headed down to the beach for the full moon party with Aunt Roo," he said. "Why don't y'all just head over to Shutters? Then we can figure everything out tomorrow."

Huge tears welled up in Maggy's eyes and spilled down her cheeks. "I just wanna sleep in my old bed tonight. With Banksy."

Riley knew when she'd been beaten. Sooner or later, Evelyn would have to know all the gory details of this endless day. Maybe it was better that she hear them all, firsthand, from the aggrieved party.

"Thanks, anyway, Parrish," she said. "And Ed. You've been wonderful. You guys go ahead to the full moon party. Don't let us party poopers spoil the fun. If Billy will give us a hand with our stuff, we'll head over to Shutters.

Mama always has plenty of groceries. I'll throw something together for dinner, and then we'll hit the hay and deal with this stuff tomorrow."

Parrish searched her best friend's face for some sign or signal. "You sure?"

"Positive."

7

After the ferry docked, Nate Milas steered his golf cart back toward Duck Inn, the cabin he'd bought at Sandy Point.

Some cabin, Nate thought, as he pushed through the unlocked door. The place had been a hunting shack, thrown together by members of his father's hunting club in the late sixties with odds and ends of leftover lumber and building supplies pilfered from construction sites around the island. The shack's title was murky, because so many of the original hunting club members had died or moved away over the ensuing years, but he'd finally tracked down the last surviving self-styled Dirty Dozen club member at his home in Pittsboro, and paid eighty thousand dollars for the property. Which was probably a hundred times what his father's pals had paid.

"All mine," Nate said, surveying the cottage. The floors were scarred oak and the walls were whitewashed planks of rough pine. The original floor plan had been simple: one big main room contained a combination living room and dining room, originally heated only by a potbellied stove installed in a huge rock-faced fireplace at the rear of the room. On either side of the living area were two high-ceilinged bunk rooms. And that was it. For the first ten years of its existence, the shack had neither electricity nor indoor plumbing. A cookhouse had been built a few yards to the east of the shack, connected to the main house by a covered walkway, and a bathhouse, with a communal shower and a two-holer outhouse had been built to the west.

Over the years, the club members had gradually (and grudgingly) upgraded the shack. Electricity and plumbing were added in the early seventies, and the cookhouse had been picked up and tacked onto the back of the original cabin in the early eighties. Bathrooms had been added to each of the bunk rooms.

But there was still no central heat or air-conditioning. And no insulation. Only one burner on the propane-fueled oven worked, and the roof leaked. The furnishings consisted of whatever castoffs the club members' wives had donated over the years. Still, it was home. For now.

Nate sat down at the dining room table, a rickety maple faux Early American number, and powered up his laptop computer. The first improvement he'd made to the cabin was having Wi-Fi installed. Now he clicked over to the Baldwin County legal advertising site and scrolled down the listings until he found the one he wanted and read it for the third time that day.

He still couldn't believe this was really going to happen. His mother had heard gossip in the past couple of years, of problems at Belle Isle Enterprises, but he'd never given them much credence. Wendell Griggs was a sharp operator. He had an MBA, and he'd learned the real estate business from this father-in-law, who also happened to be the shrewdest man on the coast, W. R. Nolan himself.

To beat back the monotony of waiting in hospital rooms during his own father's illness, Nate had started poking around at the courthouse and in online records, and he'd been dumbfounded by what he'd discovered. It was all true. Actually, things were much worse than anybody could have guessed.

Then he clicked over to his bank's Web site. Good. The funds had been transferred from his California bank to his new bank in North Carolina.

He tapped a button and the computer screen darkened. He sat back in the chair and wondered at the state of his emotions. Dread. A heavy, sick feeling of dread bored up from his belly, accompanied by an uneasy sense of guilt.

None of this was new to Nate Milas. He'd tried to quash these emotions. None of this was his doing. This was all on Wendell Griggs, who'd managed to take a thriving family business, and in the space of only two short years, driven it to bankruptcy and beyond. The stalled hotel project, the cleared but unsold new subdivision lots, and the empty and padlocked retail spaces just a block from his family's own modest Island Mercantile? Not to mention that pretentious and weird spaceship-looking home he'd had built on Sand Dollar Lane? That was all Wendell.

Not Nate's problem. Not Nate's fault. Then why, he wondered, did this whole business feel like such a betrayal?

He couldn't forget the hurt, stunned look on Riley's face when she'd been served on the ferry. Had she really been blindsided by all of this?

8

It was a closely held family secret. Although Riley's mother, Evelyn, fancied herself a dyed-in-the-wool Southerner, the truth of the matter was that her grandfather, James Thomas Riley, was an Ohio-born carpetbagger—a successful storekeeper who moved to the South in the years following the Civil War to make his fortune.

James Thomas Riley and his older brother and business partner, Charles, had made their money in timber, cutting down the longleaf pine forests of North and South Carolina and shipping the milled lumber to New York City to help supply the inexhaustible need for materials to build new factories, bridges, and apartment buildings.

In 1919, James T. and Charles made an uncharacteristically questionable decision—they bought Puquitta Island, named such by the indigenous Lumbee Indians, sight unseen, for the timber. Family lore had it that the brothers quarreled bitterly, nearly coming to blows over who was to blame upon the discovery that Puquitta's maritime forests consisted not of the highly desirable longleaf Southern pine, but mostly of thick stands of live oak, scrub pine, and red laurel.

After only one visit to Puquitta Island, the brothers forgot about their investment and turned their attention to enjoying their newfound fortunes. At the age of thirty, James married a beautiful nineteen-year-old Charleston debutante named Muriel Beacham, and a year later Earline, the first of their four daughters, was born. Charles, a confirmed bachelor, devoted himself to philanthropy and butterfly collecting.

Never one to miss an opportunity to make money, it was Charles who, in 1926, came up with the idea to build a golf course, a small hotel, and fine vacation houses on Puquitta. He'd read about Sea Island, formerly called Long Island, a resort that automobile magnate Howard Coffin was building on a barrier island down in Georgia, and didn't see any reason why such a plan wouldn't work for their homely little patch of land.

The brothers promptly dumped the ungainly Lumbee Indian name, and rebranded the property Belle Isle.

Charles hadn't actually seen the Georgia resort, so he had no way of knowing that a causeway had been built to link Sea Island to the mainland. And he'd overlooked the fact that Howard Coffin's project was served by the Central Georgia Railroad, meaning potential homebuyers and resort guests could arrive by rail or car, whereas Belle Isle, located five nautical miles off the coast of North Carolina, was accessible only by ferryboat.

While younger brother James, married with a growing family, stayed and ran the timber business from their offices in Wilmington, bachelor Charles moved to the island and set about building his new empire.

He hired a young architect, picked a prime building lot on the protected bay side of the island, on a bluff, and began construction of a residence meant to set the tone for the other homes intended for the resort. Lumber for the house was sourced from a small stand of longleaf pines and cedars in the island's interior.

The resulting house was a beauty—a Gilded Age mash-up of gambrel roofs, dormers, porches, and verandahs, all clad in soft gray cedar shingles and sporting sixty-four windows, each with its own set of distinctive shutters featuring pine-tree silhouette cutouts. It had two stories, projecting wings from either side, marble baths, high ceilings, a billiard room, library, and even a small putting green next to the carriage house. Six months after the house was completed, during a particularly cold and blustery winter, Charles fell ill from pneumonia and died.

Which was how James Thomas, J.T., came to own Shutters, and how his oldest granddaughter, Evelyn Rose Riley Nolan, came into possession of the drafty but beautiful island landmark.

Riley's heart always did a little flutter kick whenever she caught sight of the old house. Spotting the lighthouse from the ferry was a game she and Billy had invented as young children, but the first glimpse of the elegant gray-shingled mansion was her private prize.

The house was lit up, and the front porch light shone through the full darkness as Billy pulled the golf cart under the porte cochere. "Oh good," he told Riley in a hushed voice. "Mama's not back from the beach party yet."

Together they shepherded a sleepy Maggy into the house. Riley found a bowl of tomatoes on the kitchen counter and a plastic tub of pimento cheese from the Mercantile in the refrigerator. While Maggy dutifully pinpricked her finger to test her blood sugar, Riley fixed a dinner of pimento cheese sandwiches and poured herself a large glass of wine.

She took a sip and grimaced. Evelyn Nolan drank gin, not wine, which meant that the house wine at Shutters was whatever cheap, vinegary jug wine she found on sale at the Harris Teeter in Southpoint.

"Okay," Billy said, sinking down onto a chair at the Formica dinette table. "You're all unloaded. I put your suitcases in your rooms."

"Is Uncle Scott here?" Maggy asked, cramming a handful of potato chips into her mouth and chewing vigorously.

"Right here," Scott said, strolling into the kitchen with a wriggling pug under each arm. He set Ollie and Banksy down on the linoleum floor and helped himself to a potato chip from Maggy's plate.

Billy and Scott lived a short golf cart ride away in the island's former firehouse, which they'd completely restored.

"Hey, shug," he said, reaching across the table and squeezing Riley's hand in his.

Scott Moriatakis had been born and raised in San Francisco, but he'd managed to acquire an authentic-sounding Southern accent soon after meeting Billy Nolan. He was a full head taller than his partner, with streaks of gray at his temples and a neatly trimmed goatee that set off his olive skin. He was barefoot and dressed in a bright turquoise T-shirt and coral-colored skinny jeans.

"When did you get in?" Riley asked, nibbling at her sandwich.

"Day before yesterday," Scott said. "Or maybe it was day before that. I lose track of time when I'm here working."

"But he couldn't be bothered to let me know that," Billy said.

"I needed two days alone to finalize the schematics for the restaurant in Boca Raton," Scott countered. "You know what I'm like when I'm trying to finish a project."

"Say no more. He's a bear. Or I should say, unbearable," Billy told a giggling Maggy.

Scott dipped a spoon into the tub of pimento cheese and tasted it thoughtfully. "You know, this would make a nice appetizer for the Southern-themed diner Stephen wants to do in Durham."

"Mama usually serves it on Ritz crackers with some of Aunt Roo's pepper jelly drizzled over it," Riley said. She set her half-eaten sandwich down on the plate and pushed it away. And then drained the glass of piss-poor wine she'd poured herself.

"Rough day, huh?" Scott said, taking note of the wine.

"Epic," Riley said.

"Uncle Scott! Somebody changed the locks at our house," Maggy said. "Daddy's gonna be so mad when he finds out."

"No way!" Scott looked from Riley to Billy for affirmation. "Did you call the cops?"

"We did," Riley said quietly. She glanced over at Maggy, catching her in mid-yawn.

"Sweetie, why don't you take your insulin and then you and Banks can go on up to bed?"

"I'm gonna wait up for Dad," Maggy said.

"There aren't any more ferries tonight," Riley pointed out.

"Sometimes he catches a ride over," Maggy said stubbornly. "Or maybe he's got our boat over at Southpoint. You don't know."

"I'm too tired to argue with you now," Riley said sharply. "Go on up to bed like I asked. If Dad does come in, I'll send him upstairs to see you first thing. I swear."

"Come on," Billy said, tugging at Maggy's hand. "I'll walk you up. I'll even see if I can find that raggedy old Little Mermaid blankie you used to love."

"Mimi probably threw it away," Maggy said, her voice forlorn, allowing herself to be led from the room.

"No way," Billy said firmly. "Mimi never throws anything away."

"What's going on between you and Wendell?" Scott asked, as soon as Maggy was out of earshot.

"Absolutely nothing," Riley said.

"And what's that mean?"

Riley fetched the wine jug and poured herself another glass. "I don't even know where to start." She hesitated. "This was *supposed* to be the weekend we break the news to Maggy that we're separating. But Wendell pulled a disappearing act, and now all hell is breaking loose."

She recounted the day's events, including the discovery of the foreclosure notice tacked to her front door.

"Ed tried calling the sheriff's office, but the dispatcher doesn't know what's going on. It looks like we might have to wait until Tuesday to get everything straightened out."

Scott pointed at Riley's cell phone, which she'd plugged into the only outlet on the kitchen counter. "And you still haven't heard from Wendell?"

"Not a word. Maggy's furious at me, I'm furious at him, and tonight . . . when Mama finds out, well, you know . . ." Her voice trailed off.

Scott took a bottle of water from the refrigerator and uncapped it. He took a long swig. "Why do you say that? You don't think Evelyn's going to blame you for everything that's happened—do you?"

"She's sure not gonna blame St. Wendell," Riley said. "According to Mama, he can do no wrong."

"Families." The way Scott said it came out as a prolonged sigh.

She took the wine upstairs, set it carefully on the nightstand on her side of the bed, and looked around the room.

Not much had changed since Evelyn had fixed up what she called "the honeymoon suite" twenty years earlier. The floral wallpaper still had bright blue morning glories twining up sea-green stripes. The ugly marble-topped Victorian dresser that had been her grandmother's still wore a hand-crocheted doily precisely in the middle, with a nearly full bottle of yellowing Youth Dew perfume planted in the middle of it.

The mahogany four-poster bed stood on a sun-faded Oriental rug, and the forty-year-old mattress—that had been her parent's until her father flatly refused to sleep one more night in a double bed—still sagged in the middle.

That was another thing Evelyn didn't believe in spending money on—new mattresses—unless it was for her own bed.

The room was warm and stuffy, and it smelled of lemon Pledge. Riley went to the double-wide window that looked out on the back lawn—and the bay, and tugged upward on the wooden sash until it opened with a screech of protest.

Warm, humid air floated into the room, and Riley felt strangely reassured. Her suitcase stood, unopened, at the foot of the bed, but out of curiosity more than anything else, she opened the top dresser drawer.

Sure enough, she found a stack of neatly folded cotton nightgowns, right where she'd left them—how long ago? Seven, eight years?

She pulled the cotton gown over her head and let its folds settle lightly over her skin, then climbed into bed and poured herself another tumbler of wine.

Riley picked up her cell phone one more time. It had bars, and was fully charged, but what it did not have was any type of communication from Wendell Griggs.

Her mind kept going back to the boldfaced notice taped to her front door.

To the sight of her locked front door. And the face of the sheriff's deputy, who'd served her with the foreclosure notice. She wanted to scream. She wanted to throw something. Preferably at Wendell Griggs.

Instead, she found a dog-eared Agatha Christie paperback in the nightstand drawer and started reading and sipping.

By the time Riley finally drifted off to sleep, Miss Jane Marple had discovered the body in the vicarage, and was puzzling over the railway schedule to St. Mary Mead and a single, suspicious fingernail clipping.

"Riley!" A hand clamped firmly over her shoulder. "Riley, wake up."

She rolled onto her back.

"What on earth?" Evelyn Nolan was perched on the side of the bed, staring down at her slumbering daughter. She was still dressed for the full moon party, in a pair of crisp white linen slacks, a red-and-white-striped blouse, and a navy blue linen Ralph Lauren blazer. Her size-four feet were shod in sporty white kid loafers, and she wore a red silk Hermès scarf knotted at the open neck of her shirt. This was her mother's idea of beachwear. She looked like a tiny, angry robin pecking at a helpless worm. And Riley felt like that worm.

Evelyn didn't wait for Riley to reply.

"Billy told me some crazy story about your house being foreclosed? How can that be?"

Riley struggled to sit up as her mother continued to volley questions at her. "What did the sheriff's office say? Did Ed talk to the sheriff? Where's Wendell?"

She got out of bed, went into the bathroom, closed the door, threw her head back, and screamed silently. Then she scrubbed the taste of cheap white wine from her mouth, peed, flushed, washed her hands, and went back into the room.

"Well?" Evelyn's penciled-on brown eyebrows formed perfect inverted *V*s, and her face powder had settled into the deep furrows on either side of her lips.

Riley climbed back into the bed. "The sheriff's office couldn't tell us anything. Ed tried, but was unable to talk to the sheriff and, as to your last question, I have no idea where Wendell is."

"I don't understand any of this," Evelyn said. "Wendell makes a wonderful salary at Belle Isle Enterprises. Your daddy saw to that. Honey, why didn't you tell me things had gotten so bad?"

"I didn't know things had gotten bad. I still don't know that they have. There has to be some kind of a mix-up."

"I should hope so! Everybody on the island is talking, you know. According to Frances Carter, that dreadful Payne woman was going around telling people Wendell had you served with divorce papers on the ferry today. Franny told her she was mistaken, but you know how people talk."

Riley hesitated, then shrugged. "Andrea Payne is actually about half right. You might as well know, Wendell and I are splitting up."

"I can't believe you would do such a thing."

"Me? Mama, what makes you think I'm the one doing the divorcing?"

"Because I know Wendell. He would never hurt our family by doing something like that. He adores Maggy. He would never let his daughter go through a divorce."

"I notice you don't say he adores *his wife,*" Riley said pointedly.

"Don't be silly. Wendell is devoted to you, and you know it."

"Unfortunately, I don't know it. Mama, when was the last time you saw Wendell with me and Maggy?"

"You know I don't keep track of things like that," Evelyn said. "Anyway, Wendell's a busy man, trying to provide for his family. He's traveling between here and Raleigh and New York, and he's got all these plans for the new development.... Your father wasn't home much either when you and Billy were young, but that didn't mean he didn't love his family. And me."

"Except for ten days ago when he came home to pick up his dry cleaning, Wendell hasn't spent more than two nights in a row in our house in six weeks. He missed all five performances of Maggy's school play in April. We haven't had sex in seven months. *That's* how much he loves his family."

Evelyn recoiled as though she'd been spattered with hot grease.

"Don't be crude."

"It's the truth," Riley said.

Evelyn unknotted and then retied her scarf. "Is there . . . do you think . . . ?"

"Another woman?" Riley said helpfully. "He swears there isn't, but I don't believe him. And, at this point, I frankly don't care."

Now Evelyn removed the scarf and was twisting it between both hands. Riley wondered, idly, if her mother would use it to garrote her thankless only daughter.

"Now listen, young lady. I won't let you throw a perfectly good marriage away, just because your husband might be having himself a meaningless little fling."

Riley hooted. "You won't let me? Sorry, Mama. This is one thing you cannot control. Don't you think I gave it the old college try? Don't you think we've been in counseling for two years? Or rather, I've been in counseling. Wendell has been too busy 'providing for his family' to make it to any sessions since November."

"Counseling," Evelyn said with a dismissive sniff. "A waste of good money."

"Not for me," Riley said, dropping back down onto her pillow. "It was the best money I've ever spent." She took the pillow from Wendell's side of the bed and put it under her own head and gazed into her mother's disapproving gray eyes.

"Riley Rose Nolan Griggs—you need to stop this selfish behavior right now. You need to think about that little girl sleeping in that bedroom across the hall. If you go ahead with this divorce, you will break that child's heart," Evelyn said, standing to go.

"I know it, Mama," Riley said sadly. "And if I could fix that, I would. But I can't raise her to be the kind of woman she needs to be if she sees her mother settling for a marriage that's a lie. I need her to know that I deserve better. And that she deserves better, too."

"For Pete's sake," Evelyn snapped. She pointed at the half-empty wine bottle on the nightstand. "I can't talk to you when you've been drinking like this. I'm going to bed now. And in the morning, we are going to have a serious talk about life, and your totally unrealistic expectations of marriage."

She snatched up the wine bottle, took it into the bathroom, and poured the wine down the commode with deliberate ceremony before stomping out of the honeymoon suite.

"Should have done that hours ago," Riley murmured, turning over to go back to sleep.

9

Hey, Nate. Look at that crowd over there at the marina."

Annie Milas was standing in front of the large picture window in the office on the top floor of the ferry building. It was the first Saturday of summer, a bright, clear day. She'd been going over the accounting books with her son to assure him that all was well with the family business. Trying to convince him that it was time for him to get on with his life.

Nate looked up from the spreadsheet he'd been studying. He walked over to the window and looked out. A black-and-white Baldwin County sheriff's cruiser was parked at the end of the marina dock, its blue light flashing. A small crowd of people had gathered, all of them craning their necks and staring down at the water where a pale yellow Boston Whaler and a sleek thirty-six-foot sailboat were moored.

"Probably a dead shark or something washed up," Nate said dismissively.

"I don't think so," Annie said, shaking her head. "They wouldn't call out the sheriff for a shark."

"Maybe somebody vandalized one of those boats there," he mused, watching as a uniformed deputy leaned over the dock, taking photos with a 35mm camera.

The deputy was laid out flat on his belly now, his torso hanging over the edge of the concrete bulkhead, as a man hung onto his legs to keep him from falling in.

"They're not looking at the boats. That deputy is taking pictures of something in the water," Annie pointed out. "Wonder what it is?"

"I suppose you think I should wander over that way to find out?" he asked, bemused. "When did you turn into the official Belle Isle busybody?"

"I keep my eye out for trouble, that's all," Annie said. "I'd go myself, but I'm expecting a call from Wayne. He's supposed to pick up some groceries for me at the Harris Teeter when he gets to Southpoint."

"I'll go," Nate said. "But I promise you, it's probably nothing."

Nate sauntered over to the marina. The crowd had grown larger in the twenty minutes since he'd accepted his mission, and they'd been pushed back, away from the water, by the cops. Probably two dozen people were now clustered at the near end of the bulkhead. A set of police barricades had been set up to block access, and the frizzy-haired female deputy who'd been on the ferry yesterday was standing guard. From the scowl on her face it was apparent that she was praying for an excuse to handcuff or at the very least Mace somebody.

"Hey, Nate, how's it going?" A scrawny, balding, deeply tanned man with tattoo sleeves on both arms slapped him on the back.

It took Nate a moment to connect the face with a name. He'd known Marty Connor, a second-generation commercial fisherman, since high school but hadn't seen him in years.

"Going good, Marty. Real good."

"Sorry about your old man," Marty said. "Captain Joe always treated me right. He was a good dude. And your mom, she's a real nice lady. Even if she did flunk me in fourth grade. Twice."

He had the wheezy, labored laugh of a lifetime chain smoker. And although it was only 9 a.m., Marty Connor already reeked of cheap booze.

"Thanks," Nate said. He pointed toward the end of the dock. "What's going on?"

"Shiiiiit," Marty said. "It's a floater!"

"You mean, like a body? A dead person?"

"Damn straight." Marty thumped his bare, bony chest. "And I'm the one who found him. I went out early this morning, chasing redfish, but nothing was biting so I came on back. I tied up in my usual spot, and I was just kinda, you know, walking the dock, checking things out when I looked down and saw him. A guy, floating there, with some rope kinda tangled around him. Tellin' ya, man, I about crapped my Fruit of the Looms!"

"I'll bet."

"Not gonna lie," Marty said, lowering his voice. "It shook me bad. I went back to my truck—I got a bottle of Jim Beam I keep under the seat for, like, emergencies—and I hit it hard, cuz I had the shakes so bad. After that, I called nine-one-one."

Nate's eyes were riveted toward the end of the dock. There were two deputies now, and they were straining, lifting something with ropes.

"Any idea who it is?" Nate asked.

"No, man. There was a bunch of seaweed and stuff covering his face. I took some pictures with my cell phone, but after that I boogied out of there as fast as I could."

They heard a siren approaching, and both men turned to see a rusting white ambulance turning into the marina parking lot.

The driver pulled the vehicle up to the police barricade and rolled to a stop. The driver and another man got out. They were both dressed casually, in shorts and T-shirts, which Nate found strange, until he remembered that the Belle Isle Volunteer Fire Department also ran the only ambulance on the island. The two men opened the ambulance-bay doors and pulled out a collapsible rolling gurney. One paused, pulled a pack of cigarettes from his back pocket, and lit up before continuing on.

"Everybody back," the female deputy bellowed. The crowd parted, and the volunteers began pushing the gurney toward the end of the dock.

"Not in any big rush, are they?" Nate murmured.

Marty cracked a wide grin. "Hell, what's the hurry? That dude ain't getting any deader."

The morning sun beat down on the bystanders' heads. A mosquito buzzed around Nate's face, and he slapped at it until it left a black smear on the palm of his hand. Nate's shirt stuck to his back, and he began to wish he'd grabbed a hat, or at least his sunglasses, before leaving the office. After more than a dozen years in California, he still couldn't get used to the brutal humidity of the coastal South. Still, he lingered on, accusing himself of the same morbid curiosity that kept everybody else standing around on the first Saturday morning of summer.

He tried to think of something to talk about with Marty Connor. "Fishing good this year?"

"Nah. Sucks so far. My wife wants me to get a real job on the mainland, and I might have to if things don't pick up." Marty turned to study his old classmate.

"Hey. I hear you went out to California and invented some kinda Web site. Kinda like Bill Gates, or that Facebook dude, Mark Wahlberg."

Nate didn't bat an eye. "You mean Mark Zuckerberg?"

"Wahlberg, Zuckerberg, same difference. So you hit it big out there, right?"

"I did okay." Nate tried to change the subject. He stared up at the Carolina blue sky, shading his eyes from the glare. "Think it'll rain?"

"Nah. Hey, uh, word around town is you might be looking to do some hiring for the ferry, what with your dad being dead and stuff. You know, I got my commercial captain's license awhile ago."

"Good for you," Nate said, already dreading what would come next.

"What's the pay for a ferry captain these days? Pretty sweet, I bet."

"I think the pay's decent, but I wouldn't really know, because my mom handles all that stuff. But if you want to put in an application, I'm sure she'd consider you."

"Oh." Marty's shoulders drooped. "Yeah, okay. Maybe I'll do that."

They both contemplated the probability of that happening for a moment.

"Here comes the corpse," Marty said, pointing toward the bulkhead. The ambulance attendants walked the gurney with the corpse, zippered into a gray vinyl bag, toward the barricade, and the crowd silently parted to let them through. Just before the attendants passed, Marty whipped his phone from his pocket and clicked off a series of photos.

"I gotta go," Nate said suddenly. The heat was too much. It was all too much. What a depressing start to the long weekend.

"Yeah, see ya," Marty said.

10

Riley!" For the second time in a few short hours, somebody was shaking her awake. She opened one eye. It was daylight, but just barely.

"Not again," Riley groaned. She opened the other eye. Billy stood beside her bed. His face gleamed with perspiration, his thinning dark hair was pasted to his scalp, and his white T-shirt clung to his chest.

"Wake up, Riley. The sheriff is here," Billy said.

"Thank God." She swung her legs over the side of the bed and ran a hand through her own tangled hair.

"Good old Ed," Riley said, yawning. "He must have gotten hold of the sheriff last night. Now maybe we can get to the bottom of this foreclosure bullshit."

She opened her suitcase, found a pair of shorts, and pulled them on under her nightgown. "Tell him I'll be down as soon as I'm dressed, okay?"

"Riles? I don't think this is about the house."

She stood and studied her little brother's face. It was pale and drawn.

"Then, what's the sheriff want with me?"

"Sit down, okay?"

She sank down onto her unmade bed and pulled one of the feather pillows onto her lap.

Billy sat down beside her.

"Bebo, you're scaring me now. Tell me what's going on. Please?"

He took a deep breath, and then another. The room was cool, but he was sweating profusely now.

"It's Wendell. There's been some kind of accident."

Riley gripped the pillow with both hands. "Where is he? Is he all right?"

"No." Billy shook his head. "No, honey. Wendell is dead."

She hugged the pillow to her belly like a life raft. "That can't be right."

He put his arms around her, and she tried to pull away, but he hugged tighter. "It's true. I'm so, so, so sorry. That's why the sheriff is downstairs. He won't tell Mama why he wants to see you, but I know it's because . . . of Wendell. They found his body this morning. In the water, at the marina."

"That's not right," Riley repeated. "It can't be Wendell. He wasn't even on the island. It's a mistake."

"I wish," Billy said. "I was coming back from my run about an hour ago, it was still dark, and a sheriff's car went zooming past me on the loop road." He ran a hand through his damp hair, leaving it standing up in little tufts. "You never see cops here, right? So I just, kinda followed the road until I saw where they were going. And it was the marina."

"A fisherman found him. He was . . . I mean, his body was . . . tangled in some lines. I saw his face, honey. It was Wendell."

"No." She felt like screaming, but it came out as a whisper. "It's somebody else."

"It was Wendell, Riles. It was. But the sheriff, he's downstairs in the kitchen with Mama. He wants to see you. I told her I'd come get you."

Riley searched her brother's face for some tip-off, a tell. He was a notorious practical joker.

"It's true, Riley," he said softly. "You know I wouldn't kid about something like this."

"Swear it," she said fiercely, hugging the pillow so tightly she could feel sharp feather quills stabbing the tender skin of her inner arms.

"I swear. To God. Remember Ray Warren? We played T-ball together as kids. He's a member of the volunteer fire department. He was driving the ambulance, and he saw me standing there, and he told me, because he knows you're my sister. It's Wendell. They found his wallet in his pants pocket. And then they brought me over, and I identified him."

"No. No. No." She buried her face in her hands. Her eyes burned, but the tears didn't come.

Her heart was beating a mile a minute, and her chest—it felt like a lead weight was perched there.

She looked up at Billy, gasping for breath. "I can't . . . I can't . . ."

He patted her back gently. "Come on. You can do this." The palm of his hand was warm as he made circles on her back. "Slow it down. Breathe in. Breathe out."

Five minutes passed. Her cell phone dinged quietly on the nightstand, registering incoming e-mails. Without thinking, she grabbed it up. Wendell. Maybe he was e-mailing to let her know there'd been some gruesome mistake. Maybe he was waiting on the ferry dock in Southpoint right now.

The e-mail was for a Scoutmob deal for an oil change and lube job. She thrust the phone away.

"Okay?" her brother asked.

She nodded.

Billy went to the suitcase and handed her a T-shirt. "Come on, Riley. You need to get dressed and go talk to the sheriff. Please?"

She stared down at the T-shirt and some part of her brain registered that it was a hot pink walkathon shirt from some charity benefit she'd done for the television station. She folded it neatly in her lap.

"He's been down there for half an hour now. If you don't go downstairs, you know Mama's going to come up here. . . ."

"No," Riley said quickly. "Okay. I'll get dressed." She stood up, but her knees were shaking so badly she had to cling to the bedpost for support.

"Where's Maggy? Tell me she's not down there. I don't want her . . ."

"She's still asleep," Billy said quickly. "It's not even nine yet. You go on down. I'll stay up here and wait for her to wake up."

"I'm going," Riley said.

Riley found the sheriff standing in the kitchen, looking uneasy beneath the hostile glare of Evelyn Nolan, who was still in her cotton housecoat. Even to Riley, this man looked barely old enough to be a school crossing guard, let alone a sheriff.

His white-blond hair was neatly combed with a side part. He wore a baby-blue golf shirt with an embroidered insignia patch, and black Dockers. His baseball cap was tucked into his belt, which also held a leather case bearing a gold badge.

"Ma'am?" he said, as she entered the room. "I'm Craig Schumann. Sorry to barge in on you people so early."

"It's all right," she murmured. "I'm Riley Griggs. My brother said you wanted to see me?"

"Yes ma'am," the sheriff said. He glanced at Evelyn, who was pretending to wipe down the already spotless countertop. "I was, uh, wondering if we could talk, well, I wouldn't want to disturb your family . . ."

"He won't tell me what this is all about," Evelyn said. "I've explained that I'm your mother, and this is my home."

"Mama, please?" Riley gave her mother a beseeching look.

When they were alone, the sheriff gestured toward the dinette. "Ma'am, you might want to sit down before we talk."

"Did my mother offer you coffee?" Riley heard herself ask. Absurd that she should be concerned about his discomfort, when she was the one about to be given the worst news of her life.

She hadn't been a real journalist in more than a decade, but suddenly, out of nowhere, she found herself back in reporter mode, noticing the tiniest details, the mole on the sheriff's chin, the speck of mustard on the Formica tabletop, her own hands, clasping and unclasping, the sorry state of her nails, with chipped polish and ragged cuticles. Most of all, and the thing she found both shocking and unforgiveable, was her complete and utter emotional detachment.

"No, well, she did, but I don't care for any coffee," the sheriff said, blushing furiously.

Riley sat down at the table, and he took the chair opposite hers.

"My brother said this is about my husband?" she asked.

He nodded. "I'm afraid I have some bad news." He leaned forward and took a small spiral-bound notebook from his back pocket. He flipped through the pages until he found the one he wanted. He consulted his notes, then looked directly at her.

"Your husband is Wendell Griggs, that's correct? Age forty-two? And the two of you reside here on Belle Isle at 555 Sand Dollar Lane."

"My husband is Wendell Griggs. We have a second home on Sand Dollar Lane, but our legal residence has been on St. Mary's Street in Raleigh, which we just sold," she said.

"That's right." He nodded. "Okay, well." He took a deep breath and looked directly at her. "I'm sorry to have to tell you that your husband is deceased."

"I know."

His eyes widened. "You already know? Do you mind if I ask how you know?"

"My brother was out for his morning run when he saw the commotion at the marina," Riley said. "He told me just now."

"He told you your husband is dead?"

"Yes."

"Shit." He said it under his breath, then looked up and colored again. "Pardon my French. I'm just, well, your reaction isn't what I expected."

"It's not what I expected either," Riley said sadly. She stood abruptly. "If you don't mind, I think I'm going to need some coffee now."

At home she drank coffee heavily dosed with sugar and half-and-half. Today she drank it scalding hot and black, and she could already feel a blister rising on her tongue. It was the only thing she could feel.

She sat down at the table and took another sip of coffee.

"Do they know? I mean, do you know what happened? Billy said he was in the water?"

"That's right."

"I don't understand any of this. Are you saying he drowned? Because Wendell wouldn't drown. He could swim. He was an athlete. Or, he used to be."

"We don't know yet. I can tell you there was a wound on the back of his head."

Her eyes widened. "Oh God. A wound? What does that mean?"

"Again, this is all the information I have. There will be an autopsy. . . ."

Riley felt her stomach roil. She bolted from the room, making it to the hall bathroom just in time. She knelt by the commode, retching again and again, until she thought her ribs would shatter. Finally, she laid down in a fetal position on the black-and-white-penny-tile floor, resting her cheek against the cool surface.

There was a light knock on the door, which she hadn't had time to close. Parrish stepped inside. She took one of Evelyn's starched and monogrammed linen fingertip towels from a delicate silver tray on the marble vanity, ran it under the faucet, and sat down beside her best friend, pressing it to the back of her neck, and then her temples, and finally, dabbing it at Riley's lips.

"They're saying Wendell's dead," Riley said finally.

"I know, shug," Parrish said sadly, putting an arm around her shoulder. "Billy called. Are you okay?"

"I don't know," Riley whispered. "I don't know what to do, Parrish."

"Ed does," Parrish said. "He's out in the kitchen with the sheriff. He'll take care of stuff."

"The sheriff said Wendell had a . . . a wound on his head."

"That's what he told Ed, too. Do you feel like standing up yet?"

"Give me a minute." Finally, Riley pulled herself up and splashed cold water on her face.

"The sheriff said he had some questions for me," Riley said. "But I don't know anything. I don't know what Wendell was doing at the marina. He was supposed to meet us at the ferry yesterday."

"Ed doesn't want you to talk to the sheriff just yet," Parrish said.

"I already have."

"Well, don't say anything else to him. Look. Your husband is dead. We don't know how, or why, or anything. Maybe there was an accident. We don't know that yet. Now, it's been years since I practiced criminal law, but I can tell you, if this is not an accident, the first person they're going to look at is Wendell's wife."

Riley stared. "Are you saying they think somebody did this to him? It might not be an accident? That somebody *killed* Wendell? That's crazy! Who would kill him? And why? And why would the sheriff think I had something to do with it?"

"Because he's a cop. That's how their minds work. And, face it, once he starts asking questions, he's probably going to find out that you guys were about to get a divorce. And then there's this whole foreclosure thing."

Riley sat down abruptly on the commode. "Oh God. I'd forgotten about that."

"He hasn't," Parrish said. "We need to get you a lawyer."

"I don't want a lawyer," Riley said. "I didn't do anything. You know that. Ed knows it."

"Of course we do. You wouldn't hurt a fly. This is just for your own protection."

"No." Riley shook her head vehemently. "I want to talk to the sheriff. I'll answer his questions. I want him to know I don't have anything to hide. I want to know what happened. I have to be able to tell Maggy what happened."

"Not a good idea," Parrish warned.

"I don't care. I appreciate Ed's concern, and yours, but I have to do this."

"All right," Parrish said, sighing. "Where's Maggy? You haven't told her yet, right?"

"Billy's upstairs with her. She's still sleeping and, with any luck, it'll be another hour or so until she wakes up."

"Your mama doesn't know yet?"

"God, no."

She sat at the table with Ed and the sheriff, who was now sipping coffee from one of Evelyn Nolan's delicate pink-flowered coffee cups.

"Wendell was supposed to meet me yesterday at the ferry in Southpoint, before the last boat of the day. But he never made it. I kept calling and texting . . . I guess now we know why he didn't answer."

"Why didn't your husband drive down from Raleigh with you?"

"He had meetings. Most of the time, we do drive down separately, because my daughter and I stay on the island all summer, and Wendell is a weekender."

"Even for the long Memorial Day holiday?"

"Yes."

"What kind of meetings? Do you know who your husband was going to be with?"

"No." Riley bit her lip. "I didn't keep up with Wendell's work stuff. And I guess I should just go ahead and tell you . . ."

"Riley?" Ed gave her a warning shake of his head, anticipating what she would say next.

She plunged ahead anyway. "Wendell and I had been pretty much living separate lives these past few months. He hadn't actually moved out yet, but that was our next step."

"You're getting divorced?"

Riley picked at the cuticle on her thumb. "We were going to tell Maggy, our daughter, this weekend."

"When was the last time you talked to Mr. Griggs?"

"You mean, in person?" She thought back. Lately, the bulk of her communication with Wendell had consisted of e-mails and texts.

"Maybe Wednesday?" She frowned. "I'd have to look at my phone."

"What did you talk about? Did the subject of the divorce come up?"

"Not really. I guess we were both avoiding the subject. I know I told him I'd booked his trip on the ferry online. We just talked about the usual stuff. Dinner plans, like that."

The sheriff jotted something down in his notebook. "I'm sorry to have to ask these questions."

"Then don't," Ed put in. "For God's sake! She just learned about Wendell's death. She's told you what she knows."

"All right." The sheriff sighed and closed the cover of his notebook. He glanced at his watch. "I've got to get over to the mainland anyway."

Riley swallowed hard. "What happens now? I mean, with my husband's body? I need to make arrangements."

"For now, his body has been taken to the morgue at Memorial Hospital in Southpoint. As I mentioned, there will be an autopsy. That's state law. Unfortunately, as you know, this is a holiday, so that could take a few days."

A holiday. She'd forgotten about that. This was to have been the weekend to start the summer, to start getting used to the reality of divorce. Riley had forgotten. Now, she guessed, she'd start getting used to the idea of being a widow.

The sheriff set his coffee cup carefully in the sink. "Just one more thing, Mrs. Griggs. Were you aware that your husband was having financial difficulties? And that your home here was in foreclosure?"

"No." Her head was throbbing. "I didn't know anything. Last night, when we got to the house and saw the sign tacked to the door, that was the first I knew about any of this. I thought it was a mistake."

She looked up at the sheriff and realized she was crying. "A horrible mistake."

11

Mom?" Maggy's shrill voice rang out from the hallway. Riley heard her bare feet slapping against the wooden stair treads. A moment later, she stood in the kitchen doorway, dressed in an oversize T-shirt, her hair disheveled. When she saw Ed Godchaux seated at the table, she tugged self-consciously at the hem of the shirt, trying to pull it down over her bare, tanned thighs.

"Mom, there's a cop car in the driveway. What's going on? Why are Ed and Parrish here? And the cops? Has something happened?"

Riley jumped to her feet and gathered her daughter into her arms. She stroked Maggy's hair, wondering how she would find the words to break this child's heart.

And Maggy *was* her heart. Motherhood had been a hard-fought battle for Riley. She'd suffered through two first-trimester miscarriages before finally managing to carry this baby full-term.

Once she and Wendell took Maggy home from the hospital, her anxieties about motherhood hadn't ended. Her newborn had learned to sleep through the night months before Riley was able to do so without sneaking into the nursery and checking on the infant every few hours.

Riley had been driven in the early years of her journalism career. After Maggy's birth, she'd eventually funneled all that energy into motherhood, taking an extended leave from the television station. She'd only briefly, reluctantly, returned to her evening anchor position after the station's assistant manager, a sympathetic older mother herself, had pointed out that many children not only survived, but thrived in the care of a nanny or a good preschool.

Riley had a shelf of pregnancy, childbearing, and parenting self-help books at home in Raleigh, but nothing she'd ever read in those books could have prepared her for a moment like this.

Maggy pulled away from her mother's embrace, her blue-gray eyes narrowed. "It's Dad, isn't it? Tell me, Mom. Something happened to him, didn't it? That's why he didn't make the ferry last night. Tell me right now!"

Riley glanced over at Ed, who stood now, his hand on her right shoulder.

"Honey? Yes. It's Dad. He was . . . there was some kind of accident." She grasped her daughter's hand. "Dad's dead, Mags."

"No." Maggy wrenched away from Riley. She looked at Ed for confirmation. "He's not, is he?"

Ed nodded, his expression grave. "I'm so sorry, but it's true."

"Noooooo." Maggy howled, collapsing to the floor. "Noooo. Nooo. Nooo."

Riley knelt down beside the child, trying to embrace her, but Maggy pushed her violently away. "No!"

Ed stood quietly. "I'll get Parrish. We'll be on the porch if you need us."

Maggy looked up, tears streaming down her face. "What happened?" she whispered.

"We don't really know yet," Riley said. "Some kind of accident, they think."

"Oh my God," Maggy moaned. "Was he in a car wreck?"

"No. The sheriff told me they found Dad this morning. In the water, at the marina."

"What? What does that mean? Dad couldn't drown. It's the wrong guy. Dad couldn't drown. Did you tell the sheriff they made a mistake?"

Riley reached out and tucked a strand of damp hair behind Maggy's ear. "It's not a mistake. Billy was there. This morning. It was your dad."

"I don't believe you."

"It's true, Magpie."

Billy had entered the kitchen so quietly that neither of them noticed his presence. He sat down on the floor and took both of Maggy's hands in his. "I wish it wasn't true. Nobody wants it to be but it is. It just is."

"I want to see him," Maggy said.

They were sitting at the kitchen table. Riley drinking her second cup of scalding black coffee, Billy drinking a Diet Dr Pepper.

"Oh, honey," Riley said, shaking her head. "No. I know this is a shock for you. It's a shock for all of us. But that's not a good idea. Look. The sheriff said Dad had some kind of wound on his head. You don't want to see that. It's too upsetting."

"I don't care," Maggy said. "You think it's not upsetting knowing he's dead? Knowing he was in the water like that?"

"It's just that, well, the sheriff said there has to be an autopsy. I don't even know yet when we can have a service."

Maggy stuck out her chin in an expression Riley knew all too well.

"He's my father. You can't just dig a hole in the ground and bury him without letting me see him. It's not fair."

"All right," Riley said, shrugging. "I'll call the sheriff and tell him what you want. It's a holiday weekend, so he didn't know when they'd actually . . . you know."

"That's the worst idea I ever heard," Evelyn chimed in. She'd been flitting nervously around the kitchen for fucking ever, as far as Riley was concerned, ever since Billy had pulled her aside upstairs and told her the reason for the sheriff's visit.

Evelyn put down the broom she'd been using to sweep up nonexistent crumbs. She took a seat at the table, directly opposite her only grandchild.

"Listen to me, Margaret. I know you think you're all grown up, and that you can handle seeing your father like that. But you have no idea what it will be like."

"I do so. I saw Boots—after she got run over by that car at home. I'm the one who had to pick her up and put her in the shoebox and bury her. And I went to Granny Griggs's funeral, too. I went right up to the coffin, when Mom wasn't looking, and I touched her hand."

"Maggy!' Riley said, shocked.

"I'm not talking about a kitten, or an old lady whose funeral you went to when you were only seven years old," Evelyn said.

"I was eight."

"You were a little girl, and you scarcely knew your Granny Griggs, because she'd been in that nursing home for years when she passed away. This is your father you're talking about. It's an entirely different matter. Right now, you're in shock. You don't really know what you want."

"Mama?" Billy gave her an almost imperceptible look. "Why don't we let Riley decide what's appropriate for her own daughter?"

"Because she's obviously not thinking clearly right now, or she'd never even consider letting this child have her way." Evelyn's voice rose, and Riley's head throbbed even worse.

She stood up slowly, holding the edge of the table to stabilize herself.

"I'm going upstairs to shower and get dressed," she said quietly. She held out a hand to her daughter. "Come on, Mags."

12

Sunday morning, Riley was sitting at the kitchen table, staring down at a plate of cold scrambled eggs that her mother had just slid in front of her, when the doorbell rang.

"Got it," Scott said quietly. From the hallway, they heard subdued voices. Five minutes later, he was back, carrying a foil-wrapped casserole.

"What's that?" Evelyn got up to look.

"Mona Gillespie brought her Chinese chicken casserole," Scott said, placing it carefully on the countertop. "She said to tell you to bake it at three-fifty for thirty-seven minutes."

"Hideous," Billy said, lifting the foil to get a peek. "Just as I feared, topped with chop suey noodles. And almonds."

"Mona Gillespie is a dear, sweet friend," Evelyn said. "Wasn't that thoughtful of Mona, Riley?"

"Very thoughtful." Riley pushed the eggs around on her plate, clockwise, and then counterclockwise.

Five minutes later, the doorbell rang again, and then again. It had been only twenty-four hours, but word of Wendell Griggs's death had already begun to spread. The phone rang, and offerings of food began to pile up.

"Where's Maggy?" Billy asked, standing with the refrigerator door ajar, as he searched for a place to stash Sheila King's tomato aspic.

"She went to the beach with some of the Billingsley kids, first thing this morning," Riley reported. "Shane, the oldest one, had a cast-net. They seem to think they're going to catch a shark."

"Good for Mags," Billy said approvingly. "No use her sitting around the house all day with us."

"That's what I think, too. But I told her she needs to be back in time to shower and change so we can make the two-fifteen ferry," Riley added.

"You're going to town?" Evelyn asked, her coffee cup poised inches from her carefully made-up lips. "Traffic will be terrible."

"I know, but the sheriff has arranged for us to go to the hospital so Maggy can see Wendell."

"Of course." Evelyn's face radiated disapproval as she removed the plate of eggs and dumped them in the trash with deliberate ceremony.

"You talked to the sheriff this morning? Did he have any news?" Billy asked.

"Not really. He wanted my permission to take the Boston Whaler over to the mainland, so they can have somebody from the state crime lab take a look at it."

"What do they want with the boat?" Scott asked.

"They're assuming Wendell came over to the island on the Whaler since his name wasn't on the ferry manifests for the past week, and they found him close to where the boat was tied up. I told him Wendell did that sometimes, if he needed to. I guess they're looking for fingerprints or something. He was pretty vague about everything."

"Fingerprints?" Evelyn frowned. "This was a horrible, tragic accident. It's clear that Wendell must have slipped, hit his head on the dock, and fallen into the water. Why would they want to fingerprint the boat?"

Riley's headache was back. The truth was, it had never really gone away. She'd gotten little sleep the night before, and now, it felt as though a band of wire was wrapped tightly around her skull.

"They think there's more to it than that. There's another head wound—

the sheriff called it blunt force trauma. Somebody hit him. Hard. Hard enough to knock him down."

"Jesus!" Billy whispered.

"Who would want to kill Wendell?" Evelyn asked, her pale blue eyes filling with tears.

I would, Riley thought, remembering the shock and humiliation she'd suffered on the ferry, and feeling yet another wave of guilt.

"But why?" Billy gave up on finding a place for the aspic. He set the dish on the counter, alongside Sylvia Sutliff's pineapple fluff and Marilyn Butler's strawberry pretzel salad, which sat next to Cleo Metcalf's chocolate sour cream pound cake.

Why not? Riley thought. And she was immediately ashamed. Again.

"The sheriff seems to think it might have something to do with Wendell's business dealings," she said finally. She swallowed hard, blinking back sudden tears. "Maybe something connected to our house being foreclosed. I don't understand any of this."

The back door swung open with a bang, and a tall, lanky woman with damp silver hair worn in a long braid breezed into the kitchen.

"Good morning, everybody," Mary Roosevelt Nolan sang out in her husky voice. She wore a baggy, faded black one-piece bathing suit with a towel wrapped loosely around her hips and she had a pair of white rubber swim goggles pushed up into her hair as a headband.

"Hi, Aunt Roo," Riley said, grateful for the distraction of her aunt's arrival.

Mary Roosevelt Nolan was used to being a distraction. Christened such by her New Deal–loving father, her name had been shortened to Roo by her baby brother, W.R., who happened to be Riley's father.

Roo was a confirmed spinster, devoted birdwatcher and, to the chagrin of many of her relatives, a card-carrying liberal Democrat and either her sister-in-law Evelyn's best friend or worst enemy, depending on both of the women's moods. She lived in the carriage house at Shutters.

"The water felt glorious this morning, and I even saw a long-billed curlew," Roo said, helping herself to a blueberry muffin from a basket that had been dropped off moments earlier by Gretchen Lombard.

"I guess you must have loved it, since you decided to track it all across my kitchen floor," Evelyn said, mopping at the offending drops of water with a paper towel.

"Sorry." Roo shrugged and poured herself a mug of coffee. "Why are you all sitting around here on such a beautiful morning?" She pointed at the lineup of dishes on the counter. "And what's with all the food? Are we having a party I'm not invited to?"

Billy and Riley exchanged a look.

"Aunt Roo," Billy said gently. "Didn't you get the voice mail I left you last night?"

"Hell no. I hate voice mails. They're always from some telemarketer trying to sell me a time-share at Disney World. Now, you tell me, what does an old maid like me want with a condo in Orlando? They don't even have a beach there."

"Mary Roosevelt Nolan!" Evelyn snapped. "Maybe if you took the trouble to listen to the messages we leave you, you'd know what's going on around here. For your information, Wendell is dead."

Roo looked from Riley to her sister-in-law, and then back again.

"Wendell Griggs? Your Wendell?"

Riley nodded. "It's true."

Roo took a bite of the muffin and chewed slowly. "That's awful. When was this? What happened?"

"We'll discuss it later," Evelyn said. "I don't want to upset poor Riley any more than necessary."

"It's okay, Mama," Riley said, taking a deep breath. "They found Wendell's body in the water at the marina yesterday morning. He had some kind of a head wound. The sheriff doesn't think it was an accident."

"Murder?" Roo's eyes shone with excitement. "Right here on Belle Isle?"

"Roo!" Evelyn shook her head in exasperation. "For God's sake, have you no sense of propriety? My daughter has been widowed. My granddaughter has lost her daddy. We are inconsolable."

"Sorry." Roo leaned over and patted Riley's hand. "Really, sweetie, even though I never really liked him, I'm sorry about Wendell. Truly."

Riley managed to choke back a giggle. "Thanks, Aunt Roo."

"I guess I really am the last one to know. When's the service?"

"We can't plan anything until the coroner releases Wendell's body," Riley said. "Soon, I hope. For Maggy's sake, I don't want to drag things out any longer than necessary."

"Of course," Roo said. She walked over to the counter and pointed hopefully at an oval turquoise Pyrex bowl. "Is that Sylvia's pineapple fluff? It's my favorite!"

13

The tide was out, and the beach on the north side of the island was a smooth expanse of silvery-gray sand. Parrish stood in the surf for a moment, letting the gentle waves lap at her ankles, allowing her toes to sink into the gritty sand. They mostly had the beach to themselves, save for a pair of men surf-casting up ahead, and a group of kids trying to throw a cast-net.

"The water feels amazing," she called to her husband. "Come on, Ed."

He shook his head. "No, thanks. You know how I feel about sand."

She did know. Her husband had a pathological hatred of sand. He didn't mind walking on the beach with her, as they did most days when they were together on Belle Isle, but he stopped short of walking barefoot, always insisting on wearing his tennis shoes.

"Riiiight," she said. She dipped her fingers into the water and flicked some at him, but he moved away, unharmed.

She walked along behind him, stooped over, picking up stray seashells, searching, as she always did, for bits of sea glass. Which was a waste of time. She hadn't found any sea glass in ages.

"I wonder why," she muttered.

Ed turned around. "You wonder why what?"

Parrish laughed ruefully. "Did I say that out loud? Oh my God. I'm turning into my grandmother."

"You could do worse."

His comment stopped her cold. "Aww. That's so sweet."

"She was a grand old lady," Ed said, turning slightly pink.

Now she'd gone and embarrassed him. Ed Godchaux didn't like people to think he was sentimental. Or sweet.

"I was just wondering why I never find sea glass here anymore. When we first started coming to the island, when David was a baby, I could always find a piece or two. Green, blue, brown, even purple. I had jars of the stuff. But I can't remember the last time I found a piece. Can you?"

He gave that some serious thought. Everything was serious to Ed. She'd loved that about him when they'd first started dating. He'd been a seasoned thirty-two-year-old litigator, and she was just out of law school, at her first job, but he'd always treated her as an equal, never dismissed her as "just a girl."

He removed his sunglasses and polished them on the hem of his golf shirt. Ed didn't own any shirts without collars. He didn't do T-shirts. Or jeans. A logoed polo shirt and well-tailored, lightweight, Orvis fly-fishing shorts were about as casual as he got.

"I think it probably has something to do with the fact that people don't take glass to the beach anymore. They take plastic, or aluminum. And, luckily, people have gotten a little bit better about not littering and recycling."

"True," Parrish said.

"Tide patterns change, too. And remember, this beach was just dredged and renourished a couple of years ago, so that might have had an effect." He pointed to a spot in the surf, about a hundred yards offshore. "That sand bar probably catches whatever glass or good shells might otherwise wash up here."

"Very wise," Parrish said. "It still makes me sad."

"I think I saw one of your jars of sea glass out in the garage when I was putting up the screens. If you want, tomorrow I can come down early and sprinkle some around, and then you can hunt it up again."

"You'd do that for me?"

"Of course. It would be like an Easter egg hunt."

Parrish was astonished to find a lump in her throat. This was a side of Ed she hadn't seen in a very long time.

She caught up to him and put an arm around his waist, kissing him on the cheek.

He seemed caught off guard. "What's that for?"

"That's a just-because kiss."

He kissed the top of her head, and then sighed.

"What?"

"I was thinking about Wendell. Poor bastard."

"Poor bastard nothing," Parrish said indignantly. "He's left Riley and Maggy homeless. Do you really think somebody murdered him?"

Ed frowned. "I think Wendell was maybe a victim of his own ambition. I've heard rumors . . . very vague rumors, starting months ago, that he'd gotten over his skis on this Belle Isle development project with the hotel and the new oceanfront lots. And all that."

"You never said anything to me about any rumors."

"Because as far as I knew, that's all it was—rumors, gossip, innuendo."

"I still wish you'd said something," Parrish said. "Riley's been totally blindsided by all of this. Maybe if she'd known he was in financial trouble . . ."

"Hindsight is twenty-twenty," Ed reminded her. "Right now, I think the best thing we can do for Riley, and Maggy, is be there for them."

Parrish shivered and turned up the collar on her shirt.

"What's wrong?"

"I was just thinking. Somebody murdered Wendell Griggs. Right here on this island. What if the killer is still hanging around? What if it doesn't really have anything to do with the development deal? My God. What if it's somebody we know?"

"Not likely," Ed said calmly. "Whoever killed him—for whatever reason, that person is probably miles and miles away by now."

She looked at him wistfully. "Do you really have to leave so soon? We had a pretty sucky start to the weekend. Doesn't even feel like Memorial Day."

"Can't be helped. I need to go over the transcripts from the last deposition we did on the thing in D.C. before I fly out to Chicago first thing Wednesday."

"Can't one of your associates handle the Chicago thing?"

"No. The clients are paying for me, so they get me. You know that, Parrish."

She nodded. "I know it, but that doesn't mean I like it."

Ed glanced at his watch. "It's almost nine. You want to go get breakfast at the Sea Biscuit?"

Parrish slid her arm around his waist again. "Maybe later. I've got a better idea."

"What's that?"

She leaned in and whispered in his ear, letting her hand slide casually down, until it rested lightly on his butt.

His face lit up. "Really?"

"Absolutely."

An hour later, Ed reluctantly rolled onto his side of the bed and yawned. He caught Parrish's hand and kissed the palm of it.

"That was great."

She leaned over and kissed his bare shoulder. "If I ask you something, will you tell me the truth?"

"If I know it."

"Friday, when we were on the ferry, and Riley was telling me she planned to file for divorce, she said she'd wondered if Wendell was having an affair, even though he denied it. Have you heard anything like that? Did he have a girlfriend?"

"If there was another woman, do you really think Wendell would have told me? We weren't best friends, you know. Not like you and Riley."

"Men hear things. They gossip just as much as women," Parrish insisted. "I just want to know what you've heard."

Ed reached for the eyeglasses he'd left on the nightstand. "Okay. I did hear something. But you can't tell Riley. It might not even be true."

"Just tell me, for God's sake," Parrish said. "This is not a deposition. It's just us, in bed. Pillow talk."

"I played golf with a fellow down at Pinehurst, back in the fall. This guy was president of a family-owned bank in Wilmington. I mentioned that we have a place at Belle Isle, and he got this funny look on his face. Sort of a smirk, you'd probably call it. I asked him what was so humorous, and finally, he told me that he'd heard all the development going on at Belle Isle was being bankrolled by another small bank on the coast, and that the buzz in banking circles was that one of the bank's junior execs, a gal in her early thirties, was literally in bed with the president of Belle Isle Enterprises."

"That's it? Did this guy name names?"

"No. There was nothing like that. Just a buzz, no more."

"I wonder who the woman was?"

"Parrish!" His voice was sharp. "You promised not to say anything to Riley. Remember?"

"Spoilsport."

Ed leaned over and gave his wife a long, lingering kiss. "Wendell Griggs was a fool. Didn't his daddy ever tell him you don't get your honey where you get your money?"

"So he was a fool for sleeping with a banker? But it would have been okay if his girlfriend was a cocktail waitress?"

He blinked. "That's not what I meant at all. Riley is a good woman. A beautiful woman. He ought never to have cheated on her." Ed sat up and swung his legs over the side of the bed. "I would never do that to you," he said, turning to look at her. "And I know you wouldn't do it to me either."

He stood up and padded, naked, toward the bathroom. A moment later, she heard the water in the shower running, and his deep voice humming.

14

Parrish was sitting on the front porch of the cottage staring moodily out at the bay when Riley rode up on a rusty red beach cruiser with a straw basket wired to the front.

"Hey!" She opened the screened door and waved her friend in. "What's up?"

Riley collapsed onto the porch swing and Parrish sat down beside her. "Where's Ed?"

Parrish rolled her eyes. "Up in his office. He swears he's just going to answer a few 'urgent' e-mails, but we both know he'll stay up there until I physically drag him away from that damned computer."

"Just like Wendell. And yet, nothing like Wendell," Riley said.

Parrish raised an eyebrow, and Riley shrugged.

"Horrible things just keep coming out of my mouth. Anyway, sorry about the unannounced drop-in, but I just had to get out and away from the house for a little bit."

"You know you never need an invitation to show up here," Parrish said. "What's with the bike?"

"Mama took the golf cart. She and Roo are playing golf this morning.

Well, they call it golf. I call it Bloody Marys and gossip and a little putting and very little actual driving."

"Evvy's playing golf today? That's kind of cold."

"Just be happy she's out of my hair."

You want some iced tea? Or an Arnold Palmer? I just made tea and lemonade."

"Don't judge me, but I'd love an Arnold Palmer if you could just drop a thimble-full of vodka into it."

"Me? Judge? Ha!"

Riley sat back in the swing and took an appreciative look around the porch. Parrish and Ed's house wasn't particularly big, maybe fifteen hundred square feet in all, and it wasn't old by island standards. Basically it had been a 1960s concrete block bunker when they bought it, but the way the house was situated, on a knoll at the end of a cul-de-sac with the other houses built downhill, gave it the best, most unobstructed view of the bay on the island.

And, of course, in the ten years since they'd bought the house, Parrish had remodeled and refurnished it to magazine-worthy perfection. She'd covered the concrete block exterior with cedar shingles that had weathered to a soft silver, added a peaked-roof portico over the front door, put in divided-light windows, and painted the trim a deep green, Now the bunker looked like a snug New England cottage.

"Here." Parrish thrust a frosted tumbler with a piece of skewered lemon and a mint leaf into her hand.

"Thanks." Riley sipped and grimaced. "Kinda strong there, girlfriend."

"Desperate times, desperate measures. What's happening over at the Shutters? I know Evvy is driving you crazy."

Riley fluttered her hand. "Not just Mama. It's everybody. The word about Wendell is officially out. The casserole brigade started up this morning around eight and it has not let up. We have enough food to feed Pharaoh's army, and it just keeps coming. Mama's fridge and Billy and Scott's at the firehouse is full, so Roo took a bunch of stuff over to the carriage house. And the phone's been ringing off the hook . . ."

She pulled her cell phone from the pocket of her shorts. "The voice mailbox on this thing is full too. I know people mean well, and I should at least listen, but honestly, I just can't take one more ounce of sympathy."

Parrish put her hand out. "Gimme that thing. I'll listen, write down the messages from people you care about, erase the ones from the pests."

"Would you? That would be great."

Parrish went into the house and came back with a yellow legal pad and pen.

She stationed herself at the glass-topped wicker table and started taking notes while Riley slowly sipped her drink.

"Your cousin Jacky called. You're in her prayers. She wants to know when the funeral is going to be."

"Me, too," Riley said. "I'll call her when we've got everything set."

Parrish nodded and continued with the note taking.

"Julie, your neighbor on St. Mary's Street. Sends her love. Wants to know if you need anything."

"Julie?" Riley wrinkled her brow. "I haven't talked to anybody in Raleigh. How does she know about Wendell?"

"Dunno," Parrish said. She listened for another five minutes and put the phone down. "Word's out up there, that's for sure. The book-club girls want to know where to send flowers, and the principal at Maggy's school also sends condolences."

"How in the hell? . . . It's only been a day."

"Bad news travels fast," Parrish pointed out.

She picked up the phone again, listened for a moment, scribbled something on the legal pad, listened again, and scribbled some more before setting the phone carefully down on the tabletop.

"Uh, Riles? You've got three phone calls from reporters here."

"What?" Riley stopped swinging abruptly. "Who called? What do they want?"

Parrish consulted her notes. "Some guy from the Wilmington paper. His name's Bert . . . something. He left a number, wants you to call. Says he's working on Wendell's obituary."

"No way," Riley said. "Who else?"

"Nancy Olivera—from the Raleigh *News and Observer.* Same thing, says she's working on an obituary."

"I can't figure out how they know about Wendell," Riley said. "This is so bizarre. When I worked at WRAL, we'd get tips from the funeral home, or sometimes the cops, when there was a suspicious death, but I haven't even called a funeral home yet. And I can't believe the sheriff would go around notifying the media."

"Don't reporters check police reports to find out stuff like this?"

"They used to," Riley said. "But things have changed since I got out of the business. Newspapers have skeleton staffs these days. No way some reporter from Wilmington or Raleigh just happened to check the police reports in little bitty Baldwin County. Somebody must have tipped them off."

"Speaking of WRAL, you have a call from them, too."

Riley's shoulders relaxed a little. "Probably somebody I worked with back in the day, calling to offer condolences."

"You know a woman named Kelsey Kennedy? She sounds young. Like maybe she's still in kindergarten."

"Everybody who works in television today is just barely out of kindergarten," Riley assured her. "That name sounds familiar, but I don't know why."

She chewed on a piece of ice while she thought. "You must mean Kasey Kennedy. She really is a kid. Or she was. She was an intern the last summer I worked at the station. That's kind of nice that she called, I guess."

Parrish tapped her pen on the notepad. "I don't think she's calling with condolences. Says she's working on a story about Wendell's questionable financial dealings, wants to know if it's true the FBI is involved."

The iced tea glass slipped from Riley's fingers, shattering on impact.

"I'll get the broom," Parrish said, handing her the phone.

Riley touched the phone's Message Replay button and listened.

"Hi, Riley? This is Kasey Kennedy at WRAL? I don't know if you remember me, but we worked together several years ago. Anyway, I'm soooo sorry about your husband. And this is kind of touchy, I know, but I just have to tell you, I'm working on a story about your husband's business dealings with a bank in Southpoint. And I understand the FBI is investigating? So if you

could call me back, I'd really appreciate it. I'm kind of on a deadline, too. I know you know how that is!"

Parrish busied herself sweeping up the glass and mopping up the spilled drink.

"The FBI?" Riley put the phone back on the table. "And some bank in Southpoint? This is crazy."

"You have no idea what she's talking about, right?" Parrish asked, sitting beside her on the swing.

"No! And it can't be true. I'd have heard something." Riley clasped and unclasped her hands, trying to stop them from shaking.

"What are you going to do?"

Riley grabbed the phone. "I'm going to call that little bitch and threaten to sue her ass for slander if she so much as repeats one word of this shit. And then I'm calling Jim Swearingen, the station manager. He's known me forever. He'll put a stop to this crap."

Parrish gently took the phone out of her friend's hand. "Don't. Don't call the reporters. Don't call the station manager. I'm not your lawyer, but when you get a lawyer, she'll tell you the same thing. I know it's hard, but just button your lip, okay?"

"My God," Riley said, staring at Parrish. "What if it is true? What if Wendell really was involved in some kind of shady stuff? Maybe the house foreclosure is connected? The FBI—Parrish."

"I know. Scary. But we'll get it figured out. You want some lunch? I picked up sandwich stuff at the Mercantile."

"Food. Ugh." Riley grimaced. "I better get home."

"How's Maggy today?"

"Okay, from what I can tell, but she's such a funny kid. Yesterday, she was completely undone. Wouldn't come out of her room, wouldn't talk to anybody. Then, early this morning, she calmly announces she's going fishing with the Billingsley kids. Like nothing had happened."

"Wouldn't you rather have her doing that than sitting around brooding?"

"Yeah. I'm glad she finally made friends with some kids on the island. It's just . . . I worry, you know? She and Wendell were so close. Much closer than she and I are. I think she's still in shock. And I am, too. Oh my God. The FBI. What am I going to tell Maggy? What'll I tell Mama? If it's true . . ."

"Maybe it's just gossip," Parrish said, thinking back uneasily to the pillow talk she'd shared with Ed earlier in the day.

"As if this day couldn't get any worse, I'm taking Maggy over to Southpoint this afternoon to view Wendell's body."

"Really?"

"She's adamant that she wants to say good-bye to her Daddy," Riley said. "And I don't have the heart to say no. So that's the fun we've got in store for the rest of the day. Whee!"

"Call me later and let me know how it went," Parrish said. "In the meantime, I'll light a fire under Ed to find you a lawyer."

15

Mrs. Griggs?" The social worker who met them in the hospital lobby wore dangly turquoise earrings and a white lab coat unbuttoned over a lime-green blouse and coral slacks. Her skin was smooth and unlined. The name badge pinned to her coat read DIANE LOPRESTI, M.S.W.

"That's right," Riley said. She gestured toward her daughter. "And this is Maggy."

"Please call me Diane." She shook both their hands. Her grip was firm and cool, and the gray eyes behind her wire-rimmed glasses were kind, but not pitying.

"We're going to go down to the hospital's basement," Diane said, noticing Maggy's tank top. "They keep it pretty chilly down there. Can I get either of you a sweater? I keep extras in my office."

"I'm okay," Maggy said.

"All right. Did the sheriff tell you what to expect today?"

Riley's throat was dry. She coughed and coughed again. "Just that you'd be taking us to the hospital's morgue. He, um, said the autopsy hasn't happened yet. . . ."

"That's correct. So I'm going to take you into a room, and your husband will be on a sort of table, covered with a drape. We'll be the only ones there. Does that sound all right?"

Maggy's eyes were the size of saucers. Riley took her hand and squeezed it.

"Okay," Maggy said.

When the elevator stopped, they stepped into a tile-floored corridor, then paused a few yards down the hall, in front of a set of double doors. Diane swiped a plastic key card through an electronic reader and the doors swung inward to admit them.

They walked slowly down another short hallway, then paused in front of a third door. The social worker repeated the key-card procedure. The door swung open and they were in a tile-floored room.

The table was stainless steel. The sheet was white. Wendell Griggs's face was a waxy gray.

Riley felt her own breathing slow. She couldn't look. But she couldn't not, to convince herself that this was real.

The first thing that struck her was that a stranger had combed Wendell's hair, parting it on the wrong side. His beard was unshaven, at least a three-days' growth shadowed his cheeks, chin, and upper lip. He'd always been so particular about shaving, keeping a razor at work, just in case of a late-day or early evening meeting.

She stared. This had been a face she'd kissed, caressed, dreamt about. Not a classically handsome face, but strong, with a straight, prominent nose, a square chin, and cheekbones that looked as though they'd been sculpted with a hatchet.

Riley had told herself dozens of times over the past few months that this thing they'd had, their love, passion, sense of partnership, had cooled, and finally extinguished itself. She'd quit caring, or so she'd convinced herself.

It was all a lie.

Now Wendell's face, always mobile, agitated or excited, was flaccid, like old rubber. She felt burning bile rise in her throat and had to swallow, hard, to keep from gagging.

Maggy grabbed her mother's hand and held on tight. Riley gripped her daughter's hand with both of her own, fearing that if she didn't, she, the mother, the supposedly nurturing adult, would have bolted for the door.

"Okay?" Diane asked.

"Can I touch him?" Maggy whispered, turning to look at the social worker, who stood beside her, a hand resting lightly on her shoulder.

"Do you want to?"

"I don't know." Maggy's lower lip trembled.

"It's okay either way." Diane's voice was gentle. She looked over Maggy's head at Riley and nodded, then took a step backward. Riley released her daughter's hand, then did the same.

Slowly, hesitantly, Maggy reached out. Her hand was shaking, but her fingertips brushed Wendell's cheek. "Daddy," she whispered. Her shoulders shuddered as a sob escaped. "Oh, Daddy."

Maggy turned and Riley wrapped both arms around her weeping child. "He's really dead," Maggy said, lifting a tearstained face toward her mother's.

"I know," Riley said. "I know, baby."

In the car, on the way back to the Southpoint ferry dock, Maggy sat as far from her mother as she could, staring out the window at scenery she'd seen dozens of times before.

"You hungry?" Riley asked.

"No!" Maggy exploded. "What is wrong with you? You expect me to eat now? God! I wanna puke, just thinking about food."

The violence of the child's reaction took Riley aback for a moment. Was this how it was going to be between them? Anger and hostility?

She would have to deal with this the only way she knew how. With the lightest touch possible.

"Me, too," Riley admitted. "But we can't let your blood sugar get out of whack, or I'll have to turn around and go right back to that hospital. Mimi's already pissed at me, you know. That would really put her over the edge." She managed a shaky laugh. "If something happened to you, she'd kill me, and then you'd be an orphan, and you'd have to live with her until you go away to college."

"No way," Maggy shot back. "If anything ever happens to you, I'm going to live with Bebo and Uncle Scott."

"Good luck with that," Riley said.

Maggy's posture relaxed a little. "Okay. I'll eat. Can I just get a burger on the ferry?"

"Sure," Riley said.

"Mom? Mimi really is pissed at you. How come?"

"Oh, honey. That's just her way. Sometimes I get pissed at you too, in case you haven't noticed. It's a mother-daughter thing. Doesn't mean I don't love you."

"No, seriously. Tell me."

Riley glanced sideways. Maggy had pivoted in the seat and she was searching her face for the truth.

"Okay," she said, sighing. "She's mad at me because I told her—before we knew about your dad—that we were getting a divorce."

Maggy closed her eyes and looked away. "So it really was true? You guys were breaking up?"

"Afraid so. The plan was that we'd tell you together, this weekend. That's why I was so upset when he wasn't on the ferry Friday. I just thought he was ditching his responsibility."

"That is so lame that you would think that," Maggy said angrily. "He promised me he was coming. I knew he wouldn't break his promise. I *knew* something was wrong."

Something has been very wrong for a very long time, Riley thought.

"Why did you want a divorce?" Maggy asked. "I know Dad didn't want one. He told me."

"He told you that? When?"

Maggy shrugged. "Awhile ago. He picked me up after school, right after Easter, and we went out for tacos, because he knew I was mad that he didn't come to the beach with us."

How like Wendell, Riley thought. *Letting their daughter believe the divorce was all my fault.*

She chose her words carefully. "Your dad and I hadn't been happy together in a long time. We went to marriage counseling, but it didn't do much good, partly because he didn't make it to half the sessions."

"He said the marriage counselor was on your side," Maggy offered. "That she said it was all his fault. So that's why he quit going."

Damn Wendell Griggs. He was sabotaging her from the grave.

"That was his point of view. My point of view was that he was never home. But neither of us was without fault. There was other stuff too, stuff that I don't feel comfortable talking about to you right now, especially since your dad is gone. Okay? Can we leave it at that?"

"Whatever." Now Maggy was wearing her all-too-familiar stone-faced mask. Incredible that she'd perfected it at such a young age. But then, her daughter had always been precocious. She turned back toward the window. "You're probably glad Dad's dead."

"Hey!" Riley said. She made a sharp right-hand turn into the parking lot of a strip shopping center and put the car in Park.

"Look at me, please."

Maggy turned to her with dead eyes. "What?"

"That was a horrible thing you just said to me. I certainly am not glad about your dad. I was in that room back at the hospital, too. Remember? Wendell wasn't just your dad. He was my husband. For almost twenty years. Things between us were complicated, it's true. But I cared about him. I'm hurting, too. Don't make this harder on us than it has to be. Please? I know you don't believe me, but I'm on your side, Maggy. A hundred percent."

"You're on my side?" Her arms were crossed, hands locked to elbows, over her chest.

"Of course. Now more than ever."

"Great," Maggy said. "Will you do something for me?"

"If I can. If it's possible." Riley was instantly wary. *Was this some kind of a trap?* Since she'd been diagnosed with type 1 diabetes, Maggy had become expert at emotional manipulation.

"The sheriff said it wasn't an accident. So I want to know who killed Dad," Maggy said. "Promise me you'll find out who did this to him."

"Me? Maggy, you don't know what you're asking. I'm no detective. This isn't *CSI: Belle Isle*. Anyway, we don't even know yet whether it was an accident. We won't know until the autopsy."

"Promise me," Maggy said, her voice steely. "If you ever really loved Dad, then you'll do it. Promise?"

"I promise," Riley said wearily. "I promise to do whatever I can."

"And you'll tell me the truth? Even if Mimi gets pissed at you? Even if you think it will upset me?"

"Can we just take this a day at a time?" Riley pleaded.

"No. Do you promise?"

"God help me, I do."

16

Scott stood on the bottom stair of the firehouse, the strap of his battered Louis Vuitton carry-on dangling over his right shoulder, his laptop bag hanging over his left.

He'd been upstairs packing when he heard the first soft notes wafting upward. Now, as he stood in the open-plan living room in the high-ceilinged old brick structure, he looked over at Billy, his back to the stairs, hunched over the gleaming baby grand piano, his long, tapered fingers drifting over the keys.

When had he last heard his partner play? There was no room for the piano in their small West Village co-op, which was why this rather grand instrument stood in the middle of the living room of their not-so-grand converted 1920s brick firehouse.

He set the bags on the polished concrete floor and walked over to the piano. For a moment, Billy seemed lost in the music. He kept playing, finally nodding to acknowledge Scott's presence.

"That's so pretty. And sad," Scott said, sitting down on the bench. "What's it called?"

"It's 'Strange Fruit,'" Billy said, closing the lid to the keyboard.

"The Billie Holiday song?"

"About lynching," Billy said. "Which is why it really is a sad song."

"You're in a mood today."

Billy shrugged and rested his arms on the top of the piano. "What can I tell you? All day, since I woke up this morning, I've felt this sort of gray funk."

"Because of Wendell."

"The sheriff thinks he was murdered. Murdered! On Belle Isle. I can't even wrap my mind around that."

"Has there ever been a murder here before?"

"Not that I can remember. Wait, okay, well, yeah, come to think of it. When I was just a kid, not even ten, some lady who lived up near the north end shot her husband. She claimed he'd been beating her, and it was self-defense. I don't know what ever happened to her. I don't think she ever went to prison, but she moved away afterward, just abandoned her place, and for years afterward all us kids called it the Murder House."

"And that's it?" Scott asked, his curiosity piqued.

"Maybe. Mama would know. She's the one who keeps up with all the stuff that's ever happened on Belle Isle."

"Poor old Wendell," Scott said nastily.

"I thought you liked him," Billy said.

"I tolerated him. Because of you. And Riley. Wendell Griggs was not a nice man. Not somebody you'd want to have business dealings with."

"You think that's what got Wendell killed? A business deal?"

"Maybe. I'm just speculating here. For all I know, it could have been a drug deal gone wrong. Or a jealous husband. Or a botched robbery."

Billy regarded Scott with interest.

"You make it sound like lots of people could have had a motive to kill him. Maybe you're right. It's not like I loved the guy either. As long as Riley was happy, I thought he was okay. Well, maybe not all *that* okay, but at least he was a good dad."

"People keep saying that," Scott said. "But he wasn't even around all that much. He missed Maggy's birthday party last year. You and I flew down to Raleigh, but he couldn't cancel one lousy meeting to be at her birthday dinner. You're as much a father to that kid as he ever was. As heartless as this sounds, she's probably better off without him."

"I doubt Maggy feels that way." Billy twisted the braided rose-gold-and-platinum wedding band on his left hand. "The kid is devastated."

Scott patted his hand. "She's young. But she's still got Riley. And us. Maggy will be all right."

"I guess. But everything feels so weird to me right now," Billy said. "Like, nothing will ever be the same here again. That all the good times are maybe over. You ever have that feeling?"

"All the time," Scott assured him. "But remember, I'm twenty years older than you. I happen to know things won't be the same."

Billy rested his head on Scott's shoulder. "Don't talk like that. You're not even sixty."

"But I'll also never see fifty again."

Both men sighed simultaneously.

"Do you think I should be worried?" Billy asked, drumming his fingertips on the piano lid.

"About what? Hitting fifty? You're just like Evelyn. You'll never look old, Bebo."

"I mean, about money. And the company, with Wendell being dead."

"Why should you start worrying about money now?" Scott said lightly.

"Suppose this foreclosure thing on Riley's house isn't a screwup? Suppose Wendell really was broke? What's that mean for Belle Isle Enterprises? What's it mean for me? I mean, it's a family business. That means Riley, me, Mama, and Roo. And Maggy too, of course. We're all affected."

"Stop worrying," Scott said, firmly placing a hand over Billy's to quiet the drumming. "I make a pretty decent living. And there's always your trust fund, right?"

Billy looked away. "I feel guilty worrying about myself, especially considering what my sister is going through right now. But I can't stop thinking about this stuff. I mean, Wendell was such a smart guy. He had such amazing plans, for the hotel and the new development with the town houses and everything. Now what? It seemed like a sure thing."

"Like the checks would just keep on coming, right?" Scott asked.

Billy's shoulders sagged. "You make me sound like some kind of parasite or something, just living off my brother-in-law's largesse. It's my family's business, damn it! And I would have gone into Belle Isle Enterprises, I really would have."

"Absolutely."

"You don't believe me? Ask Riley what my dad was like. I couldn't do anything right as far as he was concerned. He never wanted me in the business, because he was ashamed that his developer buddies would think less of him because he had a fag for a son."

"Good ol' W.R.," Scott said.

"Screw him and screw Wendell Griggs," Billy said savagely. "This is all too depressing to think about."

He picked up a highball glass sitting on a nearby table and jiggled the ice cubes. "Here's to the good times," he said gloomily.

He took a swallow and held out the glass to his partner. "How about a Bloody Mary? A little roadie for the road?"

"Better not. I've still got to drive to the airport after I get to Southpoint, remember?"

"You really have to go? You can't wait until tomorrow?"

"I wish I could. Especially now, with all this stuff with poor Riley. But we've got the install for the steak house in Vegas on Wednesday. With the layovers and everything, I won't make it to my hotel until tomorrow morning. Tuesday's gonna be crazy, trying to get all the subs coordinated after the long holiday. I'm just praying all the furniture and window treatments were delivered Friday." Scott looked at his watch. "Are you taking me to the ferry?"

"Oops," Billy said. "I forgot to plug in the cart last night. I'll just call Mama and see if she can give us a ride to the ferry."

Scott paced up and down outside the house while Billy plucked at spent red geranium blooms from the large cast-iron planters on either side of the double front doors.

The Belle Isle Volunteer Fire Dept. Station 1 was located mid-island. It had served the community up until the 1960s, when funds had been raised to build a larger, better-equipped station. For more than forty years the old structure had lain abandoned, its roof collapsed, small trees growing up through the rotted engine bay doors, until Billy Nolan and his trust fund came up with a scheme to save it from demolition.

For the first few years after he and Scott were a couple, they'd stayed in the caretaker's cottage at Shutters during their summer visits, but after Billy turned thirty and gained access to his inheritance, he'd decided the time had come for home ownership.

He and Scott had sketched out the floor plan for the firehouse on a paper place mat over crab stew and cocktails at the Sea Biscuit, finishing the plan before their second round of Salty Dogs.

Because of historic district design restrictions, they'd had to keep to the original footprint of the old brick building. The plan was a simple one. Heavy twelve-foot-tall rolling barn doors were commissioned to replace the original doors to the engine bay. These opened into the first floor of the building, with an airy combined living and dining room, huge professional quality kitchen, and guestroom and bathroom. Rising up through the foyer was an open steel-frame stairway that led to a loftlike second floor, with the master suite and home office, both with new floor-to-ceiling windows looking out onto the bay.

That view was one Billy never tired of seeing. Although he still thought of himself as a New Yorker, every year he seemed to arrive a little earlier for his summer residence and stay a little later, last year past Columbus Day even.

It was only Memorial Day weekend now, the kickoff to the summer, and yet, here he stood under the shade of a live oak tree with Scott, watching as people zoomed past on the crushed oyster shell road. Everybody, it seemed, knew Billy Nolan. Families waved and hellooed on their way to the beach, with swimsuit-clad children clinging to the backs of their carts. Sunburnt tennis players rode past, waving water bottles and calling for Billy to join them Monday for the club round-robin. A steady stream of golfers passed too, heading back from Belle Isle's quaint nine-hole course.

"You're going to miss the best part of the summer," Billy said sadly.

Scott just laughed. "I don't play tennis. Or golf. Remember? I don't even particularly like the beach."

Billy looked stricken. "But I thought you loved it here."

"*You* love it here. Belle Isle is your happy place. And I love you, so I'm happy to be here with you," Scott said. "I know you think you're some sophisticated New York artiste, but we both know that at heart you're still a small-town Southern boy."

Billy couldn't let it go. "You have fun here though, right? I mean, we have supper club and bridge with the girls, and game night. And you love hanging out at the pool here. Right? You always say you like it here way better than the Hamptons or Fire Island."

"Well, I don't miss getting stuck in traffic on the Long Island Expressway on Fridays, and I don't miss Fire Island anymore either, since the Pines got so crazy," Scott admitted.

Billy's forehead creased with worry, but before he could pursue the matter further, Evelyn and Roo came jolting to a stop in front of them, with Evelyn honking her cart's cartoon-quality horn, and Banks and Ollie, who each took up a lap in the front seat, barking in tune to the horn honking.

"You sound like the Road Runner," Billy told his mother. "And you look like Strawberry Shortcake."

"Thank you," Evelyn said, patting her hair. She was dressed in a pale pink sleeveless cotton shirt, pale pink knit skort, pink-and-white saddle-oxford-type golf shoes, and a pink sun visor. Even her golf gloves were pink. Her sister-in-law, perched on the bench seat beside her, wore a faded Kelly green Belle Isle logoed polo shirt, shapeless khaki shorts, a sweat-dampened white bucket hat, and weird black golf sandals she'd found at the island's charity thrift shop.

"How'd you hit 'em today, Evelyn?" Scott asked, giving her a dutiful peck on the daintily powdered cheek she offered, and a head scratch to Ollie, who sat demurely in his mistress's lap. He and Billy clambered onto the third row of seats, since the two women's clubs were strapped to the middle row.

"Like she always does. Like crap," Roo said, turning around to address the men.

"I think I might take some lessons with the club pro this summer," Evelyn said, ignoring the gibe. "My drives just don't seem to have any oomph lately. Not to mention the fact that I can't find my seven iron."

"You couldn't hit the ball with a steam iron today," Roo said gleefully. "I think you probably left that club at home in Edenton. Billy, I think your mama maybe has old-timer's disease."

"I know I had that club last week. I know I did," Evelyn insisted.

"We didn't play last week because it rained, which you would remember if you weren't getting senile," Roo said.

"I'm not the one who lost her cell phone and her car keys—twice—last week," Evelyn said.

"Maybe it fell out of your bag when you hit a bump," Billy said as the cart rolled slowly along the road. Out of the corner of his eye, he saw Scott glance nervously at his watch. "Mama, put the pedal to the metal, will you? Scott's got a flight to catch."

"Plenty of time," Evelyn said calmly, maintaining her speed.

"Uh, actually, I think we're cutting it kind of close," Scott said.

Evelyn plucked her cell phone from the cup holder on the dashboard and tapped a number.

"I'll just call Annie Milas and ask her to hold the boat until we get there," she announced grandly.

17

Nate Milas sat in a swivel chair in the *Carolina Queen*'s pilothouse, fidgeting, looking out at the bay and back at the disappearing Southpoint ferry dock. He checked e-mails, chatted with the pilot, then finally gave up.

"You want anything from the concession?" he asked, pausing in the door.

"I'm good."

The midafternoon ferry was only half full. Later in the day, though, Nate knew, the boat would be at capacity with weekenders coming and going from the island. He spotted Riley and her daughter sitting on a bench on the port side of the boat. The girl was intent, reading something on her smartphone, while Riley leafed halfheartedly through a copy of *People*.

His presence on the ferry was no accident; he'd seen her name on the manifest earlier in the day. He leaned up against the rail, letting the salt spray mist his face. After a few moments, he saw the girl stand and head toward the concession stand. This was his chance.

He stood awkwardly before her. "Uh, Riley?"

She looked up, and Nate was struck by how sad she looked. Her eyes were red-rimmed, with dark bags underneath, and she wore no makeup, her hair bunched together in a careless ponytail.

"Hi," she said.

"Okay if I sit down?"

She shrugged, so he took the seat her daughter had just vacated.

"Hey, uh, I heard about Wendell."

"You and everybody else in the state."

"I'm sorry. It must have been a terrible shock."

Riley nodded, her eyes downcast.

He could feel the whole encounter going south again. Damn it, why couldn't he even speak an intelligible sentence to this woman?

He cleared his throat. "Look. I know you don't like me, but . . ."

"Like you?" She raised an eyebrow. "I don't even think about you."

Nate's face flushed. "Okay, then, I'll stop bothering you. . . ." He jumped to his feet.

"Oh, God." Riley reached out and grabbed his hand. "Shit. That was so rude of me." She looked up at him, contrite, pleading.

"You were just trying to be nice, and I was a jerk. I'm sorry. Really. Don't go."

"It's okay," Nate said. "I get it. You're upset."

"That's no excuse. Come on, sit down. Please?" She patted the bench. "Maggy isn't too happy with me right now. I could use the company."

He did as she asked.

"Why is she mad at you?"

"It's complicated. Everything with a twelve-year-old girl is complicated, and, with Maggy, it's slightly more complicated, because she has diabetes and I never know if she's being difficult because of her age or her blood sugar. Also, we've just come from viewing Wendell's body at the hospital. Up until that moment—when we saw him, she didn't actually believe he was really dead. I guess I didn't either. I mean, intellectually, I knew it had to be true. But emotionally? It didn't hit either of us until that moment. This is real. Wendell is dead. Now all we have is each other. And the thing is, Maggy was a total daddy's girl."

"Must have been tough," Nate said. "Seeing the body and all."

"It was. But you've been through this, with your dad. You must know what it's like."

He shrugged. "It's not really the same thing. My dad was seventy-eight, and he'd had a good, long life. It hasn't been easy, but my mom and I are coping. She's actually coping surprisingly well."

"And you're not? A big tough guy like you?"

"Like you said, it doesn't seem real. Losing a parent, I guess it makes you realize none of us is gonna be immortal. I've had some changes in my personal life recently, and now, without Dad, I feel sort of unanchored. If that makes sense."

"Unanchored. Is that a pun?" She laughed at her own joke, and it reminded him of the old Riley, a sunny, confident girl with an open face and a sweet, carefree manner. Damn Wendell Griggs for taking that girl away.

"Not an intentional one. I'm not really all that clever."

"How are you unanchored?"

"Like you said, it's a long story. Right now, I'm kind of between gigs. I've sold my business, and my house in California, and I'm trying to figure out what my next move will be."

"I thought you were running the ferry business."

"Not really. I've made some small suggestions about updates and marketing, but my mom is clearly the brains of this outfit."

"Annie doesn't teach school anymore?"

"This was her last year. She'd been thinking about retiring anyway, but with Dad gone, this seemed like the time to go ahead and hang it up."

"Will you stay on the island?"

How should he answer that question? Should he tell her what he'd been contemplating? No. The timing could not be worse for something like this.

"I'm not sure yet. For now, I bought an old duck-hunting camp, and I'm fixing that up for a temporary headquarters. How about you? Will you stay on the island for the rest of the summer, or go back home to Raleigh?"

Riley made a wry face. "I've sold the house in Raleigh. Thanks to the very viable island gossip mill, I'm sure you've already heard that I'm currently homeless."

"I did hear something about that."

"Maggy and I are staying at the Shutters with Mama. I can't find out anything about this foreclosure thing until Tuesday, when the courthouse opens again."

"I hope you get things straightened out," Nate said. He meant that, even though, from his personal knowledge of her situation, he doubted that would happen.

"When will you have Wendell's service?"

"That'll depend on the autopsy," Riley said. She bit her lip. "The sheriff . . . seems to think Wendell's death wasn't an accident. That he was killed. And there are all these horrible rumors floating around. Some television reporter in Raleigh left a voice mail on my phone. About an FBI investigation into Wendell's finances." She clapped a hand over her mouth, appalled that she'd just spilled out the latest chapter in her ongoing shit show of a life.

"Oh, damn. I shouldn't have said anything about that. I'm a mess. Please don't repeat what I just told you. Not to anybody." She was crying again, despising herself for being such a blubbering baby.

He felt an involuntary chill go down his spine. "I'm sorry," he said again and, after a moment's hesitation, he reached out and placed his hand over hers.

"If there's anything I can do, I wish you'd let me know. Anything at all."

"Mom?"

Maggy Griggs stood before Riley and Nate Milas with a foil-wrapped sandwich in her hand and a look of undisguised wrath on her face.

"Hey." Riley's single-syllable greeting to her daughter contained a mixture of guilt, surprise, resentment, and wariness.

Nate took a step sideways, feeling the withering heat of the girl's glowering disapproval.

"Anyway," he said, after an awkward pause. "I better get back up top. Please let me know if there is anything I can do to help out."

Maggy plopped down on the bench and eventually began sucking so noisily on the straw in her drink, Riley caught herself grinding her back molars in acute annoyance.

The minutes ticked by. The bay was calm and soon they caught sight of Big Belle silhouetted against the brilliant blue sky.

"What did that jerk want?" Maggy demanded.

"Nate? He just wanted to offer his condolences."

"How do you know him?" Maggy demanded.

"He grew up on the island, but he moved away after college. His father was Captain Joe, you remember him. Anyway, Nate and I have known each other since we were your age. He just wanted to offer his condolences," Riley said. "His father died recently, so he knows what it's like—to lose a loved one."

"So . . . somebody hit his dad on the head and pushed him into the water and left him like that too?"

Riley closed her eyes and waited a moment before replying calmly. "No. I believe his father died of a heart attack."

"So he doesn't *really* know what it's like to have somebody in his family get murdered, does he?"

Their eyes met. Maggy's were unblinking. Riley felt her right eyelid twitch rapidly. "Do you enjoy being difficult?"

"Why is that difficult? You said that guy knew what it was like to lose somebody he loved, and I was just pointing out that he probably has no idea what it's like to have your father killed, like I just did. Plus, he's an asshole. He took Shane's phone away, just because he was playing some music."

"Maggy, I swear . . ."

The girl jumped up and headed for the bow, leaving her mother twitching and cursing under her breath.

The cluster of departing passengers stood aside to allow the arriving passengers access to the Belle Isle ferry entry ramp.

"Riley!" She looked up to see Scott standing among the waiting passengers, a leather tote slung across his shoulder.

He gave her a brief hug. "How did it go at the hospital? Was it unspeakable?"

She gave a wry smile. "It was . . . unpleasant. Did you see Maggy come off the ferry just now?"

"She went streaking past me when she saw Billy standing by your mother's golf cart."

"Of course." Riley tugged at Scott's bag. "You're leaving today? Already?"

"Yes." He sighed loudly. "There are so many moving parts to this steak house install, something's bound to go wrong unless I get there a day early to sort everything out."

"Will you be back later in the week?"

"It depends on how work's going," Scott said. "And I'm sorry about that. But you know I'll be thinking of you and Maggy, right? Have you set the date?"

"Not yet. Billy will let you know as soon as I do."

The ferry sounded the five-minute warning horn.

Riley felt a hand on her shoulder and turned to see Ed Godchaux standing beside her with a briefcase dangling from one hand.

"You're leaving today?"

"Duty calls," Ed said. He looked over at Scott. "You, too? We could have driven back to Raleigh together if I'd known that."

"Except I'm driving over to Charlotte to catch a flight to Vegas tonight," Scott said.

Ed turned back to Riley. He pointed toward the parking lot. "Parrish is right there. I think the two of you deserve a cocktail."

"You don't know how desperately I need one right now," Riley said. "Will you be back next weekend?"

"Always," Ed said.

"For sure," Scott assured her.

After the men left to board the ferry, she joined Billy and Parrish in the parking lot, a few yards away from where Evelyn, Roo, and Maggy waited in the golf cart. The ferry *tooted* again, and the water around the big engine frothed as it slowly backed away from its berth with the weekenders ensconced on the upper deck.

Parrish used her hand as a makeshift sunshade and sighed audibly. "I hate Sunday nights. That ferry horn gets me every time."

"I know what you mean," Riley said. "When we were little, I'd get so sad, seeing Daddy packing up to leave on the Sunday night ferry. And then, after

Wendell became a weekender like Daddy, I used to dread Sundays. Maggy would get herself all worked up and beg Wendell not to go. I mean, yeah, I missed him during the week, but mostly I dreaded the fact that I'd be a single mom for the next five days."

"And I can remember those same Sunday nights when we were kids," Billy chimed in. "But I guess I had a different reaction. I can remember thinking, 'Okay, he's gone. I can slouch and sleep late and not pretend to care about baseball or fishing or any of that he-man crap.' It was a relief, really."

Parrish gave him a sympathetic smile. "I think fathers are always harder on their sons."

"Especially when their sons would really prefer to be whipping up a cake in their Easy-Bake Oven," Billy said. "Now, though, yeah, Sunday nights are sad, because it means Scott's leaving. Which is why I usually start the day with a Bloody Mary breakfast."

"Bebo!" Maggy called from the golf cart. "Mom! Let's go."

"Coming." Billy loped off in the direction of the golf cart.

Parrish linked an arm around Riley's waist as they crossed the parking lot. "Was it awful?"

"It was . . . surreal," Riley said, searching for the right words that could sum up the past few hours.

"How was Maggy?"

Riley rolled her eyes. "Upset, of course, when she saw Wendell. Then, after we left the hospital, she accused me of being glad he was dead."

"No way."

"She's so angry it's scary. And most of it's directed at me. I don't know what to say to her, Parrish. I can't lie about the state of our marriage. And I can't tell her the truth about what was going on with Wendell, because I don't know the truth. Get this—she made me promise to find out who killed him."

"What did you say?"

"What could I say? I told her I'd try."

Parrish nodded, then reached into the pocket of her shorts and brought out a folded sheet of paper, which she pressed into her friend's hand.

"Here. Ed flaked out on me on the lawyer front, so I made some phone calls myself."

The paper was one of Parrish's pale, seafoam-green, heavy, linen, monogrammed notecards. Two lines. A name and a phone number.

"Sharon Douglas?"

"I don't know her personally, but from what I hear, she's a ball-buster. She's younger than us, only thirty-two, but she clerked for a federal appeals court judge after she finished law school, then worked as an assistant D.A. in Atlanta. She worked briefly for the feds, and only hung out her shingle in Wilmington as a solo practitioner last year."

Riley studied the name. "Did she go to law school at Duke or Carolina?"

"Neither. University of Georgia. And don't be such a snob. I Googled her. She's the real deal. Editor of her law school review, finished first in her class. Divorced, no kids."

"Okay. Thanks. I'll call her Tuesday."

Parrish shook her head. "Sweetie? Call her tonight. I kinda went rogue on you and actually reached out to her myself after you and I talked this morning. She's expecting to hear from you."

Riley gulped. "Oh, God. You think things are really, really bad, don't you?"

Parrish studied her old friend's face. She hated keeping secrets, but on the other hand, she'd given Ed her word. "In times like these I think it's a good policy to hope for the best but expect the worst."

"Everything all right?" Evelyn asked as Riley climbed into the seat beside Billy. "Do we have a date for Wendell's service?"

"I don't know," Riley said in a voice that was louder than was strictly necessary. "People keep asking me that, but I just don't know. I don't know when the coroner will release Wendell's body. I don't know when we can have his service. I don't even know if we will have one."

Evelyn's eyebrows shot up in alarm. "Of course we'll have a memorial. A nice traditional service at the Chapel in the Pines. I have Father Templeton on notice. He can come down from Edenton any day this week. And the ladies' auxiliary have already started baking. We'll have people back at Shutters afterward. Wendell would want that."

"Whoa, whoa, whoa," Riley said. "Were you even going to consult me on any of this?"

"It's the right thing to do," Evelyn said, settling the matter. "Think about how it would look if we didn't have a service. I wasn't going to mention this, but rumors are already swirling around the island. If we don't have a funeral, people will wonder if we have something to hide."

"I can't talk about this right now," Riley said, knowing that she was only delaying the inevitable.

They were barely out of the ferry parking lot when Ollie, always on alert for trouble, gave a short bark, and without warning, hopped off Evelyn's lap and went trotting into a thicket of palmettos.

Evelyn stomped on the brake. "Ollie," she cried.

"Oh, let him go. Maybe a gator will get him," Roo said.

"Aunt Roo!" Maggy exclaimed. "That's mean."

"I'll go get him," Billy said, jumping down to go after the errant pug. "Ollie. Here, Ollie!"

Maggy hugged Banks tightly to her chest.

"Daddy's hair was wrong," she announced, in a very small voice. She swiveled around in her seat, turning accusing eyes on her mother. "Why didn't you fix his hair?"

"What on earth is this child talking about?" Evelyn asked.

Riley sighed. "At the hospital. Wendell. Somebody . . . they parted his hair on the wrong side. It was very upsetting."

"Mom doesn't care," Maggy said. Her arms were crossed, her chin thrust out in full pout.

"Maggy!" Riley shot her a warning look.

"She has a boyfriend already," the girl added.

"Fuuuccccckkk." Riley breathed it out in one long syllable, then inhaled a gnat, causing her to choke and sputter.

"Oh my," Roo said.

"What's this?" Evelyn demanded.

When she could finally catch her breath it took a moment for Riley to gather her composure.

"Nate Milas was on the ferry just now. He saw how upset I was, and he was commiserating with me, because of course, Captain Joe just passed away, too. Somebody," she said, glaring at her daughter, "has a very vivid imagination and a very disrespectful attitude right now."

"Oh, him," Evelyn said with a sniff. She stroked Maggy's hair. "Nate Milas? That man is not your mother's boyfriend, Margaret. He just steers the ferry, that's all. So you ought not to go around saying stuff like that, because it will give people the wrong idea."

Billy emerged from the palmetto thicket, bits of Spanish moss and pine needles stuck to his hair. He had the pug tucked under his arm like a football. "Got him," he said triumphantly, handing the dog over to Maggy. "He was staring down a baby possum back up in there."

He slid onto the bench seat beside Riley and banged the palm of his hand on the cart's fiberglass roof, as he would have for a slow-witted New York cabbie. "Come on, Evvy. Floor it! It's ten after five, which means I'm already two drinks behind schedule."

"Me, too," Riley muttered.

18

Sunday night supper in Evelyn Nolan's home was one of her sacred rituals. Even if dinner was an underdone tuna noodle casserole or an overdone pot roast, certain niceties were always observed. A crisply starched and ironed damask cloth covered the mahogany table, which was set with Evelyn's mother's china, silver, and Baccarat crystal. Attendance was as mandatory and set in stone as the dress code—which meant no T-shirts or shorts.

Riley changed into a sundress before dinner, and nagged a resistant Maggy into doing the same thing. And Billy, after downing two pre-dinner vodka tonics, had donned a too-small button-down oxford-cloth dress shirt worn with a polka-dot clip-on bow tie, in a deliberate—and successful—attempt to irritate his mother.

As always, Evelyn presided over the table wearing a dress, pearls, and heels. She glided into the dining room and slid a foil-wrapped casserole onto a silver-plated trivet in the middle of the table.

"There!" she said triumphantly.

"There, what?" Billy grabbed Riley's empty iced tea goblet and filled it to the rim with wine before handing it back to her. "What smells so good?"

"Dinner," Evelyn said, glaring at her son. She peeled back the foil and a cloud of steam escaped. "Andrea Payne dropped this off a little while ago. It's her beef bourguignon. She made it for book club last spring, and it's absolutely divine."

She lit the ivory tapers in the silver candelabra and dimmed the lights of the glittering rock crystal chandelier before seating herself in her chair at the head of the table.

"Andrea Payne was here? At the house? I hope you didn't let her in." Riley took a healthy swig of wine.

"Of course I let her in," Evelyn said. "Why wouldn't I let her in my home?"

Evelyn reached for Maggy's plate and deposited a large spoonful of meat, mushrooms, carrots, and onions, swimming in a sea of wine-soaked sauce.

"No, thanks," Maggy said, quickly pushing her plate away. "I had a hot dog on the ferry. I think I'll just have a roll or something."

Evelyn clucked her tongue in disapproval, but placed a yeast roll on the edge of Maggy's bone china plate.

"Andrea Payne," Billy said, topping off his own glass with the wine, "is a notorious snoop and gossip. And a royal pain in the ass. Not to mention she's a raging homophobe."

"What's a homophobe?" Maggy asked.

"Nothing we discuss at the dinner table," Evelyn said quickly.

Billy waggled a finger in his mother's direction. "Tsk-tsk, Mimi. This is what we call a teachable moment. For your information, Maggy, a homophobe is somebody who doesn't approve of your favorite uncle's lifestyle. And who writes letters to the editor glorifying the sanctity of marriage, even though she herself is on her third marriage that I personally know of."

He reached across the table and helped himself to a bite from Maggy's plate. He took a forkful of beef, chewed, and nodded thoughtfully. "I'll say this though. The bitch can cook."

Riley laughed so hard she nearly spat wine from her nostrils.

"You're not nearly as funny as you and your sister seem to think you are," Evelyn said, serving herself from the casserole. She stared pointedly at Billy's rapidly refilling wineglass.

"He's right, Mama," Riley said, pushing a bite of beef stew around her plate. "Andrea probably only came over here so she could sniff around and find some kind of malicious gossip to spread around the island. If you really are worried about what people will say about my predicament—she's the one who'll be saying it. Nobody loves dishing the dirt like that woman."

"What is our predicament?" Maggy asked.

"Now is not the time," Evelyn said in a warning tone.

Riley sighed. "Look, Maggy. I think you're old enough to hear the truth. I don't know all the details yet, but it looks like we might be in some kind of . . . financial difficulty."

"So does that mean we're broke? And homeless?"

Evelyn slapped the table with the palm of her hand, sending wine slopping over the edge of her glass. "Stop this talk right now! All of you!" She turned to Riley. "Are you happy now? Your daughter thinks she's going to be living in a shelter and applying for food stamps."

Maggy cocked her head toward her mother. "So? Are we?"

"Thankfully, no," Riley said. "We're not broke, or homeless. We have resources. And we have family, thank God, and we'll get through whatever is ahead of us, but I think you need to know we may be facing some tough times. That's all. And no matter what we do or say, there are going to be people spreading rumors that aren't necessarily true. So we have to just ignore that stuff and get on with our lives."

"Okay." Maggy gave a hopeful glance toward her grandmother. "Hey, Mimi. Did that homophobe lady bring any dessert?"

Riley stood at the sink carefully rinsing and stacking the same gold-rimmed Wedgewood plates she'd washed on dozens and dozens of other, far less remarkable Sunday nights.

As usual, Billy had fulfilled his proscribed after-dinner duties—clearing the table and taking out the trash, before beating a hasty retreat to the firehouse and, as usual, Maggy had disappeared to her own room, ostensibly to tackle her summer reading.

Which left Riley and Evelyn alone in the kitchen.

Under Evelyn's watchful eye, Riley dried each plate with a faded flour sack dishcloth and placed it on the lowest shelf of the cupboard just to the right of the sink.

"I wish you wouldn't do that," Evelyn said, shaking her head. She upended the plastic tube of rose-scented lotion she kept on the counter and squeezed a dollop into the palm of her hand.

"Do what?"

"You know what I mean. All this talk about being 'honest' with Maggy. There are some things she is too young to know about."

"I disagree," Riley said, folding the dish towel and hanging it over the towel bar at the end of the cupboard. "You know what this island is like, better than anybody. The coconut telegraph has been working overtime. And I've already started getting phone calls from reporters from Raleigh and Wilmington. I don't want Maggy being blindsided by this stuff. It's better she hears it from me."

Evelyn dropped the plastic lotion tube onto the countertop, where it bounced once. "What? Did you say it's been on the news? About Wendell?"

Riley picked up the bottle and squeezed some lotion into her own hands, rubbing it onto her wrists and forearms.

"I'm afraid so. Three different reporters left messages on my phone."

"You didn't talk to them, did you?"

"No! And I don't plan to. But the word is out. Prominent Raleigh businessman Wendell Griggs was found murdered Saturday at the resort community founded by his wife's family." She made air quotes with her fingertips. "Film at eleven," she added bitterly.

"Dear God. The scandal," Evelyn whispered.

"Exactly. And just like this lotion of yours, Mama—once it's out of the tube, there's no putting it back in."

Riley opened the door to Maggy's bedroom and peered in at her daughter, who was sprawled on the bed, typing something into her phone. The hated dress was tossed on the floor, and she'd changed into soccer shorts and a T-shirt.

"Thought you were supposed to be reading," Riley said, leaning on the doorjamb.

"I read two whole chapters. Dumbest, most boring book ever," Maggy said, looking up, tapping the open book at her side.

"And who are you texting with now?"

"Just one of the kids. Annabelle. We're thinking about maybe going shark fishing out on the beach later tonight. Shane says they'll be biting because of the full moon."

"Nuh-uh," Riley said.

Maggy shot upright. "Why not? I finished my reading. School's out. Anyway, it's boring as shit hanging around here."

"Watch your mouth," Riley said mildly. "You know the rules. And they don't change because it's summer and you're on the island. You're still only twelve, and you still aren't allowed to wander around after dark."

"Dad always let me go down to the beach when there was a full moon."

"Dad let you go with him—not with a bunch of kids," Riley pointed out.

"Shane is almost fourteen. And his mom lets him drive their golf cart all over the place."

"It's illegal for anybody without a valid license to drive one of those carts. Also, Shane's mom is not your mom."

"Unfortunately," Maggy shot back. "You are so totally unfair, it's sick. You're the reason I hardly have any friends at home."

"The answer is still no," Riley said. "And we're not going to fight about this, Maggy, because the issue is nonnegotiable. It's been a long, horrible day for both of us. Please don't make it any worse by nagging at me. You can read, watch television, play Words with Friends, whatever. You just can't leave this house tonight. Understand?"

Maggy flung herself face forward onto the bed.

Riley sighed again and started to close the door.

"Bitch." The word was muffled by the pillow, but still audible.

"I heard that," Riley said.

"Good."

Back in the bedroom she'd once shared with Wendell, Riley dug out the notecard Parrish had given her and dialed Sharon Douglas's phone number.

After the third ring, she was ready to disconnect, when a woman's voice answered.

"Hey, don't hang up." The voice was soft, Southern. "Sorry, I was just walking in the door."

"Hi, um, Sharon?"

"That's me. And you're Riley? I spoke to your friend Parrish earlier today. She said you might call."

"Is now a good time to talk?" Riley asked.

"Sure thing. Let me just get to my desk so I can make some notes while we chat," Sharon said. "But first, let me say how sorry I am about what you're going through."

"Thanks," Riley said. "I don't even know where to start, or what I should ask."

"Parrish gave me the big picture, but I'll need to hear it all from you, of course."

Riley sat cross-legged on the bed. "I think maybe we'd better talk money first. The thing is—I don't know what kind of state our finances are in. I know this makes me sound incredibly naïve, but Wendell, my husband, late husband, handled our money."

Sharon's laugh was warm. "Not naïve. Trusting. I know lots of marriages that work that way. Mine did, until it didn't."

"God, I could kick myself for being so stupid."

"Listen, Riley. We've never met, but after I talked to your friend, I Googled you. I even watched some of your television segments on YouTube. I can tell you're not a stupid woman. So just cut out that stupid talk, okay?"

"Okay," Riley said, her voice shaky.

"We can come back to the money part in a little bit," Sharon said. "Parrish said something about the FBI being involved in all this?"

"I haven't been contacted by the FBI, but yes, a reporter for the NBC affiliate in Raleigh left me a voice mail saying that Wendell was under investigation because of his involvement in a bank failure. Some small community bank down here on the coast."

"Okay. Did the reporter name the bank?"

"No. Look, Wendell was a developer, not a banker. And our bank is Wells Fargo, the branch in Raleigh."

"Parrish said your home on Belle Isle was foreclosed on by a bank. Do you know which bank?"

"I didn't pay attention to that part," Riley admitted. "The foreclosure notice is downstairs in my purse. I can get it and see."

"Let's just talk first," Sharon Douglas said. "You had no idea that a foreclosure was imminent?"

"No. Wendell and I had been more or less living apart for the past few months, and I'd told him I wanted a divorce. So, our communication has been pretty minimal. The first I knew about a foreclosure was Friday, when I got to the house and the locks had been changed and I saw the notice tacked to the front door."

"Brutal," Sharon said. "This is weird because the law requires you to have been notified in writing—and the foreclosure has to have been published in the legal organ of record in your county."

"I *never* got any kind of notice," Riley said heatedly. "But we live in Raleigh. Would the notification have been sent there?"

"Yes. The notice should have been sent to your legal residence of record. And it would have been sent by certified mail. So somebody had to have signed a return notice."

"Somebody might have, but it wasn't me," Riley said slowly. "We just sold the house in Raleigh, but I only moved out right before I came down here Friday."

"Weird. Is there anything else you can tell me?"

Riley stood up and opened her bedroom door, peering down the hallway to make sure she couldn't be overheard. The hallway was empty, and she could hear the muted sound of the downstairs television, where Evelyn was watching *The Good Wife,* another part of her Sunday ritual.

She closed the door and sat back down on the bed.

"The sheriff says Wendell was murdered. I don't . . . I can't process any of this."

"Sorry. Look, Riley, do you have access to any of your family's financial records, or your husband's business records?"

"Here? I'm not sure. Wendell had a small office in the village, next to the post office. That is, Belle Isle Enterprises has an office, and since Wendell was the president . . ."

"If I were you," Sharon said slowly, "I'd make it my business to take a look around his office."

"And look for what?" Riley asked. "I thought that's what I was going to talk to you about—about hiring you to help with all this mess."

"The thing is, Riley? I've only gone into solo practice this year. I just went through a divorce of my own. I'd love to help you out—this case is intriguing as hell. But the more we talk, the more I realize this isn't something that's going to be solved by filing some quick motions in the courthouse down there. I think there's something really fishy going on. But unless you can guarantee that you can pay me a retainer, this is as far as I can go. I just can't afford to take on a pro bono case like yours right now."

"Oh." The single syllable hung in the air.

"I hate, hate, hate this," Sharon said. "Let's do this. See if you can get your hands on your financial records. Check the filings at the courthouse down there, to see if your husband has been named as a defendant in any civil or criminal cases. Maybe—just maybe, if you do most of the legwork, I'll be able to help you out a little. Does that make sense?"

"I guess," Riley said, her voice meek.

"Call me when you have more facts, okay? And Riley?"

"Yes?"

"If the FBI does come calling, just play dumb. Got it?"

"Dumb I can do," Riley said bitterly.

An hour later, Riley tiptoed barefoot down the stairs, tennis shoes in hand, but the third step from the bottom—her old teenage nemesis—gave her away with an undeniable squeak.

"Who's there?" Evelyn called out.

Damn it! How many times had that creaky stair tread stood between her and freedom?

"It's just me, Mama," Riley answered.

Evelyn popped around the corner from the den. She was dressed for bed in her monogrammed rose satin pajamas, with her hair swathed in a silk scarf and her face coated with her favorite Lancôme wrinkle cream.

She eyed her daughter's ensemble with suspicion—shorts, T-shirt, and a UNC baseball cap. "Where are you going this time of night?"

"Parrish called and wants me to come over for a glass of wine. Don't wait up for me, okay?"

Evelyn frowned and glanced upward. She lowered her voice. "I don't like the idea of you running around by yourself this time of night. Do I need to remind you there's a murderer somewhere out there? I mean, why can't Parrish come over here?"

"No, Mama, you don't need to remind me that somebody killed my husband," Riley snapped. "Anyway, Parrish promised Ed she'd stick close to the house because her cat's been sick."

It was alarming, really, how quickly and easily she slid back into the habit of lying to her mother. Maybe there was something about sleeping here at Shutters, in her old bedroom. The next thing she knew she'd be stealing money from her mother's purse again to buy dime bags from the sketchy guys who gassed up boats down at the marina.

Evelyn shook her head, lips pursed in silent disapproval.

"Anyway," Riley said, "the sheriff told me he's sure whoever did this is long gone. If it makes you feel any better, I'll call you when I'm heading home. All right?"

Before Evelyn could voice any more protest, Riley gave her a quick peck on the cheek and hurried out the back door.

Palm fronds and low-hanging branches brushed against the side of her mother's golf cart as she bumped along the road in the growing darkness. Moths batted against the cart's headlights, and she could hear the soft calls of mourning doves echoing from the treetops. When an armadillo suddenly scuttled across the path, Riley was so startled she nearly fell off her seat.

Ten minutes later she turned off the main cross-island road and onto Sandy Point Lane. A hundred yards down she saw the lights of Whale's Tail, the Godchauxs' house, shining through the tree line.

Riley pulled the cart under the porte cochere and was soon tapping on the home's brass whale-shaped knocker.

Five minutes passed. Riley stepped away from the front portico, found a pebble, and tossed it upward, aiming at the second-floor master bedroom window. It fell far short, actually beaning her on the head.

"I suck," she muttered. "Hey, Parrish," she called, through cupped hands. "Open up! It's me!"

A minute later, the sash slid open and Parrish leaned out. "What the hell?"

"Would you please get your ass downstairs and let me in?"

"Why?"

"Just let me in, will you?"

They sat at the table in the kitchen. Parrish, dressed for bed in pajama bottoms and a camisole, sipped a cup of tea while Riley poured herself a glass of Ed's expensive Brunello.

"I talked to your lawyer friend Sharon Douglas," Riley reported. "She's nice, but she says she can't represent me unless I know I can pay her. And I honestly can't guarantee that I could."

"That's it? She wouldn't even talk to you?"

"I wouldn't talk to me either, if I were just starting a solo practice after going through a bad divorce."

"So that's it?"

"She gave me some advice. For one thing, she says I need to find out everything I can about the state of our finances, and the company finances."

"How do you propose to do that?"

Riley cocked an eyebrow and grinned.

"Oh, shit," Parrish said, shaking her head. "I know that look. That's the look that got us thrown out of the sorority house our junior year. The same look that made my daddy take away my car for three months after we ran out of gas and money during spring break in Key West senior year."

"I'm pretty sure Wendell kept all the business papers at his office in the village," Riley said. "All we have to do is go over there and take a look around. It's not like we'd be breaking and entering. I mean, it's my family business. And I'm Wendell's wife. I mean widow."

"You don't have a key to the office, do you?" Parrish asked, stirring her tea.

"Not exactly."

"How *exactly* do you plan to get in?"

"I need to find Wendell's keys. It didn't hit me until tonight, when I was talking to Sharon, that I don't know where his car is. I don't even know where our golf cart is. Wendell kept a separate ring for the island—with keys for the house, the garage, his office, and the golf cart."

"Maybe the sheriff impounded the golf cart," Parrish suggested.

"Impounded it where? This island is only three miles long. That cart has got to be here, somewhere."

"For all you know, the keys were in Wendell's pocket."

"No. The hospital gave me his stuff before I left. His wallet, his money clip with some soggy twenty-dollar bills. No key chain."

"What about his phone?"

"Come to think of it, they didn't give me his phone," Riley said. "Maybe it's on the golf cart. He was always leaving it in one of the cup holders."

"Or maybe the sheriff has it, or maybe it's at the bottom of the bay."

"Always the optimist," Riley said.

"I'm a realist. And you need to be, too," Parrish said. "Go home and get a good night's sleep. Tuesday, you can go to the courthouse and start figuring things out."

Riley stared at her. This was not the Parrish who'd been her wingwoman since childhood. That Parrish was reasonable and rational, but she was also the friend Riley always knew would have her back.

"Go to sleep? How? My life has gone completely haywire. I've been locked out of my own home. My husband's been murdered. I need some answers,

Parrish. I need to know why. You expect me to just sit back and wait to see what happens next?"

"Yes, I do," Parrish said. She ran a hand through her reddish hair, and under the light of the chandelier hanging over the table, Riley could see a half inch of gray at the roots. Parrish had scrubbed off her usually flawless makeup, and now Riley also noticed splotchy patches of acne on her cheeks and chin.

"You're not a cop, you know," Parrish said. "And you're not even an investigative reporter anymore. Even if you could get into Wendell's office, you have no idea what to look for."

"I'll know it when I see it," Riley insisted. She stood up. "Are you coming?"

"No." Parrish shook her head. "Sorry."

"Me, too."

Riley steered the cart away from Whale's Tail. The shrubbery on either side of the trail seemed to close in on her. She could smell night-blooming jasmine and something sour. A skunk? An owl hooted from the treetops.

She couldn't believe Parrish had abandoned her. Maybe she was being naïve, believing she could solve this mystery, but shouldn't her best friend have come along—out of sympathy, at the very least?

The air had gotten positively chilly after sundown. She shivered and wished she'd chosen a long-sleeved shirt—or a better best friend.

The path widened as it approached the village, splitting into two one-way roads, with a narrow swath of greenery in the middle. People were drifting out of the Sea Biscuit, lingering to chat in the parking lot.

A light wind whipped up whitecaps on the surface of the bay, where the huge full moon was reflected on the midnight-blue water. Now she was downright chilly. Riley stopped the cart and rummaged through the storage bin strapped onto the back of the cart, next to Evelyn's golf clubs. Aha! She found her mother's neatly folded windbreaker and slipped her arms through the sleeves.

She climbed back onto the driver's seat and sat looking out at the marina, where sailboats, runabouts, and skiffs bobbed at anchor. Occasionally she heard a hollow clanging as the wind knocked rigging against aluminum masts.

Two hundred yards ahead, she saw a stretch of yellow crime-scene tape fluttering in the breeze. Without thinking, she drove toward the long concrete pier that jutted out into the bay.

Riley parked and got out of the cart. Four small orange cones were arranged in a rectangle on the sidewalk. She stood, her arms folded tightly across her chest, and stared down at the concrete.

Was this where it happened? Did Wendell stand in this spot, just three short nights ago? Who was with him? A stranger? The sheriff said he'd been struck hard, in the back of the head. Had Wendell known he was in danger? Was there an argument? Who had done this?

Belle Isle's summer season was in full swing. Every mooring on the dock had a boat tied up. All but one. Was this where Wendell had arrived at Belle Isle? Why? What was he doing here?

An icy chill ran down her spine, and she stumbled, nearly knocked down, again, by the finality of this moment.

One of the rubber cones had fallen on its side. With her toe, she edged it back to an upright position. This was her reality. Wendell was really and truly gone. Their daughter needed to know why. And Riley needed the truth just as much as Maggy.

Riley gazed down into the inky waters of the bay. Waves splashed at the concrete seawall, washing up random flotsam: bits of marsh grass, cigarette butts, a faded plastic Dr Pepper bottle, and a snarl of monofilament fishing line with a red-and-white plastic bobber attached. Unbidden, a ghostly image of a body, tangled in that same monofilament, flashed in her imagination. She walked back to the golf cart.

Billy Nolan stared at the computer screen. He looked away, and then back again, but the red blinking numbers hadn't changed. Which wasn't really news. They hadn't changed in the last forty-eight hours either, and God knows he'd checked repeatedly, hoping against hope that maybe the bank had discovered an error. Maybe, he thought, trust accounts were like an old pair of jeans. Sometimes you put them on after not wearing them for months, and money magically appeared in your pocket.

Or not. He desperately needed some magic right now.

He fixed himself another cocktail and wandered over to the piano. Music had been his friend, his only friend, for so many years before he and Scott had connected. His fingers trailed across the keys, and he played a few notes, but they were jarring, discordant. Like his life.

God *damn* Wendell Griggs. Damn him and his crazy schemes. He'd never really trusted his brother-in-law, but when Wendell came to him with that plan of his, and the veiled threats, Billy told himself that Wendell would make them all rich. And not just Belle Isle rich, which everybody on the island mistakenly assumed the Nolans were, but filthy, stinking, Hamptons rich. Palm Beach rich.

The ugly truth of it was, Billy wanted to be richer than W.R. had ever thought possible. The old man was dead, so he wouldn't know, but everybody else would know. Scott would know. And that would be enough, wouldn't it?

Billy drained the highball glass, stared out the window, and was surprised to see a pair of headlights rounding the driveway at the Shutters. He snapped off the lamp beside the piano to enable a better view. The cart rolled to a stop beneath the garage lights, and he saw Riley climb out. It was nearly three in the morning. What was his big sister up to?

19

The list of Memorial Day activities in *The Belle Isle Bulletin*—helpfully forwarded to him by his mother—was long and exhausting. Farmers market on the village green! Cookout at the pool! Tennis tournament. Kiddie Karnival. Softball. Potato sack races! Shrimp boil on the beach.

"You should go!" Annie had e-mailed. "You're turning into a hermit."

"Two words," Nate muttered, as he loaded his gear into the cart. "Hell. No."

He glanced up at the bright, cloudless sky. A perfect day for fishing, which was why he'd called ahead to the marina and asked to have the boat gassed up and waiting at the dock.

Now, as he stowed his rods, tackle, and cooler in the twenty-two-foot Pathfinder, he realized he'd underestimated the amount of traffic that would be on the water on this first big holiday of the summer. There were boats everywhere. He shrugged. People and boats meant business. For the Mercantile and the ferry. And, like it or not, he was in business on this island.

At the slip next to his, a horde of kids piled onto a sleek twenty-eight-foot Cobalt ski boat. They were young, in their early teens, and noisy. Even over the roar of the Cobalt's motor he could hear earsplitting hardcore rap from the radio, and the teens themselves were laughing and goofing around.

He recognized the boat's redheaded "captain" as the oldest of the Billingsley litter. The same kid whose phone he had temporarily taken. Shane? Kid was a punk.

He busied himself dumping the shrimp into the live well. Every time he looked up, another kid was jumping onto the Billingsley boat. Now there were at least ten passengers, which meant the boat was seriously, and illegally, overloaded. Not his problem. With any luck, either the Baldwin County sheriff's marine patrol or the Coast Guard would intercept the ship of fools before anybody got hurt.

Nate started the runabout's twin Mercs and, looking over his shoulder, began slowly backing away from his berth. As he inched past the Billingsley boat he noticed for the first time that Riley Griggs's daughter, Maggy, was perched on the stern. She was clad in a bright pink bikini and squeezed in alongside three similarly dressed young girls. No sign of Riley, or any other adult in the vicinity.

He wondered, briefly, if Maggy's mother knew or approved of this outing, and then dismissed the thought. Also not his problem.

Suddenly, and without warning, the Billingsley kid jammed his boat into reverse and shot backward away from his adjoining berth, only inches away from Nate's, sending a huge jet of water splashing over his bow.

"Hey! Watch it, goddamn it!" Nate shouted.

"Sorry. My bad!" the redhead called back. The girls on the boat screamed in mock terror, and a moment later the kid was roaring away at full throttle. In a no-wake zone.

"Slow down!" Nate hollered, but the kid and the boat were long gone. He watched in disgust as the ski boat raced across the bay. "Weekenders," he muttered. As soon as the word came out of his mouth, he realized he sounded exactly like his old man.

Captain Joe was always polite, almost deferential to Belle Isle's part-time residents—at least in public. "These people pay our bills," he'd say, when Nate complained about the rich, entitled assholes who treated his father—and by extension—the rest of the Milas family, like little more than indentured servants.

If they called the ferry office and demanded that Joe hold the boat because somebody in the family was running late, Joe would calmly point out that a schedule was a schedule. If a passenger bitched at him about weak coffee from the concession stand or a clumsy deckhand, the old man would listen and nod—maybe even apologize for his employee's supposed transgression.

At home it was a different matter. After a particularly bad day at work, kindly Captain Joe would rage about the snooty wives, pampered kids, and self-important "executives" with second homes on Belle Isle. "Weekenders," Joe would snarl. "A giant pain in the ass, every single one of 'em."

Joe Milas was proud of his own business, proud that he'd instilled an early work ethic in his only child, but he'd always been insistent that Nate would go to college and get a real education—"Just in case you decide running a damn boat from point A to point B all day every day isn't what you want out of life."

Well, Nate had gotten a degree in finance, started a business from scratch, watched it go bust, and then started another business—an app called Cribb. He'd gotten rich and then gotten the shaft—first from his business partner/best friend Matt, and then from his best girl, Cassie. And now he'd ended up right back here in Belle Isle and was temporarily making a living running that same damn boat back and forth across the bay—six times a day.

But today was his day off, and he intended to spend it as far away from any and all weekenders as possible. He steered the Pathfinder toward a favorite fishing spot, a narrow, tree-lined spit of an island local fishermen referred to as "the spoon" because of its shape. Ten minutes later he'd anchored just off the back side of the spoon's tip at the mouth of a narrow tidal creek. Within five minutes he'd hooked a good-size flounder in the sandy shallows. His rod tip bent nearly double as he carefully reeled the fish toward the boat. He could see the flounder's broad, pancake shape shimmering just below the water's surface, and he picked up a long-handled net to assist in boating the fish.

Just as he was about to slide the net beneath the fish, he heard the roar of a fast-approaching boat. The Pathfinder rocked violently and his feet slipped out from under him and he landed flat on his ass on the bottom of the boat. Somehow, he managed not to drop the rod.

"Son of a bitch," he growled, pulling himself up to a standing position. He looked down at the water's surface, but the slack in his fishing line told him he'd lost the fish.

Nate glanced up in time to see the speedboat zoom away.

He had half a mind to go after the little punks, or maybe call the local marine patrol to alert them to the kids' reckless behavior.

Nah, he thought. He reached into the live well, drew out a shrimp, and baited his hook again. If there was one flounder here, there would be more. Let the punk kid be somebody else's problem. He had fish to catch.

And the fishing was good. He settled into the rhythm of casting and retrieving, forgetting about the stresses and annoyances of running a business and dealing with the public. A gentle breeze kept the heat from becoming oppressive. The sun beat down on his shoulders, which eventually unknotted and relaxed. Around noon, he ate the ham sandwich he'd picked up at the Mercantile, and washed it down with a cold beer from his cooler.

By the time the tide slacked he'd caught six keeper trout and a flounder, and it was nearing two. Time to head for the dock.

Nate caught himself smiling and humming as he raised anchor. Humming, for Christ's sake. Hermits didn't hum. Still. A bad day on the water beat the hell out of the best day spent in his windowless "executive suite" back at Cribb's offices in California.

He idled the skiff's motor and allowed the outgoing tide to ride him out of the shallow water.

When he was satisfied it was safe, he was about to start the engine when he heard it. A voice, faint, echoing over the bay's now mirror-calm surface.

"Help! Anybody? Help!" It seemed to be coming from the front side of the spoon. "Hey! We need help!"

He spotted it as soon as he rounded the tip of the spoon—the Cobalt—beached high and dry on the sandbar. Three of the kids had climbed out of the boat and were sitting glumly on the sand, while the Billingsley kid, his red hair gleaming in the unrelenting sun, stood at the stern, madly waving his arms. The girls lounged on the bow of the boat, seemingly unconcerned about their misfortune.

Nate allowed himself a small smirk of satisfaction. Served the little pissant right. Let him stay out here for another couple of hours, and maybe he'd learn a lesson or two about courtesy and safety on the water.

But then he spotted the forlorn silhouette of a slender girl, apart from the others, hunched over, head bent, her arms tucked around knees drawn close to her chest.

"Shit," he muttered. It was Riley's daughter, Maggy.

The water near the sandbar was too shallow to allow him to get much closer than a hundred yards away.

"Hey, man," the kid yelled. "We're stuck."

"I see that. Looks like you're beached pretty solid there."

"Yeah. They oughta have a marker out here or something. Now my prop's all screwed up. How about a tow back to the marina?"

It took a supreme effort on Nate's part not to laugh at the kid's audacity.

He shook his head. "Can't do it. Your boat's a good six feet longer than mine, and you're overloaded as it is."

The kid's face flushed red in anger. "So what the hell am I supposed to do now?"

Nate shrugged. "Call a marine tow service?"

"Are you kidding me? They probably charge. Like, a lot. Anyway, my phone's dead."

Nate held up his own phone. "I could call for you."

The kid appeared to be considering that option.

"I could call the Coast Guard or the marine patrol," Nate offered. "But when they show up, they're gonna do a safety inspection and they're gonna count how many life jackets you have on board."

"I got enough."

"I doubt that," Nate said. "I count ten of you. Show me ten life jackets."

"What, if I don't have enough, you're gonna narc me out?"

"Absolutely," Nate said, his expression grim. He gestured toward the lone figure sitting in the bow.

"Hey, Maggy—how about I give you a lift back to the marina?"

She lifted her head and glared at him. Her shoulders and arms and legs were burnt bright red, but her face looked oddly ashen.

"No."

"I think you probably need to come with me," he said, trying to keep his tone light. He knew the girl had diabetes, and wondered how long it had been since she'd had anything to eat or drink. "It's a busy holiday weekend. Even after I call the marine patrol, it could be awhile before they can send somebody out to give you guys a tow."

Her eyes widened, but she shook her head. "No way. I'll wait here."

"I don't think so," Nate said. "Come on. Let's go."

"You're not in charge of me!"

"That's true. But if you don't start wading out here to me in one minute, I'm gonna swim in there and drag you back to my boat myself. And then things are gonna start getting ugly."

One of the other girls on the boat approached, touched her friend's shoulder, and said something Nate couldn't hear. Maggy shook her head, but the girl leaned in closer.

"Go on," the Billingsley kid yelled, sounding annoyed. "Let him give you a ride. I don't want you to pass out or puke on my boat or something."

Reluctantly, Maggy climbed slowly down off the boat, using the ruined propeller as a stepladder. A moment later, she was paddling toward Nate's skiff, and a moment after that, he leaned over and hauled her effortlessly over the side.

She flopped onto the deck and looked up at him with murder in her eyes.

"Happy now? Since you ruined my life?"

"Delirious," Nate said. He touched her cheek, which felt surprisingly clammy. "When was the last time you ate?"

"None of your business."

"Have you checked your blood sugar or taken any insulin?"

She clamped her lips together tightly and turned her back to him. He could see her narrow shoulders were trembling.

"Hey!" Nate grasped her by her shoulders and turned her back around. "I'm not playing games here, Maggy."

"I left my insulin kit on the dock," she finally admitted. "I had a Coke and some chips at the marina."

"That was hours ago." He reached into the cooler and found another ham sandwich. He thrust it at her. "Here. Eat this."

Her eyes flared. "Ham? Gross."

"Eat it anyway."

She peeled back the wax paper wrapping on the sandwich and took a bite. And then another bite. And another.

He handed her a cold bottle of water. "You need to drink something. I think you look dehydrated."

The fight had suddenly gone out of her. She took the bottle and swigged half of it down.

Nate found a clean T-shirt in the locker under his console and flipped it to her. "Here. Put that on. You're shaking. And you're burned to a crisp. Have you ever heard of a thing called sunblock?"

"Have you ever heard of minding your own business?"

"Look. I don't know that much about diabetes. Are you okay? Do I need to call and have an ambulance meet us at the dock? And don't bullshit me. Your mom already lost your dad this week. How do you think she'd feel if you go into a coma or something?"

Maggy shrugged. "You have any orange juice?"

"I've got an orange." He got it out of the cooler, took his fishing knife, wiped it off on the hem of his shirt, and cut it in half.

She immediately sank her teeth into the bright orange flesh and began sucking the juice noisily.

"Better?"

She nodded.

"Then let's go home."

20

When the doorbell rang, Riley ignored it. She was sick of casseroles and condolences. But then it rang again. And again. If the visitor was one of Evelyn's friends, their next stop would be the back door, and there would be hell to pay.

Better to get it over with and face the music. She looked like crap, she knew, with wet hair, no makeup, and a faded tank top worn braless over baggy shorts she'd found in the bottom drawer of the dresser in her old room. Maybe, she thought glumly, her appearance would frighten away whoever was now banging insistently on the front door.

"Coming!" she bellowed, walking quickly down the hall. She opened the front door to find the person she least wanted to see on the porch of Shutters today.

Nate Milas. He was sunburnt and windblown, and he wasn't alone. Maggy stood beside him, also sunburnt with an unusually meek expression on her face. She was wearing an oversize shirt that definitely didn't belong to her.

"Hi," she said, looking from Nate to her daughter. "What's up?"

Nate had a hand clamped firmly on Maggy's shoulder. "I just dropped by to return some property of yours."

"Maggy?" She glanced at her daughter, who was busily studying her fingernails. "Why would she need returning?" She hooked a finger under her daughter's chin. "I thought you were still asleep upstairs."

"Uh, no," Maggy said, turning on the attitude.

"Where exactly did you find her?" Riley directed the question to Nate.

"Ask her," Nate said curtly.

"Maggy?" Riley's voice held a warning tone.

"I was just out on a boat with some kids," Maggy said petulantly. "We weren't doing anything. And then *he* came along and butted in." She tossed her head in Nate's direction, avoiding his direct gaze.

"What kids?" Riley asked. "You didn't say anything about going out on a boat today. Did Mimi say that was okay?"

"Mimi wasn't around. And you were asleep. I didn't want to bother you," Maggy said. "I'm fine. But I gotta pee now, if that's okay with him."

She stalked past the grown-ups and ran up the stairs, past her mother's confused gaze.

Riley turned back to Nate, who seemed to have something else he wanted to say.

"Well, thanks, I guess, for giving her a ride home," she said, her hand on the door.

"Don't you want to know what she was up to?" he asked.

"She just said she went for a boat ride with some kids. Aside from being sunburnt, it doesn't look like she came to any harm," Riley said.

"So . . . it's all right with you if she goes racing around out in the bay in a boat dangerously overloaded with a bunch of kids, being driven by that Billingsley kid, who has no business driving a go-cart, let alone a boat with a two-hundred-horsepower engine? And it's okay that the boat didn't have enough life jackets? And the Billingsley kid subsequently beached the boat on a sandbar—where your kid would still be sitting, with no food or drink—or meds—if it weren't for me?"

Nate's face was rigid with anger.

"Dear God," Riley said, letting that sink in. She glanced up at the stairs. "Is she really all right?"

"She was pale and shaky when I got her on my boat, and she finally admitted she hadn't eaten anything and left her insulin kit back at the marina. I gave her some water and a sandwich and an orange. When we got to the marina she did her insulin thing. So I guess she's okay."

Riley leaned against the doorjamb and let out a long sigh. "Thanks for bringing her home safely. I don't know what she could have been thinking. Maggy knows how to take care of her diabetes. God knows I've talked until I'm blue in the face about the importance of monitoring her blood sugar and eating properly. It's like she enjoys pushing the envelope, taking risks."

"Maybe she needs to have a responsible parent monitor her behavior."

Riley bristled. "What's that supposed to mean?"

"It means a twelve-year-old girl has no business running around this island without any adult supervision. Especially with that bunch of kids she was hanging out with. A boat is not a toy, but it is to that crowd. Shane Billingsley is trouble, Riley. If Maggy were my kid . . ."

"But she's not your kid," Riley said. "Maggy has plenty of adult supervision. Usually. Obviously, she snuck out of the house without my permission this morning. I'll deal with that, and she'll be punished. Look. I haven't been sleeping well, since all this . . ."

"Whatever," Nate said. "Sorry to have disturbed your sleep."

He turned and stomped his way off the front porch, leaving Riley standing openmouthed in the doorway.

Maggy stayed in the shower for nearly an hour, until the hot water ran out. It was one of her favorite delaying tactics.

Riley sat patiently on one of the twin beds in the guest bedroom. They'd barely been in the house four days, and already it looked like Maggy's room at home. Discarded clothes and shoes were strewn everywhere. Her suitcase was open on the floor, with most of its contents spilled around it. A damp, sandy bathing suit had been dropped on top of the mahogany dresser, along with Maggy's cell phone.

Riley picked up the phone and regarded it thoughtfully. She was still thinking through her disciplinary strategy when Maggy finally emerged from the bathroom, wearing clean clothes, her wet hair wrapped in a towel.

"We have to talk," Riley announced sternly. She patted the unmade bed. "Sit."

Maggy sat on the edge of the bed, already sensing her mother's dark mood. "I'm sorry, okay? I know it was dumb to leave my kit at the marina. And I promise not to do it again. Okay?"

"Not okay," Riley said. "It's not okay that you snuck out of this house this morning without letting anybody know where you were going. And it's not okay for you to be out in a boat with somebody who isn't old enough or sensible enough to legally operate a boat. And it's especially not okay to pull a stunt like this when you know what I'm going through with your father's death."

"Like you're the only one going through it," Maggy shot back.

"I didn't say that. I know you're hurting, too. But you have to stop this risky behavior." Riley felt her anger rising, along with the pitch in her voice. "Nate told me Shane was driving that boat like a crazy person. What if he hadn't come along after Shane beached the boat on that sandbar? You could have been stranded out there for hours and hours with no food or water. . . ."

Riley was crying now, damn it. But her tears failed to faze her daughter.

"Geez, Mom. Get a grip!" Maggy shouted. "Nothing bad happened. Why do you have to make such a big deal of everything?"

Riley grasped Maggy's shoulders and shook them. "You could have died. You know that, right? You could have died!"

"Ow!" the girl howled, twisting away from her mother's reach. "Cut it out! That hurts."

"I want it to hurt. I don't know how else to get through to you. You can't keep doing this stuff, Maggy. You just can't!"

Maggy hurled herself off the bed and onto the floor. She scuttled across the rug until she was a few feet away, then glared up at her mother, wide-eyed.

"Okay. I get it. All right? Can we just drop it now? I said I'm sorry. I won't do it again."

Riley clutched the edge of the bed with both hands, trying to regain her composure. She was breathing hard, as though she'd just run a marathon.

"That's right," she said, when she could speak. "You won't be doing that again. You're on restriction until further notice. You don't leave this house unless it's with me or a family member. Or Parrish."

"No! It's Memorial Day. I'm playing in the tennis tournament with Bebo. And the cookout. Everybody will be there. You can't lock me up on Memorial Day. It's not fair."

"You should have thought of that before you went sneaking off without my permission," Riley said. "Also? I don't give a damn about being fair."

"Fine," Maggy said. "Go ahead and ruin my life. I don't care."

"I'm trying to save your life," Riley said softly.

"Whatever." Maggy stood with hands clutched on both hips. "Can I please have some privacy now?" She held out her hand. "And my phone?"

"You can have your privacy," Riley said. "But I'm keeping your phone until further notice."

"Whattttt?" Maggy shrieked. "That's my phone. It's mine! Dad gave it to me."

"And I'm taking it away, until you can figure out how to behave responsibly."

Riley pushed up from the bed and walked unsteadily to the bedroom door, the cell phone gripped firmly in her hand.

The door slammed shut behind her, and a moment later she heard what sounded like a tennis shoe being thrown against the wooden door. "I hate you!" Maggy screamed.

21

Billy breezed through the back door of his mother's house. He was dressed in tennis whites with a racquet slung over his shoulder.

"Maggy!" he called, walking through the hallway and calling up toward the stairway. "Let's go! We're supposed to be on the courts in twenty minutes."

The house was quiet. Eerily so. He heard a door open and close upstairs.

"Maggy? Mama? Riley?"

Light footsteps.

Riley walked slowly down the stairs. She looked, her brother thought, like she'd been through the wringer.

Bless her heart, he thought.

"Hey," she said softly, as she reached the bottom stair. "Sorry. I guess I should have called to let you know. Maggy won't be playing in the tournament."

"Is she still pulling that crap about tennis being stupid?" he asked, frowning. "Where is she? I bet I can change her mind."

"I bet you could. Unfortunately, she's under house arrest. So she's not going anywhere for the next few days."

Billy glanced upward. "What'd she do? Rob a bank?"

"It's not funny," Riley said. "She snuck out of the house this morning and went out on a boat with Shane Billingsley and a bunch of other kids. They were racing around the bay, the boat got beached on a sandbar, and she was out there, with no food or water, or her meds. It's only by the grace of God—and that damned Nate Milas—that she made it back alive."

"Ohhh." Billy spun his racquet on his shoulder. "She's not sick though—right?"

"No, fortunately, she's sunburned but okay. Nate gave her some juice and fed her and got her back to the marina to pick up her insulin in time. Then he delivered her to me—along with an incredibly annoying and self-righteous sermon about what a neglectful, irresponsible parent I am."

"Well, fuck him," Billy said cheerfully.

"That's sort of what I told him," Riley said. "Now, I feel kind of bad about that. I know he meant well." She shrugged. "I'm really not having a good week."

Billy gave her a hug. "I know. I'm sorry about all of this. So Mags is giving you a hard time?"

She nodded. "It's like she's testing just how far she can push my buttons."

"How'd she manage to get out of the house without you seeing her? Did she figure out how to climb out that bedroom window onto the porch roof and slide down the drainpipe already? Damn! I didn't get around to that until I was fourteen or fifteen."

"No, hopefully she hasn't figured that out yet. As far as I know, she just waited until Mama was gone and left." She hesitated. "I haven't been sleeping, you know. Last night, after everybody else was in bed, I kind of wandered around the island on the golf cart. I had to see for myself where it happened. You know. Where they found Wendell's body."

"I saw you coming back to the house," Billy said. "I figured maybe it was something like that."

"Yeah." Riley sat on the bottom stair. "Last night, seeing the seawall, and the place where the sheriff marked it off, it shook me up. I couldn't get to sleep after I got home. When I finally did fall asleep—around dawn, I didn't wake up until nearly two! I didn't even know Maggy was gone until Nate rang the doorbell. He's right. I really am a shitty mother."

"Oh, sis," Billy said. "You know that's not true." He sat down beside her on the stair, and Riley leaned her head on his shoulder.

"Maggy's just going through the kind of crap kids do at that age. Remember what a terror I was? All the schools I got kicked out of? And, look, I survived, right? Just remember she's a good kid who's going through a bad time. I'll talk to her if you want. Maybe she'll listen to me."

"There's something I haven't told you yet," Riley said, keeping her voice low. "A television reporter from Raleigh has been calling and leaving me voice messages. About Wendell. She claims the FBI is investigating Wendell's involvement in some bank failure on the coast."

"The FBI?" Billy felt a cold shiver run down his spine. "You don't think it's true—do you?"

"I don't know," Riley said. "I don't know anything about Wendell's business dealings. Except," she said bitterly, "he somehow managed to lose our house here."

"What are you going to do?" Billy asked.

"What can I do? I'm going to the courthouse first thing tomorrow, to try to figure out the foreclosure and to see if I can sniff out anything else Wendell might have been up to. I talked to a lawyer yesterday, but since I can't guarantee I can pay her a retainer, I guess I'm going to have to try and figure this stuff out for myself."

Billy turned to look at his sister. "What can I do to help?"

She gave him a wan smile. "Keep Mama off my back. She's driving me nuts insisting we have to have what she calls a 'proper memorial service' for Wendell. She's already got everything planned. And in the meantime, I don't even know when the coroner is going to release Wendell's body. I know it's awful, but I'm dreading this whole ordeal."

"It's not awful," Billy assured her. "Why don't you just tell Mama to back off? There's no law that says you absolutely have to have a funeral if you don't want one. Especially under the circumstances."

"No law?" She snorted. "There's Evelyn Riley Nolan's law. It's the only one that matters on Belle Isle."

22

Riley's cell phone shattered the peace of the morning. "Mrs. Griggs? This is Sheriff Schumann. I was wondering if you'd have time to answer some questions for me."

It was barely 8 a.m. on Tuesday. Riley was sitting on the front porch at Shutters, sipping her coffee and watching a blue heron poking around at something in the front yard. It had rained overnight, and the air was cool and fresh. Butterflies hovered over the red salvia in her mother's flower beds, and the day would have seemed ripe with the promise of summer. If only.

"Yes," she said cautiously.

"Is now a good time?"

She looked down at her cotton nightgown and bare feet and sprang from the wooden rocking chair.

"Right now?"

"I could come over there if you like. I'm at the ferry dock in Southpoint, as a matter of fact."

"No, no," Riley said quickly. "If it's all right with you, could I meet you someplace else? My daughter is still pretty upset about everything."

"Have you had breakfast?"

"Just coffee," Riley said.

"Then let's meet at Onnalee's. Say, in an hour?"

"I'll see you there," she said.

Once again Riley was thankful for being an early riser in a house full of sleepyheads. Evelyn never came downstairs before 9:30 in the summer, and Maggy had barely shown her face outside her room since being put on double-secret probation.

She dressed quickly, not bothering with makeup or more than a cursory hair brushing, left a note saying she'd gone to town to run errands, and managed to make the 8:30 ferry.

Another reason to be an early bird was that she mostly had the boat to herself. The season had barely started, but the residents of Belle Isle had already eased into their relaxed summer schedule. Islanders who had jobs on the mainland had mostly taken the first ferry of the morning, and anybody who had shopping or errands to run in town would probably wait another hour or so.

After enduring the sympathetic inquiries of three or four neighbors, Riley found a sunny but deserted spot on the upper deck and barricaded herself behind the pages of the three-day-old *Wall Street Journal* she'd bought from a vending machine at the landing, for just that reason.

A shadow fell over the newspaper page. She looked up and saw Nate Milas, holding out a steaming cardboard cup of coffee.

He flashed her a hopeful smile. "We're fresh out of olive branches at the concession stand. I was hoping maybe this would do."

She lowered the paper. "Is that supposed to be an apology?"

"It is. I was way, way out of line yesterday. I had no right to give you parenting advice."

"True," Riley said. She took the coffee, sipped, then wrinkled her nose. "Speaking of advice, you really should do something about the coffee on this boat. It's ghastly."

"You're right," he said. "That's on my to-do list. Dad wasn't what you'd call a coffee connoisseur. He'd drink Quaker State if you put enough milk and sugar in it. Mom has finally agreed to let me upgrade everything we serve in the concession stand. I'm meeting with a coffee roaster in Wilmington this morning to sample his beans. And, for your delectation—all-beef hot dogs, chicken sandwiches made from actual chicken breasts, and fresh fruit smoothies. Coming soon."

"Fannncy," Riley said. "But don't you dare mess with the french fries."

"I would never," Nate promised, pressing the palm of his hand to his chest. "Would you mind if I sat down?"

"Only if you don't cluck your tongue and tell me how I've been in your thoughts and prayers," Riley said.

He sat down on the wooden bench beside her. "Yeah, all that sympathy stuff gets old pretty fast."

"Between the curious stares and the whispers, I'm just about over this whole ordeal," Riley said.

"Any news on the police investigation?" Nate asked. "Aw hell, there I go again, putting my worst foot forward. You don't have to answer that. I don't mean to be so nosy. But it's kinda natural, don't you think, for people to wonder? We haven't had a serious crime on the island in a long time."

"I guess," she conceded. "I'm meeting with the sheriff this morning. More questions."

"Does he have any idea what the motive could have been?"

"If he does, he hasn't told me yet," Riley said.

"He asked us for the passenger list for all of last week," Nate volunteered. "I've been gone from the island so long, I didn't know half the names, but my mom didn't spot anybody who'd seem like a likely suspect. Mostly just the usual weekenders, folks who work on the island, day trippers, and a few people who were probably renters."

"Was Wendell's name on the passenger list? They did find our boat tied up, in the marina, right near where they found his body, but I've been wondering when he came over because, as far as I knew, he was tied up in out-of-town business meetings right up until Friday when he was supposed to meet us here on the ferry."

"No, his name wasn't on the list, and I was on the ferry a lot last week and never saw him. He had booked a ticket for the same boat as you, but obviously, never used it."

"Because he was already dead by then," Riley said soberly.

"Do you have a theory—about the motive?"

She looked away. "I think it must have had something to do with money. And maybe Belle Isle Enterprises."

"What makes you think that?"

"Don't you ever read mysteries? There are three basic motives to kill somebody—sex, money, or revenge. Money's the most obvious—considering the fact that the bank was foreclosing on our house. And I know Wendell was really worried about the business. He had a lot riding on the north end development. He'd quit talking about it to me, though, because he knew I was totally opposed to what he was planning. Especially the hotel at Pirate's Point."

Riley's smile was tight. "Although I'm not ruling out sex or revenge either."

He gave her a quizzical look. "If you were opposed to the development, why didn't you fight him on it?"

"It's not that easy. My dad made Wendell president of Belle Isle Enterprises, and gave him voting control of the family corporation. My mother and brother were on his side, so I was outvoted. And anyway, I guess I was preoccupied with Maggy's diabetes diagnosis. That was a pretty scary time for me."

"How's Maggy doing, by the way?"

"She's not currently speaking to me, because I put her under house arrest after you brought her home yesterday. And she really, really doesn't like you either. Other than that, I guess she's your typical twelve-year-old pain in the butt."

"Am I getting too personal if I ask if you think Wendell was cheating?"

"I did wonder if there was somebody else, but he always denied it. We'd been basically living apart for about six months, but we'd been having problems for a while. We did the counseling thing, but it didn't take."

"So that brings you back to where you started," Nate said.

Just then the two-way radio he had clipped to the waist of his jeans squawked.

"Captain? Need you up here in the wheelhouse," a scratchy voice said.

Nate winced. "I still can't get used to being called captain. Better go."

He touched Riley's shoulder. "Hope things get worked out with the sheriff today. And if you need anything—well, give me a holler. I promise not to be sympathetic."

The early-morning rush at Onnalee's Café had subsided. Riley spotted the sheriff sitting at a two-top toward the back of the room. He was studying the laminated plastic menu, but looked up as she approached.

A waitress with a coffeepot appeared—the same thin, harried-looking woman who'd been working at Onnalee's for as long as Riley could remember.

Riley took her seat and ordered her usual: cheesy scrambled eggs, sausage patty, rye toast.

The sheriff sipped his coffee and extracted a notepad from the pocket of his windbreaker.

"Thanks for meeting me here," Riley told him, pouring creamer into her mug. "Do you have any news for me?"

"Nothing really. The coroner went over his notes with me yesterday. Like we thought, cause of death was blunt force trauma to the back of the skull," he said.

"Was it . . . quick?" Riley felt bile rising in her throat. An unbidden image of Wendell, bleeding, in agony, alone on a cold, damp seawall flashed in her mind.

"Yes," the sheriff said. "He was dead before he hit the water. You sure you want to hear all this?"

"I don't want to, but I need to. For my daughter."

"Okay, well, as best we can tell, time of death was around midnight, Thursday. There was some minor bruising to his forehead, probably from where he hit the ground after the blow to his head.

"He'd had a couple of drinks an hour or so before he was attacked," the sheriff went on. "Was that usual for your husband?"

"Yes. He usually drank scotch, although he liked red wine, too. He'd have wine with dinner, then a scotch or two during the evening," Riley said.

"We found no unusual drugs in his bloodstream—I take it he was on medication for high blood pressure?"

"Was he? I didn't know that." She felt ashamed that her husband had an ailment she wasn't even aware of.

The sheriff looked surprised. "When was the last time you saw your husband, Mrs. Griggs?"

"I'm not sure," she admitted. "Maybe two, two and a half weeks ago? He texted and said he was coming by."

"How did he act? Was he upset? Did he mention any particular problems?"

"He was in a rush. Maggy was at a friend's house, and I wanted him to stay until she got home, but he wouldn't. He claimed he had an out-of-town meeting and a plane to catch. I was annoyed because it had been two weeks since he'd seen his daughter."

"You didn't believe him? Any particular reason?"

"Not really. It was just that he'd made and broken so many promises, to both of us. To tell you the truth, I'd stopped trusting him. Which is a terrible thing to say."

"But true?"

"Yes."

"Other than rushed, how did he seem?"

Riley tried to think back to that night.

She'd gotten his text around 6:30 p.m.

You home? Gotta check mail and pick up clothes.

She'd texted right back. *I'm here, but Maggy's at Devin's house.*

Be right there.

He'd left the Jeep's motor running in the driveway, and brushed right past her when she met him in the hall, going directly to the basket on the pine console where she kept all the mail.

She was shocked by Wendell's appearance. He'd obviously lost some weight. His hair was long and unkempt-looking. In fact, his whole appearance was unkempt. He wore faded navy workout pants and a pale blue sweater that hung off his shoulders.

"Hi to you, too," Riley said. "Obviously your wife and daughter are not what you dropped by to check on. Want to clue me in about what you're looking for?"

Wendell scooped up the mail in the basket and began riffling through it, tossing aside the bills, junk mail, and catalogues.

He didn't even look up. "You gonna start that again? I don't have time for this crap, Riley. I was supposed to get a document at the office, but it hasn't come, so I thought maybe it had gotten sent here by mistake."

He tossed the mail back in the basket. "Shit. You're sure this is all the mail?"

"Yes, that's all of it. What kind of document are you looking for?"

"Never mind. It's not here."

"Something about your north-end deal?"

His shoulders sagged. "You should be happy. It looks like you might just get your way."

"What's that supposed to mean?" Riley demanded.

"What it sounds like. Where's Maggy?"

"Didn't you get my text? She's at Devin's house working on a school project. In case you're interested, she misses you. A lot."

"I miss her, too," Wendell said with a sigh.

"She should be home in half an hour. Will you at least stay and have dinner with her?"

Wendell shook his head. "Can't." Without another word, he headed upstairs. She followed him, standing in the doorway of his closet as he tossed clothes into a gym bag. Shorts, T-shirts, a summer-weight linen blazer, and at the last minute, a pair of brown loafers.

"We really need to talk, Wendell. I can't keep living like this. Either you're a husband and father—or we're done."

"Are you talking about a divorce? For God's sake, that's the last thing I want. Can't you understand—everything I'm doing is for us—for our family. I know I haven't been an ideal husband or father lately—but it's because of the deal, that's all."

"That's the problem. And it's not just lately. Don't you see? It's always the next deal, the next hot prospect. There's no end to it. The deal is your god, your family. And in the meantime, Maggy and I are an afterthought."

He whirled around and grasped her arm. "I'll change. I swear it. Just give me some time. This is the deal that will let us live as a family again, without all the pressures of finding the next deal. After this, we're set. Please?" His eyes were pleading.

Riley sighed. "I don't know. It feels like I've heard this before. . . ."

An all-too-familiar bugle call emitted from his pants pocket. Wendell plucked his cell phone from his pocket and read the incoming text. "Shit." He picked up the gym bag. "I gotta go. Call me if that envelope comes, okay?"

"That's it? You're blowing me off, again?"

He was already halfway down the stairs. "I'll call you later. Tell Maggy I love her."

She ran down after him. "The hell I will. If you leave now, you can stay gone."

He didn't even turn around. "Fuck you," he called over his shoulder.

"No, fuck you!" Riley screamed as the front door slammed in her face.

The waitress was back, sliding plates in front of them: sausage, eggs, and toast for Riley, a thick stack of pancakes swimming in butter and syrup for the sheriff. The sweet smell of maple syrup wafted across the table and made her feel queasy.

He attacked the food, slicing the stack into quarters, then eighths, stabbing it with his fork and shoveling it into his mouth. She swallowed hard and looked away. After a moment of chewing, he took a gulp of coffee and gave her a quizzical look.

"Something wrong with your eggs?"

"No. My appetite . . . comes and goes these days."

"We were talking about this deal?"

"Right. I assumed Wendell was referring to the north end development. There was a lot riding on it, and it had a lot of moving parts. The marina, condos, a retail strip, and a big hotel. He'd been working on it for a couple of years."

"I've heard about the hotel and all. Kinda controversial over there on Belle Isle, isn't it?"

"Yes. That end of the island around Pirate's Point has been largely undeveloped. Part of the project was to go on a parcel of land my grandfather had established as a wildlife sanctuary. Wendell intended to dredge for a new marina and pave roads to allow for vehicle traffic."

"Cars on Belle Isle?" he said, in mock horror.

"A lot of people were opposed to that. Including me," Riley added.

He chewed and dabbed at a spot of syrup on his chin. "Besides you, was anybody so opposed to it they might want to kill your husband?"

The question took her by surprise.

"I hadn't thought about that. The thing is, most people weren't aware of the full scope of the plan. Since Belle Isle Enterprises owned such a large percentage of the island, Wendell just assumed he'd have carte blanche to do whatever he wanted."

"Your husband knew you were against this plan?"

"Yes."

"Belle Isle Enterprises, that's a family business, correct? How did the rest of your family feel about the plan?"

"My mother was totally in favor. My brother, Billy, I don't think he'd really given it a lot of thought. Everybody had pretty much gotten used to Wendell running the show."

"And who runs it now that he's gone?"

"I don't know," Riley said slowly. "Wendell always liked to run a one-man band. He'd hire consultants and marketing and sales folks, but everything else—the big-picture stuff, it was all Wendell."

"Okay, back to that night. How did it end?"

"Not well," Riley said. "He got a text and literally dashed out of the house. I told him if he left—without even seeing his daughter, not to bother coming back."

"And what was his response?"

Her voice was barely above a whisper. "He told me to go fuck myself."

"Did he call later, apologize? Did you discuss what the document was that he was looking for?"

Riley stared down at the tepid eggs. "Now that I think of it, we didn't talk again. He e-mailed and texted, pretty much acting like nothing happened, but I texted back, telling him I wanted a divorce. After some back-and-forth and foot-dragging on his part, he finally agreed to meet us at the ferry on Friday and, after that, once we were at the house, on the island, we'd break the news to our daughter that we were divorcing."

The sheriff set his fork down on his now empty plate and took a small spiral-bound notebook from his jacket pocket. He made notes, and Riley sipped her cooling coffee.

He looked up from the notebook.

"Any idea who the text was from?"

"No," Riley said simply. "I'm guessing it wasn't good news. He cursed, put his phone away, and left."

"And that's the last time you saw him?" the sheriff persisted.

"No," Riley said. "The last time I saw Wendell was in the morgue at the county hospital."

23

There were more questions from the sheriff, but Riley had few answers. No, she didn't know where Wendell had been staying during their estrangement; no, she didn't have his cell phone; and no, she didn't know the status of her finances. As soon as she left Onnalee's, promising to contact him if she thought of anything new, she decided to bite the bullet and get her own answers.

Now, she stood in the Baldwin County Clerk's office, staring down at the civil proceedings docket book. The fluorescent lights buzzed and flickered overhead, and the air conditioner hummed. The room was quiet, except for the clicking of the nearest clerk's computer keyboard, and the dry rasp of paper pages being turned.

She'd been in lots of courthouses, back in her early reporting days, but those had been in big cities like Raleigh, Charlotte, or Asheville. There, even fifteen years ago, records were computerized.

But Baldwin was the smallest county on the North Carolina coast. Its courthouse was a modest two-story affair of beige brick with a tiny copper-roofed cupola and a weather-beaten granite foundation. There was a

Confederate memorial statue in front and overgrown azalea bushes flanking the front entrance.

The clerk's office reminded Riley of something from an old black-and-white movie. A battered wooden counter separated the public from the clerks. The floors were wooden, and the room smelled vaguely of tobacco, although a NO SMOKING sign was prominently displayed on the front counter. Rows of leather-bound docket books lined sagging wooden shelves.

She'd been standing there, motionless, for a good thirty minutes. She leafed forward and backward in the docket book, looking for some addendum, some additional document that would assure her that the foreclosure notice was just a clerical error, the result of sloppy bookkeeping, or a monumental practical joke.

But there it was, in black and white.

NOTICE OF FORECLOSURE OF 555 SAND DOLLAR LANE.

There was a lot of legalese she didn't really understand, but the net effect, it was clear, was that the owner of the listed property, Wendell Griggs, was in default to Coastal Carolina Bank on the mortgage to the tune of two million dollars and that the home was in foreclosure.

The clerk, a gray-haired woman with cat-eye glasses and a friendly smile looked up and gave her a questioning glance. "Find what you need?"

"I found the document, yes." Riley tapped a finger on the page of the docket book. "This whole thing is screwy. This says the owner of the foreclosed property was properly notified of the foreclosure. But I'm one of the owners, and I never received any notification."

"I only see one name on this notice. Would that be your husband?"

"Yes," Riley said. "But the house has always been titled in both our names."

"Not anymore, apparently," the clerk pointed out. She looked down at the notice, then up at Riley. "The property is located over there on Belle Isle?"

"That's right."

"Is that your primary legal residence?"

"Um, no. We live full-time in Raleigh. The Sand Dollar house is our vacation home."

"But y'all do get mail delivered over there on Belle Isle, right?"

"Yes, we get mail at our post office box."

"Then that's your answer. This is the address in the records, which means it was the address in the bank's records, and that's where it would have been sent."

"There's something else," Riley said. "This says the lender is Coastal Carolina Bank. But I never heard of them. And, anyway, our mortgage was paid off two years ago."

"Maybe your husband took out another mortgage and he just forgot to tell you about it," the clerk suggested.

Riley's eyes widened at that notion. But why would Wendell need to borrow more money on a house that they owned free and clear? So much more money. Two million?

"This can't be right," Riley insisted. "It just can't."

"I wish I could help you more," the woman said, shrugging. She went back to her desk, but before she sat down, she was back at the counter, looking again at the open docket book.

"Well, here's a problem right here," she said.

"What's that?"

"Coastal Carolina Bank? They're the one that foreclosed on you? I'm pretty sure that's the bank here in town that just got taken over."

Riley leaned over the counter to make sure she'd heard correctly. "Did you say it was taken over? By who?"

The clerk took a half-step backward, a subtle signal that Riley had violated her personal space.

"I don't bank there, so I don't really know, but I know the talk around town was that the bank was in some kind of trouble, so some other company came in and took 'em over."

"What exactly does that mean?"

The clerk shook her head sadly. "If you read this carefully, you'll see that there's gonna be an auction. A week from Friday at ten o'clock in the morning at the Seafarer Motel, in the banquet room."

"You're telling me . . . my house is going to be auctioned off?" Riley clutched the countertop with both hands. "In a motel banquet room?"

"I guess if you got a problem with that, you best get a lawyer."

Riley felt her shoulders sagging. "Can I have copies made of these documents?"

"Sure thing," the clerk said. "But there's a charge. Fifty cents a page." She took the heavy ledger and disappeared into an anteroom for a few minutes, then returned with the photocopies. "Two dollars and fifty cents," she said. "You want a receipt?"

"Not necessary," Riley said, setting her pocketbook on the counter while she extracted the cash from her billfold.

The clerk gave her an appraising look that took in Riley's expensive designer handbag and oversize diamond solitaire engagement ring. "I hope you don't mind my saying so, hon, but you sure don't look like the usual person coming in here on a foreclosure notice. You mind my asking what happened? You have an illness in the family or something?"

"I don't actually know what happened," Riley said.

"Maybe you need to ask your husband," she suggested.

"I'd love to, but unfortunately, that's no longer possible," Riley said. "He's dead."

"Oh, my," the clerk said, sucking in her breath. "Bless your heart."

The white brick building on Catawba Street had a portable sign on wheels—the kind usually seen at clearance and going-out-of-business sales.

BALDWIN COMMUNITY BANK. ASK US ABOUT FREE CHECKING!

Riley pushed through the plate-glass door. She was standing in a largish room with four bank tellers lined up at high counters across the back of the room. Painters were busily coating the walls with an unobtrusive shade of pinkish beige. There was an unoccupied reception desk to the right of the door, with a young woman standing beside it.

"Can I help you?" the receptionist asked automatically. And then—"Oh, Riley! Hi. How nice to see you."

For a moment, Riley couldn't place how she knew the speaker. Her face was familiar. She was in her early thirties, with long blond hair worn in a tight bun. Attractive, in a crisply professional way, she was dressed in the kind of dark blue blazer they probably handed out in banking school.

"Hello," Riley replied politely.

The young woman's face flushed. "It's me, Melody. From the island?"

Of course. Melody Zimmerman, or as Parrish called her, Belle Isle Barbie's bestie.

"Of course! So sorry," Riley said. "I guess I'm not used to seeing you anyplace but the island. And I wasn't expecting to see somebody I know here, at this bank."

Melody stood and clasped Riley's hands in hers. "Are you all right? I heard the terrible news about Wendell." Her voice oozed concern. "Is there anything at all I can do for you? I did drop a plate of my brownies by your mother's house yesterday, but she said you weren't up to seeing company."

"That was kind of you," Riley said automatically. "Everybody on the island has been so thoughtful. I'm okay, I guess. Sort of numb."

Melody clutched her hand. "What does the sheriff say, about, you know, what happened?"

"The coroner says it was a blow to the back of the head," she said, her voice steely, hoping that would shut down Melody's questions.

"Oh. I guess he must have fallen. Such a tragic accident."

"Actually, they don't think it was an accident at all."

The color drained from Melody's face, and she hurriedly changed her line of questions. "What brings you to the bank today?" she asked.

The last person Riley wanted to confide in about her foreclosure issues was Andrea Payne's best friend.

"Well, it's, uh, sort of confidential," she said. "Just some things to do with Wendell's estate. Is there a bank officer I could speak to?"

Melody smiled. "You probably haven't heard, but I've actually just been named senior vice president here. I'm thrilled, of course."

She looked around the room and whispered, "Unfortunately, our new management team didn't retain very many of the former Coastal Carolina employees."

"Congratulations, Melody. That's wonderful. Um, do you think I could talk to the bank manager, or whoever is in charge?"

"Afraid not. The manager's at an all-day meeting off-site. You sure there's nothing I can help you with? Since the changeover, I'm the employee with the most seniority." She looked around the room and pointed at a glassed-in cubicle. "We could just slip right into my new office and chat in private if you like."

Riley felt her resistance ebbing. She didn't actually dislike Melody Zimmerman, because she didn't know her well enough to have formed a real opinion.

"I guess that would be all right," Riley said.

Melody sat behind a desk with a brass nameplate, which she promptly placed facedown on the desktop. "Mr. Gardiner was let go when the new team took over," she explained. "Such a sweet man. Now, how can I help?"

Riley folded her hands in her lap. "I'm sure you've heard all the talk. My house—the house on Sand Dollar Lane—somehow, through some kind of mix-up, it's been foreclosed upon. Maggy and I have been staying with my mother at Shutters. And the thing is—I've just come from the courthouse, and the foreclosure notice says this bank—or rather, the bank this bank used to be, is the mortgage holder and that the house is going to be sold at auction next week."

"Yes," Melody said sadly. "I am aware. Very regrettable."

"Regrettable? This is a disaster. Wendell never said anything to me about taking out another mortgage."

"Maybe he forgot to mention it to you? I know lots of stay-at-home moms don't much bother themselves with family finances."

Riley felt her face growing hot with anger and embarrassment. She hated the condescending way some professional women treated women who'd left the workforce—as though they'd surrendered their brains and talent when they'd hung up their panty hose and company parking passes. Even more, she hated the way she allowed herself to feel intimidated by the opposing side in the ongoing mommy wars.

"Apparently, there was quite a lot about our finances I wasn't privy to. If you must know, Wendell and I were separated. We'd planned to tell Maggy on Friday, after we got to the island. This whole thing—it came out of nowhere."

Melody sighed. "So, you weren't aware of any of Wendell's financial difficulties?"

"As I said, we hadn't really lived together in several months," Riley said through clenched teeth. "He was obsessed with getting the development on the north end of the island going, and I knew there were problems. But he never, ever told me he'd taken out a new loan on the Belle Isle house. He must have known I'd fight him on that. And especially not for two million, which is absurd."

"Absurd?" Melody cocked her head. "You're just being modest. That house is amazing, I mean, from the outside."

"Maybe so, but the original loan was only for four hundred thousand. After my dad died, we agreed to pay off the mortgage with part of my inheritance."

Melody gave her that patronizing smile again. "Since the recession ended, property values on the island have soared. Which is good news for your family, right? I can't remember the exact figure, but I'm pretty sure our loan appraisal came in at just over two million."

"You knew about the mortgage?"

"Yes."

Riley stared at her. "Why? Why did he refinance the house? What did he do with all that money? And why didn't he tell me? It was *our* house. My father gave us that lot as an anniversary gift!"

Melody shrugged. "I'm sorry, Riley, but this was a business deal. We never discussed his personal life or the state of his marriage. Wendell happened to mention at a Kiwanis meeting that he was looking to raise some capital for the north end project, and he was thinking about refinancing the Sand Dollar Lane house. He asked me about our interest rates, which were favorable, so we did the loan. I think he liked the idea of dealing with a local bank, instead of some big, faceless entity in Charlotte."

"He had no right!" Riley cried. "This can't even be legal." She twisted around in her chair so she was facing the lobby. "I need to see the manager. You people can't auction off my house. You just can't."

Melody shrugged. “Even if he were in the office, Mr. Shumway would tell you the same thing I just did. Wendell took out the loan, then defaulted. We met with him to try and work out terms for him to meet his obligations, but it never happened, so the foreclosure process went forward. Wendell was aware of all of this. And if you must know, his obligations to the bank were much more extensive than just your house.”

“What’s that supposed to mean?” Riley demanded.

“I’m really not at liberty to say,” Melody replied. “Banking confidentiality laws, you know. In fact, I’ve probably already told you more than I should have, just out of respect for our friendship.”

She stood up and smoothed her skirt. “If you like, I can give Mr. Shumway your phone number and ask him to give you a call.” She stood by the doorway to the office and gestured toward the lobby. “I’m really very sorry, Riley. Truly.”

24

Riley sat in her car outside the Wells Fargo branch office and tried to calm her shattered nerves. She'd left Shutters that morning determined to unsnarl the snafu surrounding the foreclosure of her home, but nothing had gone as she'd planned. Tears stung her eyes, and her head throbbed so badly she felt nauseous. She closed her eyes and tried to remember meditation techniques from a long-ago yoga class.

"Think of your happy place," the teacher had instructed in her soothing, low whispers. "Picture yourself there and let your troubles and stresses trickle away like raindrops on the petal of a flower."

Happy place? Her happy place had been Belle Isle. Now when she tried to visualize herself there all she could see were storm clouds overhead and the boldface type on the foreclosure notice tacked to her front door.

The stabbing pain at the base of her skull was nearly unbearable. She found a packet of aspirin in her purse and dry-swallowed both of them, and then forced herself to go inside the bank to delve further into whatever "financial difficulties" her late husband had created for his family.

Half an hour later she stumbled out of the bank, too stunned and shaken to do anything more than collapse into the driver's seat of her car.

The clerk had been as polite and as helpful as a clerk in a small-town branch of a banking behemoth could be. It wasn't her fault that the news was devastating.

The joint checking account she and Wendell shared held only a few thousand dollars, which wasn't unusual. But when she'd asked about their savings and investment accounts, the teller had tapped a few keys and frowned.

"I'm sorry, Mrs. Griggs, but it looks like that account was closed last April."

She'd stood at the counter, her spine rigid, staring at the teller until the poor man had looked away, embarrassed for her.

"Maybe . . . maybe my husband opened another account? I mean, another kind of account?" She rattled off her social security number and date of birth, and Wendell's social security number, too.

He tapped the keyboard and shook his head. "Nothing."

Her mouth was so dry she could barely croak out the next question. "My trust fund?"

He nodded, tapped a few more keys, and a printer on the counter spat out a slip of paper with the balance.

"No." Riley stared down at it, and then looked up. "This can't be right. Eighteen hundred dollars and forty-seven cents?" She repeated her social security number but the bottom line was clear.

Wendell had looted the trust fund left to her by her grandfather and father, to the tune of six million dollars. And change.

The clerk looked over her shoulder at the next customer, willing her to move her miserable self away. "Anything else?"

"No," she'd mumbled. "Nothing else."

She'd driven straight back to the Baldwin Community Bank. Melody Zimmerman had emerged from her glass cubicle as soon as she saw Riley enter the lobby.

"Are you all right?" Melody took one look at Riley's face and quickly took her by the arm and led her to a sofa in the corner of the lobby. "I'm going to get you some coffee," Melody said.

"No," Riley said. "No coffee. I've just come from Wells Fargo. Wendell . . . he closed our savings and investment accounts there, last April. And my trust fund . . . did he transfer the money to this bank?"

Melody bit her lip and looked away. "Look," she said, her voice low. "If it were up to me, I'd happily give you that information right now. But I can't. It's against the law."

"But it's my money," Riley croaked. "He's my husband."

"I realize that," Melody said. "There are all kinds of banking confidentiality laws in play here. Without the proper documentation, I can't tell you anything about Wendell's accounts with us."

"What kind of documentation?"

"His death certificate, to start with."

"I don't have one yet," Riley said.

"I can't help you without that, Riley," Melody said.

The five-minute-warning horn sounded just as Riley boarded the 4 p.m. ferry back to Belle Isle. She hurried toward the upper deck, hoping to find a quiet place to digest the barrage of bad news she'd encountered, and was surprised to see Parrish sitting there, leafing through a magazine.

"Hey," she said. "If I'd known you were going to town, we could have gone in together," Parrish said. "What's up?"

"The sheriff called first thing this morning and wanted to ask me some more questions. About Wendell. The last thing I wanted was him showing up at Shutters with Mama hanging around listening, and Maggy right upstairs. So I agreed to meet him for breakfast at Onnalee's."

"What did he want to know? Did he have any news about the investigation?"

"I need a drink," Riley said abruptly. "You want anything?"

"Nothing," Parrish said. "I'll save our spot."

Ten minutes later, Riley was back with a plastic cup full of white wine. She took a sip and wrinkled her nose, but took another sip, and then another.

"Okay," she said finally. "The sheriff asked me a bunch of stuff about when the last time was that I'd seen Wendell, and why I thought somebody would want to kill him."

"What did you say?"

"I told him I thought it had something to do with money. And the business. At the time, I had no grasp of just how bad things have gotten." Riley stared into the plastic cup, then dumped it over the side. "This stuff is too gross, even for me."

"How bad have things gotten?" Parrish asked gently.

"On a scale of one to ten, I'd say my life, right now, is a ten in terms of awfulness. I'll just give you the condensed version. The foreclosure is legit, my house is going to be auctioned off to the highest bidder next week, and that won't be me, since I'm basically destitute."

"That bastard," Parrish said.

"Exactly."

Riley filled her friend in on all she'd learned that day.

"So . . . Wendell got a new mortgage from a bank you'd never heard of, but it's no longer that bank?" Parrish asked. "Not to mention he used your trust fund as his personal piggy bank?"

"As far as I can tell. And I guess I only have myself to blame."

"Bullshit," Parrish shot back. "This is all Wendell's fault. What he did was totally illegal."

"But it's all on me, now. I'm the dumb bunny who let her big, strong, brilliant husband take control of all our family finances. I should have known better. I did know better, but with Maggy's diabetes and all, I just allowed myself to slip into that clichéd helpless Southern belle stereotype."

"I disagree," Parrish said. "But do you really think Wendell took everything? I mean, how did he manage to access your trust fund?"

"Easy-peasy," Riley said bitterly. "When Dad set it up, he put Wendell's name on the account, too. It kind of bothered me at the time—I mean—it was supposed to be *my* inheritance—the same way he set up Billy's trust. He certainly didn't put Scott's name on Billy's account."

"I'm assuming your inheritance was a pretty substantial amount?"

"Only if you consider six million dollars substantial."

Riley paused a moment after Parrish's eyes widened.

"I'm holding out hope that maybe he just opened another account at the bank that gave him the new mortgage on Sand Dollar Lane. But I won't know anything until I get Melody Zimmerman the death certificate and the other documentation she says she has to have."

"Melody? What's she got to do with anything?"

"She was the loan officer who gave Wendell the mortgage. Apparently they were pals from Kiwanis. And now she's some muckety-muck at the bank that took over the old bank. She was perfectly sympathetic, but she says that the banking privacy laws say I can't access our financial records until I get the death certificate."

"She's probably right about that," Parrish said. "I know after my dad died, it took my mother weeks and weeks before the bank would turn over her accounts. Can you imagine? She didn't even know the passwords to their joint accounts. It took Ed forever to get everything straightened out. And then the insurance company was even worse to deal with. Hey!" She grabbed Riley's elbow.

"What about Wendell's life insurance? And a will—tell me you guys have wills."

"I've got to see if I can find a copy of the insurance policy in Wendell's office. All my papers are boxed up in storage in Raleigh. And yes, we did get wills done before I had Maggy. As I remember, it was all pretty basic. In case of either of our deaths, the surviving spouse inherits. That is, if there's anything left to inherit."

25

Billy Nolan could never keep his time zones straight. He'd tried calling Scott off and on all day Wednesday, but all his calls went directly to voice mail.

It was always like that when Scott had a big install. His total focus was on the job. When he was working he'd forget to eat, take his blood pressure meds, check his e-mail—or return his partner's phone calls.

Billy wondered what that would be like—to be capable of that kind of concentration.

At the third or fourth private school he'd been bounced out of, his parents finally took him to a shrink, who gave them the news that their son had ADHD—attention deficit hyperactive disorder. He'd read up on the symptoms on the Internet and concluded that this, finally, was the reason his head often felt like a pinball machine—with ringing bells, flashing lights, and a little metal ball that careened wildly in one direction and then the next.

Although he'd always loved music and had taught himself to play piano and guitar, the ADHD diagnosis became a gift, because it helped him recognize that music quieted the constant noise in his head.

Finally, he gave up trying to reach Scott and headed over to Shutters for dinner.

As soon as he walked into his mother's kitchen he wished he hadn't come. The tension between Evelyn and Riley was palpable.

"Where's Maggy?" Evelyn asked.

"Upstairs. I've called her twice, and she says she isn't hungry."

"Well, she has to eat, or she'll get sick."

"I'm aware of that, Mama," Riley said, rolling her eyes.

"Call her again and tell her Mimi said we're having Janice Snider's chocolate delight for dessert."

"Is that the stuff with the layers of cookies and chocolate pudding and cream cheese and Cool Whip?" Billy asked. "I friggin' love that stuff."

"It's Janice's signature dish," Evelyn replied. "And it's Maggy's favorite."

"Mama!" Riley exclaimed. "You know she can't have all that sugar."

"Hush. A little taste or two won't kill her."

Riley stalked out of the room. Five minutes later she was back with Maggy in tow.

Maggy's slight form was ensconced in a blue-and-white-pinstriped men's dress shirt with a button-down collar, which hung down to her knees. Her hair was mussed and her face was set in an expression best described as mutinous.

"Good heavens, Margaret, what on earth are you wearing?" Evelyn asked.

"She found one of Wendell's old shirts in the laundry room," Riley said, taking her seat at the kitchen table.

"But why is she wearing it?" Evelyn asked. "Has she taken up finger painting?"

"Because I want to," Maggy said. "It's Daddy's. It smells like him, and it reminds me of him. Is that okay with you?"

"Maggy!" Riley said.

"She was rude first," Maggy said defiantly. She looked over at the CorningWare dish in the center of the table. "Is that dinner?"

Riley shot her daughter a warning look and spooned a small helping onto her plate.

"This happens to be Helen Meehan's Chinese Chicken Surprise," Evelyn said.

Billy took a gulp of the vodka tonic he'd toted along in his plastic tumbler and wished he'd thought to bring a refill. "And just exactly what does Helen know about Chinese cuisine? I didn't know she'd ever been out of Baldwin County."

"I think it's called that because she tops it with chow mein noodles," Evelyn explained. "All the girls in book club just love it."

He took a taste and promptly got up and dumped the rest of his portion in the trash.

"And just what was wrong with that?" his mother demanded.

"I don't know which is worse, the cream of mushroom soup, the water chestnuts, or the Velveeta cheese goop. Don't your friends know how to make anything that doesn't call for canned soup or imitation cheese product?"

"If Bebo doesn't have to eat it, neither do I, right, Mom?" Maggy said, following suit.

Riley sniggered, which triggered an instant reaction from their mother.

"Fine!" Evelyn threw her napkin down on the table and glared at Riley. "You and your brother insult the delicious foods my friends have contributed out of the goodness of their hearts, in our time of bereavement. You make ugly comments, and then wonder why that child's manners are so appalling? I really don't know how I managed to raise two such ungrateful children. I hope you two are happy. I have lost my appetite, and now I have a screaming headache."

She pushed away from the table and swept out of the room.

Billy took a gulp of his cocktail. "Was it something I said?"

"Partly. But mostly she's just pissed at me."

"You? What did you do?"

"Nothing, really," Riley said. "Maggy, Mimi is right. It wasn't nice of Bebo to make fun of Helen's casserole, and it was rude of you to throw it away without even tasting it. Now you still have to eat something."

"Peanut butter and jelly?" Maggy said hopefully.

"Only if you have some salad with it." Riley got up and fixed the sandwich and put it on a plate along with a helping of tossed greens. At the last moment, she added a teaspoon of Janice Snider's chocolate delight. "Why don't you take that upstairs to your room? And if I were you, I would stop by your grandmother's room and apologize."

"Want a drink?" Billy asked, as soon as he was alone with his sister.

"God, yes," Riley said. "What kind of wine do you suppose goes best with Cool Whip and instant chocolate pudding?"

"The only kind Evelyn Nolan buys. Cheap stuff. Allow me."

He poured Riley a huge goblet of red wine, fetched two plates, and then plopped a mound of chocolate delight on each one.

Riley took a bite, licked her lips, and groaned. "I'd forgotten how amazing this stuff tastes."

"Huge improvement over ersatz Chinese whatever," Billy said. He leaned back in his chair. "Now, to get serious. What have you figured out about what was up with Wendell? I know things weren't great with you and him. Is there something you're not telling me?"

"Where do I start?" Riley asked.

Somehow, as his sister poured out her story, Billy managed to stay in control of his emotions. Maybe it was the massive amount of vodka he'd drunk, maybe it was the Valium he'd started taking again right after the discovery of his brother-in-law's corpse.

"All of it?" he asked, when Riley told him about her trust fund.

"He left me some pocket change," she said bitterly.

"And there's no mistake?"

She shrugged. "I've been holding out hope that maybe he transferred the money into an account at Baldwin Community Bank. But they won't tell me anything about Wendell's accounts there, because of some stupid banking confidentiality laws."

"But it's your money. Daddy left it to you."

"And he left Wendell in charge of it. But, supposedly, once I have the death certificate, they'll unlock the keys to the vault. Until then, I'll be sucking off Mama's goodwill."

"That's gonna get old fast," Billy predicted.

"It already has."

"You haven't told her yet about all the missing money?"

"No. I don't want to say anything until I know everything. But, Bebo, I'm afraid to keep looking for fear of what else I might find. We were married for almost twenty years, and I had no idea Wendell was capable of something like this. How could he do this to me? And his daughter? I thought he loved us. I thought he was a good person."

Billy was almost tempted to tell her the full extent of Wendell's capabilities. But if he told her the truth about her husband, she'd know the truth about her brother. And that he could not bear.

26

It had been nearly three years now, but the memory of that night had never dimmed.

Billy had been sober for eleven long months. Every Wednesday that summer, he'd take the late-afternoon ferry to Southpoint, then drive over to the Methodist Church hall in Snead's Ferry.

His AA sponsor was a black, tattooed ex-Marine named Calvin—an unlikely but surprisingly effective mentor for an effete New York jazz pianist like Billy.

Calvin's life—what he knew of it—fascinated Billy. Calvin usually listened more than he talked, but from snippets of information he'd gleaned, Billy knew his sponsor had seen combat duty in Afghanistan, and the inside of a prison. Prison was where Calvin had gotten sober.

He made a living as a sign painter, and he lived on the cheap, renting a tiny apartment above a Mexican restaurant in the downtown business district. Calvin's driver's license had long ago been revoked, so he got around town on foot or on a rusty beach cruiser, usually accompanied by his German shepherd, Heidi.

It was late August, a Tuesday. Scott hadn't been down that week, and Billy was lonely and restless, which was a dangerous combination for a recovering drunk. He took the afternoon ferry to town, picked up the battered, maroon Delta 88 he kept in the marina parking lot to run errands and, like he'd done hundreds of times before, set off for the Harris Teeter.

He was in the produce department when he spotted a display table heaped high with limes. Limes.

Only a lifelong drunk would see limes, abandon his cart, head directly for the checkout, and then make a beeline to the nearest liquor store for a fifth of Grey Goose and a liter of tonic water. He bought a bag of ice at a convenience store, along with a sleeve of plastic cups and a cheap knife, and poured himself that first drink. The first in nearly a year.

He drove around the countryside with the Olds's windows rolled down, a John Coltrane CD playing at top volume, sipping and savoring life. He felt so fine he couldn't remember why he'd ever wanted to quit drinking. It was nearing dusk when he tipped the last of the tonic water into his cup and was suddenly struck with the reality of what he'd just done. The tonic water was gone and so was his hard-won sobriety. The half-empty bottle of Grey Goose was rolling around on the passenger-side floorboard. And then it came to him. The hangovers, the blackouts, the shame, the ruined relationships, the self-hate, all of the damage his drinking had done.

Without hesitating, he dialed Cal. "I fucked up," Billy cried, when his sponsor answered.

"Where are you?"

"I don't know. Maybe ten miles out of town?" He'd stared out the window, searching for a landmark, but all he saw were more farm fields.

"Did you take a drink?"

"Yeah. I'm such a fuckup."

"It's called a relapse, man. It happens," Cal said calmly. "What triggered it?"

"I don't know. Scott's not here. I'm bored, I'm lonely. I saw limes at the store, and all I could think about was how good a drink would taste. I'll tell you what else. I'm fucking tired of being sober. It's too damn hard."

"Yeah, man. It is hard. That's the point. You been livin' on that pink cloud. You got complacent, let down your guard."

"If Scott finds out, he'll leave me," Billy sobbed.

"This ain't about Scott loving you. It's about you loving you, Billy. I think we need to meet, bro."

"Can't we just talk like this?"

"I don't think so. Is it safe for you to drive?"

"Yeah. I haven't had all that much. Just a couple of stiff ones."

"That's a lot," Cal said sharply. "You need to get out from behind the wheel before you do something bad."

"I've already done something bad," Billy said. "Anyway, I'm way out in bumfuck Egypt."

"Come over to my place," Cal repeated. "I'll make you some coffee and get you sobered up."

Billy sat in his car in the alley behind the Mexican restaurant, with the car's engine running, staring up at the single light burning in the second-floor window. He sighed and poured vodka up to the rim of his plastic cup. Most of the ice cubes had melted, and the tonic water was gone. He took a sip, sucked on the lime slice, and tried to gather the courage to get out of the car and face the music.

Five minutes later his cell phone rang.

"I see you sitting down there in your car," Cal said. "Come on up. The coffee's on."

"Forget it. This is a waste of time." Billy started the car.

"No!" Cal yelled. "Don't go. I'm coming down."

A minute later his sponsor scrambled down the steel staircase, with Heidi following on his heels. Cal was barefoot, dressed in raggedy jeans and a paint-spattered T-shirt. He reached in the open window and made a grab for the keys.

Billy batted his hand away. "I'm gone, man." He threw the car into Reverse and started to back out.

"The hell you are." Cal ran around and yanked the passenger's-side door open, sliding into the seat. The dog barked and dove onto his lap.

"Get out," Billy said plaintively. "I can't do this. Just get out, okay?" He was slowly backing the car out.

"I'm staying right where I'm at," Cal said stubbornly. "You can do it. You've got almost a year sober. You know how many guys quit before they do that? A lot. Most don't make it as far as you have."

The dog scrambled into the backseat with one sharp bark.

"And this is where I quit," Billy said, lifting the cup to his lips.

Cal snatched the cup from his hand, spilling vodka and ice cubes all over himself and the floorboards.

"Jesus! Look what you did."

"Good riddance," Cal said, tossing the cup out the window. "You don't need that shit anymore, Billy."

"That's what you think." Billy put the car in Drive and looked over at his sponsor. "Get out, Cal. I mean it."

"I'm not leaving this car," Cal said.

"Suit yourself." Billy floored the accelerator and the car blasted out of the alley and onto Main Street. A few minutes later he was back on the county road, doing seventy miles an hour. The wind whipped through the open windows and the fields and farmhouses became a blur.

"Slow the fuck down," Cal commanded.

Billy sped up to eighty.

Cal crossed his arms over his chest. "What do you think you're doing, brother?"

"I'm out of tonic water. And ice," Billy replied. "I will drink straight vodka, if I have to, but everything's nice with ice, don't you think?"

Cal didn't take the bait. "You say you're afraid Scott will leave you if he finds out you're drinking again. Is that what you want?"

"I'm not talking about this," Billy said. "And leave Scott out of it."

"Okay, I'll do the talking. You fucked up, yeah. But you don't have to keep drinking. You can save your sobriety. Save yourself," Cal said urgently.

"Maybe I don't want to be saved," Billy said. "I suck at sobriety. But I am great at being a drunk. It's the one thing I'm good at. Like playing the piano.

Practice makes perfect, and I've been a practicing drunk my whole life." He shoved the CD back in the player and turned the volume as high as it would go, drowning out Cal's reasoning and his sanity.

Cal reached into the cup holder and grabbed Billy's cell phone. He scrolled through the numbers, nodded, and held the phone up for Billy to see.

"What do you think you're doing?"

"I'm calling Scott. Maybe he can talk some sense into you." Cal's finger was poised on the screen.

"No!" Billy grabbed for the phone, but Cal jerked sideways. The next thing Billy knew, the Olds veered off the road and onto the shoulder. A massive oak tree loomed in his headlights. He slammed on the brakes. Too late.

The first thing he heard when he regained consciousness was a soft whimpering. With effort, he looked over to check on his passenger. But Cal was gone. Billy's view was obscured by what looked like a tree limb, and what he could see of the seat was covered with bark and leaves and bits of sparkly glass pebbles. He felt a warm liquid trickle down his cheek, reached up to touch it and stared at the blood covering his fingertip. His head felt as though it had been pummeled with a sledgehammer. He passed out again.

He had no idea whether minutes or hours passed before he came to again, but he was cold, his head throbbed, and there was a sharp, stabbing pain in his chest. He moved slightly and cried out in pain. He gritted his teeth, and with supreme effort managed to wrench open the heavy car door. He pulled himself out of the vehicle and propped himself up on the open door.

Moonlight spilled onto the crumpled hood of the Olds. Now he heard the whimpering again. He staggered toward the source of the sound. Heidi, the German shepherd, was crouched down on the grass, her muzzle pressed close to the motionless head of her master.

Billy stood for a moment, rooted to the spot. "Cal!" he cried, rushing to his friend's side. He knelt down in the heat-seared grass and, with a trembling hand, gingerly touched Cal's neck, feeling for a pulse. The dog whined, a high-pitched keening sound that chilled Billy's soul. She nudged repeatedly at Cal's shoulder with her snout.

Billy stroked her fur, and she turned her head slightly, looked up at him with deep, liquid eyes, hesitated, and then licked his hand. "He's gone, girl," Billy said softly. "He's gone."

His phone rang. The sound was muffled, and he was still disoriented. He walked in circles until he found it where it had landed on impact, a few yards from the car. He picked it up and saw that the missed call was from Scott.

"Oh, God," he moaned.

He would never forgive himself for what happened next. Billy started walking. He didn't look back, didn't allow himself to think about Cal. Cal was dead. And Billy was alive. He had to get away. His panic rose with each step that carried him away from the accident site. And it *was* an accident, he told himself. He kept to the side of the road, darting into the underbrush to hide each time he saw the headlights of an oncoming vehicle.

When he was well away, he took out his phone and called the only person he knew who wouldn't ask questions, wouldn't judge, wouldn't lecture. He called Wendell Griggs and told him the truth. Or a version of the truth. It didn't really matter, because Wendell would eventually figure out his own truth.

"Where exactly are you?" Wendell's voice was curt, businesslike.

"I don't know," Billy wailed. "I'd been drinking a little bit. It's dark, and there aren't any houses around."

"Pull it together, goddamn it," Wendell said. "What road are you on?"

"The county road. Maybe six, eight miles from town."

"Did you pass the Pak-n-Sak?"

"Yeah. I guess it's a mile or so back."

"I'm leaving the island now. I'll pick you up there in half an hour, but make sure you don't let anybody see you."

"I won't."

He was hiding behind a Dumpster in the Pak-n-Sak parking lot when the black Jeep pulled in. Billy jumped into the front seat and Wendell sped away.

"How much farther?" Wendell asked.

Billy's head was throbbing, and he pressed bloody fingertips to his temples. "Not sure."

"A mile? Two?" Wendell gave him a sideways glance. "Jesus, you're a mess! There should be some wet wipes in the glove box there. Clean yourself up."

Billy did as he was told. "I think it's not too much farther. Better slow down. Wait. Yeah. Right up there. That's the tree."

Wendell pulled the Jeep a few yards off the shoulder of the road and cut the headlights and then the engine. Billy started to get out of the Jeep.

"Stay here," Wendell said.

Moonlight illuminated the maroon Olds, and he could see the silhouette of the dog, still crouching by a lifeless form. Billy didn't want to see any more. He closed his eyes and slumped down in the seat.

Ten minutes later, Wendell was back in the car. He pulled back onto the roadway and headed toward town.

"How was Heidi?" Billy asked as they pulled away.

"Heidi? Who the . . ."

"The dog," Billy said quickly. "Cal's dog. She jumped in the car with us. She was in the backseat when it happened. Is she okay?"

"What do you care?" Wendell's eyes were trained on the road. "It's taken care of."

They rode in silence.

"Here's what's gonna happen," Wendell said suddenly. "Listen up, Billy, because this is important."

"I'm listening."

"My boat is at the marina in town. I'm taking you back to the island, and I'll drop you at your place. You look like shit, by the way. Is anything broken?"

"My head is killing me. I might have a concussion. And maybe a cracked rib?"

"You'll heal. Unlike your friend back there. You're gonna stay in your house, not see anybody until the cuts and bruises are gone."

"What are you going to do?"

"I'm gonna take care of it. When the police call about the accident, you're gonna tell them Cal must have borrowed the Olds without your permission. He knew you always hid the keys under the floor mats. How do you happen to know that guy anyway?"

"He was my AA sponsor," Billy said.

Wendell gave him a sharp look. "I wondered why you were on the wagon."

27

Riley tiptoed out of the darkened house on Friday morning. The sandy road was damp with dew as she walked east toward the village. The island was still slumbering, but she heard birds twittering awake in the treetops and, as she walked, sunlight began to filter through the deep green canopy overhead.

She stopped once in the middle of the road, closed her eyes, and inhaled deeply, taking in the scent of pine needles, wisteria, and even the faintest tang of skunk. "Live in the moment," she whispered. "That's all you can do. Just live in the moment." Today was the day she'd decided she would make the arrangements for Wendell's memorial. His body still hadn't been released, but what did that matter? It was a chore that she wanted to put behind her.

As she mounted the wooden stairs of the Mercantile, lights flickered on inside, and a young woman in jeans and a turquoise Mercantile T-shirt unlocked the door and gestured for Riley to come inside.

The old worn floorboards creaked beneath her feet as she passed the shelves of gourmet groceries toward the back of the store, following the irresistible smell of fresh-ground coffee and baked goods.

Riley stood in front of the display case, eyeing the temptations. There were rows and rows of cookies, frosted cupcakes, and brownies. A swinging door from the kitchen opened, and a baker in a black T-shirt and a white apron emerged with a large sheet pan balanced on one shoulder.

When he lowered the pan to the marble countertop, she realized the baker was actually Nate Milas. Without looking up, he slid the glass display case door open and began arranging muffins on flat baskets.

She gave a discreet cough. "What can I get you?—" he started, and then stopped when he realized that Riley was the customer.

"Well, hello," he said. "Welcome to the Mercantile."

"What are you doing here?" she asked. "Don't tell me you're a baker now."

"Nah. I'm just free labor. I help my mom out here some mornings when she needs an extra set of hands. One of our college kids who works the morning shift can't come in until eight today."

The kitchen door swung open, and Annie Milas bustled through, carrying cartons of milk and half-and-half, which she set on the countertop coffee station.

"Hi, Riley," she said, joining her son. She was at least a foot shorter than Nate, her silver hair pushed back from her face with a knotted blue bandana, and an easy smile.

"Did Nate tell you about today's muffin specials? Blueberry oatmeal, apple raisin, banana maple, and strawberry cream cheese. And I've got orange marmalade and bacon cheddar scones that should be out in about five minutes."

"They all sound amazing," Riley said. "But for now I think maybe just a fruit cup—and a large coffee."

"You don't know what you're missing," Annie teased.

Riley took her order out to the porch and found a small round table facing the water. She sipped her coffee and thought about the day ahead. As she was spooning up the last strawberry in her fruit cup, Nate appeared on the porch carrying an insulated coffee carafe and something wrapped in wax paper, which he presented to his only customer.

"Mom wanted to know if you'd help her out by giving this a taste. It's a dried cherry and pecan scone. She's testing a new recipe."

"Twist my arm," Riley said. The scone was still warm from the oven. She nibbled an edge. "Mmm. Tell Annie she's got a winner. I wouldn't change a thing."

"I'll let her know. I don't really get the whole concept of a scone. I'm a biscuit and sausage gravy man myself." He took the chair opposite hers and poised the coffeepot above her mug. Riley nodded, and he poured a refill.

"How's Maggy doing? Is she still under house arrest?"

"I think I'll grant the poor kid early release. Her grandmother has been on her case, and she's really missing her dad. She's had a pretty miserable week."

He looked at her closely. "How about you? Have things gotten any better in your world since I saw you the other day?"

"No," she said flatly. "My house is going on the auction block."

He didn't act surprised. "Will you try to bid on it?"

"I'm not sure I can. . . ."

Before Riley could explain, Annie Milas pushed the door open and stuck her head out. "Nate, sorry to interrupt, but Wayne just called from Southpoint. He says it's urgent."

"It's always urgent," Nate said, standing up. He turned to Riley. "Thanks for the input on the baked goods."

"I better get back to the house myself. Thanks for the scone, Annie. Two thumbs up."

Nate followed his mother into the Mercantile. Customers had begun wandering in, looking for caffeine and carbs. Summer Fridays were insanely busy, and today looked like it would be even busier than usual.

Annie glanced over at Nate. "Did you tell her?" She nodded toward the porch and Riley, who was polishing off the rest of her scone.

"I didn't get a chance," Nate said. "Every time I think the time might be right to let her know, something comes up."

He pointed toward the bay, at the approaching ferry. "Wayne was calling to say we're short a deckhand today. I better get over to the landing."

He leaned over and gave his mother a peck on the cheek.

Miles Kenton's bulk filled his leather wingback chair. He was about Riley's age, she knew, because the Kentons had a summer cottage on Belle Isle, and his father, Miller, had been friends with Riley's father, W.R. But the funeral home director looked much older, with his shiny bald head, rumpled suit coat, and suspenders.

"Your sweet mama called to let me know I'd probably be hearing from you today," he said.

"Yes," Riley said. "She's been a busy little bee helping with arrangements."

Miles gave her a benevolent smile. "You know, it's been my family's privilege to bury three generations of Nolans. And I knew Wendell from Kiwanis. He was a fine man. You have my condolences."

"Thank you," Riley said.

"Had you and Wendell discussed any kind of plans?"

"We hadn't discussed anything lately," Riley said in what she was sure was the understatement of the day.

"Will you be wanting Wendell buried in the family plot on the island?"

Riley considered the idea briefly, then nodded. If nothing else, the family plot, under a moss-hung oak tree in the churchyard on Belle Isle was free. Free was key right now.

Miles nodded. "Your mother mentioned a nice mahogany casket—maybe something with brass fittings, along the lines of the Mercury model she chose for your father?"

"No."

"No?" Miles raised an eyebrow.

"My mother isn't making Wendell's arrangements," Riley said firmly. "I am. And I don't want any mahogany casket. I don't want a casket at all. I want Wendell cremated. We'll have a small memorial service in the Chapel in the Pines, and that's it."

"Surely you'll want to have family calling hours here, say from two to four, the evening before the service?"

"Absolutely not," Riley said.

Miles shifted his bulk, and the springs in the chair squeaked a mild rebuke. "We'll respect your wishes, of course, but for a man of Wendell's stature in this community, it's usual for folks to drop by and pay their respects to you and your family. You might not think so, but it's really a comfort to the family in situations like yours."

"Folks have already dropped by. In droves," Riley said. "I'm exhausted by their kindness. Overwhelmed. As to my situation, you know that the sheriff believes Wendell was murdered. So nothing about this death is usual. Also, for now, economics is a factor."

"Your mother indicated she'd be taking care of all expenses," Miles said, frowning at the unwelcome topic of money.

Riley's mind flashed back to her bare-bones bank account. "All the more reason to keep things simple."

"I see." He picked up a pen and made some notes. "Of course, you're the widow, so we want to honor your wishes. Although, from knowing Evelyn, she is not going to be happy about your choices. Now, we can handle the cremation as soon as the coroner releases the remains, and then you can decide when you would like the service. We'll need to have some floral sprays at the chapel. And you'll want some type of urn. If you'll step into the other room, I can show you some different choices."

Riley rested her hands lightly on the desktop. "Miles? Let me be clear about something here. I don't want a casket. I don't want any floral sprays. I especially don't want an urn. I cannot imagine any circumstances under which I would want to display the ashes of my deceased husband. As far as I'm concerned, you can put Wendell Griggs's ashes in a Duke's Mayonnaise jar, and we'll bury that in the family plot. Okay?"

Miles Kenton's lips pursed, and then suddenly, unexpectedly, he grinned.

"A Duke's Mayonnaise jar? That's a good one. That would put your mama in an early grave for sure."

Friday afternoon, the *Carolina Queen* was at full capacity. Nate designated himself a floater, making coffee behind the concession stand, loading and unloading the baggage bins, and taking a turn in the pilothouse.

He was surprised to discover he actually enjoyed interacting with the passengers, especially those who were embarking for Belle Isle instead of returning to the mainland.

People were mostly in vacation mode, happy and relaxed. There was an infectious air of anticipation from the weekenders who chatted about their plans: golf dates and beach outings, tennis matches and family reunions. The younger kids, sensing the excitement of their elders, raced up and down the metal stairs between decks, leaning over the railing, exclaiming about the dolphins following in the boat's wake and the looming spire of Big Belle on the horizon.

Longtime islanders greeted him by name, asked for the local fishing report, congratulated him on his return to the island, and asked after his mother.

Nate had been apprehensive about returning home, wondering if he'd feel out of place in his childhood home after so much time away, but today, he began to wonder if maybe it really was possible to go home again. He cautioned himself, though, warning that the events of the upcoming weeks could totally change his perspective on life on a small island.

The two men who shared a booth in the main deck were both in a pensive mood.

"Parrish said Riley made Wendell's funeral arrangements today," Ed Godchaux told Scott Moriatakis. "I hate to speak ill of the dead, but what a bastard he turned out to be."

"I feel the same way," Scott said. He hesitated. "Frankly, I never liked Wendell."

"You know, we actually liked him the first couple of years they were married. He seemed like a good match for Riley. Had a decent golf game, fit right in with most of our friends, and he was a good dad to Maggy. And, of course, Evelyn and W.R. were crazy about him," Ed said.

"Yeah, Wendell Griggs was the son W.R. always wished he'd gotten instead of Billy," Scott pointed out. "Wendell was the whole package as far as W.R. and Evelyn were concerned—a big, good-looking former jock they could parade around the country club and count on for a grandchild. He was all the things their own son couldn't be."

"I never thought of it that way," Ed admitted. "I think that, deep down, those two probably were proud of Billy's talent and his music, but they were from that generation that just couldn't accept having a son who didn't want what they wanted from life."

"I've always believed that's why Billy started drinking. It was always clear to him that no matter what he did, he could never measure up to his old man's expectations," Scott theorized. "So why try?"

"God, the things we parents do to fuck up our kids," Ed said with a sigh. "And, mostly, we do it out of love. I frankly don't know how David turned out as well as he has. Parrish and I had no idea what we were doing. In fact, at the time, she wasn't even sure she wanted to have a child, because she was so focused on her career."

"Lucky you," Scott said bitterly. "Billy and I would have loved to have a family. It's not at all uncommon for couples like us to have kids now, but that whole thing came too late for us. I'm looking at turning sixty in a couple of years, and Billy's nearly forty. We're too old now to be changing diapers and joining the PTA."

"I hear ya," Ed said. He glanced at the families milling around the crowded lounge. "I see these gray-headed fellas like me, pushing strollers and trying to keep up with their new young trophy wives, and it makes me tired thinking about it."

"Me, too," Scott said.

The *Carolina Queen*'s horn gave a long loud blast, the signal that docking would start in five minutes. Around them, voices rose in happy anticipation and people began gathering their belongings in preparation for arrival on Belle Isle.

"Right on time," Scott murmured. "Let the fun begin."

28

On Saturday morning, Riley dropped by Parrish's to update her on the plans for Wendell's service.

"All you have to do," Parrish said, "is show up and play the we-we card."

"Which is what?"

"The widow card. That's what my mama used to call it, after my dad died. Widows get a hall pass for at least the first year after their husbands are gone. You're expected to be helpless, dazed, and confused. Nobody's supposed to upset you, and you're allowed to cry anytime you want. That's called playing the we-we card. And nobody did it better than my mother."

"I don't have to play it. I'm already living the dazed and confused part," Riley said. "And I've just about cried my tear ducts dry."

"Hang in there," Parrish said, giving her a hug. "We're gonna get you through this, together. Evelyn's not going to make things easy, though."

"She tried to dictate the arrangements," Riley said. "By the time I got to the funeral home, she'd already called Miles Kenton and picked out the casket."

"Dear, thoughtful Evvy," Parrish said. "What exactly did she have planned?"

"You know. Mahogany casket with bronze mounts, funeral sprays, two days of family visitation. Your standard overblown three-ring circus. If Mama had her way, we'd have Wendell lying in state under the gazebo on the village green."

The two friends shuddered in unison.

"I put the kibosh on all that crap," Riley said. "Wendell will be cremated, we'll have a short, simple service in the chapel, and then private interment in the family plot. It sounds cold, I know, but I just want this ordeal over with."

"You leave it to me," Parrish said firmly. "If you want, I'll take care of everything."

"Really?" Riley felt herself tearing up. "That would be amazing. Mama will have a fit, but . . ."

"I can deal with Evelyn, and she'll never know what hit her."

Riley's cell phone rang. "It's Roo," Riley said to Parrish. "Hello?"

"Thank God you're home. I've been trying to call you all morning," Roo said. "Your mama and Maggie went into town first thing this morning, and I'm the only one here. You've got a visitor waiting."

"I'm at Parrish's. Could you please tell whoever it is that I'm not up for company today? I'll sneak around to the back door. Just tell them I've got a headache or something."

"I can't," Roo said, her voice fraught with anxiety. "Come right away and bring Parrish with you. It's a G-man!"

As soon as Parrish pulled the golf cart up to the front steps at Shutters, Aunt Roo came scuttling out of the dim recesses of the porch. She met Riley at the bottom step.

"I told him you were staying with a friend, and I didn't know when you'd be home, but he said he'd just wait," Roo said. "What do you think the FBI wants with you, Riley?"

"Probably just some questions about Wendell's death," Parrish said.

"Oh. Right." Roo seemed disappointed. "He's mighty young looking. I didn't think they hired boys that young to work as G-men, so I made him show me his badge. It looks like the real thing, though."

"Tell him I'll be right in, would you please, Roo?" Riley said.

"So it's true," Riley said, as soon as her aunt had gone inside the house. "The feds really are looking into Wendell's business dealings."

"You don't know that," Parrish warned. "Maybe it really is about his murder."

"You're not talking to my elderly aunt, here," Riley said. "The FBI doesn't normally get involved in homicides. I remember that much from my reporting days. I can't do this by myself. Will you come with me? You're a lawyer. You know how to deal with this kind of stuff."

"I haven't practiced criminal law in years and years," Parrish reminded her.

"You're a lawyer, that's all I care about." She turned pleading eyes on her best friend.

"All right." Parrish relented. "Have you got any money?"

"What? No! You know I'm broke."

"Give me a dollar," Parrish said. "That's my retainer. Now you're my client and everything you tell me is privileged. If you really want me to help, you need to just keep quiet and let me see what we can find out from him."

Riley took out her change purse and dumped the contents into her friend's outstretched palm. "Here's seventy-five cents. I'll have to owe you the rest."

The visitor was in the living room, seated on an oversize tufted Victorian sofa. He stood when the two women walked into the room. He was compact, with an athletic build and neatly combed brown hair, dressed in pressed and starched blue jeans, an open-collared shirt, and a navy-blue blazer. He was very young, Parrish decided. Like, right out of the academy young.

"Mrs. Griggs?" He looked from Parrish to Riley, unsure who was whom. He split the difference and extended a hand with a business card between the two women. "I'm Special Agent Aidan Coyle. Sorry to drop in unannounced. I tried to call ahead, but your phone didn't seem to be turned on."

"I'm Riley Nolan." Riley took the card, gave him a nod, and handed it to

Parrish. "And this is my good friend, Parrish Godchaux, who also happens to be my attorney."

"Oh." Agent Coyle offered a weak smile.

"What can we help you with, Agent Coyle?" Parrish asked, as the three of them took seats on Evelyn Nolan's grandmother's supremely uncomfortable velvet and horsehair sofa.

He removed a cell phone from his inside coat pocket and placed it on the carved mahogany tea table. "Do I have your permission to tape this conversation?"

Riley looked at Parrish, who took out her own phone and placed it beside the FBI agent's phone. "As long as you don't mind if we do the same thing." She tapped an icon on the phone's screen and sat back in her chair.

Special Agent Coyle was only a few years older than her son, David. This was one instance where her middle-aged status might be to her advantage. "Go ahead." She nodded at the phone, as though she were agreeing to loan him the family sedan for a trip to the Steak 'n Shake.

"Well, uh, the agency is interested in Mrs. Griggs's, that is, Ms. Nolan's husband's dealings with Coastal Carolina Bank."

Parrish crossed her legs and leaned forward. "And why is that?"

"Why are we interested? Uh, because the bank failed."

"And that was because of Wendell Griggs?" Parrish cocked one eyebrow, questioning how that could be so.

"Mr. Griggs and his, uh, interests, had a substantial loan portfolio with Coastal Carolina Bank. Those loans, which are in default, represented a substantial percentage of the bank's debt," Agent Coyle said.

"Of course, we'd like to be as helpful as we can. Did you know anything about Wendell's dealings with that bank?" Parrish asked, looking directly at Riley.

"Not until I learned that Wendell had taken out a mortgage on our home here on Belle Isle with them. I'd never heard of Coastal Carolina Bank until then," Riley said.

"You weren't aware of the mortgage? Even though your name is on the document?"

"That's what she just said," Parrish pointed out.

Coyle frowned. "You didn't sign loan papers for a mortgage for the home at Sand Dollar Lane, in the amount of two million dollars?"

"I did not," Riley said firmly.

"What can you tell me about Oceanview Partners?"

"Nothing. I've never heard of it before."

Agent Coyle consulted a notebook he'd pulled from his pocket. "Fiddler's Creek Enterprises?"

"There's a Fiddler's Creek here on the island," Riley said.

"Belle Isle Landings Corp.?"

Parrish was making notes of her own, on the back of a magazine she'd spotted on the coffee table. "Agent Coyle, are these corporations that Wendell Griggs was involved in?"

He appeared not to hear her question. "Ms. Nolan, how involved were you in the financial dealings of Belle Isle Enterprises?"

Riley started to answer but Parrish cut her off. "My client was not involved in the day-to-day dealings of the company and, in fact, she and her husband were estranged at the time of his death, so she really can't answer any of these questions."

The FBI agent considered Riley for a long moment. "Are you friends with a woman named Melody Zimmerman?"

"Melody Zimmerman?" Riley shot Parrish a questioning look. Parrish shrugged.

"I wouldn't say we were friends. More like acquaintances," Riley said.

"What's Melody Zimmerman got to do with this?" Parrish asked.

"She works at Baldwin Community Bank, right? The one that took over Coastal Carolina?" Riley asked.

"That's our information," Agent Coyle said carefully. "Would you say she was a friend of your husband's?"

Parrish put a hand on Riley's arm before she could answer. "Ms. Nolan doesn't really know who her late husband was or wasn't friends with, because they were estranged, as I told you earlier." She stood up and looked down at the FBI agent, like a schoolteacher losing patience with a wayward student.

"Was there anything else we can help you with?"

"I guess not," the agent said, putting his notebook and phone away. "You have my card, so if you remember anything about those companies I asked about, maybe you could give me a call?"

"Of course," Riley said.

29

What the hell was that all about?" Riley asked, when the FBI agent had puttered away on his rented golf cart.

"It sounds like the feds are interested in Wendell's role in that bank failure," Parrish said. "Why was he doing business with a small local bank like that, anyway?"

"I really don't know," Riley admitted. "We always did all our personal banking at Wells Fargo."

"And what's up with the question about Melody Zimmerman?"

"She's something important at Baldwin Community Bank. And she worked at Coastal Carolina before the new bank took it over," Riley said. "She also told me she worked with Wendell on some real estate deals, including the mortgage on our house. They were friends from Kiwanis."

"That's pretty interesting," Parrish said. "Hey. You don't think there was anything going on between Wendell and Melody—right?"

"Melody?" Riley dismissed the notion. "She doesn't exactly strike me as the home-wrecker type. Anyway, she's totally not Wendell's type."

"What makes you say that?"

"I don't know. She's attractive enough, in a quiet kind of way. . . ."

"You're right. Wendell was a major star-fucker. He always wanted to be orbiting around whoever was the main attraction in a room," Parrish said. "Nobody would ever say that about Melody Zimmerman."

"Maybe it wasn't romantic," Riley said slowly. "Maybe it was strictly business. The question is—what kind of business?"

"That's for the FBI to find out," Parrish said sternly.

Evelyn and Maggy came back from town on the midafternoon ferry. Mr. Banks had been washed and groomed and had Carolina-blue toenails and a blue-and-white Tarheels bandana around his neck. Maggy had a sleek new haircut, too—with a hot-pink streak on the right side.

"Look what Mimi let me do!" Maggy exclaimed, walking into Riley's bedroom.

"Mimi let you dye your hair pink?" Riley gave her mother an astonished look.

Evelyn stood in the doorway gazing fondly at her granddaughter. "Peg Meecomb's granddaughter Ainslee has a new shop in town, and I wanted to give her the business. I hope you don't mind. Ainslee says all the girls are getting their hair done that way."

Riley couldn't decide what was more surprising—that her mother had indulged Maggy in such a radical hair style—or that she was seeking Riley's permission—even retroactively.

"Sure," Riley said. "I think it's cute. What's the name of Ainslee's shop? Maybe I'll get my hair dyed pink, too."

"Mom!" Maggy shrieked. "You can't. I'll kill myself."

"Joking," Riley said quickly. "Just a joke. I would never."

"You better not. Gabrielle Martin's mom went out and got her nose pierced. It's like she thinks she's young or something. And Gabrielle was, like, totally humiliated."

"I can promise you right now, I will never get my nose pierced," Riley said.

"Okay. Cool." Maggy bounced off the bed. "So... am I off restriction now?"

"Yes. As long as you can be respectful and follow the rules here. And did you thank your grandmother for taking you and Banksy into town today?"

"Yes, ma'am," Maggy said. "Thanks again, Mimi. You rock!" She turned to her mother. "I'm gonna meet Annabelle at the pool. Is it okay if we just get dinner at the snack bar?"

"Make sure you eat all your exchanges and test your blood," Riley said. "And I want you back here before dark. Understood?"

"Got it."

"My God!" Riley rolled her eyes. "I don't know how anybody survives the emotional roller coaster of raising a teenaged girl. Yesterday she was a zombie. Today, it's like I have my old Maggy back."

"Get used to it," Evelyn said dryly. "You were the same way at that age."

Evelyn lingered in the doorway, looking apprehensively at her daughter.

"For goodness' sakes, Mama, come on in," Riley said finally. "It's your house, you know."

"Just for a minute," Evelyn said, sitting down with her spine ramrod straight. "I think I need a nap after all the excitement of the past week."

"That was very sweet and generous of you, treating Maggy and Banks to a new hairdo today."

"Ainslee promised it'll wash out in a few days. It's just some kind of organic beet-juice dye. Anyway, it's nice to see her smiling again," Evelyn said. "I'm afraid I've been kind of hard on Maggy lately. And you."

"We've been kind of hard on each other," Riley said. "And I'm sorry about that. It's been a difficult time for us all. Since Wendell died, well, I've had to face some pretty ugly truths about the things he did. I've been dreading telling you, because I know you thought of Wendell as your son but, believe me, Mama, he wasn't what you thought. He wasn't what any of us thought."

Evelyn's expression changed. Her jaw tightened. "If this is about the foreclosure, I'm sure that was all a mistake. Wendell would never do anything to leave you in dire straits. If you like, I'll go into Wells Fargo with you next week, and we'll get it straightened out. The branch manager there has known our family for years."

"I wish it were that simple," Riley said. "But it's no mistake. And there's more. My trust fund . . ."

"That's enough," Evelyn snapped. "I won't listen to this. Wendell wouldn't have done those things. Your daddy was a wonderful judge of character. He trusted Wendell, knew he would always take care of you, would run the family business the way it should be run after he was gone."

She jumped up, eyes blazing. "Whoever killed Wendell, that's the person responsible for all of this. And in the meantime, I won't have you dishonoring your husband's fine name. Wendell was Maggy's daddy. She worshiped that man. If you want to help your daughter get through her grieving process, you'll stop going around saying horrible things about Wendell Griggs."

"I wish I could," Riley whispered. But Evelyn was out the door and down the hall. A moment later, the familiar slam of her bedroom door reverberated through the house.

30

Saturday evening, Riley was sprawled out on the flowered chintz sofa in the library, engrossed in a book she estimated she'd first read when she was Maggy's age. It was a Helen MacInnes international espionage novel and, even without the spidery handwriting proclaiming it the property of Earline Riley on the flyleaf, she knew it had been her grandmother's.

Despite her gentle ways, Nanny had been a voracious reader of mystery, suspense, and spy novels. The pine bookshelves in the library were lined with her Book-of-the-Month selections; heavy on the likes of Margery Allingham, Daphne du Maurier, Victoria Holt, and Phyllis A. Whitney.

How many Saturday nights in her youth had she spent in just this same position, reading these same comfortingly familiar stories of murder and intrigue? As a bookish preteen, Riley had found these fictional worlds endlessly fascinating, but now that she'd been unwillingly thrust into such a world, all she wanted was out.

The front door opened and closed with a bang. "Mom, I'm home," Maggy called out.

"Did you have fun with Annabelle?" Riley called.

"It was okay." Maggy's footsteps receded.

Riley read on. At ten, Evelyn returned home, poked her head in the library, and announced that she was headed to bed.

"I'm gonna read for a while, and then I might take a ride around the island, just to get out of the house," Riley said. "Okay?"

Evelyn shuddered. "I wish you wouldn't go out this late. You know, as long as the person who killed Wendell is at large, I don't think I'll ever feel completely safe here again."

"I'll lock up the house, and I'll have my phone with me. And I'll take a heavy flashlight. And a can of Mace. Okay?"

"Go ahead," Evelyn muttered. "Nobody pays attention to me."

She'd known her destination as soon as she got in the golf cart. If she hadn't already known the spot by heart, the sight of a handful of faded and crushed roses was enough of a reminder that Maggy, too, had been drawn to this spot.

Riley stood on the seawall at the marina and gazed down into the inky waters of the bay.

She hurried back to the golf cart and sat, her hands shaking so violently she was afraid to drive. Suddenly chilled, she lifted the backseat bench and riffled through her mother's assorted golf paraphernalia until she came up with Evelyn's pink windbreaker again. After donning the jacket, Riley clenched her hands tightly in her lap, closing her eyes, waiting to reclaim her composure, before she drove back toward the village.

Not wanting to attract attention to herself, she pulled the cart around to the back entrance of the Belle Isle Enterprises building.

It was a simple, nondescript, white wood-framed building, circa 1940s. Her great grandfather hadn't believed in showy, and her own father, W.R., hadn't seen any need to upgrade the company headquarters. Wendell had commissioned a design from the same architect who'd designed the Sand Dollar Lane house for an impressive two-story building that he felt would be more appropriate for the company headquarters, and had made plans to tear down the old building four years ago, but the shaky economy had put that scheme on hold.

Back here, there were none of the quaint, vaguely period streetlamps or fanciful façades that composed the rest of the shops in the village. Instead, an industrial-strength halogen lamp was mounted on the roof, sending a pool of harsh light onto the pavement below.

Riley sat in the cart and tried to think of a plan to gain entry into Wendell's office. To her own chagrin, she realized he'd never given her a set of keys to the office. She'd searched Shutters for an extra set of keys, to no avail, and no key chain had turned up in the effects the hospital had given her along with Wendell's billfold and wristwatch.

She thrust her hands into the pockets of her mother's borrowed jacket. The fingers of her right hand closed on something metal.

When she withdrew her hand from the pockets she saw that she was holding a key ring. There was no fob, just three plastic bar-coded cards—she had to hold them up and squint to read the fine print: Harris Teeter, the Baldwin County Public Library, and Ace Hardware. There were three keys as well, all bearing faded labels in Evelyn's distinctive flowery handwriting. *Shutters. Golf locker. Office.*

Riley grinned. Bless Evelyn Nolan's orderly, obsessive-compulsive soul.

She pulled out her cell phone and sent a text to Parrish.

Meet me at the office?

She fit the office key into the lock of the heavy steel door, but the tumblers didn't turn. Now she grasped the ugly handle hard with her left hand and with her right, jiggled the key, left, then right, then left again, until finally, the key turned in the lock.

She paused for a moment. At one time, Wendell had talked about having the same kind of security system he'd used at Sand Dollar Lane installed here at the office. Riley couldn't remember if he'd actually followed through on that plan.

Holding her breath, she opened the door and stepped inside, waiting for the shriek of an alarm or flashing lights. But all was quiet.

She walked quickly to the front window that looked out on the village green and closed the old-fashioned venetian blinds, then drew the curtains too, before snapping on the light in the office.

The outer office wasn't a large room, maybe ten by fourteen feet. The walls were painted planks, and the floor was linoleum, although Wendell had installed a thick Berber carpet in an effort to class the place up. Various postcard-worthy color photos of Belle Isle dotted the walls: a scenic shot of the Big Belle lighthouse, views of the harbor, the beach, and some village shops, along with slightly fuzzy old black-and-white enlargements depicting the early days of the island. Her favorite of all the photos was one of her great-grandfather James and his brother, her great-uncle Charles, posing with shovels planted in the sandy soil in front of a large RILEY BROTHERS REALTY sign. Her grandfather's massive oak desk stood near the center of the room, used now as a receptionist's desk, although Wendell had actually fired his receptionist more than a year earlier, claiming she was incompetent.

In the interest of being thorough, Riley opened and closed the desk drawers, finding nothing besides forgotten pencils, pens, paper clips, and rubber bands. There was a filing drawer, but the only thing it held was a pair of worn flip-flops and a stained coffee mug.

She went into the inner office, and in the half-light from the outer office found the desk and turned on the lamp. Wendell's desk was as tidy as Wendell himself. Large, sleek, contemporary, and made of some rare African wood she couldn't pronounce.

Riley sat down in the ergonomic chair. The desktop was bare, except for a phone and a sterling picture frame that held a studio portrait of Maggy that she'd had taken for Wendell's Father's Day gift two years earlier. The picture showed Maggy in profile, in a pensive pose, her hands resting lightly in her lap, her face tilted up toward the light. Riley's face softened as she touched the photo. Her girl had changed so much in two short years. Hadn't they all?

She was about to open the top desk drawer when she heard the back door creaking open.

Now there were footsteps, light ones, in the hallway, coming her way.

"Riles? Come out, come out, wherever you are."

Parrish was dressed in black: black yoga pants, black tank top, black-and-pink running shoes. "How'd you get in here?"

"Through pure, dumb luck, I found Mama's jacket in the back of her golf cart, put it on, and in her jacket pocket magically found her key ring with a key to the office," Riley said.

"Luck of the Irish," Parrish said, looking around the room.

She cleared her throat. "As your attorney, and as an officer of the court, I feel obliged to tell you that what you're doing right now could be considered obstruction of justice. Or maybe tampering with evidence. I warned you I know squat about criminal law, right? But that much I vaguely remember."

"Okay," Riley said. She pointed at the three-drawer file cabinet against one wall. "I've been warned. Now get busy going through those files while I ransack Wendell's desk."

"Any idea of what we're looking for?" Parrish pulled out the first file in the first drawer, which was labeled ARCHITECT'S RENDERINGS. It was thick, with lots of folded blueprints.

"Not really," Riley admitted. "I guess it would be too obvious for Wendell to have a file labeled 'Shenanigans,' huh?"

"Or 'Foreclosure.' I'll look though, just in case," Parrish said.

Riley slowly opened the shallow top desk drawer. It contained all the things you'd expect to find: small stainless mesh baskets, with the contents neatly sorted. Paper clips in one, rubber bands in another, postage stamps, three different sizes of Post-it Notes. There was a stapler and a tape dispenser. She was about to close the drawer when something caught her eye.

She picked up the container of paper clips and stirred it around with her forefinger, then picked up the object.

Riley slipped the white-gold band onto her thumb. "Oh, God." She choked back a sob.

"What?" Parrish dropped the file she was holding and rushed over to the desk. "What is it?"

"Wendell's wedding ring," Riley whispered, holding up her hand.

"Oh, Riles," Parrish said with a sigh.

"It was tossed in with a bunch of paper clips. I almost missed it, but then I realized one of these things is not like the other."

"Did you know he'd stopped wearing it?"

"No. The last few times I saw him, he was in and out of the house in a hurry, or we were bickering. I guess I never even noticed. How's that for some kind of subliminal message?"

"What do you think it means?"

"Well, he's known the marriage was over for a while now. Maybe he took it off after our last unpleasant encounter. Or maybe he quit wearing it months ago. Maybe his girlfriend objected to it."

"I still think this was a bad idea. Maybe we should stop looking," Parrish said. "This is too hard on you. Who knows what else we'll find? Let the local cops sort it all out."

"No." Riley shook her head vigorously. "If the cops were any good, they would have searched this office already. I can't count on them for answers. If it makes you feel any better, we'll put everything back where we found it before we leave tonight."

Parrish picked up the ring from the desk blotter where Riley had placed it. She held it up and read the inscription aloud. "'AAFY.' What's that mean?"

"Always and forever yours. He used to write me the sweetest notes when we were dating, and he always signed like that. Always and forever yours, Wendell. I wonder if he took it off after he realized always wasn't going to be forever."

"What are you going to do with it?" Parrish asked, handing it back.

Riley tucked the ring into the jacket pocket. "Keep it. I'll give it to Maggy at some point. Probably."

"Look at this," Riley said, holding out a file folder. "I know you were joking about a foreclosure file, but here it is."

Parrish took the folder and examined the documents. "Wow. It's the mortgage for Sand Dollar Lane. Which you, apparently, signed."

"Somebody signed it, but that's not my signature," Riley said. "And did you notice the copies of all the foreclosure notices there, too? Whoever signed my name on that mortgage must have also signed that I'd received those notices."

Parrish set the file aside and picked up the one she'd just put down. "This might be something."

"What?"

"Articles of incorporation for a company called Sand Dollar Development Corp." Parrish traced a line down the document. "You're the chief executive officer."

"What the hell?" Riley said. "Wonder what it means?"

"Dunno. But the business address is a post office box in Wilmington."

"I guess that could be something important," Riley said, going back to her search of the desk. "There's a copy machine over there. Better make a copy."

"A copier? That's so old school," Parrish chided. She whipped her smartphone from her bra and clicked off a couple of exposures.

"Hey, Riles," Parrish said a minute later. "I found four more articles of incorporation with you listed as chief executive officer."

She waved a batch of documents in the air. "They've all got different names, but their mailing address is that same Wilmington post office box. Let's see. You're also CEO of St. Mary's Holdings, Fiddler's Creek Enterprises, Oceanview Partners, and Belle Isle Landings Corp. Aren't those the companies the FBI agent asked about?"

"Yeah," Riley said. "Come to think of it, he did ask me about those names."

"Who's Samuel Gordon?"

"Beats me. Why?"

"He's listed as the agent of record on all these articles of incorporation."

"I never heard that name, and I'm pretty sure I never heard Wendell mention him," Riley said. She took out her own smartphone. "Let's Google him . . . what was that name again?"

"Samuel Gordon. Spelled like it sounds."

Riley typed the name into the search engine and frowned down at the phone.

"He was a lawyer in Wilmington."

"Was? Did he get disbarred?"

"Worse. He's dead. I'm looking at his obituary. He died six months ago.

At the age of eighty-two. I think you better make copies of all those corporation documents."

"I'm on it."

Riley went back to searching the desk drawers. The contents were nothing unusual or very interesting. Until she opened the bottom right file drawer.

A pair of tan-and-white golf shoes sat atop a stack of envelopes. She lifted the shoes out and looked at them. Wendell's, undoubtedly. His feet were unusually small for a man, a size seven, and wide—he wore a D width, which meant most of his shoes had to be custom ordered. She set the shoes on the desktop.

The entire bottom drawer was filled with unopened mail. Riley scooped up a handful of envelopes. They all had those telltale windows. Bills. Utility bills, credit card bills. And there were official-looking letters from the same source. Coastal Carolina Bank. Dozens of missives from that bank. Dunning letters.

Riley exhaled slowly. "Parrish. I think you better look at this."

31

Parrish picked up a handful of envelopes and let them drift down onto the desk blotter like oversize pieces of confetti. "Wonder what this is all about?"

"Only one way to find out," Riley said. She grabbed an envelope and started to rip.

"No!" Parrish snatched the envelope away. "That's tampering with the U.S. mail. For sure, that's a federal offense. You can't open any of these."

"Watch me," Riley said. "According to those articles of incorporation you found, I'm CEO of every one of the companies this mail is addressed to. Wendell's dead. I'm not. It's as simple as that."

"I doubt the sheriff is going to see it like that," Parrish said. "Or that baby-faced FBI agent."

Riley fixed her with an annoyed glare. "When did you get to be such a rules follower?"

"When I was sworn in to the bar," Parrish said. "I happen to have an aversion to prison."

"And I have an aversion to homelessness and poverty," Riley shot back. She opened the top desk drawer and withdrew a wicked-looking brass letter-opener. "Now. Are you in or are you out?"

Parrish knew she'd been overruled. Again. "God help me. I'm in."

She picked up a stack of envelopes and began sorting them into piles. "Let's at least get a system going. Five different companies. Five different piles. We'll put them in order by date, oldest to newest. Put the bills in one stack, the notices from the bank in another. Got it?"

It took them an hour to sort all the pieces of mail. "There must be a couple of hundred bills and notices here," Parrish said. "Some of them are postmarked as long as a year ago."

"I know," Riley said. She gathered up the first batch of bills and sat cross-legged on the floor. "I'll start with St. Mary's Holdings."

"And I'll do Sand Dollar," Parrish said, taking the desk chair Riley had vacated.

Riley slit open the first envelope and withdrew a single sheet of paper. She furrowed her brow as she read the fine print. "It's an overdue payment notice. From Coastal Carolina Bank. There's a loan number, and a balance of three million. Jesus! Do you suppose I'm liable for all this debt?"

"Hopefully not. You didn't sign any loan documents and, from what I can tell just glancing at what we've seen so far, the indebtedness is corporate, not personal. But again, I mostly don't know what the hell I'm talking about here." Parrish held up the notice she'd opened. "Mine is an overdue payment notice from the same bank. A loan number, and a balance of one point three million."

For the next hour the room was quiet except for the sound of envelopes being opened.

At some point, Parrish walked into the reception area and came back with an adding machine. "Good idea," Riley said. "I suck at math. There's a calculator in that top desk drawer there. Hand it to me, will you?"

The women began tapping away at their respective keyboards,

unconsciously setting up a cadence that made the room sound like a busy corporate office.

Riley yawned loudly and glanced at her watch. "Holy crap. It's past midnight. I'm gonna make us some coffee."

"Good idea," Parrish said. "Otherwise we'll never get through all this stuff."

They worked their way through two pots of coffee, and at 2 a.m., split a slightly stale packet of cheese crackers Riley found in the long-gone-receptionist's desk drawer.

"Gawd," Riley moaned, sprawling backward onto the carpet. "I don't know whether to laugh or cry. I've opened past-due bills from grading contractors, architects, civil engineers, surveyors, landscape designers. And that doesn't even include the credit card charges. It looks to me like when Wendell got one card maxed out, he'd just get himself issued another card to another corporation. By my count he had six different Visa cards, two MasterCards, three Discover cards, and two Amexes." She consulted the legal pad she'd used to keep tally. "Over eighty thousand in credit card debt."

"Did you get a total for the bank loans for the three corporations you checked?" Parrish asked.

"Oh, yes. It's at six million."

"I've only got three point two million for the two I looked at," Parrish reported.

Parrish tapped a pen on the desktop. "I think all these companies Wendell set up were dummy corporations. He probably knew he couldn't get a bank as small as Coastal Carolina to underwrite all these loans to one individual."

"So he created five different companies to spread out the risk, and listed me as CEO, but why did he need all that money?"

"For this," Parrish said, holding up the file folder. "It looks like he went on a spending spree, buying land here on Belle Isle. What did he want with more land?"

"Beats me," Riley said.

"I gotta take a potty break," Parrish said. "Where's the bathroom?"

"That doorway in the outer office," Riley said, pointing. "The light's on the wall, just to the right of the sink."

A minute later, Parrish opened the bathroom door an inch. "Hey, there's no toilet paper or paper towels in here."

"That's Wendell," Riley groused, standing up. "He always assumed toilet paper just magically appeared in a bathroom. Hang on, I'll get some from the supply closet."

The closet was located in the back entrance hall. As a child, Riley and Billy had loved accompanying their father to the office on Saturdays and raiding it for pens, paper, staplers, and supplies they used to play "work" in the kneehole beneath the receptionist's desk.

She swung the door open and groped around in the dark for the pull chain to turn on the light.

The wooden shelves inside were stocked as they'd been when Riley had "shopped" there decades ago. Reams of copy paper, ink cartridges, boxes of company stationery. Sitting on the bottom shelf were a pair of long-outdated IBM Selectric typewriters, and beside them were stacks of toilet paper and paper towels. She grabbed a roll of each and was about to close the door when she saw a large framed object pushed to the back of the closet.

Riley tucked the rolls under her arm and pulled the frame from its resting place, then delivered the supplies to Parrish, who was still in the bathroom.

"Look what I found in the storeroom," she said, when Parrish walked back into the office.

"'Belle Isle Master Plan Phase II,'" Parrish said, standing back to look at the frame. It was a large document, five feet by three feet. "I take it you've never seen this before?"

"It was shoved way in the back of the supply closet. I've never laid eyes on it before," Riley said. She dragged the plan over to a bare space on the outer office wall and, with effort, managed to hang it from a nail protruding from the wallboard.

"Looks like you found its former home," Parrish said. She perched on the edge of the desk and gazed at the plan.

It showed Belle Isle's developed south end, with areas designated as home sites, the marina, village, golf course, and shopping area. But the most detailed and ambitious portions showed the island's now largely undeveloped north end.

"Look at this," Riley said, gesturing at the picture. "Hotels. A second marina. An eighteen-hole golf course. Two huge retail 'villages,' condos, apartments. An airstrip, for God's sake! It looks like a mini Hilton Head Island."

"Apartments?" Parrish stood closer to the plan, her finger tracing the color-coded designations. "We've never had apartments on the island before."

"Or hotels. Or parking decks, or any of this crap," Riley said, her voice dripping disgust.

"I take it Wendell never discussed any of this with you?"

"Never! We had a knock-down, drag-out fight about the fancy boutique hotel deal he'd lined up. He knew exactly how I felt about any kind of high-density development on the north end. And cars on the island! My grandfather deeded all that land into a nature conservancy for a wildlife preserve. After the last blowup Wendell and I had over it, I thought the idea was dead."

"Doesn't look like it from this," Parrish said.

"This, this . . . thing is ten times worse than anything I knew about," Riley said.

"I always thought your family owned all the undeveloped land on Belle Isle."

"We did, originally. But when it looked like the whole project would go bust, back in the thirties, my great-uncle sold off some plots on that end of the island to a couple of unsuspecting rubes from up in the mountains. Back then, it was considered the equivalent of selling 'beach-front swampland' to tourists. Over the years, Granddad and my father managed to buy some of it back, but there were half a dozen holdouts. Some of them eventually built houses up there, others just passed it down in the family, or bought more desirable lots mid-island and on the south end. All of those holdouts lived up in the mountains in western Carolina, or had family from there. The Holtzclaws, the Funderburkes, and the Milbanks. They were pretty clannish. Dad used to refer to them as the Bug Tussle Mafia."

"I recognize some of those names," Parrish said.

"The Holtzclaws go all the way back to my great-grandfather's time," Riley told her. "Porter Holtzclaw was a dentist, but he's been dead for ages. Mrs. Holtzclaw was a little older than my dad. Every year he'd drive up to the mountains with a whole case of Carolina roasted peanuts, which were her favorite. He'd take her out to dinner and wine her and dine her, then try to talk her into selling out. And every year, she'd just smile and say, 'Not yet.'"

"You know, I think I saw a file folder labeled 'Holtzclaw,'" Parrish said, opening the middle file drawer and riffling through it.

"Here it is," she said, flipping the folder open. She picked up a photocopied sheet of paper. "Josephine Holtzclaw?"

"That's her."

"She died in September. This is her obituary. She was ninety-two years old."

"Let me see that," Riley said, reaching for the paper.

"I only met Miss Josie a few times, but I remember even as a kid knowing she was a pistol. This says she's survived by her son, Porter Jr., of Malibu, California. Kind of sad." She looked up. "You know which house is theirs, right? That big spooky old wood-frame house with the partially collapsed dock at the mouth of Fiddler's Creek."

"Miss Josie doesn't own it anymore. According to this deed, the house and the land it sits on is now owned by Fiddler's Creek Enterprises. Wendell apparently bought it from the son not long after the old lady died. That must be some house, because he paid four and a half million for it."

Riley's jaw dropped. "That's crazy. Four and a half million for that dump? Dad used to say the only thing holding it together was spit and termites. Nobody's lived there for years and years. He used to bitch and moan because he had to have the driveway mowed and cleared every year, just to keep it from being a fire hazard. At first he used to bill Miss Josie, but since she never paid, he just kept doing it as a public safety precaution."

"Wendell probably didn't care about the house," Parrish said. She stood in front of the master plan and studied it closer. "Show me where the Holtzclaw house is."

Riley slid her finger along the glassed-over map. "Okay. Here's Fiddler's Creek, and here's where it widens into the bay, right at the edge of the nature preserve." She tapped the juncture between river and bay. "This is about where the Holtzclaws' place is. How much land did you say came with the house?"

"Quite a bit. Fifty acres. Which explains why Wendell paid the price he did. That tract looks like it sits right in the middle of his planned phase two."

"If you were going to build a marina and some hotels and another golf course, you'd definitely need that chunk of land," Riley said.

"What were those other names you mentioned? The holdouts?" Parrish asked, opening the folder again.

"Um, the Funderburkes and the Milbanks."

"Yep," Parrish said. "They're not holdouts anymore. Wendell bought their land, too. Let's see. Looks like he paid two-point-six-million dollars for a house and nine-acre tract owned by the Funderburkes, and just under two million for the Milbanks's property, which was only three acres."

"Unbelievable," Riley said. "My grandfather used to love to tell how his father and uncle only paid eighty thousand for this whole island. And the locals in Southpoint thought it was hilarious how much they'd overpaid."

"Who's laughing now?" Parrish said.

"Not me." Riley yawned widely. "I don't know about you, but my brain is about fried. And there's still so much that doesn't make sense. So Wendell sets up all these dummy companies and talks one bank into loaning him over nine million dollars? Shouldn't somebody at that bank have realized they were being scammed? I mean, the two of us figured it out, and we're not exactly rocket scientists."

"Maybe somebody at the bank was in on the scam," Parrish said.

"Somebody like Melody Zimmerman? I just can't wrap my mind around her and Wendell—together. Why would she take a risk like that?"

"That," Parrish said, snapping off the desk lamp, "is probably what the FBI wants to know, too. Come on, let's get outta here. I'm dead on my feet."

32

Scott opened the spice cabinet and sighed heavily. He'd designed a state-of-the-art kitchen for the old firehouse during the extensive restoration, and laboriously labeled every drawer, shelf, and cupboard in the room.

But labels were only a suggestion as far as his chronically disorganized partner was concerned. The spice shelf that he'd spent hours alphabetizing during his last stay a month earlier was a jumble of jars and bottles. Now the allspice was shoved in next to the dill weed, the mustard seed next to the cinnamon and the tarragon—where was his tarragon? And the white peppercorns?

This was supposed to be a lazy Sunday morning on the island. He and Billy had most of the day ahead of them before he had to catch the 3:30 ferry back to the mainland.

Although Scott was a much-in-demand commercial kitchen designer, the truth was that he was rarely home long enough to cook, so Billy had assumed that role. Fortunately, Billy brought the same creative flair and sense of inventiveness to his cooking that he'd developed with his music.

But Billy was still lounging in the living room with the Sunday *New York*

Times that he'd picked up at the Mercantile, and Scott was craving an omelet. Easy enough—if he could just find the damned tarragon.

Scott padded down the long hallway to the living room in his stocking feet, stopping short of the doorway when he heard Billy's voice.

"Yeah, Kenny, I know I told you no gigs this summer, but I've changed my mind. Why? Money, of course. Now, we've sublet the place in the Village until September because Scott's gonna be mostly on the road so, ideally, any jobs would be within driving distance of here."

Kenny, Scott knew, was Billy's longtime booking agent. It was news to him that Billy had decided to go back to work.

"Jesus, Kenny. Here is the coast of North Carolina. Don't you have a map? Okay, yeah. Just about anyplace in the South would work, but if the job pays air travel, I'd be okay with that."

Billy listened for a moment. "Uh-huh. Yeah, I know those guys. I filled in for their piano player at a New Year's gig in the city a few years back. Corporate work? I guess if that's the nearest thing available. Exactly what kind of convention are we talking about? So, let me get this straight. The job's in Charlotte, first week of July. Easy-listening cocktail music, two hours. My regular rate? Plus gas and hotel, right?

"Okay, so that's set. You can fax me over the contract. What else have you got for me?"

"Yeah, yeah. Like I told you, I'm willing to lower my standards. Weddings, deb parties, bar mitzvahs. Road shows? Yeah, I sat in for *West Side Story* in Atlanta a couple of years ago. The money's not bad. So you'll let me know? Thanks, man."

"Billy!" Scott yelled, walking into the living room just as his partner was putting his phone down. "Where are my white peppercorns?"

"In the cabinet, right next to the black ones," Billy said, picking up the Arts section of the paper.

"Were you on the phone just now?"

Billy lowered the paper and looked at him. "You were eavesdropping, weren't you?"

"Maybe a little," Scott admitted. "Why didn't you tell me you were going to go back to work?"

"I don't know. It didn't seem all that important. You're gone so often, and there's not that much going on here, I just thought it might be a good idea to keep my name out there, you know, so my public won't think I'm dead or retired."

"That's the only reason? I heard you telling Kenny you'd do weddings and deb parties. You always said you hate working society gigs."

"I still do," Billy said. He folded the paper in half. "Okay, if you must know, things are a little tight for me, finance-wise."

Scott sank down onto the black-leather-and-chrome sofa. "How tight? No bullshit. Tell me the truth."

"Truthfully? I'm flat busted." Billy slouched down on the sofa, not wanting to meet his partner's searching gaze.

Scott tipped a finger under Billy's chin. "Tell me what happened."

"Three words. Wendell fucking Griggs."

Scott's eyes widened, but he kept quiet.

"You can't tell Riley, okay?" Billy said quickly. "She's got enough on her mind without worrying about me."

"I'd never," Scott swore.

"Okay, here it is. A little over a year ago, in early spring, Wendell called and asked if he could take me to lunch. I was curious, of course. I mean, we've never been what you'd call lunch buddies. I was here on the island, helping Mama open up the house, so I met him for lunch at the club. I knew he was working on some big deal on the north end, and I knew Riley was dead set against it, but hell, I wanted to see what he had planned.

"It was beyond anything I would have imagined. I knew he'd been talking to the hotel people, but now there was the hotel, and a whole new retail shopping village, apartments, condos, another golf course, and marina. It was wild. If anybody else had come up with that scheme, I would have told them they were nuts. But it was Wendell Griggs! He had everything laid out, renderings, maps, financing."

"But he needed a little more financing," Scott guessed.

"He had an eye on a tract of land—it belonged to the Holtzclaws, and he and my dad had been trying to buy that parcel for years. Old Miss Josie had gone into a nursing home, and Wendell told me he had an option to buy the land—but he needed to move fast—faster than the bank would take to free up the financing. It would be an investment for me—a great investment with a guaranteed return of twenty-five percent interest."

"So you gave him the money."

"Why wouldn't I? He's family. It was a sure thing," Billy said bitterly.

"How much?"

"Everything I had left in my trust fund. A million and change. Which is why this piano man is hitting the road again."

"I wish you'd talked to me before giving Wendell any money," Scott said with a sigh. "You know, you don't have to do this. I've still got my work."

"No way. I'm twenty years younger than you. I'm not gonna be a kept boy toy."

Scott didn't bother to argue the point. "At least, tell me you had a lawyer draw up some kind of loan document, some kind of promissory note, anything on paper."

"Nothing," Billy said. "Strictly a handshake. Wendell called it a gentlemen's agreement."

Of course, there'd been nothing gentlemanly about his financial arrangement with Wendell Griggs. And virtually nothing he'd just told Scott about his meeting with Wendell was true, because the truth would mean the end of everything Billy cared about.

From the moment he'd sat in that ruined car, faced with the knowledge that he'd caused Calvin Peebles's death, he'd known he owed a terrible debt to his brother-in-law. There were no nights Billy didn't grapple with the seeds of the guilt and self-hatred that had been sown that night.

He'd climbed in and out of the bottle half a dozen times since then, but on that chilly early spring day he was cautiously celebrating three months of sobriety.

As soon as he answered the door that day and saw Wendell standing there, holding a liter bottle of Stolichnaya, Billy felt his grip slipping away.

"Hey, buddy," Wendell said, flashing his huge salesman's smile. "I was in the neighborhood and I thought I'd drop by and see how you're hanging."

Billy nodded at the bottle of Stoli. "Do you always just happen to have a bottle of vodka when you're tooling around the island?"

The smile dimmed only a little. "My mama taught me it's rude to drop in on somebody empty-handed. You are gonna invite me in—right?"

Billy swallowed hard. "Do I have a choice?"

Wendell pretended to look hurt. "Did I come at a bad time?"

It had taken him a little while to get down to brass tacks. Wendell hadn't been in the firehouse since the restoration was completed, so now he asked for a tour, feigning interest in every last brass doorknob and hand-forged hinge.

They'd ended up in the living room. The floor-to-ceiling sheer curtains were open and the sunlight illuminated trees outside just beginning to bud out.

"I didn't realize what an unbelievable view you have here," Wendell said, settling himself on the sofa. "I might want to get the name of the architect you worked with, for when we get cooking on the north end development. There's an old smokehouse on one of the lots, and seeing this gives me an idea we might just want to save it instead of tearing it down."

"There was no architect," Billy said flatly. "I came up with the ideas and Scott drew up the plans. But thanks."

"I didn't know you were such a talented designer," Wendell said. "Maybe I'll hire you to consult on the smokehouse."

"I doubt anybody would pay me for my ideas," Billy said coolly. "But I'd be happy to take a look at it if you like."

"That'd be great!" Wendell exclaimed. "In fact, the reason I stopped by here today has to do with the north end. I've got a little investment opportunity I think you might be interested in."

"I don't know," Billy said slowly. "I've sunk most of my working capital in the firehouse. Everything cost a hell of a lot more than I'd anticipated."

"You don't have to tell me about construction and development costs. I'm living it twenty-four-seven right now. But here's the thing, Billy. I really don't think you want to miss out on this deal. It's kind of a once-in-a-lifetime opportunity. You know what I mean?"

There was no threat, no bullying, nothing so gauche. Everything was implied. And Billy knew the rest was just a formality.

"I've got an option on the Holtzclaw land. You know the house, right? The old lady's finally gone into a nursing home, and I think I've about got her son persuaded to sell. The thing is, I gotta move fast, before he changes his mind. There's no time to go to the bank, so naturally, I thought about you, thought I'd give you first shot at a sure thing."

Billy swallowed hard. "How much?"

"One point two million," Wendell said quickly.

"For that falling down wreck on Fiddler's Creek?"

"It's not the house. It's the land. It's the lynchpin for the whole project, especially the new marina."

"Marina? I thought you were just talking about a hotel and some new houses."

"No, man. This is big. The hotel's the anchor, then we'll have the new marina, condos, apartments, a new retail village, luxury estate lots, all of it. It'll be the biggest thing to hit this coast in the past twenty-five years."

"How does all that affect the wildlife sanctuary?"

"No biggie," Wendell said. "Your grandfather left it in the family trust. We'll do a land swap, move the sanctuary to another part of the island. It's done all the time."

"Does Riley know about this?" Billy asked.

He shrugged. "Your sister and I have a difference of opinion on some of the fine points, but she'll come around. Anyway, what she doesn't know won't hurt her, right?"

There it was, the implied threat, again. In the end, he'd had no choice but to write the check and swallow his fears. And after his visitor left, as Wendell knew he would, Billy had cracked open the Stoli and swallowed it, too.

"The money's all gone. You know that, right?" Scott said gently.

"I do now. Six weeks ago, Wendell came back to me, and he seemed panicky. Not like himself at all. He said the hotel people were threatening to pull out of the deal. He wanted more money, to sweeten the pot, offer them more incentives. I told him I was tapped out, and asked about my investment. He beat around the bush, but finally told me that if the hotel went south, all bets were off." Billy gave Scott a curious look.

"You already knew about the hotel thing, didn't you? I mean, the seafood and steak restaurant, that was going to be your baby, right?"

"Right. 'Was' being the key word. I only found out after Darren Cruikshank, the chef, called me, as a courtesy, to tell me the Belle Isle project was off. He's putting his steakhouse in a hotel down in Lauderdale instead."

"What happened?" Billy asked. "Wendell swore up and down this was a sure thing."

"A sure thing is never a sure thing where real estate development is concerned. Darren told me that in the end, the hotel's finance committee decided the demographics weren't a good fit. So they pulled the plug. Wendell borrowed millions to buy all that land. The bank that did most of the financing is now out of business, and the bank that assumed that loan portfolio—which includes Riley's house—is going to auction all of it off."

"That bastard Wendell. I swear to God, if he weren't already dead, I'd kill him myself," Billy said. "My only regret is that somebody beat me to the punch."

33

Nate tied up the skiff at the Holtzclaw dock. Or, what was left of it. He tugged at the line to make sure the piling wouldn't turn to dust at his touch, and was amazed when it held. He studied the weather-beaten silver decking, which had so many missing and rotted boards he was already having second thoughts about his mission.

He looked down at the swirling brackish waters of Fiddler's Creek. The tide was up, and a mullet flopped lazily at the edge of the muddy creek bank, where the partially submerged hull of an old metal johnboat had become one with the oyster bank.

Then he shrugged and jumped onto the dock. A new wooden gate had been erected at the end of the dock, with a stern NO TRESPASSING sign tacked to it. Nate ignored the sign and easily clambered over the gate. If all went as he hoped, he'd own this dock and the fifty acres that went with it by the end of the week.

He picked his way carefully down the dock toward solid land, testing each plank before putting his full weight on it. He didn't dare look up until he'd reached the grassy shore.

The rambling wooden farmhouse loomed tantalizingly close before him, thirty yards away, but an ugly new six-foot-tall chain-link fence with a sturdy padlocked gate and yet another NO TRESPASSING sign had been strung across the back edge of the property.

"I'm too old for this crap," he muttered to himself, shoving one foot into a link and laboriously climbing up and over the fence.

Once he was on the other side he paused and studied the house. The old structure hadn't been occupied in at least twenty years, and even when he was a boy, the Holtzclaws, who lived somewhere in the mountains, didn't mix much with Belle Isle's weekenders or the locals.

But the house, which rose three stories high, with wide tin-roofed porches extending across the back, was a landmark on the winding Fiddler's Creek, where its profile was visible for miles.

As Nate picked his way across the weedy yard dotted with blackened fire circles and piles of trash from unauthorized campers, he noted the telltale metal pins and pink-flagged surveyor's tape. He turned and looked back at the water's edge. The property sat at the widest opening of Fiddler's Creek in a natural oxbow, with half a mile of deep-water frontage and easy access to the ocean. No wonder Wendell Griggs had been willing to lie, cheat, and steal to get his hands on this prize.

But right now it was the old house he was drawn to. He put a foot on the bottom step of the porch and tested, then climbed onto the porch. A trio of ancient rocking chairs with rotted split-cane seats were upended against the wall, and he saw that most of the row of windows were broken out. Beer cans and the remains of a Styrofoam cooler were heaped at the far end of the porch. There was a door in the middle of the wall, and it hung partially open.

Nate frowned. This place was a magnet for vandals and kids. It was a wonder it hadn't burnt down. He'd need to do more to secure the property as soon as the sale was complete.

The old floorboards groaned as he walked toward the door. He pushed the door inward, and the rusty hinges rasped loudly.

"Hello?" A woman's voice. "Who's that?"

Riley Griggs didn't look the least bit guilty to be caught trespassing. She was standing in front of a massive rock fireplace, her hands on her hips. "Nate. What are you doing here?"

She was dressed in faded blue jeans, a cornflower-blue T-shirt, and sneakers, with a baseball cap jammed down over her hair. She had her cell phone in her hand, and Nate guessed she'd been photographing something when he'd busted in on her.

"I could ask you the same thing," he said easily.

"I asked first," Riley countered.

He gazed around the high-ceilinged old room. It had been handsome once, not fancy or grand, but the island-milled cedar walls were a soft silver, and the pine floors gave it a rough sort of dignity. Exposed wiring dangled from the ceilings and walls, where light fixtures had been ripped away and stolen, and soot blackened the granite masonry of the fireplace.

"This old place has always fascinated me," Nate admitted. "My buddies and I used to sneak over here and fish off the dock as kids. You could almost always catch a mess of flounder or the occasional big red when the tide was right, and the blue crabs that hung around those pilings were the biggest and sweetest on the island."

"My dad used to bring me over here to visit Miss Josie when I was a little girl," Riley said, her expression taking on a dreamy quality. "Dad said she was partial to girls because she didn't have any of her own, just the two sons who didn't come to the island that much."

She pointed to a partially burnt-out skeleton of a sofa. "She always kept a cut-glass jar of sour lemon jawbreakers on a coffee table that used to be there. I thought they were the most exotic thing in the world."

"Is that what you're doing here?" Nate teased. "Looking for jawbreakers?"

"No," Riley said. "I guess I wanted to see for myself what my husband bought with the money he stole from my trust fund, before somebody else buys it from the bank."

"You're saying Wendell took money from your trust fund? And you didn't know about it?"

"It turns out there was a lot he was doing that I didn't know about," Riley said.

He was at a temporary loss for words. Should he tell her what he was planning? To what end?

"I'm so sorry," Nate said. "Have you talked to a lawyer? Is there anything you can do about it? That's gotta be some kind of bank fraud, right?"

Riley held up three fingers and ticked off the answers to his questions. "I've talked to a lawyer, but since Wendell apparently cleaned out all my savings, I can't actually afford to pay her a retainer. And, anyway, who do I sue? Wendell? He's dead. Besides, my father saw fit to put Wendell's name on my trust account, so it appears he had full legal access to my inheritance."

"Unbelievable," Nate said. "Do you want to talk about it?"

"Not particularly," Riley said. "I really did just want to take a good look at the house. Wendell intended to tear it down, you know. I wasn't privy to many of the details, but I did know he planned to build a second marina here, with condos and apartments and all manner of marvelously hideous 'improvements' to the island."

Nate pushed at one of the worn wooden floorboards with the toe of his shoe, surprised that it didn't give way.

"At first glance, it looks like the house is in pretty rough shape, at least from the outside, but it's not nearly as bad as I expected in here." He pointed upward. "High ceilings, and it doesn't look like the roof has leaked. And the floors seem solid. How old do you think it is?"

"I know my great-uncle sold the property and the house to the Holtzclaws sometime in the early thirties, so it was probably built in the twenties, by the looks of the place. My grandmother told me this was originally built as a sort of boardinghouse for all the construction workers who were brought over to clear the land and build the first homes."

"I never knew that," Nate said, intrigued. "So this house is old, but not as old as your parents' house. Not anywhere near as fancy either, from what I can remember of Shutters."

Riley cocked her head and appraised the sly grin on his face. "What do you remember about our house?"

"I remember being totally intimidated the first time I showed up to take you out," he said.

"By the house, or my mother?"

"Both, now that you mention it. Your mother was pretty imposing. And Shutters was easily the fanciest house I'd ever been in. Marble floors, crystal chandeliers, and a wood-paneled library." He whistled at the extravagance.

"That's only because my great-granddad built the house as a sales tool to sell the rest of the lots and spec houses in the early days when he and my great-uncle were trying to get Belle Isle up and running," Riley said.

"According to Parrish Godchaux, you're currently a multi-multimillionaire, so I bet you wouldn't find Shutters quite so fancy now, and anyway, I seriously doubt there's much that intimidates you these days."

"Not true," Nate said, looking directly at her. "You intimidate me."

"Me?" Riley scoffed, gesturing at herself. "Look at me. I'm a forty-two-year-old widowed has-been. I don't even intimidate our twelve-pound pug puppy."

"I sincerely hope you don't believe that," Nate said. "You're beautiful, intelligent, and talented. And don't give me that crap about being washed up. I've seen your television work, and I know about the regional Emmys you've won. You were really good at what you did."

"Oh! You're telling me you saw my work while you were out in California making your first million?" Riley taunted.

"I made my living off the Internet," he reminded her. "You should try Googling yourself. You'd be surprised by how many video clips of your work there are floating around out there."

"That was a long time ago, back in the days when I was actually a serious journalist. A lifetime ago. Haven't you gotten the memo? Middle-aged women are officially invisible."

"Not to me," Nate said.

Riley took a half step backward. "If I didn't know better, Nate Milas, I'd think you were trying to hit on me."

He closed the gap between them. "What if I was? What would you do?"

Riley felt something she could have sworn she'd forgotten: a warm tingling in her scalp that traveled all the way down her spine. And then she had the oddest sensation. Her give-a-shit up and left.

They were standing only inches apart, so close she could see the gray stubble on his chin and the laugh lines worn into his deeply tanned face. Her eyes met his. They were warm and kind. She took a deep breath. "I might just let you."

Nate reached out and tilted up the bill of her baseball cap. He placed his hands on either side of her face and tilted it up so that his lips met hers.

The kiss was tentative at first. But when she didn't protest, or back away, he pulled her closer, flattening his body against hers, kissing deeper, teasing her lips apart with his tongue.

"Okay?" he murmured.

She wrapped her arms around his neck. "So far, so good."

34

As she sank further into Nate's embrace a tiny part of her brain—the only part of her body not preoccupied with the pleasure of being in a man's arms again—kept insisting that one of them would have to come to their senses soon and break away.

After all, they were standing in an abandoned house, in broad daylight, making out like a couple of horny teenagers.

But then, Nate's hands slid slowly, slowly around her waist, slipped under her T-shirt, and were definitely headed north, while his lips were unmistakably headed south, hovering now around her collarbone.

"Whoa," she whispered.

He looked up, genuinely puzzled. "Whoa? Does that mean slow down?"

"It means," she said, catching his right hand just as it reached her right nipple, "what's going on here?"

Nate nuzzled her neck. His breath was warm on her skin. "Well, I was hitting on you, and I thought it was going pretty well."

"Yeah, it was going great until you suddenly went from hitting on me to swinging for the fences," Riley said.

Nate sighed and stepped away. "Too fast. My bad."

"Again," Riley said.

They both laughed, temporarily breaking the tension of the moment.

"It's getting late, and I really want to see the rest of the house," Riley said abruptly, heading for the stairway.

"Are you running away from me?" Nate asked.

"Absolutely," she called over her shoulder.

He caught up with her on the wide second-floor stair landing. She was standing in front of the open door to a bedroom, with her hand clapped over her nose and mouth, pointing inside the room.

"Gross," Nate said, peeking inside. He kicked at a mound of rotting trash, walked inside, and quickly retreated, pulling the door closed.

"It looks like a family of raccoons moved in here after the Holtzclaws moved out." He pointed toward the ceiling, where a hole had been chewed in a section of rotting boards.

"This stench!" Riley made a gagging sound in the back of her throat.

Nate moved over toward a window and tugged at the sash, but it didn't budge, so he took a step backward and kicked out the glass.

Riley raised an eyebrow, but he pointed at the rotted window frame and she nodded in agreement.

"Are you okay?" he asked. "I kinda want to keep going and see the rest of the space up here."

"You go first," she said, pointing down the hallway.

In all, they discovered that the second floor held six bedrooms but only two bathrooms, both of which featured cracked and stained porcelain tile floors, wainscoting, and enormous cast-iron claw-foot bathtubs.

"No showers, just like Shutters," Riley noted. "And I guess the concept of creating a master bath never occurred to the Holtzclaws. My dad used to say Dr. Holtzclaw was so cheap he squeaked when he walked."

"I can tell now that it was built as a boardinghouse," Nate said. "And it would probably take a couple hundred thousand dollars to at least make it livable. Probably another reason Wendell decided it was a teardown, aside from the fact that the location and the deep-water access makes it a perfect spot for the marina he was planning."

She regarded him with surprise. "You sound like a prospective buyer."

Nate looked notably uncomfortable.

"You dodged the question earlier, when I asked you why you were here. That's it, isn't it? You're interested in buying this property."

"Yeah," he said. "That is why I'm here."

Her eyes narrowed as she processed that information. "You're a single guy. Why do you need a house like this? Never mind. Don't tell me." She shook her head in disgust and headed down the stairs.

"Wait up," Nate called, but she was taking the stairs two at a time in her haste to get away from him. "You asked me a question. At least let me try to explain."

She stood by the front door, glaring at him. "If I stand here and listen, are you going to tell me the truth? Or are you going to hand me a load of bullshit, like every other man in my life?"

"I will tell you the truth. You're not going to like it, but I promise, I will not lie to you."

"Go ahead," she said. "I can't wait to hear it."

"Can we back up a little, to earlier? Starting with what happened in the living room?" he asked.

"Yes. Let's do start with that kiss. And end with it, too. That was a mistake. I should know better. I do know better, but you caught me at a weak moment."

"Why?" he asked. "What's wrong with me kissing you—and you kissing me back, if that's what we both want?"

"You want a list? Let's start with the fact that my husband's ashes aren't even buried yet. And I don't even know you. Yeah, I used to, a long time ago, I thought. But I don't know you now, and I don't even know if I want to. The last thing I need right now is a hot fling, especially with another smooth operator, wheeler-dealer like you."

"Hold up!" Nate said, his face reddening. "I know my timing sucks, but didn't you tell me you and Wendell were getting a divorce? I can slow down if that's what you want, but let me be clear about something, Riley. I'm not looking for a hot fling, as you put it. I really care about you. Your situation sucks right now, and I'd like to help you out, if you'd let me."

"No way," she shot back. She gestured at the house. "You do what you're gonna do with this place. Buy it, tear it down, build an amusement park, if you want. I'll take care of myself, thanks very much."

Nate stood in the open door of the decrepit old house. He watched while she climbed onto the golf cart she'd parked under an old carport. Riley didn't look back, and this time, he didn't call out to her. He'd blown it—his last chance to tell her all of it—the whole thing. She'd find out for herself soon enough, and that would be the end of his stupid folly, of thinking that he could have it all—the island, the girl, the family, the life.

35

Parrish parked the car on the street in front of the Baldwin Community Bank. She smoothed the skirt of her navy Prada suit and tucked a loose strand of hair into the severe French twist she'd fashioned earlier that morning.

Then she turned to her best friend, sitting in the passenger seat. "We're agreed, right? I'll do the talking. I'll be calm but firm, and hopefully we'll manage to snow her into giving us what we want. But you need to know, this might not work. In fact, it probably won't work."

"It'll work. You look terrifying in that suit, and with your hair pulled back like that," Riley said admiringly. "If you showed up in my office, I'd totally pee my Spanx and then spill my guts."

"Let's hope so. It's a good thing for you that Ed had this old briefcase stashed in the downstairs coat closet. I haven't carried one of these things in years. Also, you do know you're the only person in the world who could get me back into panty hose and heels in June, right?"

"I'll owe you forever," Riley vowed.

"Okay." Parrish nodded to herself. "I'm psyched. Let's do this."

Parrish's black Ferragamo high-heeled sling-back pumps clicked across the marble floor of the bank. Tellers turned their heads to watch her progress as Parrish made her way toward the glass-walled office on the far side of the room.

"Uh-oh. Looks like the FDIC," one of them murmured to her coworker.

Melody Zimmerman was on the phone when the two women glided into her office and seated themselves opposite her desk.

She looked startled to see her visitors and held up a finger to indicate she was otherwise engaged.

"We need to talk," Parrish said loudly.

Melody frowned, but hurriedly ended her conversation.

"Parrish, Riley, what a nice surprise! What can I help you with?"

Parrish opened her black leather briefcase, took out a document, and placed it on Melody's desk.

"That's a certified copy of Wendell Griggs's death certificate. Now, I'd like you to get us all the records and balances for any and all accounts Wendell had here—either jointly with his wife, Riley Nolan Griggs, or in his own name," Parrish said.

"Well, uh," Melody stammered. "I'm not sure that's strictly kosher."

"I'm acting as Riley's attorney in this manner, and I can assure you that it is indeed the law," Parrish said, handing her another slip of paper. "And here's Riley's social security number, in case you need it."

Melody glanced at Riley, who nodded in agreement. Reluctantly, she powered up her computer and started typing. Five minutes later, she tapped a button and the black box on the console behind her desk began spitting printouts.

She handed the papers to Riley without comment.

There was a checking account in Wendell's name only, and the balance was nineteen hundred dollars. Riley handed the paper across to Parrish, who studied it and frowned.

The next account was for Wendell Griggs doing business as Belle Isle Enterprises, and the balance hovered just under sixteen thousand dollars.

"That's it?" Riley asked, stunned. "No savings account, nothing with my name on it?"

"No," Melody said, looking distinctly uncomfortable. "And you already know about the foreclosure on your home, right?"

"Yes," Riley said bitterly. "I think everybody on Belle Isle knows about that now."

Parrish gave Melody a stern look. "Somebody forged Riley's name on those mortgage documents."

"I'm sure you're mistaken," Melody said.

"We found a copy of it in Wendell's office. It's not my signature," Riley said. "And there's no way I'd agree to a two-million-dollar mortgage on that house. Nobody in their right mind would pay that for it."

"She's right," Parrish said. "When it goes up for auction, it'll go for pennies on the dollar."

"I hope you're wrong about that," Melody said. "The bank's appraisal was for two point one million, which is why we made the loan. Property values on the island are strong, and the auctioneer we've hired to conduct the sale seems to think it should bring a healthy price."

"And the auction is this Friday?" Riley asked, biting back tears.

"Yes, the auctioneer will be selling off all of Coastal Carolina's distressed loan portfolio, and I'm sorry, but that does include your house along with several other parcels on the island."

She paused. "I don't know if you were aware, but Coastal Carolina also made a one-point-nine-million-dollar loan to Wendell for the purchase of the Holtzclaw property on Fiddler's Creek. That's another of the assets that will be liquidated."

She gave Riley a sympathetic smile, which Riley immediately wanted to slap off her face. "I'm so sorry, Riley. I hope you know the matter is completely out of my hands."

"Hmm," Parrish said, looking dubious.

Parrish extracted another document and placed it squarely on top of the death certificate. "As you'll see, this is a list of corporations which we understand received several million dollars' worth of real estate loans from this bank, to buy property on Belle Isle. I want to know the status of all those loans."

"I can't . . ." Melody started to object.

But Parrish was ready with yet another document. "That's a copy of the articles of incorporation for those companies. You'll see that Wendell made Riley an officer in each one, without her knowledge."

Melody looked over the list of corporations. "Well, yes, the bank did do business with these companies, but I'm not aware that Wendell Griggs had anything to do with any of them." She tapped the typed sheet she'd been given. "This man, Samuel Gordon, he's the agent of record, and he's the one I dealt with."

"You dealt with the lawyer from Wilmington?" Riley broke in.

Parrish shot her a stern look.

"Yes," Melody said cautiously. "I was vice president of lending at Coastal Carolina Bank at the time. But I had no idea Wendell was behind these companies. Are you sure of your facts?"

"We found these documents in files in Wendell's office at Belle Isle Enterprises," Parrish said. "And since Riley's never met this man, I can assure you she had no idea Wendell was involving her in any of these real estate schemes of his."

"I wouldn't call them schemes," Melody objected. "We made these loans in good faith to Mr. Gordon. It was unfortunate that he later defaulted on them, but we absolutely did our due diligence before writing this business."

"Default?" Riley blanched.

"Yes." Melody sighed. "Mr. Gordon's credit history was impeccable, and the projects he presented us with all showed great promise for Belle Isle. Most importantly, we're a community bank, and we believe in investing in our community. So we were devastated to hear that shortly after our deal was concluded, Mr. Gordon was diagnosed with a fast-moving cancer. The poor man was dead within weeks." She shook her head in sorrow. "Just tragic."

"How tragic are we talking about?" Parrish asked. "Put a number on it, please."

Melody donned a pair of glasses, turned to her computer, and started tapping. Riley stole a glance at Parrish, who sat perfectly erect in her chair, looking positively terrifying.

"Total amount of the package came in at around nine point six million," Melody reported.

"And what happens now, with poor Mr. Gordon deceased?" Riley asked. "Especially since your old bank was shut down?"

"Not shut down," Melody said quickly. "None of our customers experienced any losses because their deposits were insured by the FDIC. Baldwin Community has assumed all of Coastal's assets, and of course, its liabilities and loan portfolio."

"That's a pretty big loss for one little bank like this," Parrish noted. "Forgive me, Melody, but if you were the loan officer, and those loans turned sour, I'm a little surprised you got to keep your job with the new entity."

Melody's face turned scarlet with indignation. "You might be a good lawyer, Parrish, but you obviously know nothing about the banking business. It happens that I was the top producing loan officer for the past three years among all of Coastal Carolina's branch banks. I've summered on Belle Isle my whole life, and Baldwin's executive committee recognized my ability to help with the transition to the new bank management."

"You're right, I don't know a lot about banking," Parrish said, maintaining her serene composure. "But I'm pretty good at doing Internet research, and before we came over here today, I did find an article in a banking trade magazine that speculated that the source of Coastal Carolina's failure was specifically due to bad loans to those five companies, which amounted to a disproportionate amount of the bank's total losses."

"That's a gross oversimplification," Melody said heatedly. "But since we're all friends here, I'm going to let it pass. Riley is understandably emotional and grief-stricken right now, but I'm really surprised at you, Parrish." She glanced pointedly at her watch.

"I hate to have to ask you to leave now, but I've got an out-of-office meeting I need to prepare for. Are we all done here?"

"Not quite," Parrish said. "There's just one more thing. I was wondering why Wendell chose to suddenly close his business and personal accounts last year at Wells Fargo, where he'd banked for many years, and transfer everything over to a dinky little bank like Coastal Carolina, with only four branches, all in little Podunk towns up and down the coast."

Melody began picking up files from her desk and transferring them into a messenger bag. She unplugged her cell phone, put it in an outer pocket of the bag, and added some pens and a calculator.

"That's no mystery," Melody said. "Wendell and I were in Kiwanis together. After I was named executive loan officer here, I mentioned to him that we had favorable commercial loan rates, and how much we'd love to have his business. I think he was tired of the endless bureaucracy of dealing with a megabank like Wells Fargo. As he said, he was just an account number to them. Here at our bank, he was a treasured customer."

"Nothing more than that?" Parrish asked.

Melody looked up, her eyes narrowed. "What are you implying?"

"Were you sleeping with my husband?" Riley blurted out. "Were you in this together?"

Melody Zimmerman zipped her messenger bag and stood up. "I'm not going to dignify that with an answer. I'm leaving now. I'll let you find your own way out."

36

She waited until they were back in the car. "That was not cool what you just did back in there," Parrish said. "At all. The agreement was that you were going to listen and let me do all the talking."

"I couldn't help myself," Riley said. "She was just so . . ."

"Professional? Yeah. Melody's very good. Very banker-ish. And very believable, too."

"Did you believe her?"

"Up to a point," Parrish admitted. "I was at least willing to give her the benefit of the doubt, up until she got to that business about the lawyer from Wilmington, and what a good risk it was, loaning him nearly ten million dollars."

"Maybe he looked good on paper?"

"Uh-uh. Remember that obituary clipping we found in Wendell's files? Samuel Gordon was eighty years old. I find it hard to believe a man that age is going to put together a big, long-term real estate deal—and that a small bank like this would risk making a loan that size to an octogenarian."

"It's illegal to discriminate based on age," Riley reminded her.

"On paper," Parrish retorted. "But you and I know firsthand the reality of things like age and sex discrimination."

"You're right," Riley said, thinking about her own professional prospects as a middle-aged woman. "So, how do you think Wendell pulled it off? Was Melody in on it? Do you think she was sleeping with Wendell? And what's the connection to the old guy in Wilmington?"

"I don't know," Parrish said. "That's for the FBI to figure out. Our more immediate concern is what to do about getting your house back."

"You heard what Melody said," Riley said. "My money's all gone. Even if you're right, and Sand Dollar Lane does sell for pennies on the dollar, it'll be more pennies than I can scrape up."

"Don't you have the proceeds of the sale from the St. Mary's house?"

"I had half the proceeds. I had to split it with Wendell. The rest of my share went to the down payment on the new house. Which I can't even move into until August."

"What about your mom? I bet she'd help out if you asked."

Riley got a pained expression. "She'd be my absolute last resort. I know everybody thinks she's the dowager countess of Belle Isle, but the reality is that she's a seventy-two-year-old widow living on a fixed income. A very nice fixed income, mind you. Daddy left her enough money to keep up the house in Edenton, and of course, she has Shutters, which she owns free and clear, and her stock in the family corporation. But think about what Wendell's done to the business! I just can't go to her to bail me out."

"What about Billy? Your dad left him a trust fund too, right?"

"Yeah." Riley shook her head. "I don't know what kind of shape Billy's in financially. He hasn't always exactly been very responsible with money. I think he's gotten a lot better, since he's been with Scott, but he must have spent a ton of money buying and fixing up the firehouse. I think Scotty's the breadwinner."

"It won't hurt to ask, right? Parrish asked. "Anyway, I think you should get the family all together—Evelyn, Billy, and Scott, hell, even your Aunt Roo. Lay it all out for them and see what they say. That auction is Friday. There's not a lot of time."

"I guess I could do that, but I really think it's a waste of time. Mama won't hear a word against Wendell. I've tried, but she's just turned a blind eye to all of it, convinced there's been some clerical error."

Parrish started the car. "If you want, I'll talk to her. We can show her the documentation, prove the kind of shenanigans Wendell pulled."

"Maybe," Riley said, still not entirely convinced. "She does respect your judgement—way more than mine, that's for sure."

She pointed at the dashboard clock as Riley backed away from the bank. "We just missed the noon ferry, you know. Where to now?"

"Onnalee's," Parrish said. "I need to pee, get out of these damned panty hose, and get some lunch—in that exact order."

Riley and Parrish found a booth near the door, and while Parrish was in the bathroom shedding her panty hose, Riley ordered lunch—a Cobb salad for herself and a grilled cheese sandwich for Parrish.

After Parrish returned, the waitress had just brought their food when the front door opened and Nate Milas walked in.

Riley's eyes met his for a moment. Nate stopped in his tracks, like a deer caught in headlights. The hostess approached, offered him a seat, but he shook his head, turned on his heel, and left as quickly as he'd arrived.

"What was that about?" Parrish asked.

"How am I supposed to know? Maybe he decided he wasn't hungry." Riley reached over and snagged a french fry from her friend's plate.

"Don't give me that," Parrish said. "I saw the look on his face when he saw you, and I saw yours, too. You practically turned green. There's something going on between the two of you, isn't there?"

"No."

"Liar." Parrish pushed her plate away. "You can have the rest of those fries if you want."

"Sweet!" Riley reached for the plate and Parrish grabbed her hand. "First tell me what happened. I know you, Riley Nolan."

"It was nothing," Riley insisted. "I mean, he wanted it to be something, but it's not."

"Spill it," Parrish said. "You owe me that after what I did for you back at the bank."

Riley looked around the packed café. "God, I wish you could get a drink in here."

"Quit stalling."

"Okay, but it's not exactly earth-shattering stuff. I ran into Nate out at the Holtzclaw place yesterday."

"What were you doing there?"

"I wanted to see for myself what Wendell was up to. After all, it was my inheritance he used to buy it. And when you see the place, especially from the water, it all makes sense. It's got a ton of waterfront access, at the deepest, widest part of Fiddler's Creek. It's the perfect spot to put that damned marina to go with the hotel Wendell was planning, which explains why he paid so much to buy the property. He didn't care about the house at all."

"So, what? You rode around and just kinda checked it out?"

"I borrowed Mama's golf cart and went over, but Wendell must have put up a new gate, because it was padlocked tight."

"Then how'd you get in?"

"Bolt cutters."

"I wish you hadn't told me that," Parrish said.

"Anyway, I rode down to the house and went inside."

"You broke in? Jesus, Riley. You're on some kind of criminal streak, aren't you?"

"No. The back door was standing wide open. I think kids and vandals have been hanging out there. There was trash all over, and you could see where people had made fires. I was walking around, checking it out, taking pictures with my cell phone, and Nate walked in and scared the hell out of me."

"What was he doing there?"

"He didn't want to tell me at first. He gave me some line about how he used to love to go fishing there as a kid, and he just happened to be riding around in his boat and decided to see the house for himself."

"And then what?"

Riley shrugged. "He started telling me how beautiful I was and how talented, and he said he'd seen clips of my work from when I was an anchor. Then the next thing I knew, he was hitting on me."

"Just like that."

"He said some other stuff."

"So what, he just jumped your bones right there?"

"Not exactly. He kissed me."

"Did you kiss back?"

"I don't remember."

"You are such a liar. How was he?"

"He's definitely improved with practice."

"I knew it!" Parrish crowed.

"Hush!"

"What happened next?"

"Same old Nate Milas," Riley said, wrinkling her nose. "One minute he was kissing me, the next minute he was heading for second base."

"Well I certainly hope you let him have his way," Parrish said.

"Really? You think I'm that big of a slut? I'd just drop to the floor and do the deed with some random guy in an abandoned house? In broad daylight?"

"Why not? He's single and so are you. He's rich and successful, and easy on the eyes, and you said yourself he's a good kisser."

"Nate Milas is just another guy on the make," Riley said flatly. "He finally admitted he'd gone out there because he wants to buy the Holtzclaw place. He even said he didn't blame Wendell for wanting to tear the place down, because that was the smart thing to do."

Parrish studied her friend. "Riles, you know all that property is going to be auctioned off this week. Somebody is going to bid on it, and the reality is that that somebody is probably going to be a developer. Maybe they won't build a hotel and all that other stuff Wendell wanted to do, but it really is inevitable. Don't you think it would be a good thing if that buyer is Nate Milas? He's a local boy who made good. His family has been on the island almost as long as yours. He's not gonna want to foul his own nest."

"No," Riley said vehemently. "That's just the point. Mama always says there's nothing worse than new money. Nate is hot to prove to the world that he's not just Captain Joe's kid. He'll pave the roads, mow down the wildlife sanctuary next door, put in a marina, and God knows what else. It's the perfect spot for another ferry landing. Before you know it, Belle Isle will be like Myrtle Beach or Panama City Beach: pancake houses, golf courses, and high-rise condos. It'll be nothing like what my great-grandfather intended. The island you and I grew up on, the one I thought Maggy would grow up on, will be gone forever."

"That is not going to happen on Belle Isle, and you know it," Parrish said. She signaled the waitress for their check. "This is just you, panicking and throwing up roadblocks to your own happiness."

"No, this is me trying to save my own life," Riley retorted. "I've already let one man ruin it. I'll be damned if I'll give Nate Milas a second chance."

37

Aunt Roo looked around at all the somber faces gathered at the big mahogany dining room table at the Shutters. Evelyn sat at the far end in her customary Chippendale chair, and Riley sat opposite her in the chair where Roo's brother, W.R., had presided. Billy sat across from Roo, and Parrish sat beside him.

"This better be something good," she said, stirring the ice in her Manhattan. "I'm missing poker night."

"Roo is right," Evelyn said. "Dinner was very nice, so, Parrish, thank you for bringing that delicious lobster. But why all the urgency, Riley?"

"I'm thinking it's bad news," Billy said. "Why else would we all be here on a Wednesday night?"

Riley looked desperately at Parrish. They'd settled on a game plan for this dreaded meeting, but Riley was already starting to chicken out.

"I realize I'm an outsider here tonight," Parrish said finally, "but Riley asked me to come because she's got something really difficult to discuss with all of you." She looked pointedly at Riley, who nodded.

"Okay, here goes," Riley said. "You all know that Sand Dollar Lane has been foreclosed on, and is going to be auctioned off by the bank on Friday, along with all the other land Wendell bought for the north end development. And, well, the thing is, I can't bid on the house, because I'm broke. It turns out that Wendell not only took out a new mortgage on our house without telling me, but he also emptied my trust fund to buy some of that land."

"Now, Riley," Evelyn said, frowning.

"It's true, Evelyn," Parrish said gently. "From what we can tell, Wendell went on a spending spree assembling all the land for the marina, hotel, and golf course he was planning. He closed down Riley's trust account at Wells Fargo, and used some of the money to buy the old Holtzclaw property on Fiddler's Creek. I've seen the bank records. Wendell really did take out a two-million-dollar mortgage on Sand Dollar Lane, then defaulted on it, which is how the foreclosure came about."

"Two million dollars!" Roo exclaimed. "I didn't know the house was worth that much."

"It's not," Riley said. "He must have bribed some appraiser to give such a wildly bloated value. Daddy gave us the lot, but we only paid four hundred thousand dollars for the house when we built it."

"Can't you go to the bank and tell them it was all a mistake? That Wendell had no right to take your money?" Roo asked.

"Afraid not, Aunt Roo," Riley said. "The bank that made him all those loans actually went out of business when Wendell defaulted, and they've been taken over by a new bank. That bank, Baldwin Community Bank, is liquidating those bad loans and selling the whole portfolio at an auction in Southpoint the day after tomorrow. My house will be auctioned off then."

"It's definite, then?" Evelyn asked, looking at Parrish.

"I'm afraid so."

"Well, I'm sorry to speak ill of the dead, but I never trusted that husband of yours," Roo told Riley. "He had shifty eyes."

"Roo, for God's sake," Evelyn said.

"Well, he did," Roo insisted.

"The thing is," Riley interrupted, "I don't know where else to turn. I've started to look at going back to work in Raleigh, in the fall, when Maggy's school starts. The new house will be ready by then. But in the meantime, I was wondering if maybe you all might be willing to loan me the money to help buy back Sand Dollar Lane." She turned pleading eyes to her mother. "If it were up to me, I'd just let it go. But it's Maggy's home."

She bit her lip. "The other night I went into her bedroom to check on her, and she was gone. I tried calling her cell phone, but she didn't answer. Just as I was getting ready to start calling her friends, I caught her sneaking back into the house. It turns out she's been riding her bike over to the house late at night, after we've all gone to bed, and crawling in through a window in the laundry room. Maggy admitted that she sleeps in our bed, because she said the pillow smells like Wendell. She misses him dreadfully, and that house, and its memories, are all she has left of him. You've been wonderful letting us stay here, Mama, but it's such an imposition."

"Oh, Riley," Evelyn started, then she burst into tears.

"Well for goodness' sakes," Roo said.

Billy knelt by his mother's side, putting an arm around her shoulders. "Now, Mama," he started, "I know you thought the world of Wendell, but you heard what Parrish said. It really is true. I think we have to find a way to help Riley, if we can."

"That's just it," Evelyn sobbed. "There's nothing I can do. I—I don't have any money either." She buried her face in her napkin. "I've been such a silly old woman."

"Mama?" Riley rushed over. "Please don't cry. Can you tell us what happened?"

"I'm so stupid," Evelyn insisted. "I've ruined everything. Everything your daddy and granddaddy worked for." She lifted her head and looked around at her family.

"He told me it was a sure thing. That I would get my money back, with interest, and nobody would have to know. And, like the old fool I am, I believed him."

"Who, Mama? Who told you that?" Billy asked, patting her hand.

But Riley knew, of course.

"It was Wendell, wasn't it?"

Evelyn nodded, too overcome for a moment to speak.

Parrish got up and silently fetched the bottle of wine she'd brought from the kitchen, refilling all the empty glasses at the table.

When she'd downed a glass of Parrish's Silver Oak cabernet, and after she'd gone upstairs to repair her makeup, Evelyn sat back down at the head of the table.

"Wendell came to me, last fall, and said he had finally managed to talk the Holtzclaw boy into selling him their house and land. It was something my daddy, and then W.R., had been working on for as long as I can remember. Miss Josie strung W.R. along for years, but she never would sell. And after she died, one son wanted to sell, but the other boy didn't. Then the son who was the holdout died of a heart attack. I don't know how Wendell did it, but he finally got that Holtzclaw boy to agree to sell. But he wanted an awful price! Fifteen million! Wendell said this was the chance of a lifetime. But the bank would only give him so much, and he was still short. He said another buyer was waiting in the wings, and if he didn't come up with the money, we would lose out, and some other developer would swoop in and get that land."

Evelyn looked around the table. "Belle Isle Enterprises has always been the majority property owner on this island. When W.R. married me, my daddy made him promise he'd never let the island get taken over by an outsider." She shook her head. "I thought of Wendell like my own son. He came from such a nice family. I can't understand what happened to him."

"How much money did you give him, Mama?" Riley asked.

"Not as much as he wanted," Evelyn said. "He told me he needed another five million, which was preposterous! I went to my stockbroker, and asked him to sell some of my stocks, but he said the market was down and it was a terrible time to sell. So, then, Wendell had another idea. He said I should take out a mortgage on Shutters."

"If you did that, you really are an old fool," Roo said, draining her wineglass and sliding it across the table to Parrish for a refill.

Riley's stomach twisted, knowing what would come next.

"Wendell said I should take out a balloon note. I'd never heard of such a thing. So I went to the manager at Wells Fargo, and he explained it. The bank would lend me three million dollars, and I would pay the interest only on that amount, for three years, but then, at the end of that time, the balance of the mortgage would be due."

Evelyn took a deep breath. "Wendell showed me the plans for the marina and the condominiums and the new subdivision. The lots on the creek would sell for nearly a million apiece, and he said he already had commitments from three buyers. He promised I'd have my money back in a year—with interest. And, in the meantime, he'd help me pay the monthly interest on the loan."

"You really did it? You mortgaged Shutters?" Billy asked, looking queasy.

She nodded. "For the first three months, Wendell did what he said. But then in April, he said he couldn't come up with the money, because he'd had some kind of a shortfall, due to expenses. He promised to make it up the next month, but May first came and went, and he didn't send my check. And then, well, you know. He was dead."

"What did you do?" Riley asked. "How did you pay?"

"I sold some of my stock, and my broker gave me the dickens about it, but I didn't know what else to do," Evelyn said. "I kept telling myself that something would change, and it would be all right, but then we found out your house had been foreclosed on, and all I could think about was losing this house."

Parrish cleared her throat. "Evelyn, if you don't mind my asking, exactly how much interest are you paying?"

"It's forty thousand dollars," Evelyn said. "Every month." She turned to Riley. "I'm so sorry, honey. You don't know how sorry. I believed Wendell instead of my own flesh and blood. And now I've ruined everything. This house—this was to be yours and Billy's after I'm gone. And Maggy's. It was all I had to give you. And now it's gone."

"You haven't missed a payment, though, have you, Evelyn?" Parrish asked.

"Well, no. But I've been dipping into my principal to pay that interest, and W.R. told me I should never, ever, do that unless it was an emergency."

"I'd say keeping a roof over your head is an emergency," Parrish said.

"You haven't ruined anything, Mama," Riley said, hugging her mother again. "And it's not your fault. Wendell fooled all of us. We'll figure this out, somehow, and anyway, nobody wants to lose this house, but the most important thing is that we have each other, right?"

"That's true," Evelyn said tearfully. "And right now, I'm realizing how important that really is."

Billy cleared his throat. "Uh, as long as Mama's coming clean about her questionable judgment regarding Wendell, I guess now would be a good time to admit that I did the same thing."

"Oh my God," Riley cried. "You didn't! Why?"

"Same old story," Billy said. "He came to me, said his hotel deal was in jeopardy, and if he didn't get the money to buy some additional land, the whole north end project would go up in flames. He swore me to secrecy and promised it would be strictly a short-term loan, and he'd pay interest. Long story short, I cleared out almost everything in my trust fund and gave it to him."

He looked over at Riley. "I'm so sorry, sis. If I had the money, I'd give it to you. You know I'd do anything for Maggy."

"I don't know whether to laugh or cry," Riley said, looking around the table. "He took us all in. Every single member of this family got ripped off by my husband."

"Except me," Roo said brightly.

"Of course not," Evelyn said.

"What? You think because I dress like a bag lady, I'm the poor relation? Well, the joke's on you, Evelyn Riley. I've been playing the stock market for years. I bought Facebook at seventeen and change when it was in the toilet."

"I'm amazed," Evelyn said, shrugging. "All these years I've been buying you lunch at the club."

"And that's why I'm rich and now you're poor," Roo said cheerfully. "And by the way, Wendell did try to hit me up for money, but I told him, no way, José. 'Neither a borrower nor a lender be,' that's my motto."

"Good for you, Roo," Billy muttered, getting up to go look for the vodka bottle.

"And in the meantime, Evelyn," Parrish said, "if you like, I could go to the bank with you and see if they'd be willing to renegotiate that balloon note. They'll do that sometimes, under some circumstances."

"I'll go with her," Billy said quietly.

All heads turned in his direction. "It's great of you to offer, Parrish, but

I'm her son. I'll go to the bank with Mama and explain that she took out that note under duress. We can work something out."

"Thank you, son," Evelyn said, tearing up again. "But what are we going to do about Riley's house?"

"I'll just have to tell Maggy the truth," Riley said. "Or a version of it. I can't tell her the full extent of what Wendell's done. Not until she's older, anyway. I'll think of something."

"Well I'll be damned," Roo said loudly. "Here I sit, and it's like I don't even exist with you people. Did nobody think to ask me if I'd like to help buy back Riley's house?"

Riley was, for once, speechless.

"Roo, you just told us neither a borrower nor a lender be was your motto," Billy said.

"I'm not talking about a loan. This would be a gift. To Riley and Maggy."

"Oh no, Roo, I couldn't take your money," Riley demurred.

"I don't know why not. Except for Evelyn, you and Billy are all the family I've got left. And from the looks of things, I don't believe Billy's going to be giving me any great-nieces or nephews. Right around the time you were born, I bought FedEx stock. Made a killing on it, too. I've had that money set aside for both of you, for years now. I'd just as soon give you your share now, while I'm alive and able to enjoy your kissing my butt every day out of gratitude, than wait until I'm cold and in the grave."

"I don't know what to say," Riley said, astonished.

"Then it's settled. I'll take the ferry into town tomorrow and get you a cashier's check. Now, then." Roo tapped her cheek. "Just give me a little sugar and then get this old girl another Manhattan. That fancy wine is giving me a headache."

38

Gnats swarmed as Nate Milas plunged into the tall grass at the creek's edge. But he'd come prepared this time, coated himself in bug spray, wore long sleeves and work boots. Still, it seemed that every time he inhaled he got a mouthful of no-see-ums.

He glanced back at the dock to make sure his Pathfinder was securely tied. It was a typical steamy June day, and his shirt was already sticking to his back. The tide was out, and when he saw the thick oyster beds that lined the steep bank, his mouth watered for the taste of oysters the way they'd eaten them as kids—pried open with a jackknife, coated with hot sauce, and popped right in the mouth, fresh out of the creek. He took out his cell phone and clicked off a couple of photos.

He knew from his reading that the oyster fishery was making a comeback on this part of the coast, and had tucked that fact away. Now, it was an added attraction to the plan that was coming together in his head.

Nate unfolded the survey map of the Holtzclaw property that he'd bought at the county courthouse the previous day. As he walked the property, he marveled that this island jewel had gone untouched for so many years.

According to the survey, the parcel contained just under fifty acres, and of that there was more than a thousand feet of creek frontage.

Gazing down at Fiddler's Creek, he could envision a multitude of deep-water moorings, more floating docks, and a heavy-duty boat lift. There was also enough high ground for drydocks, trailer parking, and room for whatever outbuildings would be needed.

Heading away from the river, he walked past the house toward the hard-packed road that led onto the property. For the first time, he noticed a large barn-type building, half-hidden by a dense stand of overgrown azalea and camellia shrubs, and nearly smothered by a thick wisteria vine growing up from the north corner of the structure.

He found the barn door, but it was fastened with a new-looking padlock. He stood back from the building a few yards and took some photos. He didn't actually need to see inside. The sloping tin roof was rusted, but intact. With any luck, the rest of the structure, built of the same weather-beaten cedar as the house, was sound. The barn, which didn't appear on the survey, was a huge plus.

He hiked up the drive toward the main road, noting the new gate—and the damaged padlock. He'd idly wondered how Riley had gotten onto the property, and the lock confirmed his suspicions. He smiled despite himself. She was maddeningly stubborn and opinionated, but Riley Nolan wasn't one to let a little thing like a locked gate keep her from her mission.

Nate turned back around and returned to the house. After his confrontation with Riley, he'd been too depressed to complete his exploration on Sunday, but now there was plenty of time.

He climbed the stairs to the third floor. The roofline here was steeply pitched, but on each side of the central hallway were tucked two more bedrooms with a bath connecting each. He photographed each room, then walked through the rest of the house, documenting nearly every inch.

The kitchen wing was located in a shed-roofed addition on the side of the house. It looked to have been added sometime in the sixties or seventies, with cheap roll-vinyl flooring and outdated harvest-gold appliances. A shattered window over the rust-stained, cast-iron sink looked out onto the creek. He looked up at the ceiling and saw evidence of more raccoon activity, and water damage from a leaky roof. None of this mattered. The space was large, and once gutted, he felt sure it would accommodate a commercial kitchen.

Nate walked out onto the porch. This was the money shot. The house was on high ground that allowed panoramic views of Fiddler's Creek, with the Atlantic Ocean not a fifteen-minute boat ride away. After snapping more photos, he made his way back to the dock.

He'd intended to leave, but the scent of the hot sun beating down on the salt-soaked boards was too much of a siren call. Nate always kept a fishing rod and a rudimentary tackle box in the skiff. He fetched the rod and fastened a chartreuse jig onto his line.

The tide was wrong, and the trout probably preferred live shrimp, which he didn't have, but Nate didn't particularly care one way or the other. He settled himself on the edge of the dock with his legs dangling over the edge and cast his line into the middle of the creek, letting the line drift toward a deep spot in the bottom before setting the bail of his reel. He leaned back, closed his eyes, and inhaled the scent of mud and marsh and salt, occasionally giving the line a gentle bump.

He found his mind drifting too, back to his pirate days.

They were fourteen years old. Too young for real jobs, too old to be bossed around by parents or babysitters. There were four in his crew, island boys all, no summer people or weekenders allowed. Unlike the rich brats who spent their summers lounging around pools or swatting at tennis balls, they were the sons of working-class families. Pete Davenport's mother was a single mom who cleaned houses on the island for a living. The Mayo twins, Bobby and Corey, lived in a modest cottage in the village. Their alcoholic father was the groundskeeper at the golf club, and their mom had been missing in action for as long as the twins could remember.

Nate was the captain of the crew—not because he was clearly from a higher socioeconomic class, but only because he'd managed to save enough money from mowing lawns to buy a leaky old Montgomery Ward aluminum johnboat with a fifteen-horsepower Johnson outboard.

Most mornings they'd meet up at the marina, pool their money to buy gas, Cokes, and chips, and set out to sail the seas. They knew the salt flats of the bay and the winding creeks like they knew their own home phone numbers.

They spent their summers on the water, fishing, crabbing, and casting for shrimp, which they'd either sell to the bait house or use themselves, and generally getting into the kind of mostly innocent trouble boys got into. They explored the wildlife refuge, hung out at the dump, shooting rats with Pete Davenport's BB gun, and talked about the cars they would buy and the girls they would screw when they got older.

That fall, they all started high school on the mainland. Nate played JV football, and then baseball in the spring, and the rest of the crew played truant. When summer rolled around that year, Captain Joe decided he was old enough to work as a deckhand on the *Carolina Queen,* and the Mayo brothers found work as caddies, while Pete Davenport was forced to attend summer school in a doomed effort to save his failing grades. Nate hung with his friends on weekends, when he wasn't working, or went into town to lift weights at the high school gym with the rest of the football team, but predictably, the crew drifted apart.

There was one last memorable escapade, the Labor Day weekend before school started. A camping trip was organized, and the crew took the johnboat and an old Boy Scout pup tent and some mildewed sleeping bags out to Lighthouse Key, the marshy island that was home to the Big Belle lighthouse.

Corey Mayo had swiped a bottle of Jim Beam from a golfer's bag, and they'd had themselves a high old time around their campfire, roasting hot dogs and passing the bottle around until the four of them either passed out or puked.

And that was the last hoorah for Nate's crew. Sixteen, it turned out, was the age when their differing interests and temperaments set the crew adrift for good.

Before their senior year of high school, Pete's mother remarried and moved with him to Orlando. The last Nate heard, he was selling used cars in Tallahassee. Corey Mayo dropped out of high school, drifted on and off the island, and eventually ended up in prison for car theft. His brother, Bobby, enlisted in the Army and served honorably in Operation Desert Storm. He'd come home from the war suffering from PTSD, gotten married, and had a baby on the way when he'd killed himself on a cloudless May day in Fayetteville, North Carolina.

And Nate Milas had gone off to college at Wake Forest, started one doomed business, then moved to California with his best buddy and girlfriend to start up a new enterprise, a real estate app called Cribb.

The johnboat had developed a slow leak while he was away at school, and when he'd returned home to the island at Christmas break, he discovered it had sunk at its mooring, ruining the outboard and ending their pirate days forever.

He found his own success as improbable as the Mayo brothers' failure. He'd thought about the crew a lot since his return home to Belle Isle. What, really, was the difference between himself and those fourteen-year-olds? An intact family, yes, that was part of the equation. His parents had been loving, but strict. Annie Milas, a teacher herself, had kept on top of him about his studies, and Joe, who'd never gone to college, had passed along his own demanding work ethic.

Luck and timing were factors, too. What if his sophomore-year roommate hadn't been Matt Seaver, a computer nerd who shared Nate's fascination with the Internet? What if, after he'd been dumped by Riley Nolan, he hadn't met Cassie Barnes, who was as brilliant at business as she was beautiful? And what if the three of them hadn't landed in San Carlos, with some of the highest real estate prices in the country, and been totally frustrated in their efforts to find a condo they could afford?

The intense heat was making him sleepy. He yawned. Yeah, luck and timing, and a decent family, and yeah, he had to hope his own smarts and hard work had something to do with it.

Things were lining up again, he felt, now that he was home. All he lacked was a partner, somebody who would help him build a new dream from the ground up. He'd have to forget about Riley Nolan, though. She'd made it crystal clear that they had no future together.

Nate felt a tug on his line. He sat up and started reeling, watching as the silvery shadow of a nice five-pound trout skimmed through the water. Hmm. Luck and timing again. Maybe this was an omen.

39

Left to her own devices, Maggy would sleep until noon. Friday morning, Riley went into her bedroom and sat on the edge of the bed. She looked down on her sleeping daughter's face. She was sun-browned, and her toffee-colored hair was lightened, too. Her pale pink lips were slightly ajar, and the room was quiet except for her deep, even breaths. Her hot-natured daughter had kicked off all the covers and was sprawled sideways on the pink-sprigged sheet.

"Hey, Maggy," Riley called softly. "Sleepyhead."

Her daughter sat up in bed, stretched, and yawned. "What time is it?"

"It's still early. Just barely eight."

"Good." Maggy launched herself backward onto the mattress. "See ya, Mom."

"Honey, I just wanted to let you know I'm going into town this morning, to try to buy back our house."

Maggy's eyes widened. "Oh, Mom. That is so awesome. I'll get my old room back, and we won't have to share a bathroom. . . ."

"Wait. I said I'd try. The house is being sold at an auction, and that means that if somebody else comes along with more money, I might get outbid."

"Then you just outbid them. Right? I mean, it's our house."

"Not anymore," Riley said. "It belongs to the bank now. Look, there are some things I need to tell you. I thought you were too young to understand before, but now, I really don't have a choice. I'm sorry, baby, but you're gonna have to grow up in a hurry today."

Maggy clutched her hand. "What, Mama? Are you sick?"

"No, baby, that's not it. I'm healthy as a horse, and I'm not going anywhere. It's about your dad."

"Oh." Maggy crossed her eyes. "That again."

"Just listen. Your dad made a big mistake. Several big ones. I know you want to think he was perfect, but he wasn't. None of us is perfect, including me, which is okay. And it's good that you want to remember what a great dad he was to you, and how much he loved you, because that part about your daddy is true, and nothing can change it."

Maggy nodded. "But there was bad stuff too, wasn't there? Stuff he did that hurt you and made you cry, which is why you were going to get a divorce, right?"

"That's true. I don't want to dwell on that. I want to move ahead with our lives. But I have to deal with the fact that his bad choices, and some dishonest things he did, are going to affect our family for a long time to come."

Tears filled her daughter's eyes. "I know, Mom. BeBo told me a little bit, when we went for ice cream yesterday."

"He did?" Riley was again taken by surprise at her brother's sudden streak of maturity.

Maggy nodded. "Yeah. Dad took your money that Granddad left you, and BeBo's, and Mimi's too, didn't he?"

"I'm afraid so, sweetie. I think he intended to pay it back, and he had his reasons. He thought he was doing it for the business, but it turned out to be a really bad thing."

"And that's why we're poor and have to live with Mimi," Maggy concluded.

"We're not really poor," Riley protested. "But it's true we'll have to change the way we live. And we may not get our old house here back. Your Aunt Roo is being incredibly generous and giving me some money to try to buy it, but I just don't know if it will be enough. Either way, we'll always have a place to live here on Belle Isle. And when we get back to Raleigh in the fall, I'll have to get a job."

"That's cool," Maggy said. "But what about my new school? Can I still go?"

"I think so. Anyway, let's worry about one thing at a time."

Since the auction was to start at 10 a.m., she took the 8:30 ferry and was waiting outside the bank when the doors opened. As promised, Roo had gone to her bank the previous day to make arrangements for the money, but the teller had informed her that such a large withdrawal would require the signature of a bank officer, who was out of the office until late in the day.

"They said they'd have the cashier's check ready for you at the receptionist's desk first thing Friday," Roo reported.

"It's for five hundred and fifty thousand, and I'm sorry it's not more," she added. "I took a flier with one of those damn dot-coms in the nineties. Myspace. Phooey!"

"That's more money than I ever could have hoped for," Riley told her aunt. "And I can never thank you enough."

At nine o'clock, she rushed inside the bank and made a beeline for the receptionist's desk. "I'm picking up an envelope for Riley Nolan," she told the elderly man.

He fumbled around the desk for a full five minutes, mumbling her name over and over. "Riley Nolan. Riley Nolan. Riley Nolan." After he'd turned over the same piece of paper for the third time, she wanted to scream.

"Nothing here," he said with a shrug.

"Can you go ask one of the tellers?" Riley said tersely. "I'm sort of in a hurry."

By now customers were streaming into the bank, and the line at each teller's window was five or six deep, yet the old man waited patiently at the end of the longest line.

"Come on, come on," she muttered, glancing again at her watch. It was 9:20. She'd studied the online auction rules and catalog the night before, and knew she'd need to register and present her proof of funds before being given a bidder's paddle.

Finally, twenty minutes later, the old codger sauntered over. She reached impatiently for the envelope.

"Sorry. Need to see some ID," he said. She produced her driver's license and he studied it for what seemed like an hour.

"That's a nice likeness of you," he said finally. "Hey! I know you. You used to be the TV lady from WRAL. Riley from Raleigh. Whatever happened to you, anyway?"

"I fell down a rabbit hole and lost my way," Riley told him.

The parking lot at the Seafarer Motel on the highway was packed. She found a spot at the far edge and managed to wedge her car in between a Mercedes with South Carolina tags and a tricked-out RV with Florida tags. If she'd had any notion that a bank-owned real estate auction in an obscure corner of North Carolina would be of little interest to the outside world, she now knew better.

Signs in the lobby pointed to the Admiral's Conference Room. She could hear the buzz of voices as she sprinted down the narrow hall toward the room. It was 9:55 a.m.

Riley was still gasping for breath as she hurriedly filled out the paperwork for her bidding paddle and presented a photocopy of her proof of funds. The clerk barely looked up as she handed her a numbered cardboard paddle.

"They're fixin' to start," she said, motioning to another couple who'd just arrived at the table.

The conference room was lined with rows of folding chairs. A stage had been set up at the front of the room, with a wooden lectern front and center. A large easel held a blown-up cover photograph of what she recognized as an old gas station from the next town over. She looked around for an empty chair but, finding none, claimed a spot standing against the wall.

A woman walked up to the lectern and tested the microphone. "Can y'all hear me?" she drawled. "In the back, can y'all hear?"

Assured by the crowd, she nodded and sat down at a long table at the edge of the right side of the stage.

A short, bandy-legged man dressed in starched and pressed blue jeans, a bright yellow logoed polo shirt, and an enormous ten-gallon cowboy hat took her place at the lectern.

"Okay, all right, welcome everybody. I'm Colonel John Fowlkes, and I'll be your auctioneer today. That lovely lady at the table over there is my able assistant and wife, Miss Martha. She'll be keeping the bidding and me straight today, so y'all mind your manners and we'll have us a great auction."

Members of the audience laughed appropriately at the colonel's seasoned patter.

"In case you're new to these auctions, be advised that all properties are in 'as is' condition, with no warranties about condition stated or implied. If you're the successful bidder, proceed immediately to Miss Martha to make arrangements for payment and completion of paperwork.

"The first item in our auction today is number zero-zero-one. It's a concrete block structure, built around 1963, located out on the county highway, with two hundred feet of highway access. Formerly used as a gas station, what you do with it today is your business. We'll start the bidding on this fine building at five thousand. All right, here we go.

"Who'll give me five thousand?"

Half a dozen hands shot up into the air.

"That's a start, folks. Now six. Who'll give me six? Seven? Gimme seven for this outstanding commercial property. Good. Eight? I have eight. Nine? Gimme nine, now folks."

There was a pause in the bidding.

"Nine? Get serious here, folks, this is a two-thousand-square-foot building with prime highway access. Wake up, people! Did y'all not have your Wheaties today?"

A couple of bid paddles went up.

"That's more like it," the colonel said. A few minutes later, when the action slowed again he shook his head sadly. "All right, we're stalled at twelve five. Is that it? Only twelve five?" He glanced over at his wife. "Call the sheriff, Martha, this is a crime right here!"

She shrugged, and he hammered the building down. "Twelve five it is, and bidder two eighty-eight, you just bought yourself a gas station. See the lady!"

The Sand Dollar Lane house was not at the top of the catalogue, which was a relief. It was on the last page of the four-page catalog, with a thumbnail-size bad color photo and a brief description:

Stunning custom-built waterfront Belle Isle manor house with every luxury. Five bedrooms, including master suite with ocean-view balcony, four baths, gourmet kitchen, formal living and dining room, media room, three-bay garage, professional landscaping, patio with outdoor kitchen, fire pit. Minimum bid: $400K.

Riley didn't know whether to laugh or cry at the last line. They'd spent four hundred thousand dollars building the house six years ago, and Wendell had refinanced it for an astonishing two million dollars, and now it was being auctioned off, as Parrish had warned, with a minimum bid of less than a quarter of that. But if the bidding went higher, past half a million dollars, she'd be forced to drop out.

She scanned the room looking for a familiar face, but she was too far at the back of the room to see much more than the backs of other bidders.

The morning dragged on as Colonel Fowlkes sold off a convenience store, half a dozen condos in an ill-fated complex in Wilmington, a fire-ravaged duplex in Southpoint, and eleven builder's lots in an unfinished subdivision the next county over.

Riley was surprised at how cheaply some of the properties sold for, while others, based on description alone, fetched double the price she'd expected.

There had been no time for breakfast that morning, so at noon she wandered out of the room and into the motel's modest coffee shop, where every stool at the counter was full, and every table occupied.

She was turning to leave when she saw Nate Milas heading directly toward her, a determined gleam in his eye.

Her pulse raced as he grew near. His hair was newly cut, he was clean-shaven, and dressed more formally than she'd seen him over the summer, in jeans, a pale yellow dress shirt, and a well-cut linen sport coat. He wore polished oxblood loafers on his sockless feet. He looked like what he actually was, a wealthy entrepreneur with a head full of plans and a pocketful of cash.

There was no place to run and hide, so she stood her ground.

"Riley, can we talk? Please?" He stood so close she could smell the starch in his shirt.

"What about? Your plans to buy up all the land on the island and turn it into Milas World?"

"That's not what I want. At all. I'm sorry that Wendell drove you into debt buying all that land, but there was nothing I could do to stop him."

She stared. "You knew what he was doing? Buying all that land for the north end?"

"Well, sure. I'd been watching the land sales records in the weekly newspaper, and I saw that he was making a run at most of the undeveloped property. And overpaying, from what I could tell."

"Hindsight is twenty-twenty," Riley snapped.

"I heard the rumors around town, six months ago, that he was in over his head," Nate said. "I went to Wendell, offered to partner up with him, invest some capital, if he'd be willing to change the scope of what he'd planned."

"And what did Wendell say to that?"

"Said he wasn't interested in having a partner, and that he knew exactly what he was doing. In short, he told me to buzz off."

Riley felt herself doing a slow burn. "So you sat back and waited for it all to blow up in his face. And now that it has, you get to swoop in and scoop it all up at a bargain price. It's a happy day for you, right?"

"No! It's not like that."

"You're not here to bid on the Holtzclaw place?"

"Well, yeah. It's an amazing property. There's nothing else like it on this part of the coast."

"You don't plan to live in that house. You'll knock everything down and build a marina, and when you're done with that, you'll mow down the nature sanctuary. . . ."

"No, you're wrong," Nate protested.

"No marina? On the widest part of the creek?"

"Hell yeah, there'll be a marina . . ."

"See?"

"Look," Nate said. "You saw that room in there. There are a dozen or more guys waiting for the Belle Isle lots to come up. That's what they'll do with the land if they get it . . ."

"And I'm supposed to believe that you're different?"

"I *am* different," Nate said. "That island is my home. My people have been on Belle Isle almost as long as yours."

"There's a big difference," Riley said heatedly. "My family came and they stayed. You? This is just another deal for you. You'll do your thing, then you'll head back to Silicon Valley."

"You're wrong," Nate said. "I don't know how to make you believe it, but you are."

Riley looked at him with contempt. "God knows, I can't stop you. I don't even know if I want to try. Just do me a favor. Stay away from me and my family."

40

She settled for a lunch of a candy bar from a vending machine and a tepid cup of free coffee from the hospitality table in the lobby.

By the time Riley got back to the conference room, it had cleared out enough to offer a seat on the back row, but she was too nervous to sit.

At 3 p.m. Colonel Fowlkes announced, "And now, we'll start with the parcels I think a lot of you have been waiting on. Folks, this is an extraordinary opportunity, in fact, I'd call it a once-in-a-lifetime chance to own a large tract of land on Belle Isle, which, as you may know, has been exclusively owned and developed by one family for nearly a hundred years."

Riley saw several heads in the room turn and stare knowingly in her direction. She looked down at her catalog, unwilling to meet their curious eyes.

The auctioneer coughed discreetly. "Due to a tragic set of circumstances, these tracts are being auctioned off today, and you will note each parcel does have a minimum bid, as well as a ten percent buyer's premium."

He placed a survey map on the easel. "This first item is a twelve-acre tract containing an as-is home, with ocean views on the island's beautiful north end. It has recently been rezoned for commercial development. The previous owner has already done some clearing of land, and word has it that there has been some interest in that land from a prominent national hotel chain. Now folks, we have a set minimum bid of three million, and I'll remind you that we will only be recognizing prequalified bidders for this lot. Everybody else, you're welcome to stay for the show."

Nobody moved, but there was a ripple of laughter from the audience.

"All right. Looking for three million for oceanfront acreage. I said three, but I'd prefer four." Four hands shot up. Riley recognized Nate's silhouette and his raised paddle.

"Now four. Good. Five is better." One bidder dropped out, but three paddles stayed in the air. The bidders were Nate, a silver-haired man with a leather-wrapped ponytail and extravagant signet ring, and a man who looked to be Middle Eastern.

"Now six. I have six. Seven? Who'll give me seven million for a piece of paradise over there on Belle Isle?"

Ponytail man shook his head regretfully and lowered his paddle. Nate and the other bidder hung tight. The auctioneer acknowledged them with a nod.

"Go eight. We're talking prime oceanfront commercial property. I need eight."

"Seven-five," Nate called.

The Middle Eastern man shrugged and lowered his paddle, and the auctioneer hammered Nate's bid down at seven point five million.

Colonel Fowlkes beamed. "That's a great buy, buddy. Seven point five million, sold to number eight twenty-three."

The rest of the island parcels sold quickly, and though the signet-ring man and the Middle Easterner bid vigorously, Nate managed to win the next three properties.

Riley had been keeping score, scribbling his purchase prices on her paddle, and by her estimate, Nate's buying spree had already cost him sixteen million, with the Holtzclaw property up next.

Now the colonel went into overdrive. "Friends, this next lot has no equal in this state, maybe the whole coast. I'm talking about the Holtzclaw property, a pristine fifty-acre parcel with a one-hundred-year-old farmstead, barn, and the best part, a thousand feet of prime, deep-water frontage on Fiddler's Creek, a fifteen-minute boat ride from the ocean. I don't need to tell you how rarely something like this comes on the market, but I'm gonna anyway. Minimum bid is six million."

Bidders who'd stayed on the sidelines earlier suddenly came awake. "All right then, who's gonna steal this for six million?" the colonel yelled. Eight or nine paddles shot up.

"Let's go six. Now seven. Now eight. You betcha. Eight is chump change for a property like this."

Three bidders stayed in; Nate, ponytail man, and a woman Riley hadn't noticed before, with a long mane of dark hair and an armful of jangly gold bracelets.

"I need nine million. And that's peanuts, y'all. This land is appraised at sixteen million, without any improvements at all."

"Nine," Nate called. The other bidders dropped out.

"Sold to number eight twenty-three," the auctioneer announced.

Riley added Nate's latest purchase to his total, a breathtaking twenty-five million.

The next three parcels were small zero-lot-line lots scattered around the village, and Nate stayed out of the bidding, allowing the dark-haired woman to scoop them up for less than ten thousand apiece.

Riley scarcely paid attention to the bidding. Her palms were starting to sweat because the next lot up was her own house.

The colonel put an enlarged real estate listing photo of the house on his easel.

"This is a one-of-a-kind home, mid-island, oceanfront. Custom-built for an executive of Belle Isle Enterprises, designed by a fancy New York architect whose name I can't pronounce. Now, friends, you've seen the catalog description, but that doesn't do this home justice. This is easily a two-million-dollar home on the very desirable Sand Dollar Lane, but we're going to start crazy low at four hundred."

"Dollars?" a man with a sweat-stained tractor cap called, earning a round of laughter.

"Hey, buddy," the colonel called. "I do the jokes here. It's four hundred thousand, American dollars. Who's gonna start us out?"

Riley looked around, and to her dismay, eight paddles popped up. Hers was the last to be raised.

"I see you guys know value," the colonel said. "Four ten. Now four fifteen. Now four twenty, now four twenty-five." Three or four paddles dropped out, but there were still three other bidders besides Riley, whose heart was racing.

"Four thirty. Four forty, four forty-five," he called. "Who'll stay with me at four fifty?"

One bidder shook her head and lowered her paddle.

The colonel had hit his stride. "Four fifty-five, now four sixty, four sixty-five, now four seventy, and seventy-five . . ."

Riley was afraid she might hyperventilate. Every muscle in her body was tensed. Roo's check was for exactly five hundred and fifty thousand—but with the buyer's premium tacked on, she could only go as high as five hundred.

"I've got four eighty, gimme four eighty-five, now four ninety." Riley's eyes were riveted to the competition–the dark-haired woman and an older man with a large bald spot on the back of his head.

"Drop out, drop out, drop out," she whispered. "Please drop out."

"Four ninety-five," the auctioneer called. But the other paddles stayed in the air. "Five hundred," the auctioneer shouted, "now five-oh-five."

Riley left her paddle on the chair and fled the room. She couldn't bear to see who would win her house away from her.

41

Ed Godchaux's face lit up when he saw Riley trudge onto the upper deck of the ferry.

"Riley!" he called, patting the bench beside him. "What were you doing in town?"

She took a seat beside her best friend's husband, and her mood lifted—infinitesimally. "Parrish didn't tell you?"

"We've been missing each other all day. What's going on?"

Before Riley could answer, they heard a familiar voice.

"Riley, Ed! The gang's all here."

Scott dropped down on the bench beside them, and the five-minute horn blasted. "Whew! Made it in the nick of time."

"Doing some shopping in town?" Scott asked.

"In a manner of speaking," Riley said. "Unfortunately, I'm coming home empty-handed."

"What were you looking for?" Ed asked.

"My house."

"Oh, shit," Scott said. "The auction. Was that today?"

"Afraid so," Riley said.

Scott snapped his fingers. "That's right. Billy told me Roo stepped in with an amazing contribution. But no go?"

"Nope. I had to drop out when the bidding reached five hundred thousand, because there was a ten percent buyer's premium."

"How much did it end up selling for?" Ed asked.

The ferry's horn blasted again, and they moved slowly away from the dock. Riley glanced discreetly around and was thankful not to see Nate. He was probably still back at the auction, buying up every last square inch of the island.

"I don't know. After I'd reached my limit and there were still two others bidding, I didn't have the heart to stick around. All I knew was I didn't have enough."

"God, honey, I'm sorry," Scott said. "I know you're heartbroken. Again."

She shrugged. "I don't mind so much for myself. But Maggy had her heart set on it. She thinks of that house as the embodiment of her dad. We had a talk this morning, and I did warn her that I might not be successful, but I just don't know how she'll take the news."

"Maggy's a bright kid. She'll understand," Scott said.

"Hope so. Anyway, as my dad used to say, it's Friday afternoon and the sun is officially over the yardarm. I think I'm more than ready for an adult beverage. Can I get you guys anything?"

"Let me go," Ed said, half-standing.

"Tell you what, if you buy, I'll fly," Riley said.

"I'd love a beer," Ed said.

"Make it two." Scott handed her a twenty-dollar bill, and Riley made her way downstairs.

The main cabin was typically crowded for a Friday, and it seemed that most of the passengers had the same idea as Riley. She had two beers and a plastic cup of wine clutched in both hands and was about to return to her seat when she felt a tap on her shoulder.

"Riley!" The voice was all too familiar. Andrea Payne, aka Belle Isle Barbie.

"Hello, Andrea," Riley said. She could feel her molars grinding already.

Andrea's Botox-frozen face folded into an expression so sad it would have been comic in any other setting.

"Oh, my gosh," she said, hugging Riley close, causing her to spill half an inch of wine on herself. "I guess you didn't see me at the auction earlier. Graham and I decided at the last minute to bid on one of those building lots in the village. Can you believe we got ours for less than ten thousand? But my heart just went out to you, you poor thing, when I saw that you had to drop out of the bidding for your house. That must have been devastating. And then when it sold right after you left, for just over five hundred thousand! You were so, so close. I can't even imagine how that must have felt."

"It would have felt pretty shitty if I'd hung around to see it," Riley agreed. She leaned in close. "But Andrea? Could you do me a favor?"

"Anything!" Andrea exclaimed.

"Could you kindly fuck off?"

Andrea's eyes goggled. "I beg your pardon?"

Riley raised her voice so there could be no mistake about her sentiment. "I said, fuck off!"

Heads turned. Riley smiled serenely and made her way back to the top deck.

Evelyn, Roo, and Maggy were waiting in the ferry parking lot.

"Did you get our house back?" Maggy asked, catching sight of her mother and bouncing up and down on the rear seat with Banks clutched tightly in her lap. "Can we go in tonight?"

Riley sat down and wrapped her arms around her daughter's waist. "Honey, I'm so sorry. We just didn't have enough money."

Maggy lowered her head, but Riley could see her bottom lip was quivering, and her eyes welled up with tears. "It's all right, Mom. I know you tried."

"I did, sweetie. And Aunt Roo was so wonderful to help us out, but we just came up short."

"Oh, Riley," Roo said. "I don't know what to say. That's just dreadful."

"Maybe the other person won't really have enough to buy the house. Maybe they'll back out," Evelyn said hopefully.

"I don't think so. All the bidders had to present proof of funds before they'd issue us a bidding number," Riley said.

"Well, whoever it is that did buy it, we'll never speak to them," Roo said.

"They'll be shunned on this island," Evelyn agreed. "Totally shut out of book club, supper club, mahjong, bridge club, garden club . . ."

"And poker club," Roo added. "We will make them rue the day they messed with the Nolan women."

"And if they have kids," Maggy said ominously, "I'll . . ."

"You'll be nice to them. We'll all be nice to whoever buys Sand Dollar Lane," Riley said firmly. "We had some wonderful family times there, and nobody can take that away from us. But it was just a house. We'll get another house, and we'll make new memories. Right?"

"Whatever." Maggy crossed her eyes. "But I'm going over there tonight, and I'm cutting down my tire swing Dad put up for me. And you can't stop me."

"And when was the last time you got on that tire swing?" Riley asked.

"I don't care. It's mine. Dad made it for me, and I'm not gonna have some weird new kid using it."

"All right," Riley said, settling back on her seat. "Maybe you've got a point. And maybe while we're over there cutting down your tire swing we'll grab my staghorn fern by the back patio and dig up my David Austin rosebushes too."

42

A week later, Maggy stuck her head in the library doorway. "Mom, Parrish is here. She said for me to tell you to put on your bathing suit on the double."

Riley slammed down the lid of her laptop computer, not wanting her daughter to see what she'd been working on all morning. "When did you get back?"

"A little while ago. And yeah, I had some lunch, and yeah, I tested my blood. And no thanks, I don't want to go hang out with you old ladies. I'm meeting the kids at the pool."

"I guess that answers all my questions." Riley stood up and stretched. She'd been sitting at the desk for what seemed like hours, scanning industry Web sites, making notes to herself, and looking for job listings. She was actually glad to have a diversion.

"We're not going to the pool?" Riley asked, as Parrish turned her golf cart in the opposite direction of the country club.

"Too crowded. I dropped Ed off for his golf game this morning, and the parking lot at the club was already full. I could hear a million screaming brats, all of them intent on peeing in the shallow end. Anyway, I thought it would be fun to revisit our old stomping grounds."

"The north end? Why do you wanna go there? It's gonna be too depressing."

"We haven't been to the beach together all summer, and Fourth of July is next weekend," Parrish said. "You can't stay locked up inside forever. Come on, it'll be fun. I packed the cooler with cold drinks and some snacks. We can park our chairs on the beach and take a walk and then come back and bust a chill."

"Bust a chill?"

"That's what David calls vegging out," Parrish said. "He called this morning. He and Amanda are coming for the long weekend. It's pathetic how excited I am at the prospect of seeing him."

"Not pathetic at all. I think it's sweet."

Parrish pulled the cart into the small parking lot at the north end dune walkover. "I'll get the cooler bag if you grab the chairs."

They climbed the stairs to the boardwalk and paused at the landing to look out at the water. Turquoise waves rolled lazily into the shore, and a flock of seagulls swooped and dove over something on the water's surface. Not a soul was in sight.

Riley inhaled deeply, closed her eyes, and took in the smell of the salt water and the faint scent of beach rosemary. The sun beat down on her head, and the soles of her feet in their flimsy flip-flops were superheated from the sunbaked decking.

"Man," she said, breathing out. "I forget how amazing this is. Every winter, back in Raleigh, when it's cold and gray and dreary, I wish I could be right back here, just soaking up all this sunshine. You were right. This is just what I needed."

"I'm almost always right," Parrish said. "You need to keep that in mind."

They parked their gear on a level patch of sand. "Come on," Parrish said, after spreading a towel on her chair. "Let's go exploring."

The tide was out, so they splashed through ankle-deep water, stooping occasionally to pick up shells, or stopping to marvel at a school of dolphins dipping and cutting through the waves on a path that paralleled theirs for so long the two friends joked that they were being followed.

At the far north tip of the island, where the ocean met the river, the shoreline receded into a rocky jetty. The two women clambered over boulders slick with algae, then climbed onto the seawall and gazed toward the maritime forest just ahead.

"Take a good look now," Riley advised. "Because a year from now, this will probably be either a Howard Johnson's or a Motel Six."

"Stop being such a pessimist. Did Nate Milas actually buy this parcel? I thought your grandfather left it in some sort of trust."

"He did, but Wendell was scheming to do some kind of land swap to move the sanctuary to a piece of swamp in the middle of the island—a piece without that all-important waterfront access," Riley said. "He said that was a condition the hotel people insisted on. They claimed they'd keep the preserve, but they just wanted to pave what they called 'access trails'—otherwise known as roads—through it."

"And did Wendell manage to do that?"

"I'm not sure."

"Well, before you start assuming this is all gonna turn into a HoJo, maybe you should do some research. Maybe you could actually have a discussion with Nate."

"Not happening," Riley said flatly.

"You're going to have to talk to him sooner or later. He now owns a big chunk of this island. What he does is going to impact your family's business, and vice versa."

"Don't remind me." Riley pressed onward, drawn toward the wildlife sanctuary just ahead. A bronze plaque marked the entrance to the area.

DEDICATED TO THE MEMORY OF EARLINE RILEY, WHOSE LOVE OF NATURE INSPIRED ALL SHE KNEW. Beneath the words was a silhouette of Riley's grandmother. As always, she placed the palm of her hand on the sign. "Hi, Nanny," she whispered.

She'd always thought the wildlife sanctuary was the most magical spot on the island, and it still held a powerful sway on her imagination. She stepped over the trunk of a sun-bleached live oak, so battered by wind that its branches were nearly parallel to the sandy soil.

The temperature dropped noticeably once she was beneath the tree canopy.

"Here," Parrish said, catching up. "Bug spray."

As they wandered among the live oaks, red cedars, and bay laurels, they heard a loud flapping sound and looked up to see a pair of snowy egrets rising from the top of the canopy.

"Remember when we were in Girl Scouts and Roo brought us out here to count species for our bird-watching badge?" Riley asked.

"I'd never seen a cedar waxwing before," Parrish said. "And I'll never forget when we climbed that tree and peeked inside that huge nest and saw all those just-hatched white ibis."

"Remember how we'd make little fairy houses in the crooks of the live oaks?" Parrish asked, leaning against a tree trunk.

"And plan which tree we'd live in after we ran away from home," Riley said. "And then Billy did run away when he was nine and Daddy tried to make him join the swim team, and that lasted about two hours, until he got hungry and scared when he heard a hoot owl."

As they got deeper into the maritime forest, they pushed aside branches of holly, yaupon, and wild olive, flinching when catbrier branches scratched their bare ankles.

After thirty minutes, they emerged from the undergrowth to find themselves in a wide, sandy area.

"Son of a bitch," Riley exclaimed. The exposed roots of bulldozed old-growth live oaks reached like ugly tentacles into the sky. Blackened tree stumps poked from the soil, and a huge stack of newly cut trees had been scraped to one side of the land like so many pickup sticks, where a bright yellow Bobcat was apparently stuck in a patch of mud.

"Oh, no," Parrish said, looking around in dismay. "Do you think Wendell did this?"

"Who else? I'm pretty sure this is the start of the Pirate's Point tract, where the hotel was supposed to go." She did a quick about-face. "Let's go back to the beach. This is too depressing."

"Speaking of Wendell," Parrish said, as they returned to their gear, "have you guys figured out a succession plan yet?"

"That'll be up to Mama. You know, Wendell liked to think of himself as a one-man show. For now, Bruce Boore, who ran the office in Wilmington and handled the sales and marketing end of things, is coming down on Monday. He's been doing the nitty-gritty stuff, dealing with the tenants in the village and fielding inquiries about lot sales and stuff. And I guess he's been staving off our creditors. I've been dreading all those credit card statements we found in Wendell's office."

"You won't be liable for all those debts," Parrish said. "At least, I don't think so."

"If I am, I am," Riley said. "I've already lost my house, so what else are they gonna do to me? They can't get blood from a turnip, right?"

She reached into the cooler bag Parrish had provided and brought out a thermos bottle, which she opened.

"Margaritas! Nice touch," she said, pouring a stream of the chartreuse drink into an insulated plastic tumbler and offering it to her friend.

"Not for me, thanks," Parrish said hastily. "The older I get, the more I realize I can't drink in the heat of the day without earning myself a wicked headache."

"I can," Riley said, taking a swig of her cocktail. She stood up, stripped off her bathing suit cover-up, and began applying sunscreen. She glanced over at Parrish, who was uncapping a bottle of water, still dressed in her calf-length gauzy cotton caftan.

"Aren't you hot in that getup?"

"Nope," Parrish said, ratcheting down the back of her chaise longue and tilting her sun hat over her face. "We fair-skinned redheads have to be careful of too much exposure, you know."

"You're not the least bit fair skinned, and you're not a real redhead either," Riley said.

"Sun is very aging," Parrish said airily. "But if you want to end up looking like a piece of beef jerky, go right ahead."

"Aging," Riley said with a sigh. "That again."

Parrish tipped her sunglasses down. "What's going on?"

"I've started job hunting. That's what I was doing when you showed up at the house."

"And?"

"And nothing. You know what a tiny market Raleigh is. There *was* an opening for a consumer affairs reporter at WRAL."

"Perfect!"

"Yeah, for a twenty-four-year-old Asian bombshell two years out of Duke and a graduate degree from Columbia," Riley said. "Jade Kang. Can you believe it? And that's her real name. I even went so far as to call my old program director." She shuddered. "I groveled. It wasn't pretty. He was very nice and promised to 'seriously consider' me, but I knew it wasn't gonna happen."

"Aw, man, that's so unfair. And shortsighted. You would have been ratings dynamite again. Nobody in this state had a following like you."

"Had," Riley said. "Past tense."

"But you've got until August when school starts to find something, right?" Parrish asked.

"That's only a little over a month away. I'll tell you, I've even started looking outside the Triangle. I was thinking maybe I could go into a smaller market, say Roanoke, Virginia, or Columbia, South Carolina."

"And how would that affect Maggy?"

"Exactly. That kid has been through so much this past year, with the diabetes, then Wendell, and losing the house. She's been a trouper, but I just can't pack her up and drag her to a strange town, especially with no family or friends for a support network."

"You know I'm always just a phone call away," Parrish said. "Have you thought about trying something totally different?"

"Like what? Aerospace engineer? Journalism is all I know. I'm too damn old to reinvent myself."

Parrish lunged forward and took a swipe at Riley's drink.

"Stop talking like that! If you're too old, then so am I. And I can't stand to think we're done already—at forty-two."

"You can go back to lawyering anytime you feel like it," Riley said. "But you won't have to. You can sit back and restore houses all you want. Ed is Mr. Perfect. Steady Eddie. He'd never do you like Wendell did me."

Parrish put her sunglasses on and sank back into her chair. "Nobody knows what somebody else is capable of."

43

The listings on TVJobs.com were depressing. They were either geographically impossible or economically laughable. Sunrise coanchor in Pierre, South Dakota. General assignment reporter in Naples, Florida. Investigative team leader in Newark, New Jersey.

Riley clicked over from the listings, searching for a response to any of the feelers she'd put out to old friends and former colleagues in broadcasting. Nothing. Crickets.

She heard footsteps coming down the hall toward the library, and quickly closed her laptop. She hadn't told anybody but Parrish about her plan to return to work, and wasn't eager to share that news just yet.

"Riley?" Evelyn's voice called. "The sheriff is here, and he'd like to speak to you."

"I'm in the library, Mama," Riley called.

Craig Schumann trailed Evelyn into the room. He held his baseball cap in his hands, and his white-blond hair still held its imprint.

"Sorry to barge in on you," he started. "I was on the island on business, and I did try calling, but I only got your voice mail, so I decided to drop by to fill you in on our progress."

"Whoops. I guess I left my phone upstairs," Riley said, standing. She pointed to one of the wing chairs that flanked the fireplace. "Why don't you have a seat? I'm anxious to hear what news you have."

"So am I," Evelyn said, starting to sit in the other chair.

"Uh, Mama, maybe the sheriff wants to talk to me in private," Riley said.

He turned and gave the older woman an apologetic smile. "If you don't mind."

Evelyn sniffed. "Why would I mind being kicked out of a room in my own home?"

Riley watched her leave. "Sorry about that. Are there any new leads on who killed my husband?"

"I can't get into any specifics," the sheriff said. "I can tell you that, based on new information from the coroner, we've widened the time frame in which we believe he was assaulted."

"How so?"

"Since the body was found in the water early Saturday morning of Memorial Day weekend, we assumed it had taken a couple of days for it to wash up," he explained. "However, the coroner took a look at the weather and tide patterns on the island in the week leading up to the murder, and he now believes your husband could have been killed as late as Friday evening."

"Forgive me, I don't understand the significance of that," Riley said.

"It just means that he could have been killed either Thursday *or* Friday evening. More work for me, because it considerably increases the number of suspects."

She let that sink in. "Are you telling me that I'm a suspect?"

He shrugged. "You, and everybody else who was on the island Friday night. And we know from the ferry manifest that at least a hundred and twenty more people arrived here on Friday. That's in addition to the folks who were already here."

"But I told you where I was," Riley objected. "Parrish and Ed Godchaux dropped me off here at Shutters around eight p.m. My daughter was with me. We didn't leave the house. And my mother came in when she got home from the full-moon party. I'm not sure what time, but well before midnight. I was still sleeping the next morning when you arrived to tell me Wendell's body had been found."

He uncrossed and recrossed his legs. "The problem is, theoretically speaking, you could have left here, after everybody in the house was asleep, killed your husband, and then returned in plenty of time."

"And why would I do that?" Riley asked.

"Seems to me you'd have plenty of reasons. Let's see, he'd driven you into debt, emptied your trust fund, and you suspected him of having an affair."

"I didn't know any of that until after he was killed."

The sheriff smiled. "So you say."

"Wait. Who told you I thought Wendell was having an affair?"

"Just some folks I've talked to around town."

"Are you referring to Melody Zimmerman? She's the only one I've accused of sleeping with my husband. And, by the way, she didn't deny it."

"I'm keeping an open mind," the sheriff said.

Riley was dumbfounded. "Are you really telling me I'm your number one suspect? That's . . . mind-boggling."

"Not necessarily number one," the sheriff said. "But you were a reporter once. I'm sure you know we don't consider this a random stranger-to-stranger homicide. This island is small and fairly close-knit. A stranger—any stranger, would have stood out. No, ma'am, I feel sure whoever killed Wendell Griggs knew him, and from the impact of the blow to the back of his head, meant to do him harm."

"Lots of people on this island besides me knew Wendell, and could have wished him harm," Riley pointed out. "I take it you know about his questionable business dealings."

"Oh, yes," the sheriff said. He gave her a stern look. "You know you had no business ransacking your husband's office. Tampering with what might be evidence in a homicide investigation only makes you look guiltier."

"I didn't 'tamper' with anything. I made copies of financial records that I had every right to know about—both as Wendell's widow and as somebody who was victimized by his fraudulent activities."

He shook his head in disgust. "This is what happens when amateurs go blundering around, trying to play detective. You have no way of knowing what evidence you might have destroyed."

Riley refused to be cowed by him. "How long did it take you to search that office, Sheriff? If I'd waited around for you, whoever killed him could have gotten into that office just as easily as I did, and removed any incriminating evidence."

"The fact is, I did search the office, and my people are following up on what we found. And since you bring it up, we're aware that your husband borrowed heavily from several of your family members, which also makes them suspects."

"You mean my mother and my brother?" she asked incredulously. "My mother is seventy-two years old. She's no murderer. Anyway, dozens of people must have seen her at the full-moon party that Friday night."

"Oh, sure, plenty of people saw her that night, and even saw her leave the party shortly after ten p.m. with your aunt," he agreed. "But we have the same problem with your mother that we have with you. She could have easily left the house under cover of darkness that night or even Thursday night after she supposedly went to bed."

"My mother was the last person who would have killed my husband," Riley said. "She adored Wendell, believed in him totally, despite all the evidence that he was a rat. In fact, she was furious when I told her I intended to divorce him. As far as Evelyn Nolan was concerned, Wendell Griggs was her second son. Hell, she thought he was the second coming."

"Sometimes people say one thing and do another," the sheriff said. "Your brother, for instance."

"And what's that supposed to mean?"

"The first time I interviewed him, he told me he was at his home, that old firehouse, all night Friday, after he arrived on the island. But when I started asking around the past couple of weeks, at least two people told me they remember that he arrived at the full-moon party alone, around eleven p.m."

"Billy went to the party that night?" Riley was dumbstruck.

"Yes, ma'am. And when I went back to see him today, and questioned him a little closer, he finally did admit that he lied about going out that night, because he didn't want his uh, boyfriend, to know he'd been partying."

"Scott happens to be Billy's husband," Riley said. "And I suppose Billy might not have wanted his partner to know he'd gone out, not because he'd decided to run out and kill Wendell, but because Scott's very concerned about my brother's drinking problem."

"So you acknowledge he does have a drinking problem?"

"I'm afraid so," Riley said. "My mother is in denial about it, but I'd say it's an open secret that Billy is a high-functioning alcoholic. And he may be that, but he is *not* a murderer."

"We'll see," the sheriff said. "Of course, his whereabouts on Thursday night are unaccounted for, too. He says he was on the mainland, doing errands for your mother, but nobody else can vouch for him."

"And I'm sure nobody can place him anywhere near that marina either," Riley said, doing a slow burn. "Because he didn't kill Wendell. If you really want to figure out who did kill him, take a look at his business associates."

"We are doing just that," Sheriff Schumann assured her.

"And what kind of an alibi does Melody Zimmerman have for those two nights?" she asked.

"You think she could have killed your husband? Why is that?"

"She was his loan officer at the bank that went out of business when he defaulted on several million dollars in real estate loans," Riley said. "He'd always banked with Wells Fargo before, and then suddenly he closes out all our accounts there and switches over to this tiny community bank? Where his friend Melody, from Kiwanis, happens to be vice president of lending? Don't you find that kind of odd? Because I do."

"If she was having an affair with him, why would she kill him?"

"I don't know," Riley admitted. "Maybe because he was the reason her old bank went under? I don't know all the ins and outs of the banking business. That's for you people to investigate."

"Which we are doing. As is the FBI," the sheriff assured her.

"Ask the FBI to tell you who Samuel Gordon is, why don't you?" Riley asked.

"I don't have to ask. I already know. He was the lawyer in Wilmington who set up those dummy corporations, presumably for your husband. I've left several messages on his answering machine, asking him to call me, but he hasn't responded yet," Schumann said.

"I wouldn't hold my breath waiting to hear from Mr. Gordon," Riley said. "Unless they have long distance in heaven, that is." She stood up and gave the sheriff a sweet smile. "As one amateur detective to another, I'll give you a tip. He's dead."

44

After the sheriff was gone, Riley opened her laptop, intending to continue her job search. But she was still seething from the injustice of being considered a suspect in Wendell's murder. She was fed up with being his victim. If the sheriff couldn't find his killer, maybe she'd have to take matters into her own hands.

She sat back and thought about Melody Zimmerman. Not a very likely looking murderer but, as she knew, looks could be deceiving. What, exactly, did anybody know about the woman, beyond the fact that she worked at the bank and was perpetually overshadowed by the showy, nosy Andrea Payne?

Riley decided to start her search with a call to her best friend, but her phone rang just as she was picking it up.

"Hey," Parrish said. "Word on the street has it that Sheriff Schumann paid you a visit this morning. Did he have any news?"

"Wow, that was fast. I guess I shouldn't underestimate the power of the coconut telegraph. How'd you hear?"

"I saw Evvy in the village. She was pretty ticked off that she'd been banished from her own home."

"She'd be even more ticked off if she knew Sheriff Schumann considered her and me and the rest of her family prime suspects in Wendell's murder."

"Evvy?" Parrish laughed. "Get real."

"That's what I told him. I also told him he should take a good look at Melody Zimmerman's motive and alibi."

"Damn!" Parrish said. "You know, this totally slipped my mind. Ed told me awhile back that he'd heard through the grapevine that Wendell was having a fling with some young chick who worked at a bank. No names mentioned. He said it was strictly locker-room stuff."

"Parrish!" Riley said. "You're just now mentioning this?"

"I know, but he swore me to secrecy at the time, and anyway, I didn't think it had any bearing on his murder, and I didn't want to hurt you."

"I bet the chick was Melody. That's why I was getting ready to call you. What do we know about her?"

"Not much. She lives in a kinda nondescript seventies cottage on the south end. I think it actually belongs to an elderly relative who lets her live there rent free in return for keeping it up."

"That's all?"

"Don't rush me," Parrish said. "Okay, here's something else. I was just reading the Belle Isle Country Club's online newsletter. Her picture was posted as being a new member."

"Just now? But I see her there all the time."

"She probably either used her relative's membership or sponged off Andrea Payne."

"Okay, that's something," Riley said. "How much does it cost to join the club these days?"

"We've been members for so long, I have no idea what the initiation fee is."

Riley opened her laptop's browser and pulled up the Belle Isle Country Club's Web site. "Hang on, I'm looking. Hmmm. No mention of the fees. I guess it's considered gauche to put it out there for the unwashed public to see. Sort of a 'if you have to ask, you can't afford to join' mind-set."

"I'll text Ed and ask him to find out, and then I'll call you back," Parrish said.

"Cool. In the meantime, I'm gonna see what I can find out about Melody online."

Melody's LinkedIn profile wasn't terribly informative. She'd attended college at UNC-Charlotte, and her current job description was vice president of lending, Baldwin Community Bank. Her Facebook listing wasn't much better. Photos of dogs, funny dog videos, a few selfies of Melody and Andrea Payne at the beach, and some glowing color photos of Belle Isle sunrises. Riley tapped the sunrise photo to enlarge it. It was fairly generic, showing a glowing orange orb casting a molten glow on the surf. There was a strip of beach, but it could have been almost any strip of beach on the East Coast. On the far right corner of the image, she could just make out the arm of a familiar-looking wrought-iron chair. She maximized that detail.

"That bitch," she fumed. The chair was one of a pair she'd personally dragged home from the Hickory Furniture Mart sample sale and placed on the master bedroom balcony of the house at Sand Dollar Lane. If she'd had any doubts before, they were gone now. The only way Melody Zimmerman was snapping sunrise photos that included that chair was if she'd spent the night in that master bedroom. And Riley was certain she hadn't stayed there alone.

"Gotcha," she muttered. She took a quick screen shot of the photo, just in case Melody decided to delete the photo in the near future. Other than that one slipup, Melody was disappointingly discreet with her social media posts. Her relationship status was single, and Riley couldn't find a single photo that included anybody who even remotely resembled Wendell Griggs. She didn't seem to have an Instagram or Twitter account.

Most of the hits she found for Melody were professionally related. Items from banking publications announcing her job promotions, a couple of items from her college alumni magazine, and a brief profile from a "Women in Banking" newsletter.

Riley scribbled some notes. Melody was thirty, a hometown girl who'd grown up in Southpoint, and had a degree in business administration. The profile noted that her first job out of college was at a law firm in Wilmington.

Had she worked for Samuel Gordon, the lawyer who'd set up Wendell's dummy corporations? The article didn't mention it. She might have to do some more digging. After leaving the law firm, Melody had worked as a clerk at a Bank of America branch in Wilmington before starting to climb the career ladder at first Coastal Carolina Bank, and now Baldwin Community.

Her phone rang, and it was Parrish.

"Ed talked to one of his buddies on the club's membership committee. Initiation fees are pretty steep these days—like twenty-five thousand!"

"Wow. How do all these young families we see hanging out at the club afford that kind of a hit?"

"I've wondered the same thing," Parrish said. "I think it was something like five thousand when we joined, and at the time I thought that was all the money in the world."

"I think Daddy probably fronted us our initiation fee as a wedding gift," Riley said.

"Ed's friend also told him that Wendell was one of Melody's three member sponsors, the others being Andrea Payne, and somebody named Myrtice Zimmerman. She's probably the relative who owns the house Melody lives in."

"Twenty-five thousand dollars is a lot of money for a single woman, especially one who doesn't even own her own home here," Riley said. "What kind of money do you think a vice president of a small community bank makes these days?"

"Not that much," Parrish said.

"So, she either has a sugar daddy or an outside source of wealth we don't know about," Riley mused. "I Googled her and didn't come up with any useful info. However, I did find a possibly incriminating photo on her Facebook page that must have been shot from the balcony outside my master bedroom. At sunrise," she added.

"So, that's interesting, but it isn't exactly a smoking gun," Parrish pointed out.

"I know. What are you doing in the morning?"

"I was going to go grocery shopping in town. Ed will be in on the late afternoon ferry, and David and Amanda are coming down, too. I'm ridiculously excited because I haven't seen him since Mother's Day."

"What's the occasion?"

"Helloooo? Riley? Tomorrow's Friday. And Sunday is the Fourth of July."

"Already? I guess I've lost track of time. I feel like I've been living in some weird alternative universe ever since Maggy and I got here Memorial Day weekend."

"You've had some stuff going on," Parrish said. "Why were you asking about my plans for tomorrow?"

"Just wondering if you'd like to come along on a little stakeout operation."

"What? You're going to follow Melody Zimmerman around? How do you plan to do that? She knows you, Riley. She'd spot you in a minute. Anyway, what do you hope to accomplish?"

"I just want to see who she sees and what she does on a typical day in the life," Riley said. "No biggie."

"That's what you say now," Parrish said warily. "I know you, Riley Nolan. You've got something else up your sleeve. Something that could get us both in hot water."

"With whom? My dad's dead and so is yours, so it's not like our parents are gonna put us on restriction or take away our cars for missing curfew. You said Ed won't get here until late afternoon. What could it hurt for us to do a little après-shopping sleuthing?"

"I just know I'm gonna regret this," Parrish said.

"No you won't," Riley assured her. "It'll be just like old times when we used to stalk cute guys back in high school. What time do you want to pick me up for the ferry?"

"Lord help me. I'll see you at nine fifteen."

45

Riley hopped on Parrish's golf cart Friday morning and gave her the thumbs-up sign. "Let's roll."

Parrish studied Riley's appearance. Red-and-white-striped tank top, denim boyfriend jeans, and sandals. "I'm surprised you're not dressed in a blond wig and dark glasses to go incognito."

Riley donned the sunglasses she'd perched on top of her head. "See? I'm fairly anonymous just like this. It doesn't take much."

"Hah!" Parrish said. "You still get recognized as the TV chick everywhere you go." She handed Riley a sun visor that had been hanging from the cart's rearview mirror. "Here. Put this on."

"Don't kid yourself. People in town and on the island know me, but that's because of my family, plus I grew up here and I've been coming here my whole life. To the rest of the world of broadcast journalism I'm just another over-the-hill hag. Literally, I am yesterday's news."

"I take it the job search has yet to turn up a big-bucks offer from one of the networks?"

"The search hasn't even yielded a callback from my agent," Riley reported.

"But you just started looking last week, right?"

"Right. Now can we talk about something else? Like a game plan for the stakeout? I was thinking we go by the bank, to make sure Melody's there. It has a big plate-glass window, so we should be able to see her from the street."

"Then what?"

"We find a good parking place for your car—in the shade so we don't roast to death, then we take turns watching in shifts. We can use my car to go to Harris Teeter."

"What exactly are we waiting for?" Parrish asked, as they sat in her car under the sparse shade afforded by a crape myrtle across the street from the Baldwin Community Bank.

"If Melody comes out, we follow her, see where she goes, and what she does," Riley said.

"Brilliant! Maybe she'll lead us to the two-by-four she used to wallop Wendell in the back of the head," Parrish said, rolling her eyes.

"Do you have a better plan?"

"Yes. Leave the stakeouts to the cops."

"I would if the cops were interested," Riley said. "Go on, get your groceries, and run your errands."

"I'll be back in an hour," Parrish said.

Shortly after eleven, Parrish popped the trunk of her car and stashed her groceries in the cooler she kept there. She slid onto the passenger seat. "Anything exciting to report?"

Riley yawned. "Nothing."

"Let's ditch this and go get some lunch," Parrish urged.

"No way. I want to see where she goes at lunchtime. Maybe she'll meet an accomplice or something. But you go, if you're hungry. Just bring me back a sandwich."

"Nope. I said I'd take a shift and I will. See ya."

Riley was back in forty-five minutes. "Any movement?"

Parrish was sipping from a bottle of water. "She went out right after you left and came back twenty minutes later with a takeout bag from Onnalee's. Melody's quite the dedicated banker."

"She didn't meet anybody?" Riley asked, disappointed.

"I followed her, but she must have called in her order, because she stood around at the front of the café, alone, waiting for her food, then walked directly back here. It's been pretty busy in there," Parrish said.

"Hmm." Riley handed a paper-wrapped sandwich to Parrish. "That's chicken salad with lettuce and tomato."

Parrish took a bite and chewed. "Thanks."

"Maybe you're right. Maybe this is a total waste of time."

"Not entirely," Parrish said, delicately wiping her hands with a paper napkin. She took out her cell phone, tapped the screen, and scrolled through her photo feed. "Take a look at that."

Riley removed her sunglasses and stared at the photo. "That's Melody, all right. What am I missing?"

Parrish shook her head. "I forget you're totally not into fashion." She took the phone away and maximized a frame that showed Melody walking out of the café.

"See that cute little dress she's wearing? That's a Jason Wu, from his spring collection. Sarah Jessica Parker wore the same thing, but in green, in last week's *People* magazine. I looked it up online. It retails for eighteen hundred dollars."

Riley squinted at the dress. "For that? Really?"

"Um-hmm. Those pumps she's wearing? Those are Louboutin."

"Even I've heard of them," Riley said. "What, something like two hundred, two hundred fifty dollars a pair?"

"In your dreams. Those are ostrich skin, six hundred dollars, on sale. Also? That tote bag where she stashed her lunch? Calfskin, Prada. Two thousand dollars easy."

"You're sure it's not a knockoff?" Riley asked. "I mean, I bought a knockoff Kate Spade bag down on Orchard Street the last time I was in New York for forty dollars."

"Yeah," Parrish said. "Bootleg. Ugh. I've been meaning to talk to you about that purse. You need to quit carrying that thing. It's an embarrassment."

"Oh." Riley studied the photo again. "Who knew?"

"I did," Parrish said crisply.

Riley did the math. "She's walking around wearing over four thousand dollars' worth of stuff."

"More than that," Parrish said. "I can't see the logo from these pictures, but it looks like those are Chanel cat-eye sunglasses. That's another six hundred dollars. I also can't tell about the watch from this distance, but just based on what she's wearing today, Melody likes timeless, classic style. If I had to bet, I'd say that's a Cartier tank wristwatch, and they start at around two thousand dollars. Let's say she's wearing, conservatively, nearly seven thousand dollars' worth of designer goodies. They must be giving away free samples to the employees of this bank."

"Damn, Parrish, you're good at this."

"I keep up," Parrish said. "Here's the thing I've been thinking about. Melody is a very clever girl. She's definitely got expensive taste, but she's careful not to wear anything too flashy, like one of those giant blinged-out Louis Vuitton logo bags that all the rappers carry. Nope, it's understated and quiet."

"Like Melody," Riley said. "The question is, how does somebody who works at a community bank in Southpoint, North Carolina, afford all that stuff?"

"Not to mention a twenty-five-thousand-dollar country-club membership," Parrish reminded her.

Riley thought about it. "Even if she was Wendell's mistress, it's hard for me to imagine him buying that stuff for Melody. I mean, he liked to think he was always buying top-of-the-line, but you said it yourself. He was a star-fucker. He totally would have gone for the Louis Vuitton, and not the Prada. Just look at the fancy purse he gave me for my birthday. I never said anything, but it was way too ostentatious for my taste."

"So she shops for herself. Wonder what kind of car she's driving these days," Parrish said.

"Nothing fancy," Riley said, pointing toward the parking lot. "I noticed her pulling into the ferry parking lot Memorial Day weekend. It was a perfectly ordinary silver compact."

"Too bad."

Shortly before four o'clock, Parrish walked briskly back to her car and got in the driver's seat. "Whew. Somebody was in the ladies' room at the drugstore. I thought I was going to wet my pants. Anything new?"

"Nothing. It's almost quitting time," Riley said. Let's hang around and see if she goes someplace else, or heads back to the ferry. Is that okay?"

"Yeah. Ed texted me just now. He got tied up in traffic leaving Raleigh, so he'll be doing well to make the seven o'clock ferry."

"What time will the kids be here?"

"I'm not sure. They're flying on a buddy pass because Amanda's dad works for the airline. They're supposed to call when their flight gets into RDU. So I'm just having boiled shrimp and a nice green salad tonight. They can eat that whatever time they get in."

A flash of silver caught her eye, and Parrish pointed across the street, at a silver Kia about to make a left turn out of the bank parking lot. "That looks like Melody now."

"Follow that car," Riley said, grinning. "I've been waiting my whole life to say that."

Parrish pulled away from the curb and did a quick U-turn.

"That was subtle," Riley said.

"It was that or lose sight of the Kia," Parrish said. She slowed down and hung back by half a block. "You know, following a car without being spotted isn't as easy as they make it look on TV."

"That's because very few cop shows are set in towns with a population of just under three thousand," Riley said. "You're doing fine. If Melody spots us, so what? We had a totally legit reason to be in town, grocery shopping for the holiday weekend."

"True," Parrish agreed. "We've even got the Harris Teeter bags to prove it."

"Damn," Riley said, pointing at the Kia. "She's turning left. She's headed for the ferry. Guess she's not planning on leading us to her accomplice. Or the murder weapon. Still, the day wasn't a total failure. We figured out Melody's come into a buttload of money recently."

"And probably not because she got a bonus from the bank. You want me to turn around and drop you at the car?" Parrish asked.

"Yeah. I'll meet you at the ferry. Save me a seat as far away from Melody as possible. And order me a drink, will ya?"

46

They'd gotten the text at eleven o'clock the night before.

No open seats on any flights. Headed back to apt. Sorry.

"Hey," Ed said softly. "Parrish. Come on. It's not the end of the world."

"I know," she said, sniffing. "I'm being stupid. But I can't help it. I had the whole weekend planned out with the kids."

Parrish sat up and reached for a tissue to blow her nose. "I haven't seen our son in two months, and he'll be back in school in early August, and then he'll probably go home with Amanda for Thanksgiving."

Ed looked puzzled. "This isn't like you. Is something else going on that's making you so emotional?"

"No! I mean, I guess maybe seeing what all Riley has been going through, first Wendell being murdered, and then all this money stuff. And now the sheriff actually told her she's a suspect. It just has me thinking about how important family is."

"I'm your family," Ed said, dropping a kiss on her neck. "And I'm sorry David and Amanda had a change of plans, but look—I'm here now, and I'm staying 'til Tuesday."

"You are? Really? I thought you had depositions."

"One of the associates can take the damn deposition," Ed said. "Why be senior partner if you can't delegate authority?"

"That's great," Parrish said.

"And I'm going to make more of an effort to cut back on all my hours and travel. And I promise not to get myself killed or to bankrupt us. Okay? Will that cheer you up?"

She punched his chest lightly. "You're terrible. Don't even joke about it. I haven't even told you the latest developments."

"Tell me over breakfast," Ed said, standing and tugging at her hand. "Let's ride over to the village."

They got their food and sat at a table by the Mercantile's front window while Parrish detailed what she and Riley had accomplished the day before. She was careful not to mention their previous raid on Wendell's office.

"I don't like the idea of you two following that woman," he said, frowning. "What if she figures out you're stalking her? And Riley needs to be careful about making accusations she can't prove. If Melody is as smart as you think, what's to stop her from suing Riley for slander?"

"You sound like such a lawyer," Parrish said.

"I am a lawyer, and so were you, so you know better," he said. "I thought she was going to hire that woman in Wilmington to represent her."

"She was sympathetic, but Riley's got no money for a retainer," Parrish said. "So I'm just helping out a little."

He looked over his glasses at her. "Have you been studying up on criminal law while I've been away?"

"Eat your breakfast and read your paper," Parrish said.

Ed sat at a table in the café, happily devouring his favorite everything bagel with cream cheese and lox, reading the Sports section of *The New York Times,* while Parrish nibbled at an apricot croissant and leafed through a magazine from the Mercantile's newsstand.

"Ed and Parrish! Where have you two been hiding all summer?"

Parrish knew the voice without looking up, but silently prayed she might be mistaken.

"Hi, Andrea." Ed, ever the Southern gentleman, doffed his baseball cap. He gestured at the empty chair at their table. "Would you care to join us?"

Parrish gave him a swift, vicious kick in the shin.

"Oh, no, you're too sweet," Andrea cooed. "I'm just going to pick up a cake I ordered, and then I have to run. It's my Thomas's birthday and we're having fifteen three-year-olds for his party this afternoon. It's a *Star Wars*–themed party, and I've got to go home and finish putting together the light sabers. Can you imagine? Total bedlam!"

"Totally," Parrish said, turning back to her magazine as though it was the most fascinating thing she'd ever seen.

"Okay, well, toodles," Andrea said.

"Toodles," Parrish said under her breath.

"What was that kick for?" Ed rubbed his calf absentmindedly.

"For trying to inflict Belle Isle Barbie on us for one minute more than is absolutely necessary," Parrish said. "That woman is a pestilence."

"That seems kind of harsh," Ed said, turning back to his newspaper.

"You and your good manners," she said, standing. "I'm going to get another cup of tea. Do you want a coffee refill?"

He held out his mug without looking up. "Thanks."

The Mercantile hummed with activity. Shoppers trundled carts across the wooden floors, kids clamored at the candy counter for treats, and the cash registers beeped with a constant flow of purchases. Parrish stood patiently at the counter in the café until Annie Milas came over to take her order.

"Hey, Parrish," Annie said, eyeing the empty mugs she held out. "Let's see, Earl Grey tea for you, French roast for Ed?"

"You've got a great memory," Parrish said, looking around. "How do you keep everything straight, as busy as you are?"

"After all those years of teaching school, this is like child's play," Annie said. "Is your son here for the weekend?"

"He and his girlfriend were supposed to be," Parrish said. "But they canceled at the last minute."

"That's how it is with sons," Annie said. "Believe me, once there's a girlfriend in the picture, everything changes."

"So I hear. I really envy you, having Nate move back to the island."

"I never thought it would happen, after all the years he spent out in California. I liked Cassie, his ex-girlfriend, but she was a city girl, and she always made it clear she had zero interest in hanging around here. Of course I was grateful when Nate came home to be with Joe after he got sick, but I was totally shocked when he announced he wanted to move back here for good."

"It must be nice, having him working in the business with you," Parrish said.

"It's been kind of fun, but now he's got his own business plans, which is fine," Annie said. "We were kind of getting in each other's way and, besides, he's way overqualified to be running a ferry or making ham biscuits here in the café."

"I heard Nate bought a big chunk of real estate on the island," Parrish said innocently. "The scuttlebutt I heard says he's going to build a big new resort hotel, a bunch of condos and shops on the north end, and a new marina. . . ."

"Don't believe everything you hear," Annie said. "Nate's not interested in picking up where Wendell Griggs left off. He's always loved being outdoors, but I think the years he spent working in California really changed him. He's got a new appreciation for what we have here on Belle Isle, and he says he intends to make sure any project he undertakes will be sensitive to the environment." She laughed. "Joe joked that California turned Nate into a total hippy granola head."

Annie lowered her voice. "When people hear what he's trying to do, especially with the old Holtzclaw place? They're going to be blown away. I'm blown away, and he's my son."

"Sounds intriguing," Parrish said. "Can you give me a hint?"

"Nothing's finalized," Annie said. "But Nate's been in Chapel Hill and Morehead City all week, meeting with folks from the Institute of Marine Sciences. He'd kill me if he knew I was talking out of turn like this, but you know how proud mamas are."

"I do," Parrish said. "Is Nate thinking he'll sell the Holtzclaw property to the university? That land must be worth a bundle. Can the university afford something like that?"

"Sell it? No. He's not only going to donate the land, he's going to build it out, too. The old house will be a dorm and classroom building, and there'll be a place to dock the boats they use for research, but the center would focus on the fishery and bringing back commercial oystering and crabbing. . . ." Annie clapped a hand over her mouth. "See? There I go, running my mouth about stuff I'm not supposed to talk about. Nate says I couldn't keep a secret if my life depended on it. But it just makes me so mad, you know, folks saying he's going to pave the island and turn it into another Myrtle Beach. People have been making snide comments about it all week, and I'm just fed up."

"I'll bet," Parrish said.

"Excuse me, Annie?" The voice was shrill and unmistakable. *There she was again,* Parrish thought. Belle Isle Barbie, like a toenail fungus that got under your skin and would not go away.

Andrea Payne thrust a white cardboard cake box at Annie Milas.

"Look at this cake your baker did," she said. "I can't serve this at Thomas's party. Is that supposed to be Chewbacca?"

Andrea poked at a lump on the cake. "Look at this, Parrish. It's hideous!"

"Looks like Chewie to me," Parrish said.

"It looks *nothing* like Chewbacca," Andrea cried. "It's like a big, brown, chocolate turd. And I cannot serve this to those children." She shoved the box across the top of the display counter at Annie Milas.

"This is atrocious. And I am not paying for it until you fix it."

Annie looked down at the cake. "I'm sorry you're unhappy, Andrea, but my cake decorator doesn't work on Saturdays."

"You have to fix it," Andrea insisted. "The party's in an hour."

"All right." Annie shrugged. She turned around, picked up a plastic spatula, scraped the offending chocolate Chewbacca off the top of the cake, and dropped the mound of chocolate in the prep sink. "Anything else?"

Andrea stared down at the cake, speechless for all of thirty seconds. "I want my money back."

Annie stepped over to the cash register, opened the drawer, and removed two twenty-dollar bills, which she placed in her outraged customer's outstretched hand. "Happy to be of service."

Belle Isle Barbie snatched the cake box from the counter and marched out of the café.

Annie watched her exit, then glanced over at Parrish, who was trying to choke back a laugh. "There's just no pleasing some people."

"But I notice she took the cake with her," Parrish said. She heard a polite cough and turned to see that a line was forming at the counter. She paid for her refills and turned to go.

"Oh Lord," Annie said worriedly. "I wonder how long that woman was standing there? I hope she didn't hear any of what we just talked about. Nate hates for other people to get in his business. Even his mama."

"I won't say anything, but I can't guarantee that she won't," Parrish said.

She hurried back to the table and slid Ed's coffee in front of him.

"Where'd you get to?" he asked.

"Just gathering some intel," Parrish said. "Are you done with your breakfast? I need to go by Shutters and see Riley."

47

Mama, please?" Maggy clasped her hands together prayerfully. "Annabelle's mom says it's totally cool for me to spend the night over there. She's, like, a nurse and everything. And that way, you can go to the beach party tonight with Ed and Parrish and not worry about me. Please?"

"Yes," Parrish chimed in as she walked in the kitchen door. "You could go to the party with Parrish and Ed tonight. In fact, you must."

Riley turned and shot her best friend the death stare. "Who asked you to put your oar in the water?"

"I did," Maggy said. She flashed Parrish a hopeful look. "Can you talk to her? She won't listen to me."

"I just think you need to get out of the house tonight and have some fun for once," Parrish said. "You can't drape yourself in black and play the sad widow for the rest of your life."

"Yeah!" Maggy said.

"It's not that," Riley said. "I don't feel like being around a big crowd of people who are all going to be talking about me behind my back—'Poor Riley, bless her heart, lost her husband and her house, blah, blah, blah.' It gets old, fast."

"Oh, grow up," Parrish said. "I'm sorry to break it to you, sweetie, but you are officially no longer the talk of Belle Isle."

"And who is?" Riley offered her friend a blueberry muffin, but Parrish refused.

"It's a toss-up between Ginny Cranshaw and Nate Milas. Ginny was on the same ferry as Ed last night. She's sporting a huge new diamond—at least three carats, and she's definitely had her eyes done. Word is both the plastic surgery and the rock were a consolation prize from Woody after his latest affair with one of his surgical nurses."

"Parrish! Shh!"

"Too late, Mom. I already know about Dr. Cranshaw," Maggy said. "Holly said her mom found a bunch of texts from one of his girlfriends on his phone. So gross!" She reached across the table and clutched Riley's hand. "So can I do it, please?"

"I'm just not sure," Riley said. "I've never even met Annabelle's mom."

"She's super nice," Maggy said. "She took Annabelle all the way to D.C. for the Justin Bieber concert this year."

"Well, that definitely qualifies her for mother of the year, in my book," Riley said. "But you're still not spending the night with Annabelle until I talk to her super-cool mom and tell her about your diabetes and explain about your food and injections. . . ."

"Okay, great. I'll have her call you when she wakes up." Maggy jumped up from the table, planted a kiss on Riley's cheek, hugged Parrish, then dashed out the kitchen door with her backpack in hand.

"Wait! That wasn't a yes," Riley called, but Maggy was already pedaling down the path on her bike.

Parrish poured herself a glass of orange juice from the pitcher on the table. "And now you're free to go to the party with us tonight."

"I don't want to horn in on your time with the kids," Riley said. "What time did they finally get in last night?"

"They didn't. David texted at eleven that they couldn't get on any flights. It happens sometimes, when you're flying on a buddy pass. Especially on holiday weekends. Stupid me. I should have just told him to put a ticket on my Amex card."

"Oh, Parrish! I know you're bummed. And after you'd made all those plans, too."

"I've been crying like a big baby all morning long. Ed thinks I'm a menopausal mess. Which is why I'm glad you can go out with us tonight. I think we both deserve some fun."

"I never said I wanted to go," Riley said. "And I definitely never said I thought it was okay for my daughter to spend the night with a woman whose name I don't even know, and who apparently doesn't get up before eleven a.m. on Saturday."

"Relax," Parrish said. "Maggy introduced her to me at the pool this week. Her name is Chantelle and she seems perfectly nice."

"We'll see. And, by the way, thanks for meddling in my business."

"You're welcome," Parrish said. "So, it's settled. You're coming tonight."

"Nothing is settled," Riley said. She hesitated. "You said the other hot topic beside Ginny Cranshaw's facelift is Nate Milas? What's the latest?"

"I thought you didn't care about Nate Milas. Didn't you tell me you told him to stay away from you and your family?"

"That doesn't mean I don't want to know what kind of skullduggery he's up to now," Riley said. "If it affects this island, it affects me. Now spill it, because I know that's why you came over here."

"Since you insist," Parrish said impishly. "I had a fascinating conversation with Annie Milas at the Mercantile just now."

"Do tell."

"She told me Nate's been in meetings in Chapel Hill and Morehead City all week."

"Yippee. Probably lining up his dredging and demo permits."

"Actually, he's putting together plans to turn the Holtzclaw place into some kind of marine fisheries research facility. Annie said he's donating the land to UNC and building it out with docks for their boats and stuff, and that old house will be turned into classrooms and dorms. . . ."

"He's giving it away?" Riley asked. "You're sure he's not selling it?"

"That's what Annie said. She said Nate turned into a hippy-dippy conservationist while he was living in California. She was all worked up because she said she's sick of people insinuating he wants to turn Belle Isle into Myrtle Beach."

"Of course she'd defend him and put a positive spin on it. She's his mom. What else would you expect?" Riley said.

"You've really got it bad for Nate, don't you?"

"You're nuts," Riley said. "He's an arrogant ass."

"I like him. I've always thought he was a decent guy, and this seals the deal as far as I'm concerned. I don't understand why you're so suspicious of his motives. As far as I can tell, he wants what you want."

"I'm suspicious of him because I know him better than you do," Riley said. "And, unless he wants to keep the island the way it's always been, he definitely does not want what I want. I guarantee when he bought up all this land Wendell assembled, he had an agenda, the same as Wendell. He may have figured a way to put a happy, shiny spin on it for his mom and people like you, but it's there."

"You're hopeless," Parrish said. "Seriously, Riles. All this anger and bitterness is warping you. It's a holiday weekend. I'm trying not to be sad about missing David and Amanda. Come to the party with us tonight, okay? Forget all this drama. Let it go for one night and try to enjoy yourself. Will you? For me? Please?"

Riley got up and stared out the kitchen window at the bluff and the water below. Sailboats skimmed across the surface of the bay and the sky was an amazing blue. Carolina blue. She'd been so busy trying to salvage what was left of her life, she'd forgotten to savor the beauty right outside this window. Maybe Parrish was right.

"Okay, I'll go," she said, turning around to face her friend. "But I refuse to have fun."

"Deal," Parrish said. "We'll pick you up at seven. Try to look cute, would you?"

48

Nate collapsed into the armchair in front of the television. He had an ice-cold bottle of Corona in one hand and the remote control in the other. He heard the sound of tires crunching on the crushed-shell driveway outside his cabin, then light footsteps on the cabin's front porch. He didn't move. He didn't need to because he already knew who the visitor was.

Annie walked in without knocking. "What are you doing? It's time to go."

"Go? I'm not going anywhere," Nate informed her. "I'm beat. I've been in meetings or on the road all week. I just want to sit here, by myself, drink a beer, and watch a ball game."

His mother didn't move. She tried staring him down.

"Did I mention the 'by myself' part?" he repeated.

"Yeah, I'd like that, too," Annie retorted. "I've been up chopping vegetables and making salads since five a.m. because the café's prep chef didn't show up for work. And we've been slammed all day."

"So go home. You're the boss. You've earned a night off. And so have I."

"I can't, remember? We're catering the big party tonight. Wine and appetizers for a hundred and fifty people. Somebody has to take all of it out to the south beach and set up and serve."

"Nooooo," Nate groaned.

"I had a couple of the deckhands from the ferry take the tent out to the beach and put it up earlier. Now I need tables delivered and set up, the grills carried down there, and the big coolers with the food and wine and ice dragged down from the parking lot to the tent."

"I thought that's why you have staff at the café," Nate protested. But he knew it was a lost cause. Resistance was always futile where Annie Milas was concerned.

"Those skinny little college girls can't lift those heavy coolers," his mother said. "I can trust 'em to pour wine and serve, but somebody has to do the heavy lifting and man the grills."

"And you think that somebody should be me?"

"Who else?"

They could hear the steel-drum band warming up when they arrived at the south beach parking lot shortly after eight. Golf carts were lined up nose to nose, with more parked on the sandy shoulder of the road.

Men in colorful tropical-hued shirts and shorts, and women in their finest beach-casual cocktail wear strolled toward the boardwalk over the dunes, coolers and beach chairs in hand. Riley, Ed, and Parrish joined the parade.

Riley paused at the top of the dune and looked out at the spectacle below. Festive white party lights were strung from the corners of a large blue-and-white tent, attached to tall poles planted on the beach. The sky was already turning amethyst, and a breeze stirred the sea oats. Plumes of pork-scented smoke billowed up from a huge grill set at the edge of the tent. A hundred or more people were scattered around the bar and buffet tables. She heard laughter and froze for a moment.

She was already feeling panicky, having second thoughts. She'd promised Parrish she'd come, but that was a mistake. She wasn't ready yet. As if she could read her thoughts, her best friend tugged at her hand. "Come on. It'll be fun."

Riley stepped out of her gold sandals, leaving her shoes with all the footwear left by other partygoers. Her toes sank into the soft sand, still holding on to the last traces of the sun's warmth.

He saw her standing alone, at the edge of the dunes, frowning. She wore a long dress of some kind of pale pink gauzy fabric with a hem that fluttered in the breeze. The dress tied around her neck and showed a surprising amount of bare shoulders and cleavage—for Riley Nolan, anyway. Her dark hair was twisted into a braid that hung down her bare back. She looked like the same teenaged girl he'd spotted on this same beach so many years ago—ethereal and unattainable. Then and now.

That first time, she'd been with a group of her girlfriends from Raleigh. Nate knew she was a Nolan, and that her family were the original developers of Belle Isle, where he'd lived his whole life. He'd never noticed her before, but then, up until he'd turned fifteen, he'd never paid any attention to girls.

It was the summer of 1988, and she and her three friends had set up camp not far from this same stretch of sand, their lounge chairs arranged in a circle. They were giggling and drinking Diet Cokes from cans, and they all wore tantalizingly miniscule bikinis, except Riley, who wore a comparatively modest one-piece suit. Even now he could picture those summertime girls, their bodies shimmering with coconut-scented lotion. They had a suitcase-size boom box and they were listening to the huge hit of the summer, Robert Palmer's "Simply Irresistible," doing their best to copy the dance moves from the MTV video. He hadn't worked up the nerve to ask her out until the next summer, and had been astonished when she'd said yes.

After that summer, whenever he heard "Simply Irresistible," he thought of Riley Nolan.

She used to look good to me, Nate thought, *but now I find her simply irresistible.*

He held his breath for a moment. He was sure that if Riley spotted him at the party she'd turn around and leave. But she followed her friends onto the beach, stopping occasionally to speak to people, but never lingering. He remembered what she'd said on the ferry, right after Wendell's death, about not wanting people's pity. He watched her unfold a beach chair before heading over to the table where the bar was set up.

"Excuse me. Can I get one of those pork sliders?" A balding man with a sunburnt nose pointed toward the grill, and Nate went back to slicing and serving.

Riley drifted around the party, sipping her wine, making pleasant chitchat. Why was this so hard? Most of the people here she'd known for years. They were her neighbors. She knew their families, and they knew hers. She wasn't actually mourning Wendell. In fact, her rage at the predicament he'd left her in frightened her at times, it was so intense. So why did she feel so emotionally exposed tonight, her wounds still so raw?

"Are we having fun yet?" Billy approached, sipping a pale green concoction with a paper parasol and a hot-pink hibiscus blossom sticking out of the top of his cup.

"It seems weird, being at a party," she admitted. "I feel sort of guilty for even thinking about getting on with my life."

"You shouldn't feel guilty," Billy said. "Wendell never did, that sorry son of a bitch." His words slurred together, and his eyes were slightly glassy.

"How many of those umbrella drinks have you had tonight?" she asked.

"Too many, apparently," Billy said. "Scotty and I had words about it. And then he left. Now I don't even have a ride home."

"Scott worries about your drinking," Riley said. "I wish you'd cut back a little."

"Pfffft," he replied. "Hey, you look really pretty tonight, Riles." He plucked the hibiscus from his drink and tucked it behind her left ear. "I like your hair this way."

She touched the braid self-consciously. "Maggy taught me how. She'd seen a picture in one of her magazines."

"Where is the Magpie tonight?" he asked, looking around. "Is she over at Roo's, watching Animal Planet?"

"She's spending the night with her friend Annabelle. Against my better judgement. I left a voice mail message with her mom, just to check in, but the woman still hasn't called me back."

"Helicopter mom," Parrish said, walking up with Ed and handing Riley a glass of wine.

"She'll be fine," Billy said. "They're twelve-year-old girls. What kind of trouble could they get into?"

"Lots. When I think back to the kind of stunts we pulled at that age, I realize now why Mama went gray-haired while she was in her thirties," Riley said.

"Yeah. Remember that time we wanted to go to town to the movies, but we didn't have enough money for the movie and the ferry ticket?" Parrish asked. "So we rode our bikes over to the marina, then climbed inside one of those big empty Rubbermaid luggage totes and got ourselves loaded onto the boat without paying? What movie was it that we were so desperate to see?"

"It was *The Goonies*. And I still have nightmares about being locked up in small places like that," Riley said. "Remember how Captain Joe caught us trying to sneak onto the boat on the way back to the island?"

"And he threatened to call your daddy and tell on us, but instead he made us sweep out the snack bar for a whole week," Parrish said.

Ed looked from his wife to Parrish. "You were stowaways?"

"We were small for our age," Riley explained. She examined the plate of appetizers Ed was balancing on top of his plastic wineglass. "That looks amazing. I think I'll go get something to eat. Anybody want anything?"

Billy jiggled the ice cubes in his now-empty cup at his sister.

"Don't make me call Scott and rat you out," Riley said. "Go get some food and try to sober up, okay?"

She was walking toward the buffet table when one of the musicians stepped a little ways apart from the rest of the band. He raised a trumpet to his lips and played a slow rendition of "Taps." Riley turned and walked, as though in a trance, toward the ocean. The sky was an ombre patchwork ranging from palest purple to deep, midnight blue, and hanging low on the horizon was a staggeringly beautiful silvery moon.

Applause rippled through the crowd. She stood very still, gazing up at it. The day's worries and troubles slowly receded, and she was only aware of the sound of her own breathing and the sensation of waves lapping at her ankles and that luminescent moon, spilling liquid beauty.

The line for food had temporarily slowed. At the sound of the trumpet solo, Nate turned away from the grill for what seemed like the first time that night. He automatically scanned the crowd, wondering if she'd already left. And then he spotted her. She was silhouetted in the moonlight, standing in ankle-deep water, her face tilted up to the sky. He must have been staring at her for a good five minutes until a voice broke in and brought him back to reality.

"Hey, man, are there any of those shrimp-skewer things left?"

"Oh, yeah," he said. He reached for his tongs and placed two kabobs on an outstretched plate.

"And could I get some of that grilled pineapple salsa on the side?"

Nate scooped a spoonful from the cast-iron skillet he'd shoved to the side of the massive grill and dumped it on the customer's plate. He heard coins clinking in the tip jar one of the college girls had placed prominently on the buffet table to his right, but still he watched Riley Nolan until she reluctantly turned her back on the moon and started to walk toward the food tent.

She was starving. The line at the buffet table had dwindled to less than a dozen people. Riley took a plastic plate and helped herself from trays of appetizers lined up on the long table: cheese and crackers, crab dip, bacon-wrapped blue cheese–stuffed dates, and fruit skewers. But it was the pork-scented aroma emanating from the grill that drew her like a magnet.

Finally she reached the front of the line. The server had his back to her, slicing a charred slab of pork tenderloin. His head and torso were wreathed in smoke that poured from the grill.

"Medium or well-done?" His tongs were poised over the sliced meat.

"Medium, please," Riley said, extending her plate toward him. Her eyes stung from the peppery smoke. She coughed and blinked and realized too late that the server was Nate Milas.

He was wearing a flowery Hawaiian-print shirt, jeans, and latex disposable gloves, and he needed a shave.

"Want a shrimp kabob?" he asked gruffly.

"Oh, uh, sure," she said.

"Pineapple salsa?"

"That sounds good," Riley said. She extended her plate again, and he heaped it with shrimp and grilled fruit.

"Nate Milas!"

Andrea Payne bore down on them like a guided missile. Riley started to escape, but it was too late.

"Is it true then?" Andrea demanded, addressing the server. "About the new marine research facility you're going to build?"

"I don't know what you're talking about, Andrea," he said, keeping his voice low.

"Oh, come on now. A little birdie told me you're donating the Holtzclaw property to UNC!" Andrea exclaimed. She turned to Riley. "That was one of the pieces of land Wendell bought, just before he was killed, wasn't it? Isn't it nice that something so wonderful could come out of your personal tragedy?"

Riley felt her face flush deep red.

"Where did you hear that?" Nate asked.

"I have my sources," Andrea said. "Come on now, don't be so mysterious."

"I can't talk about it," Nate said flatly. "And I really wish you wouldn't either."

"You're just being modest," Andrea said. "I heard your mother telling Parrish Godchaux all about it at the Mercantile this morning."

Nate's expression remained deadpan. "Can I get you a shrimp or something, Andrea?"

"No, thanks, I never eat food from a grill. So unsanitary." She looked from Nate to Riley. "Toodles, you two."

Nate shook his head. "I don't know who I'm going to kill first, my mother or Andrea Payne."

"I vote for Barbie," Riley said.

"Who?"

"That's what we call her. Belle Isle Barbie," she confessed.

"Why's that?"

"Because she's skinny and has plastic boobs. Don't be mad at your mom," Riley said hastily. "Parrish told me about the conversation she had with Annie this morning at the café. Your mom was just sticking up for you."

"How did the topic even come up?"

Riley stared down at her plate of food as she felt her cheeks burn. She forced herself to meet his eyes. "I might have told Parrish how angry I was that you were going to tear down the wildlife sanctuary and pave the island. And then, this morning, I guess Andrea was eavesdropping when Annie told Parrish the truth, that you were donating it to UNC."

"Nothing's finalized yet," Nate said. "The university trustees have to vote on it, and it'll have to go before the county commission for approval."

"I think I owe you an apology," Riley said. She hesitated. "Can I buy you a drink? When you're done here?"

"I'm done right now," Nate said. There was nobody left in the food line. The platters of food had been emptied of everything but the lettuce leaf garnishes and the occasional lonely orange slice. He set the tongs on the table and stripped off his apron and latex gloves. "Your place or mine?"

49

You seem to forget I don't have a place of my own," Riley said.

"I don't really feel like hanging around here much longer," Nate said. "What would you think about going to the Duck Inn?"

"Is that a new bar on the island?"

"It's my cabin. We could go there, unless you think it's too, uh, private."

"That sounds fine," Riley said. "Let me just tell Parrish I'm leaving. I need to make sure she gives Billy a ride home. He shouldn't be driving tonight."

"In the meantime, I'll let Annie know I'm clocking out. Meet you back here in five minutes?"

"Sure thing. Can you do me one favor?" Riley asked, handing him her plate. "Save this for me. I didn't have dinner tonight, and I'm starving."

She found Parrish and Ed sitting on their beach chairs at the water's edge, holding hands and gazing up at the moon.

How lucky they are, Riley thought.

"Hello, young lovers," she said, smiling down at them. "I'm gonna head out. Will you take Billy home?"

Parrish frowned. "You're leaving already? It's not even ten o'clock. How are you getting home?"

"She didn't say she was going home," Ed pointed out.

"If you must know, I'm going to go have a drink with Nate," Riley said.

"Doesn't the bar at the Sea Biscuit close down at nine?" Parrish asked.

"Mind your own business," Riley told her.

"Are you cold?" Nate asked as he backed the cart out of the south beach parking lot.

Riley sat on the bench seat beside him with her arms wrapped tightly across her chest.

"A little," she admitted. "I forget how fast temperatures drop on the island after the sun goes down. Even in July."

"Here." He handed her the Hawaiian shirt Annie had issued him earlier in the night.

"Thanks," she said, pulling her arms through the sleeves and buttoning it up. Nate immediately regretted his generosity because the shirt covered her lovely bare neck, shoulders, and chest.

"Won't Annie be mad at you for leaving her to do all the cleanup by herself?" Riley asked.

"Her café girls can handle the cleanup. And I'll come back early in the morning to break down the tent and load out the tables and chairs. Anyway, what's she gonna do, fire me?"

"You two seem to work so well together," Riley said.

"Annie and I have our moments," Nate said, steering the cart through the dense tunnel of greenery that led to his cabin. "After I'd been back here a few weeks, helping out, she let me know she was quite capable of handling the Mercantile and the ferry without any meddling from me."

"Was that when you decided to start your own business here?"

Nate turned to look at her. "Can we talk about this without you wanting to throw something at me?"

"Yes," Riley said solemnly. "I'm ready to listen, if you're ready to talk."

"Let's wait until we get to the cabin, okay?"

"Sure," Riley said.

The road veered sharply to the left and transitioned into more of a narrow path. The undergrowth was so dense here that it nearly shut out the moonlight. All around them were night sounds: the thrum of cicadas, croaks and peeps of tree frogs and peepers, and a lonely whip-poor-will.

"I don't think I've ever been to this part of the island," Riley said. "Where exactly are we?"

"This is Sandy Point, and you wouldn't have been here unless you were a duck hunter," he said. He made two more sharp turns and finally steered the cart into a clearing.

"Here we are," he announced.

The cabin was unassuming, built of unpainted cedar. Its foundation sat on sturdy tree stumps, and the tin-roofed porch was held up by stout cedar trunks, bark and all.

Nate got out of the cart and grabbed a backpack, and Riley followed suit. "Watch out for that first step. It's pretty steep," he warned. She climbed onto the porch, and he held the screen door open. "Welcome to Duck Inn."

"This is so cool," she said, turning around in the living-dining-kitchen room. "So, what? Rustic?"

"Primitive? Manly? Barbaric?"

"It's not barbaric at all." She laughed.

"Make yourself at home," Nate said. "I grabbed a couple of bottles of wine from the party—do you like white or red? Or I've got cold beer if you want that."

"White's good," she said. "Would you mind if I looked around? I've never been in a hunting cabin before."

"Go ahead," he said, opening a wooden cupboard to search for something resembling a wineglass. "It's only two bedrooms, so I don't think you need a guided tour."

The room on the right held two sets of built-in pine bunk beds, but Nate was obviously using it as storage. Neatly labeled cardboard moving boxes were stacked against the walls, and in one corner of the room leaned half a dozen fishing poles, assorted tackle boxes, and two beautiful old shotguns.

There was a bathroom with a sink and commode and a shower stall lined with what looked like galvanized metal sheeting. The fixtures were ancient and rust-stained and the vinyl flooring was peeling.

She crossed the living room to the other bedroom, which he'd obviously fixed up for himself. There was an unmade double bed and nightstands made from upended wooden wine crates. An old pine dresser spilled clothing, and a faded oval braided rug covered the wooden floor. The bathroom was clean but basic.

"I wasn't expecting company, so it's kind of a mess," Nate called from the living room. "I thought I was going to spend a quiet night at home until Annie shanghaied me into helping out at the party."

She walked back into the living room, and he handed her a pint jelly glass filled with Chardonnay and gestured to the sofa—the nicest piece in the cabin, it was made of soft glove leather and looked expensive.

"I haven't had a whole lot of time to do anything with the place," he said, taking a seat beside her. "I was staying at my parents' house, until one day Annie announced that she thought it was absurd for a grown man to be living with his mama. This place was available, and the price was right, so I bought it." He took a long drink from his bottle of beer.

"I'm in the same position, you know," Riley said. "Except my mother is delighted to have Maggy and me under her roof—and under her thumb."

"But it's probably good for Maggy, having family around now, right?"

"Maybe," Riley said. "I really do admire the relationship you and Annie have. It seems so easy and natural for you to work together. I love Evelyn, but if she and I had to be together in a business, I'd have to kill her for sure."

"Did you ever think about working in the family business?" Nate asked.

"You mean Belle Isle Enterprises? That was never an option for me. My great-grandfather Riley started the business with his brother, and then when Mama married my father, he turned it over to my dad."

"And then you married Wendell and your father turned it over to him to run," Nate said.

"Daddy used to brag that he chose Wendell before I did," Riley said, swirling the wine around in her glass. "Wendell was already working for Daddy when we met. He used to say he saw my photo on Dad's desk and was, quote, 'intrigued by my beauty,' end quote. Typical Wendell bullshit."

"The beauty part wasn't bullshit," Nate said, touching her chin lightly. "I always thought you were the prettiest girl on the island when we were teenagers, but you're even more beautiful now."

"You thought I was pretty? That's so sweet. I didn't think you knew I was alive."

"I didn't pay much attention to girls until I was fifteen, but believe me, I knew who you were. I kinda had a crush on you. But it was clear you were way out of my class."

"Hah! I guess I was too busy being the super-nerdy Beta Club president-slash-school newspaper editor, until my senior year of high school. But believe me, that summer, all my girlfriends had the hots for the hunky deckhand on the ferry, because we thought you looked exactly like Don Johnson."

"Who?"

"The guy who played Sonny on *Miami Vice*. You always had that same stubble he had."

Nate laughed. "That's because I was too lazy to get up in time to shave before I went to work, and my dad wouldn't allow his employees to have beards, because he said only bums had beards."

Riley sipped her wine. "I was just remembering—that summer, my girlfriends and I would always try to get down to Southpoint in time for either the early-morning ferry or the last one of the day, because we figured out that's when you'd be working."

"Because I had football practice during the day," Nate said.

"I thought you were sexy as hell back then," Riley said.

"I've still got the stubble," Nate pointed out.

She reached out and ran a finger down the graying stubble on his jawline. "And I think maybe I've still got the hots for you."

"But earlier, at the Holtzclaws, you accused me of everything just short of burning down this precious island of yours."

"I know," Riley said with a sigh. "And I want to apologize for the way I treated you. I've been a total bitch. Suspicious and paranoid."

"Not bitchy, but you sure made it clear you wanted no part of me or anything I wanted to do here. What made you change your mind?"

"It was something Parrish said. She told me I was bitter and unforgiving, and she was right. And then, when I heard what Annie told Parrish about your donating the Holtzclaw property to the university, it made me realize who you really are and what you want. Why didn't you just tell me that the day we were together?"

"It wasn't a done deal yet. It still isn't. I think it will happen, and I'm excited about it, but it's early days yet. And, let's face it, you wouldn't have believed me anyway."

"I do now," Riley said. "Parrish was right, damn her. You do want what I want."

She inched over beside him on the sofa, until she was close enough to smell the wood smoke on his skin and hair and clothes.

"Riley Nolan. Are you trying to put the moves on me?" Nate pretended to be shocked.

"If you have to ask, I must be doing it wrong," Riley said, leaning in to kiss him.

She'd known this would happen, from the moment she'd asked to buy him a drink back on the beach. Maybe even before that.

Her kiss was tentative at first, and tender.

Riley felt his lips curve beneath hers, into a smile, and then he was holding her face between both hands and the kisses became deeper and more insistent. She slid backward onto the sofa, pulling him down with her, and they were lying sideways, facing each other, the space between them disappearing, the old fears and distrust dissolving.

She ran her hands up under the back of his T-shirt, craving the feel of his warm skin beneath her splayed fingertips. His shoulder muscles knotted at her touch. She slid her hands around to his chest, felt his rib cage, brushed one nipple with her thumb. He inhaled sharply, and she felt him smiling again.

Nate nibbled at her earlobe and found the hollow in her throat. She inched his shirt upward, letting the palms of her hands rest lightly against his erect nipples.

He kissed her deeply, his tongue teasing hers, while his hands found her breasts, gently pushing them upward until they spilled from the deep V neckline of her dress. His lips found one nipple, kissed it, teased it, nipped at it, and she rolled onto her back to allow equal time for the other nipple.

Riley let her hand slide down his abdomen until it was resting squarely on the crotch of his jeans. His response was immediate. He reached for the hem of her dress. It was still damp and sandy from where she'd stood in the waves, a lifetime ago, watching the moon spill silver onto the night.

Nate tugged the dress upward, past her hips. He stopped suddenly, propping his head on one hand, gazing down at her. There was that smile again.

"You keep doing that," Riley said.

"I smile when I'm having a good time," he said, trailing a fingertip down her chest, toying with her nipple again. "Don't you?"

"Maybe, but I can't remember when I've had as good a time as this," she said truthfully, kissing him again, rolling his T-shirt up, then pulling it over his shoulders as he very helpfully raised his arms to allow her to remove it entirely.

She gazed down at his sun-browned chest, at the golden and silver curls of hair, and then at the dark line of hair that extended below his navel, toward his groin. Her fingertips followed the trail, pausing at the metal snap of his jeans.

"And we're just getting started," Nate promised. He reached behind her neck and expertly untied the halter top with one hand. He'd always been good with knots. A moment later, he yanked the dress over her head, tossing it to the floor. Riley curved herself into him, yearning to feel the warmth of him pressed tight to the entire length of her body. Moments later, he'd done away with her panties, his knee parted her bare legs, and his hand was sliding down and into her, and when she moaned very softly she could feel his smile grow wider, matching hers, because she was having a very, very good time.

Riley cupped her hands on Nate's butt, drawing him closer, feeling the bite of the metal snap over his swollen fly digging into the sensitive flesh of her belly. She reached around and managed, with both hands, to unfasten the snap and slide the metal zipper slowly downward. She tugged at his waistband, hooking her thumbs into the fabric of his briefs and jeans, rolling them down over his narrow hips past his erection and then to his knees, before using her toes to push them around his ankles.

Nate stood, kicked off the rest of his clothes, and pulled Riley to her feet. He placed a hand on either side of her face, resting his forehead against hers. "Do you have any idea how long I've wanted this?" he asked.

"No," Riley whispered, kissing him lightly. "How long?"

"Since the first time I saw you prancing around in that one-piece bathing suit of yours, on the beach, with your friends. You were all dancing around, trying to copy the girls in that Robert Palmer video."

She buried her head in his chest. " 'Simply Irresistible?' " Oh, my God! You saw that? I was such a klutz. I would have died if I'd known somebody saw us."

"Nobody saw you but me," Nate said. "But if I'd known what was under that bathing suit of yours . . ." He ran his hands slowly down her back, grinding his hips into hers. "I've always wanted you, Riley. Always."

"I was just a stupid, naïve girl the first time we were together," Riley said. "I didn't want you then, or maybe I did, but I was too dumb to realize it. But I do now. I've wanted you for a while, but I just didn't know it until now. Right now." She kissed him and felt the heat and need within her building to a fever pitch.

"You're sure?" he asked. "No second thoughts?"

"I'm sure." Riley looked up at him, suddenly shy, through lowered eyelashes. "I think I'm ready to smile again."

50

Nate rolled onto his side and draped an arm over Riley's side, caressing her breast. He pressed his lips to her ear. "You finally had your way with me, after all these years. Was it worth the wait?"

His beard tickled her cheek, and she could feel his erection pressing into her side. She slid just out of his reach and turned to face him. "The question is, was I worth your wait?"

He cast his eyes downward. "You can't tell?"

"I don't know if I'll ever stop smiling," Riley said.

"Then don't," Nate said, closing the space between them, running his hand down her flank. He started to slide his leg between her legs. "I bet I can find a way to keep us both smiling. All night long. Tomorrow, too."

"I can't stay," she said. "You know that. It must be after midnight now."

"So? Do you have a curfew?"

"Mama will be wondering where I am."

"You're forty-two years old, Riley. Tell her you met a charming man on the beach, took him home, and seduced him."

"Who seduced who?" she said playfully.

"You kissed me first," Nate pointed out. "I was just being polite."

She yawned widely. "I certainly do love your good manners." She sat up in the bed, clutching the sheet to her chest and glancing around the darkened room.

"I wonder what happened to my clothes?"

"You don't need no stinkin' clothes," Nate growled, dropping kisses on her shoulders. "You're gorgeous just like this."

"That's very nice," Riley said demurely. "But it might turn some heads if I ride home naked in your golf cart. Just think what Belle Isle Barbie would have to say about that! The coconut telegraph would be working overtime."

"Who cares?" Nate reached over and turned on the lamp on the nightstand.

"I do. I have a twelve-year-old daughter, remember?" Riley clapped her hands over her mouth. "Oh my God! Maggy! I completely forgot about her."

"You forgot you have a kid?" Nate walked into the living room and returned with her dress and panties.

"No! She was spending the night at her friend Annabelle's house. I left messages for the mother, but she never called me back."

"So?"

"So I've never met this woman. Her name is Chantelle. I needed to explain to her about Maggy's insulin, and her exchanges . . ."

"Why can't Maggy tell her?" he asked.

"She could, but who knows if she will? Oh my God. I am the worst mother ever!"

Riley grabbed her clothes and began dressing. "My phone! I don't even know where my phone is. What if she tried to call? What if Maggy was sick. . . ."

Nate walked calmly into the living room. Through the open bedroom door she saw him pull on his discarded jeans and walk out the front door, barefoot.

A moment later she heard the screen door slam and he was back, handing her the phone. "It was in the cup holder in the cart."

Riley took the phone and examined it. "No text messages. I guess that's a good sign. But there's one missed call and a voice message. I don't recognize the number, but it looks like a Durham area code."

Riley tapped the message and turned on the speaker.

The caller was a woman, with a slight Southern accent. *"Hi. This is Chantelle Roberts. Sorry we've missed each other. I just wanted to let you know the girls finally settled down and went to bed. Maggy checked her blood sugar and everything's fine. I'll have her call you in the morning. Thanks so much for letting her spend the night. I think they've had a real good time."*

"Thank God," Riley said, exhaling loudly. "If something had happened tonight while I was here . . ." She shuddered. "I would never forgive myself."

"But nothing did happen," Nate pointed out. "What does Maggy do about her diabetes when you're not around? Like, when she's at school?"

"She knows how to test her blood and she gives herself insulin. But this is different."

"How?"

"At school her teachers know about her diabetes and they know what to do if she's in trouble. There's a trained nurse in the school clinic. . . ."

"And there was a responsible adult parent tonight at her friend's house," Nate said. "And nothing bad happened."

"But it could have," Riley insisted. "I'm sorry, Nate, but you've never had kids, especially a sick kid. You wouldn't understand."

"Okay, okay," Nate said. He moved behind Riley and knotted the tie of her halter dress, stopping to nuzzle her neck again.

"I'll take you home, dressed, if you insist. But what about tomorrow night? Can we do this again?"

She turned and put her arms around his neck. "That would be lovely, but let me see what's going on at home. Okay? I'm supposed to go to a cookout at Parrish's house."

Nate kissed her deeply and sighed. "After? Before? Doesn't matter to me. I just want to be with you."

"We'll see," Riley promised. She walked into the living room to look for her shoes and spotted her half-empty wineglass and full plate of food.

"You never did feed me last night," she said accusingly.

"No, I did something a lot better for you," he said.

"Way better," she agreed.

51

Maggy burst into the kitchen door at eleven Sunday morning, her eyes shining with excitement. "Mom! I had the best time ever at Annabelle's last night."

"Who's Annabelle?" asked Scott. He'd arrived thirty minutes earlier with his brunch contribution, a batch of blueberry scones fresh from the oven, but no Billy.

"My new best friend," Maggy said, sitting down at the table across from her grandmother and beside her great-aunt Roo. "She lives in Durham, so after school starts back, we can probably hang out on weekends and stuff."

"I'm glad," Riley said, handing her daughter a plate. "Did you eat this morning?"

"Yes, Mom," Maggy said, rolling her eyes. "And I tested my blood, and I took my insulin. Can I just have some strawberries?"

"Help yourself," Riley said. "Can I ask what you did at Annabelle's that was so fabulous?"

"Chantelle let us order takeout pizza. Two different kinds."

Mimi set her bone-china coffee cup down on its saucer. "Young lady, does Annabelle's mother have a proper name?"

"I don't know, Mimi. Everybody just calls her Chantelle. Even Annabelle. And Chantelle said I should call her that."

"What is this Annabelle's father's last name?" Evelyn asked.

Riley tried to signal to her mother to abandon this line of questioning, but Evelyn Nolan was not someone to be deterred.

"I don't think Annabelle has a father," Maggy said. "But Chantelle's girlfriend's name is Micki. Spelled with an *i*. She's cool too, but she had to work this weekend."

"Girlfriend?" Evelyn said, frowning.

"Domestic partner," Maggy said. "You know, like Bebo and Uncle Scotty."

Scott turned his head and discreetly spat a mouthful of French-press coffee into his linen napkin.

"Ohhh," Roo said. "You mean this Chantelle is a lesbian. I didn't know there were any lesbians on Belle Isle."

Scott coughed violently, and Riley could see his back heaving with suppressed laughter. She passed him a glass of water and he took a sip, shooting her a grateful look.

"Do you know those girls, Scott?" Evelyn asked.

"Um, no, Evvy," he said politely. "Actually not every gay person in Carolina knows every other gay person."

"Hmm," Evelyn said.

"Where is Bebo this morning, Uncle Scott?" Maggy asked. "We're supposed to have our first doubles match at noon."

Scott cut his eyes at Riley. "He's got a bit of a headache this morning, Mags. But I'll make sure he gets there in plenty of time."

"Ohhh." Maggy nodded knowingly. "A hangover. From the party last night, right?"

"How was the party, Riley?" Evelyn asked, skillfully changing the subject.

"It was nice," Riley said. "I've never seen such a beautiful moon. It looked like it would drop into the ocean it was so huge and low over the water."

"You must have had a good time. I didn't hear you come in until after midnight," Evelyn said.

"Was it that late? I guess I lost track of the time," she said. She felt her phone buzz in the pocket of her shorts, signaling an incoming text message.

She jumped up and ducked into the butler's pantry.

The text was from Nate.

Dinner tonight?

I'll get back to you, she typed.

After Maggy had gone upstairs to change for her tennis match, Riley started clearing the brunch dishes.

"Um, Mama, don't count on me for dinner tonight," she said. "Parrish and Ed want me to come over before the fireworks, and I said I would because she's upset that David and his girlfriend had to cancel their trip."

"Just tell them to come over here," Evelyn said. "You know I always plan for extras for Sunday supper."

"Sunday?" Riley groaned inwardly. "This long holiday weekend has me all mixed up. I was thinking today was Saturday."

"No. It's Sunday," Evelyn said. "I'm doing a tenderloin. Ed loves my tenderloin."

"I'll ask," Riley said. "But the thing is, Parrish bought this gorgeous salmon filet when we went to town Friday, and I know it won't keep another day. It won't hurt for me to miss supper here this one time."

"We always have family supper on Sundays, Riley," Evelyn said. "You know that. Why would you make other plans?"

"Maybe I want to make other plans," Riley snapped. "Good God. It's just one Sunday. Billy and Scott will be here, and so will Maggy."

"It's not the same if everybody isn't here," Evelyn said, tears welling up in her pale blue eyes. "All I ask of you children is one night a week. Why is that so difficult?"

"Fine!" Riley said, throwing her hands up in defeat. "Fine. I'll be here. I'll eat the damn tenderloin, and then I'll go out."

"Good," Evelyn said. "And what about Parrish and Ed?"

"No," Riley said. "Parrish and Ed are not related to us by blood or marriage, so you don't get to guilt trip them into making a command appearance here."

Riley was waiting on the front porch when Billy pulled up in his golf cart. His hair was still damp from the shower, and the bags under his bloodshot eyes were impressive.

Riley hurried down the steps and snatched the plastic tumbler from her brother's hand, dumping the contents onto the lawn.

"Hey!" he protested. "That was Sprite."

"Sprite and what?" Riley demanded.

"Ice cubes. You can smell my breath if you don't believe me."

"No, thanks," Riley said. "You want to drink yourself into a coma at home, be my guest. But I don't want your niece seeing you shitfaced before noon. She happens to love you, Billy, and she's already had enough loss in her life this summer."

"Geez. Would you chill? I just told you I'm stone-cold sober, Miss Breathalyzer."

"For a change," Riley said.

Behind them, the screen door opened, and Maggy ran down the steps, racquet in hand. "Ready, Bebo," she said. Billy had the cart rolling down the drive before Riley had a chance to say good-bye.

She waited until Evelyn and Roo had gone off to play bridge and the house was empty. Riley took her phone out to the bluff and sat in one of the oversize Adirondack chairs.

Nate picked up on the first ring. "Hi," he said. "I was hoping you'd call. Are we set for tonight? I could pick up a steak at the market to grill over here, or if you wanted to eat out . . ."

"I can't tonight," she said. "It totally slipped my mind that today is Sunday."

"You don't eat dinner on Sunday?" He laughed at his own joke. "Have you joined some weird religious cult?"

"Sunday dinner with the family at Shutters is Mama's religion," Riley said.

"Can't you get out of it, just this once?"

"I tried. It's pretty much a nonnegotiable issue with her."

Silence.

"I'd invite you to join us, but I really don't want to subject you to the whole family just yet," Riley said. "Mostly, I just want to keep you to myself for a while longer."

"You mean, you don't want Maggy to know you're seeing me," Nate said. "It's okay. I guess I get it."

"This is not what I want," Riley said, sounding as miserable as she felt.

"How about later, after dinner, for the fireworks?" he asked.

"Perfect," she said eagerly. "Mama hates fireworks, but Roo loves 'em. I'll get her to take Maggy, who'll want to be with her friends on the beach at the club."

"And where will you say you're going?" he asked.

"I'll lie like a rug," she said cheerfully. "I'm sure Parrish will cover for me with Mama. It'll be like we were college kids again."

"I don't suppose you want me to pick you up?" Nate asked.

"No!" It came out a little faster and a little more emphatic than she'd intended. "I'll meet you—how about at the Mercantile?"

"Under the cover of darkness?"

"I don't like this any better than you do," Riley said. "I'll be there no later than eight. Okay?"

"See you then," he said.

Riley was about to dial Parrish when her friend walked out onto the lawn and dropped down onto the chair next to her.

"It's really uncanny how you always know when I'm about to call you," Riley said. "It's like you have some kind of superpower."

"More like I'm super curious to hear how things went with Nate last night."

"Fine."

"How fine?" Parrish studied her face carefully.

"I think you could say very fine."

Parrish sighed happily. "You slept with him. Finally! Thank God."

"I never said that," Riley said.

"You don't have to. I can tell by the look on your face. I'm so glad. Nate Milas is a good guy. A great guy. He's twice the man Wendell Griggs ever hoped to be."

"He's sweet," Riley admitted. "I hate to admit it, but you were right. It felt so good, letting go of all that . . . stuff . . . I was carrying around. I can't get over how easy it is, being with him. I'd forgotten how much fun he was, back when we were in college."

"I just love being right," Parrish said. "It makes my whole damn week. When are you seeing him again?"

"He wanted me to have dinner with him tonight, but I told him I couldn't."

"And why not?"

"Because it's Sunday. And you know how Mama is about Sunday supper."

"Just tell her you made other plans," Parrish said.

"I tried. And she laid that 'I never ask much of you children' crap on me, and of course, I caved."

"Of course," Parrish said. "Everybody always caves in to Evvy. And that's *her* superpower. She brandishes guilt like a light saber."

"You're just lucky I told her she couldn't guilt trip you and Ed into coming tonight."

"Us? How did we get roped into this?"

"I tried to tell her that I needed to have dinner with you guys, because you're sad about the kids not coming, but then she insisted you could just have dinner with us. Because Ed loves her tenderloin."

"No offense, but your mother's tenderloin is indistinguishable from shoe leather."

"I know. But since you don't have to suffer her cooking tonight, I thought you could do me one other teensy little favor."

"Which is?"

"Cover for me. I told her I was going to watch the fireworks from your house."

"But instead you and Nate are going to have your own private fireworks."

Riley found herself smiling again. "Something like that."

Nate had one hand on the golf cart's steering wheel and the other draped across Riley's shoulder. It was twilight, and the cicadas were already tuning up.

"This isn't the way to your cabin," she said.

"I know." He leaned over and sniffed her hair. "You smell nice. Is that the same perfume you wore in college?"

"I can't believe you remembered," Riley said.

"There is nothing I don't remember about you," Nate said.

"If we're not going to your place, where are we going?" she asked.

"To watch the fireworks. At the Holtzclaw place." He handed her a can of insect repellant. "You'll need that."

A new padlock had been installed on the gate since Riley's last visit. "We should have a pretty good view from the dock," Nate said. He produced a flashlight and trained it on the newly mowed yard, pointing in the direction of the creek.

"Is that dock safe to walk on?"

"It is now. I spent the morning over here, putting down new decking and cleaning up around the place."

There was a light shining from the end of the dock, and as they drew closer, she saw that Nate hadn't just nailed down a few boards. He'd also set up a pair of chaise longue chairs with a low table between them. A citronella candle burned in a jar, and an ice bucket held a bottle of wine.

"This is perfect," Riley marveled. "You managed to do all this in just one day?"

"I sort of started planning this from the minute I bought the place," Nate admitted. "The hard part was figuring out how to get you to stop hating me long enough to see what I see."

"You amaze me, you know that?" Riley said.

He opened the wine and poured two glasses. "First things first," he said, wrapping his arms around her waist and kissing her deeply.

As if on cue, a burst of silver-and-gold rockets shot upward from a barge anchored out in the sound, lighting up the inky night sky.

"It's starting!" Riley said.

Somehow, they ended up on the same lounge chair, and then, eventually, on the newly repaired dock. "I should have put an air mattress out here," Nate grumbled. "We'll be picking splinters out of our asses for a week."

Riley stood and pulled on her shorts. "My hair is a disaster," she said ruefully.

"Your hair is beautiful," Nate said, running his fingers through it.

They stood watching the fireworks until the grand finale, which featured a huge, waving American flag surrounded by cascades of Roman candles.

"Time to go," Riley said. "Maggy will be getting home from the club, and I don't want to have to answer too many questions from Mama."

Nate started to say something, but stopped himself.

"I'm headed out in the morning," he said, after they started back toward the Mercantile.

"You mean to Southpoint?"

"For starters. I've got meetings with some of the marine-ecology faculty in Chapel Hill, then I'm going to Charlotte to meet with some architects and talk to the finance guys, and then I'll head to Morehead City to tour the research facility there."

"Finance guys?" she said.

"Yes. Buying the land was just the first step. There will be some development on this end of the island, you realize that now, right?"

"I guess." She looked away.

"But it won't be anything like what Wendell was planning. We'll do a medium-density mixed-use project at Pirate's Point. A much smaller boutique hotel, more like an inn, really. Some retail, and some town houses built around a sort of village green space. I'm also going to talk to some of the forestry folks at the university, to see if there's some kind of mitigation we can do to that portion of the wildlife sanctuary that Wendell started clearing."

"Really?"

"No promises," Nate said. "Those were old-growth trees he knocked down, and you can't exactly go to a nursery and buy that kind of thing."

“When will you be back?” she asked.

“Week after next, I hope,” Nate said.

“That long?”

“Meet me in Charlotte next weekend,” he urged. “I’ll get a suite at the Ritz-Carlton, and we can have some nice dinners. It would do you good to get away from the island for a few days.”

“You don’t know how much I’d love that,” she said wistfully. “But what would I tell Maggy? And Mama? And, anyway, I’ve got stuff I need to do here.”

“Like what?”

“For starters, I need to get serious about looking for a job. Maggy starts back to her new school in a month. I’ve got to find a way to pay for her tuition.”

“A month?” Nate said, startled. “Summer’s just getting started. *We’re* just getting started. Labor Day isn’t until September.”

“As Maggy would say, ‘get in the now.’ Lots of the private schools, including hers, start in early August, because they let out in May.”

“Sending kids back to school before Labor Day is un-American,” he said. They’d arrived at the village, and he pulled his golf cart alongside hers.

Riley glanced around the lot, which was almost empty because the fireworks had ended nearly an hour earlier. Nate was kissing her, even before she could give him the “all clear” signal.

“You know what I wish?” he said, when she reluctantly started to get out of the cart.

“What?”

“I’m headed out on the first ferry tomorrow. Every summer, I’ve watched guys like your dad, and Wendell, and Ed Godchaux head back to work after the weekend, and for years I’ve watched wives and girlfriends sending them off and then picking them up the following Friday. Just once, I wish there was somebody waiting for me on Friday when the ferry docks.”

52

Scott was sitting on the chair opposite the sofa when Billy opened one bleary eye on Monday morning. He was dressed for travel, and his overnight bag stood by the door.

"Oh, God," Billy moaned, jumping off the sofa and heading for the bathroom. "I overslept. What time is it? Don't worry. I can take you to the ferry. Is there any coffee?"

"It's seven. Riley is going to take me to the ferry. And there's coffee in the kitchen."

Scott stood outside the bathroom door, waiting.

"See?" Billy said, drying his hands and face with a towel. "I'm all set."

"Too late," Scott said. "But we need to talk before I leave."

"Again?" Billy lurched toward the kitchen and the coffeepot.

"Your drinking is out of control. I think you need to go back to AA," Scott said.

"No, I need to go back to work," Billy said. "I've been thinking about this a lot, since, well, Wendell. I can't just hang around the island all summer being Evelyn's glorified houseboy. I've got a gig this week. That's a good start, right?"

Scott walked over to the counter, to the half-empty jug of Stoli, and dumped its contents into the sink. "This is a good start, Billy. Spending one entire day sober. That's a good start. When was the last time you went twenty-four hours without a drink? Do you even know?"

Billy glugged down half a mug of black coffee, then poured a refill. "You make it sound like I'm a big lush," he protested. "Okay, yes, I like a cocktail most days. Who does that hurt? You're gone all week. I get bored."

"I was here this weekend. I got off the ferry Friday night, and you met me with a cocktail in your hand. You were wasted both Friday and Saturday night, and both mornings you made yourself a Bloody Mary before I'd even gotten up."

Scott pointed at the now-empty vodka bottle. "That was a new bottle on Saturday. Face it, Billy, you've gone off the rails. You need help."

Billy took the coffee into the living room and sat down at the piano, flexing his fingers before starting to do scales.

"What I need is a job and a source of income," he said. He looked up at Scott. "Can we not fight about this anymore? It's giving me a headache."

They heard the firehouse's front door open. Riley poked her head around the corner. "Scotty? Are you ready?"

Scott sat down beside Billy on the piano bench and put his hand over his partner's on the keyboard. "No more fighting. I've got to go. Will you think about what I just said? Please?"

Billy sighed deeply. "I'll try."

Scott set his suitcase on the back of the cart beside Evelyn's pink-and-white golf bag, then joined Riley on the front seat.

"Did you talk to him?" she asked.

Scott nodded. "I tried. He seems to think that if he goes back to work, that will be some kind of magic cure. He does have a paying gig this week. I forget where. I told him he needs to go back to AA, but he's still in denial."

"What will you do if he doesn't get sober?" Riley asked. "Have you thought about that?"

"Look at these wrinkles on my face. Look at my new bald spot," Scott said, turning to his sister-in-law. "I don't think about anything else. But I don't know what to do. I'd threaten to leave, but if I do, what happens to him?"

"Maybe he figures out how to be a responsible adult?" Riley suggested.

"Or maybe he just locks himself up in that damn firehouse and drinks himself to death," Scott said.

Riley looked stricken. "Please don't talk like that."

She pulled the cart into the ferry lot.

"You don't have to wait," Scott said. "You can just pull up to the front and I'll jump out."

"That's okay," Riley said awkwardly. "There's, um, somebody here I want to see for a minute."

"Is it the same somebody you were with last night?" Scott asked.

"How do you know about that?"

"Relax. Nobody else saw you. We left the club late after the fireworks, but I had to go back, because your brother left his phone in the bar. I was passing by, and I happened to catch a glimpse of you two in a clinch."

"Oh, God," Riley moaned, covering her face with both hands.

"I won't say anything," Scott assured her. "He's a good guy. I'm happy for both of you."

Riley gave him a grateful smile. "You're a good guy too, Scotty. The best other brother a girl could ask for."

"He's standing right over there, in case you were wondering." Scott pointed toward the porch of the Mercantile. "Damn! He looks fine in a suit."

Nate's face lit up like a Christmas tree when he saw her climbing the front steps of the Mercantile. He had on a well-cut charcoal summer-weight business suit and dress shirt, with an unknotted tie looped around his collar.

"You came!" He grasped both her hands in his.

"I can only stay for a minute," Riley said. "But I'm glad I got to see you dressed in a suit. As Scott said, you look mighty fine."

"For the bankers," Nate said. "Take a good look, because it's the only one I own, and it's the same one I used to wear in California when I had to meet with the venture-capital investors." He glanced down at his well-polished wingtips. "These shoes are already killing me."

"Very nice, but I think I prefer you in shorts and a T-shirt," Riley said.

"Or nothing at all?"

"That, too," she said.

They heard the *Carolina Queen*'s horn blast from across the parking lot.

"I better go," Riley said. She leaned in and tried to give him a quick peck on the cheek, but Nate pulled her to him, wrapped his arms around her waist, and kissed her deeply. "Thank you," he said. "See you in a couple of weeks?"

"Call me," she said. Her cheeks were cherry pink as she jogged back to the parking lot.

53

Riley stared at her own reflection in the bathroom mirror. The old silvering was peeling away, leaving moody, discolored freckling on the glass, which did her own moody, discolored skin no favors.

She wasn't typically a vain person, not by broadcast journalist standards, but since she'd gotten her first television job twenty years earlier, she'd always been aware that her looks were as important a professional asset as her reporting skills.

Riley knew she'd been blessed with good genes, but in her business, DNA was never enough. To that end, over the years she'd had her teeth capped, her hair colored, and as a fifth-anniversary gift from Wendell, her slightly beaky nose reworked. She'd had Botox and dermabrasion and, since having Maggy, she'd lost and regained the same cruel twenty pounds half a dozen times over.

Now, though, none of that was enough. Even though the current stress in Riley's life had reduced her to her lowest weight since college graduation, with the advent of high-definition television, every inflamed pore, wrinkle, sag, bag, or pimple was magnified in the cruelest detail.

And, to add to the indignity of her chosen profession, social media now made it possible for every snarky bitch on the planet to become a self-appointed media critic, which meant that the most unflattering screen captures and on-camera blunders went viral almost the moment they occurred.

She pulled her hair back into a sloppy ponytail and frowned. The video clips attached to her résumés were all at least five years old. If and when she managed to score an interview for any of the half-dozen jobs she'd applied for—even the off-camera ones—she'd have to have some minor cosmetic miracles performed.

"Why are you staring at yourself like that, Mom?" Maggy stood in the bathroom doorway, scowling. "Are you, like, a narcissist or something?"

"Narcissist? Where'd you learn a word like that?"

"It's on the stupid vocabulary list I have to learn for school. It means somebody—"

"I know what it means, sweetie. And no, I don't think I'm a narcissist. But if I'm going to get a new reporting job, I have to look good."

"You mean you have to look good for your new boyfriend?"

Riley felt a cold shiver run down her spine. "What are you talking about?"

Maggy held out her cell phone. The photo had been shot from a distance, but the subject matter was unmistakable—Riley Nolan, caught in a passionate embrace with a tall man in a dark suit.

Nate had been gone a week, and they'd talked every night, but she knew that photo had been taken the previous Monday, when she'd seen him off at the ferry.

"Where did you get this?" Her hands shook with fury. Riley tapped the trash-can icon on the bottom of the phone's screen and deleted the photo.

"Cute, Mom. Real cute. But it's too late. Everybody on the island has seen this. And now everybody knows my mom is a big ol' ho."

"Stop it!" Riley said, her voice steely. "I want to know where you got this photo. Right now."

"No biggie," Maggy said. "Shane Billingsley saw you making out with that Nate dude at the Mercantile last week. The same one you said was just a friend. And I know you've been calling him every night. I can hear you talking to him. And it makes me want to puke!"

"Margaret Evelyn Griggs, you will not speak to me this way," Riley said.

"Okay. I won't talk to you at all," Maggy said, turning away. "Ho."

"That's it." Riley grabbed her daughter by the arm.

"Ow, cut it out," Maggy cried. "Let go."

"I'll let go, once we're in your room," Riley said, clamping her fingers tighter around her daughter's forearm. "Now, march."

Maggy's bedroom looked and smelled like a toxic waste dump. Riley shoved her rudely inside and slammed and locked the door behind them. In response, Maggy flung herself facedown on a bed-shaped mound of clothing.

Riley stood with her spine against the wall, praying for some kind of composure or inner knowledge to help her deal with this newest single-parenting nightmare.

"Turn over and look at me, please," she said, trying to sound calm.

"No." Maggy's voice was muffled.

"Do it," Riley said. "Or I'll turn you over myself."

Maggy sat up on the bed, her arms crossed defiantly over her chest, glaring at her mother. "Mimi knows you're a ho too," she announced.

"First of all, I am not a ho," Riley said. "So I'd appreciate it if you'd stop using that word."

"Whatever. What you're doing is gross. I mean, how are you any different from Dr. Cranshaw, sleeping around with his nurses?"

"First of all, unlike Dr. Cranshaw, I'm not married."

"Yeah, but you were. And you were practically in that guy's pants even before we knew Dad was dead."

"Margaret!" Riley bit her lip. "You know that even if your dad were still alive, we wouldn't be together. You admitted to me that Dad told you we were probably getting a divorce right after Easter. And I was *not,* emphasize *not* in Nate Milas's pants."

"I don't care. It's disgusting! He's disgusting, the way he looks at you. Like, even on the ferry when we were coming back from seeing Dad's body, he was hitting on you. You think I didn't know that? I'm not stupid."

Riley tried to think back to that time on the ferry, then remembered that Nate had approached to offer his condolences.

"He was not hitting on me. He was being kind and sympathetic."

"I saw the way he looked at you. And Mimi told me that even though he's like, super rich now, he used to be poor, and you used to go out with him, until he barfed all over you at some big party."

Riley sighed. "Mimi doesn't have any right to tell you stuff like that. And your friends don't have any right to take pictures of people and share them without permission. It's called invasion of privacy."

"So, what, you're gonna have Shane arrested?"

If only, Riley thought.

"Most importantly, neither you nor your friends have any right to call me something as hurtful as what you just did."

"Well, it hurts me for you to go around acting like you do," Maggy retorted. "If there's nothing wrong with what you're doing, why are you sneaking around with him all the time? Why do you only talk to him late at night, when you think nobody can hear you?"

Good question, Riley thought ruefully. Why was she so intent on keeping her relationship with Nate secret?

Riley sat gingerly on the edge of the bed. "I'm a grown woman, Maggy. And I'm single. And Nate is single and he is somebody really special to me. And yes, he makes me happy, in a way that I haven't been happy in a long, long time. Aren't you tired of me being sad all the time? I am. I'm ready to be happy again, and I hope that you want that for me, too."

"Not with him!" Maggy cried. "He's a prick, and I hate him, and I hate you."

She found Evelyn in the library, dusting the bookshelves. Her mother frowned as Riley walked in. "What was all that door slamming I just heard from upstairs? Are you fussing at Maggy again?"

"As a matter of fact, I was," Riley said. "She just called me a disgusting ho because one of her friends shared a picture of me kissing Nate Milas at the ferry last week."

Evelyn shook her head. "Well, she's upset, naturally. Honestly, Riley, what were you thinking?"

"Me? I was thinking I'm a grown woman—a *single* grown woman, by the way, who is allowed to have a relationship with a single grown man without having everybody in my life freaking out and calling me names."

"You're a widow, for God's sake. We haven't even buried Wendell yet! And I did not raise my daughter to act like this, going around necking with some man in public at seven o'clock in the morning. It's indecent. Have you no sense of propriety at all?"

"We weren't necking, Mama. He kissed me good-bye. It was at the ferry. People kiss each other hello and good-bye all the time. I saw you and Daddy do it a million times, growing up. And I'm not scarred for life."

"Your father and I were married. And I seriously doubt you ever saw him put his tongue in my mouth in public, for God and everybody to see."

Riley felt her face get hot. "So you saw that picture, too."

"I did. And I found it revolting. So it's no surprise that your daughter would, too. You might not care that Wendell is dead, but Maggy is still mourning her father. I would think you would be just a little sensitive to her feelings before you go cavorting around like some gay divorcée."

Riley was struggling to keep her temper. "No, the timing of this isn't the best in the world. But we don't live in the past. I'm not Queen Victoria, and I'm not going to wear black and hang scarves over mirrors for the rest of my life just because my soon-to-be ex-husband got himself murdered."

Evelyn threw her dust rag onto the tooled-leather desktop. "Nobody expects you to throw yourself on some funeral pyre, Riley. But I don't think it's too much to expect for you to wait a decent amount of time before you start dating again, out of respect for Wendell."

"Respect for Wendell? For the man who bankrupted me, stole from me, stole from my family, and who, by the way, was sleeping around on me? I'm sorry, Mama, but yes, that is too much to expect. I didn't go looking to find somebody new. It just happened. And I can't believe I got this lucky—that this man, this wonderful, kind, decent, caring guy, wants to be in my life."

"You obviously see something in Nate Milas that I can't see," Evelyn said with a sniff. "Yes, he's been successful in business, but that hardly makes him suitable for somebody like you. You can call me a snob if you want, but it's the truth and you know it. And have you forgotten how he ruined your debut? I haven't and, no matter what, I'll never forgive him for humiliating our family that way."

"Okay," Riley said wearily. "I give up. I do. Unfortunately, I don't have the financial resources at the moment to allow Maggy and me to find a place of our own here on the island. Out of respect for your insane dislike for him, I won't bring Nate around here. But I'm not going to keep our relationship a secret any longer. I'm going to keep seeing Nate, and I'm going to create a new life for my daughter and me."

"Do as you like," Evelyn said, carpet-bombing the desktop with Pledge.

"I intend to," Riley said.

54

Riley's cell phone rang, and, when she saw that the caller was Porter Burroughs, she grabbed it. Porter was her longtime agent. The agent she'd been calling and e-mailing for a month. Riley hit the connect button.

"Riley!" Porter's booming voice reflected his roots in shock radio. "How are things at the beach?"

"Oh, you know, sunny and beachy. I've been hoping I'd hear back from you. Getting a little anxious, you know?"

"Yeah, sorry about that. One of my client's contracts expired, and we got involved in a bidding war. Pretty exciting stuff, but also crazy-making. Bottom line is she's gonna be evening anchor at the number-one station in a top-five market. And I'm gonna be one happy son of a bitch when I cash that commission check."

"How nice for both of you," Riley said, feeling long-dormant pangs of professional jealousy. At one point in her career, she, too, had aspired to that kind of a career trajectory. Now she'd be happy just to be able to pay her mounting bills.

"Has anything turned up for me?" she asked.

"Honey, you know everybody in the business loves you, right? You've got class, experience, smarts . . ."

"And a forty-two-year-old face," Riley said.

"Yeah. Don't take this wrong, but one of my clients down in Florida just flew to Mexico for a little tune-up. Fabulous results. It's like a spa, right? You stay two weeks, get a little R-and-R and some ice packs, and boom! When you come back, you're ten years younger. Only ten thousand dollars. Think about it, okay?"

"I just thought about it. But I don't have ten thousand dollars, Porter, which is why I really need for you to find something for me."

"Did I say I haven't?"

"Does that mean you have an offer for me?"

"I'm getting to that. You know there's just not a lot out there right now. I do have an assistant line producer opening in Huntsville, Alabama. . . ."

"Nothing out of state. Remember I told you that?"

"Which is why I'm calling to tell you about a great opportunity. It's right near you, in Durham. That's near you, right?"

"Right," she said cautiously. "Tell me more."

"It's a new concept for that market. A lunchtime magazine format, heavy on women's interest. It's an owner-operated ABC affiliate, four times a week . . ."

"I'll take it," Riley said. "What's the pay?"

"Welllll, it's not what you're used to making," Porter said. "But they're building it from the ground up, so I'd say if ratings are okay, we can go back and renegotiate at a later time. The main thing is to get you back on the air and your foot in the door."

He named a salary so low that Riley was momentarily too stunned to speak. "Porter, I can't survive on that. I'm a single mom now," she said.

"I thought about that, but we'll get you lined up to do some commercials, endorsements, and some voice work. There's actually a vinyl siding company in town that wants to hire you to do Riley from Raleigh commercials. You'd do live shots, travel around to home shows, that kind of thing. Money's decent. And one of the sponsors for the show is a snazzy local women's boutique, so your wardrobe is comped."

"All right," she said finally. "When do they want me to start?"

"Second week in August."

"Okay, Maggy's school starts back around then, too."

"I'll send you the contract," Porter said.

She fixed herself a sandwich and a glass of iced tea and went out on the front porch to have lunch and compile a mental list of all the things she'd need to accomplish as soon as she got home to Raleigh.

It had been an unusually cool and rainy week, and Maggy had been moodier than ever, bored and hostile toward every adult she encountered. Riley was actually grateful she'd gone to town with Annabelle to see a movie. She was grateful too, that Evelyn, who wasn't currently speaking to her, was at her garden club.

She went back to worrying about things she could control.

Job one would be getting all her furniture out of storage, where it had been since selling the St. Mary's house back in May. Job two would be getting moved into the new house.

Riley frowned. She'd agreed to a leaseback agreement with the sellers, who didn't want to vacate the house until their new home was completed. Her agreement was that she'd move in August fifth. That hadn't been much of an issue in May, but now, with starting a new job and a new school, she'd really need to get into the house sooner. She'd have to call her real estate agent to ask if she could speed up the move-in date.

School clothes for Maggy. She'd always gone to public school before, but the new, exclusive, private middle school she was starting required uniforms. Boxy navy blazer with an embroidered crest, pale yellow blouse with Peter Pan collar, gray kilt, navy knee socks, and black-and-white saddle oxfords. Thank God she'd ordered everything back in the spring.

The last item on her list was the one that was the hardest. Leaving Nate. They'd discussed it briefly on the phone during his two-week absence. He'd be in Raleigh and Chapel Hill on business in the fall, but it wasn't the same thing. And she knew most of his focus would be on starting up his projects on Belle Isle. And there was Maggy to think about, too.

Riley looked up when she heard the unusual sound of a car approaching on the driveway that encircled the house. It was a Baldwin County sheriff's cruiser. As soon as it parked she saw that the driver was Craig Schumann, aka Sheriff Shoe, and his companion was Special Agent Aidan Coyle.

She picked up her phone to call Parrish but, out of the corner of her eye, she saw a golf cart right behind the police cruiser. Parrish. This superpower thing of hers was helpful, but super creepy.

The two men turned around to see who was joining them, and Riley saw the sheriff frown when he recognized Parrish come hurrying up the walkway.

The four of them sat around the polished mahogany dining room table, with Parrish's cell phone placed right beside her tumbler of iced tea.

"I hope you're here to tell me you've made some progress on solving my husband's murder," Riley said.

"We have," the sheriff said cautiously. "Of course, I'm not at liberty to give you any specifics. But we had some questions we wanted to ask, if that's all right."

Riley glanced at Parrish for approval.

"Ask away," Parrish said.

Agent Coyle took a printout of a color snapshot from the inner pocket of his windbreaker and slid it across the table to Riley.

It showed a deeply tanned man with a thick mane of silver hair and a neatly trimmed goatee. He wore a Western-style denim shirt with a bolo tie. The man was laughing and holding a cigarillo between his thumb and forefinger.

"Ever seen this man before?" Agent Coyle asked.

"No," Riley said.

"You seem pretty sure of that," the FBI agent said.

"This guy kind of reminds me of Harlan Sanders," Riley said. "I'd remember if I'd ever seen him."

Sheriff Shoe wrinkled his forehead. "Harlan Sanders?"

"Colonel Sanders—the Kentucky Fried Chicken founder?" Parrish said. "Yeah, you're right, Riley, he does look like the guy on the chicken bucket."

"Who is he?" Riley asked.

"That's Samuel Gordon, the Wilmington attorney who set up the dummy corporations for your husband," Agent Coyle said.

"What kind of law did Samuel Gordon practice?" Parrish asked. "I've been a lawyer in this state for nearly twenty years, and my husband has been practicing for more than thirty years, so we know a lot of lawyers."

Agent Coyle said, "Our records show he moved to Wilmington in 2002, and set up a solo practice the next year, following admission to the bar."

"Moved from where?" Parrish asked.

The FBI agent took a notepad from his windbreaker and flipped some pages. "Laurel Springs, Mississippi. He had a law practice there for many years."

Parrish did the math. "He died at eighty. Which means he moved to this state at the age of sixty-seven and started practicing law here?"

"So?" Sheriff Shoe said.

"So most men that age are retiring," Parrish said. "They're not picking up and moving to another state and taking that state's bar exam to start all over again. Do you know anything else about this guy?"

"Married and divorced twice, the last time in 1992," Agent Coyle said. "No children, no survivors other than a distant cousin who hadn't seen him in forty years. One interesting thing, his law license in Mississippi was suspended for a year after a client accused him of commingling funds from an escrow account. The suspension was lifted after a year."

"I wonder why he moved to Wilmington," Riley said. "And how he knew Wendell? I mean, Belle Isle Enterprises has a sales office there, but Wendell hadn't spent a lot of time there in the past few years."

"We don't know how they knew each other, but we know now that they did," Agent Coyle said. "We searched Mr. Gordon's records and found an agreement signed by Gordon and your husband, stating that all assets of those dummy corporations were actually owned by Belle Isle Enterprises."

"Maybe Melody Zimmerman was the connection," Parrish said.

"We talked to her," Sheriff Shoe said. "And she strongly denies having anything but a strictly professional relationship with Wendell Griggs."

"She's a liar," Riley said. "There's a photo on her Facebook page that I can tell was taken from the balcony of my bedroom on Sand Dollar Lane. And I also know from Facebook that her first job was as a clerk in a law office there."

"But she didn't work for Samuel Gordon. We checked," the sheriff said.

"Maybe she knew him through some other connection," Parrish said.

"Okay, I'm still not convinced this lawyer had anything to do with killing Wendell Griggs," the sheriff said impatiently. "I mean, he was already dead."

"Then how can we help you today, Sheriff?" Parrish asked.

"Tell me about your brother's relationship with your late husband," the sheriff said.

"Billy? He and Wendell got along okay, I guess. They weren't best friends, but they weren't enemies either," Riley said. "But I told you before, Billy is the least violent person I know. He would never . . ."

"Your brother has an alcohol problem, isn't that correct?"

Riley glanced at Parrish.

"What bearing does that have on Wendell's death?" Parrish asked.

"Do you have any idea of how many violent crimes are committed by people under the influence of drugs or alcohol?"

"Billy's not violent when he drinks. He just gets happy. And sleepy. And he didn't have any reason to kill Wendell," Riley said.

"Your husband owed him money, correct?"

"Yes. I think Billy invested money in Wendell's hotel project."

"We looked into your brother's finances. He was basically broke," the sheriff said. "The money he inherited from your father, that was all gone, right?"

"My brother doesn't discuss his finances with me," Riley said. "But even if he was destitute, that wouldn't change things. Billy's partner, Scott, is a very successful restaurant designer. They have money. And, as I told you before, neither of them had a reason to kill my husband."

"That you know about," the sheriff said. "Where is your brother today, Mrs. Griggs?"

"It's Ms. Nolan. I believe he's working out of state this week. Billy is a jazz musician."

"And his partner, Scott Moriatakis? He's what you people call a weekender? Comes and goes but works someplace else?"

"Yes. His full-time residence is in New York, but he travels constantly for work. Didn't he tell you this already when you questioned him?"

The sheriff ignored her question. "And your husband owed him money too, because he'd also invested money in the hotel project that fell through?"

This was the first Riley had heard about Scott investing in the Pirate's Point hotel project. "Where did you hear that?"

Riley felt Parrish kick her under the table.

"Scott doesn't discuss his finances with me either," she said quickly.

"Is he on the island now?" the sheriff asked.

"No. As you said, Scott's mostly a weekender. You have his contact number, correct?"

"Yes," the sheriff said. "There's one more thing. The Baldwin County Coroner's office is ready to release your husband's remains. Call Cleo Carter at this number. They'll need to know what mortuary you're using."

He stood up abruptly, ripped a page out of his notepad, and handed it to Riley. "Mrs. Griggs, Mrs. Godchaux, that's all we have now. But we'll be back in touch."

Riley and Parrish stood on the porch at Shutters, watching the police cruiser roll slowly down the driveway toward the main road.

"Good thing I saw that cruiser leaving the county garage in the village," Parrish said.

"So that's how you knew to come without my calling you," Riley said.

Parrish smiled blandly. "It's my own secret bat signal." Her expression turned serious. "Did you know Wendell owed money to Scott?"

"No!" Riley said. "Billy never said anything about it to me. I wonder if he knows Scott loaned Wendell money? And I really wonder how the sheriff knows."

"It sounds like they really do suspect either Billy or Scott," Parrish said.

"Which shows you what an idiot that sheriff is," Riley said. "You've known both of them for years. Does either one of them strike you as a killer?"

"Of course not. Nobody we know strikes me as a killer," Parrish said. "Except maybe Evelyn. That didn't come out right," Parrish said hastily. "What I meant was, your mother is a force of nature. And when people don't bend to a force of nature, well, sometimes they get mowed down. I totally don't think Evelyn bashed in Wendell's head and killed him. If she wanted him dead, she would have poisoned him."

"She'd like to kill me right now," Riley said. "And so would Maggy."

She quickly brought Parrish up to date on her confrontation with her mother and daughter over her relationship with Nate Milas.

"You were right to stand up to both of them," Parrish said. "Good for you for finally growing a set."

"Nate and I have been talking almost every night while he's been gone," Riley said. "But I don't know how we can keep up a relationship once Maggy and I go back to Raleigh. Especially since I'm starting my new job as soon as I get back."

"You got a job!" Parrish squealed. "I knew you could do it. That's fabulous."

"We'll see. The money sucks, and it's some new start-up women's interest magazine format, sort of like my last job at WRAL. And I'm a little nervous that they were willing to hire me without an interview. I mean, who does that? But I don't have any choice. And my agent promised that if the ratings are okay we'll go back and renegotiate."

"So you'll be amazing, and you'll get offers for something better," Parrish said.

Riley sighed and looked at the scribbled note in her hand. "I guess it's time to throw a funeral, huh? God, how I dread it."

Parrish put her arm around her friend. "Don't worry. I'll get you through it."

55

Riley was almost dressed for the funeral. Thank God she'd thrown a simple navy-blue linen sheath into her suitcase when she was packing for the summer. As she was pawing through her jewelry case looking for something to dress it up a little, she picked up a strand of huge freshwater pearls.

They'd been a gift from Wendell's mother, Beatrice, and although she'd been touched by the sentiment, Riley had secretly found them a bit gaudy. Today though, it seemed appropriate to wear them for the last time. And then she'd pack them up, along with her engagement and wedding rings, and save them for Maggy, who loved bling.

As she searched the case for her pearl earrings, Riley spotted the amber-colored pill bottle Parrish had pressed into her hand the night before. "Here. I think you're gonna need this."

"You know I don't like drugs," Riley said hastily, trying to give the bottle back.

"Don't be ridiculous. Who doesn't like drugs? Anyway, it's not like it's quaaludes or meth, honey," Parrish said. "It's just a little something to take the raw edge off your nerves tomorrow."

"Isn't that why God invented wine?"

"Wine is for *after* the service," Parrish said. "And I promise, I'll have plenty for you back at my house afterward. But you need to dose yourself with these an hour beforehand if you want to survive this ordeal with your wits intact."

Riley was fastening the pearl necklace when Maggy burst into the room. Her daughter was wrapped in a towel, and her hair was dripping wet.

"What's this supposed to be?" Maggy brandished a pale purple frock.

"A dress?"

"I get that it's a dress, Mom, okay? When I got out of the shower just now I found it laid out on my bed."

Riley took the dress and frowned. It was a girlish lavender floral print, with a deep ruffle at the hem and a high neckline. She held it up to her daughter. The hem hit Maggy two inches below the knees. It reminded Riley of something from *Little House on the Prairie*. All it needed was a matching sunbonnet.

"I think I know what this is about," Riley said. She walked out into the hallway and hollered, "Mama!"

Evelyn popped her head out of her bedroom door. "I'm right here, Riley. You don't have to shout."

Riley held out the dress. "Do you know anything about this?"

Evelyn's face softened. "Isn't it darling? I knew Maggy didn't have anything suitable to wear to her daddy's service, and there wasn't time to take her shopping in Wilmington. Frieda Heard orders all her grandchildren's clothes from this online store. I had to guess at Maggy's size and pay extra for overnight shipping, but I think it's perfect, don't you?"

"Perfect?" Maggy shrieked. "It's hideous. I wouldn't be caught dead in that thing."

Evelyn turned her head and gave Riley an expectant look.

"Would you please explain to your child that it's rude to speak to her elders like that?"

"I will. But in the meantime, I really don't think this dress is right for her."

"What's wrong with it?" Evelyn asked, stepping out of her bedroom wearing a severely cut long-sleeved black dress. "I'll have you know I paid a hundred and seventy-five dollars for that dress."

"If you like it so much, you wear it," Maggy retorted.

"Margaret? That's enough," Riley said. "Take the dress and go to your room. I'll be there in a minute."

"I'll go," Maggy muttered. "But I am not wearing that rag."

When she'd heard the bedroom door slam, Riley returned to the subject at hand. "I'm sorry Maggy was disrespectful. She's obviously upset. But about the dress. It's at least two sizes too big, and it's not her style at all. She's twelve, Mama, not four."

"Fine," Evelyn snapped. "I was just trying to help." She started to walk away, but Riley caught the sleeve of her mother's dress.

"I know you were, Mama, and I really do appreciate all you've done for Maggy and me. So let's try not to fuss at each other so much. Especially today. Okay?"

"Whatever you want, sweetheart," Evelyn said, turning a critical eye to her daughter. "But it's already after two. Don't you think it's time for you to change before we leave for the chapel?"

Riley found the pill bottle right where she'd left it, on her dresser. She swallowed two tablets and tucked the bottle in her pocketbook, along with her grandmother's red leather-bound Bible. "Help me, sweet Jesus," she whispered.

"Maggy!" Riley stood in the main floor hallway at the bottom of the staircase. Evelyn was already waiting outside in the golf cart, tooting the horn every thirty seconds. "We need to leave for church now. Right now!"

"Coming!"

Maggy walked slowly down the stairs. She was wearing an old dress of her mother's, which Riley had rigged to fit with strategically placed safety pins and duct tape. And over the dress she wore her father's old pinstriped dress shirt. The shirt was buttoned and there was a suspicious, wriggling bulge in front.

"You look very nice," Riley said. "What's that you've got under your shirt?"

"I had a big lunch," Maggy said, brushing past her and motoring toward the front door.

"Not so fast." Riley clamped one hand on her daughter's shoulder.

"Moooom. We're gonna be late."

Evelyn tooted the horn again.

"See?"

"Lose the shirt. And the puppy," Riley started, and then changed her mind. Maggy had been through enough. If wearing Wendell's clothing and clutching the puppy he'd given her gave her comfort, so be it. "Never mind."

Maggy's eyes widened. "Really?"

"Really. Just make sure Banks doesn't poop in the chapel, or your grandmother really will blow a gasket."

"Thanks, Mommy." Maggy smiled for the first time that day.

Evelyn pulled the golf cart alongside the porch and stared at her granddaughter. "What on earth?"

"Mama?" Riley gave her a warning look. "We'd better get to the chapel. I need to give Father Templeton the readings."

"I never," Evelyn muttered under her breath as they pulled away from Shutters. "I really never."

The Chapel in the Pines had been designed and built in the 1950s by Riley's great-grandfather from plans he'd sketched on a two-by-six piece of lumber. The foundation was of granite from a nearby quarry and the board-and-batten pine walls had been cut and milled right on the island. The large stained-glass window behind the altar had been donated by Evelyn in memory of her parents, and it depicted stylized versions of creatures found on the island—mockingbirds and herons, deer, chipmunks, squirrels, and raccoons set in a border banded by native flowers; dogwood, wild rose, dune daisies, and rudbeckia.

The altar had been carved by a local boat builder, and today it was dressed with a pair of huge silver urns overflowing with deep-blue hydrangeas and ferns.

The nondenominational chapel could only seat sixty people, but today every pew was packed, with dozens of people standing along the side aisles.

Parrish greeted them at the door. "Okay?"

Riley took a deep breath. "Okay."

"The rest of the family is up front on the right," Parrish whispered. "Father Templeton is in the sacristy. Did you bring the readings?"

"Right here." Riley held up the Bible. "They're all marked."

"Good. I already briefed him on what you want. If he goes any longer than thirty minutes, I've threatened to unplug his mike. I forgot to ask, does anybody in the family want to say a few words?"

"No," Riley said firmly.

"I do," Maggy said.

"Oh, no," Evelyn said, looking horrified. "I don't think that's a good idea."

"It'll be fine," Riley said. She glanced at her watch. "Let's get this show on the road."

The organist played Bach's "Jesu, Joy of Man's Desiring."

It took awhile to make it to the front of the church. People stopped and hugged them, whispering words of comfort and encouragement in their ears. Billy was sitting on the aisle in the first pew, beside Scott, who was seated beside Ed Godchaux. Aunt Roo sat at the end of the pew, resplendent in a vivid purple muumuu and flower-decked straw hat. Billy and the rest of the family slid down the pew, and the three of them sat down, with Riley seated next to Billy, and Maggy between her and Evelyn.

"How you doin'?" Billy asked.

Good question. She'd felt a weird sense of something—detachment—settle over her during the short ride to the church. "I don't know why, but I feel kinda numb," Riley said.

Billy gave her a sly wink and patted the pocket of his sport coat. "Me, too." He slid his hand into his pocket and showed her the top of the sterling silver flask that had been W.R.'s. "Want some?"

"No, thanks, I'm good."

True to Parrish's word, Father Templeton stuck close to the script he'd been given.

"In the Gospel of John, we are told that, 'in my father's house, there are many mansions,'" the priest intoned.

Mansions, Riley though grimly. Mansions in heaven. If that's where Wendell was headed, and she had her doubts about that, he'd be happier than a hog in slop. But down here on Belle Isle, he'd somehow managed to mortgage their own mansion right into oblivion.

She felt her eyelids flutter and close just as the priest was starting to remind the congregants of the fleeting nature of life. At some point she must have actually nodded off, because Billy elbowed her in the ribs.

"Wake up," he hissed. "We're getting to the good stuff."

What followed was such a tender and glowing eulogy—for a man Riley was fairly sure the priest had never met—that Riley could only conclude it had been written by Evelyn.

"Who's he talking about?" Billy asked, giggling at his own humor.

"Shhh." Riley just managed to suppress her own giggle.

"In Ecclesiastes, we are reminded that to everything there is a season," Father said. "And a purpose under heaven."

Riley had found the verse underlined in red in her grandmother's Bible. It was one of Nanny's favorite pieces of scripture, and she'd quoted it so often that Riley could almost recite it from memory.

"'A time to live and a time to die. A time to plant, and a time to pluck up that which is planted . . . a time to weep, and a time to laugh, a time to mourn, and a time to dance.'"

Wendell's time, Riley wryly reflected, had come, but not soon enough. How much destruction had the son of a bitch left in his wake? And what else would she discover in the weeks to come?

Riley heard a muffled sob and looked over at Evelyn, who was softly crying into a linen handkerchief. She reached over Maggy's lap and took her mother's hand and gave it a gentle squeeze. After a moment, Evelyn squeezed back.

The priest droned on through the rest of the verses from Ecclesiastes.

"'. . . And also that every man should eat and drink, and enjoy the good of all his labor because it is the gift of God.'"

This last elicited another fit of giggles from Billy Nolan, which earned him a death stare from his mother.

Finally, Father Templeton got to the verse Riley had been waiting for. It was the one Nanny had underlined and starred in the Bible, and though her grandmother was dead and buried before Riley met Wendell, it was the verse that rang truest for her.

"'I said in mine heart, God shall judge the righteous and the wicked: for there is a time there for every purpose and for every work.'"

Riley nodded in solemn agreement. Wendell's judgement might come in heaven, but down here on earth, she'd judged for herself, and her verdict would never win him a pass beyond the pearly gates.

"Wendell's daughter, Maggy, would like to say a few words."

"Ready?" Riley asked, turning to her daughter.

"I think so," Maggy whispered. "Could you hold Banks?" She unbuttoned Wendell's shirt and Riley saw that the puppy was sound asleep. She gently transferred the sleeping pug to her own lap.

When she reached the altar, Father Templeton helped her to the pulpit, then stepped aside.

Maggy extracted a sheet of lined notebook paper from the breast pocket of the shirt and slowly unfolded it. She took a deep breath and cleared her throat.

Her voice was low but the words clear. "My name is Margaret Evelyn Griggs. I am Wendell Griggs's daughter. And I know a lot of you think you know my dad, but I bet none of you know how special my dad was.

"My dad did a lot for this island. Even before he met my mom, Dad came to work here for my granddaddy, and he helped build a lot of houses on this island. He did a lot of good things that people don't know about, too. In Raleigh, where we live, he and I cleared a nature trail that runs through our neighborhood so that people in wheelchairs could be in nature. He and some other dads gave the money for a new soccer field at my school, and my dad drove the bulldozer when they were making the field okay for us to play on.

He paid for the Big Belle lighthouse to be painted too, and hardly anybody knows that."

Maggy looked down at her paper. She bit her lip and continued. "My dad taught me a lot. He told me to always go to the net in tennis. He taught me how to ride a bike and how to do fractions. And he let me drive the golf cart sitting on his lap starting when I was a really little kid. Almost every Saturday when he was home, he and I went to the Waffle House or the Mercantile for breakfast so my mom could sleep late, and he taught me that scrambled eggs always need hot sauce. And the most important thing he told me was that you can tell a lot about a person by the way they treat their dogs.

"This year . . ." Maggy's voice trailed off for a moment. "This year I got pretty sick and we found out that I have diabetes, and I had to go to the hospital and stuff and get shots and not have candy and Cokes anymore." She sniffed and looked down, and then back up again. "My dad wanted to surprise me, so one day he came to the hospital, and he brought me a puppy for my very own. And the nurses yelled at him, but Dad told them to back off, so they did. And then my dad crawled into the hospital bed with me, and I decided to name the puppy Mr. Banks, because Mr. Banks was the dad in *Mary Poppins,* which is my favorite movie, except for *Star Wars,* which my dad took me to when the new one came out because his dad took him when he was a kid."

Maggy gripped the lectern with shaking hands. "My dad had to work a lot, so lately he wasn't home that much, but almost every night, he called me to tell me good night, and say that he loved me."

She seemed to be staring directly at Riley. "I know some people are saying bad things about my dad. But they're not true. My dad loved me, and he loved my mom, and he loved Belle Isle. And I wish he weren't dead."

She folded her paper and put it back in her pocket. "That's all I wanted to say."

Father Templeton put a kindly arm around the child's shoulder. "Thank you, Maggy, for such a beautiful, heartfelt tribute."

Maggy nodded wordlessly and left the altar, but instead of joining her family in their pew, she leaned in without a word and took the now-awake

Banks from her mother, then continued down the main aisle and out the door of the chapel.

"I'll go get her," Evelyn said, but Riley shook her head. "Let her go, Mama. She just needs a little more time to grieve."

56

On Saturday morning, Riley sat up in bed and met the bemused eyes of her best friend. She looked around the room. "Why am I in your guest bedroom?"

"I certainly wasn't going to put you in my bed," Parrish said. "I love you like a sister, but even I have certain limits."

"No. Seriously."

Parrish handed her a mug of coffee and grinned. "There are so many ways I'm tempted to answer that question."

"You're really enjoying yourself at my expense, aren't you?"

"Hugely."

"How about just telling me the truth?"

"Spoilsport. Okay, the truth isn't all that exciting. You managed to make it through the service all right, although Billy did have to shake you awake at one point. And then afterward, when everybody came back here for supper, you fixed yourself a plate of food and guzzled down approximately three glasses of white wine like a pro."

"Oh, no." Riley flopped back onto the bed. "It was those damn pills of yours. Mama started in on me about my dress, and I just couldn't take it. I popped two pills right before we left for church . . . and as soon as we sat down I started feeling kind of weird. You know, like my give-a-shit had up and gone . . ."

"Good God, Riles. You took two Xanax followed by about a quart of pinot grigio? No wonder you were zonked out of your gourd."

"What exactly did I do? Or do I even want to know?"

"You didn't attempt a pole dance or pick a fight with your mom, if that's what you're worried about. Mostly, you just got really, really mellow and went around telling everybody how much you loved them. Including Andrea Payne and what's-her-name."

"Belle Isle Barbie and Melody Zimmerman? Who invited those two?"

"You did. Along with Father Templeton and the organist, who nobody'd ever met before, and various other random funeral-goers. Fortunately most of them had the good sense not to show up. Except, of course, for Andrea and Melody, who waltzed right in here like they were your long-lost cousins."

"Oh, no. I'm so, so sorry."

"Don't be. It was excellent comic relief."

Riley took another sip of coffee. "I didn't . . . say anything about Wendell, did I? Anything bad?"

"Not that I heard," Parrish said. "You definitely didn't say anything the two of us were thinking."

"That's a relief. But wait. Oh God! Did Maggy notice how strangely I was acting?"

"Relax. She wasn't here. As soon as we got out of church, Ed tracked her down."

"Where'd she go after she left the chapel?"

"Ed said she was sitting on the seawall, near the marina. Just sitting there, staring out at the water."

"Where they found Wendell's body," Riley said. "I'm afraid she's obsessed with that."

"Yeah. They sat and talked for a while. She was pretty emphatic about not coming back over here afterward, so Ed took her over to the Mercantile and got her an early supper, then took her back to the Shutters. We didn't think you'd mind."

"Mind? I'm incredibly grateful to Ed for being so sensitive to Maggy's mood. I'm so grateful to both of you. I don't know if we could have survived yesterday without the two of you."

Parrish said, "We didn't do anything you wouldn't have done for us." Changing the subject, she asked, "So what are you going to do with the rest of the day?"

Riley looked around the room and spotted her clothes, neatly folded on an armchair near the bed. "I feel like doing something useful. Now that I'm starting a new job, we only have a couple of weeks to figure out how we prove Melody Zimmerman killed Wendell."

Parrish sighed. "You've got another screwball plan, don't you?"

"What would it hurt if we just took a ride over to Melody's cottage and took a look around?"

"Oh, no," Parrish said. "I am not breaking into that woman's house. At least we had a key to get into Wendell's office, and he was your husband. This is an entirely different crime. It's called breaking and entering."

"Who said anything about breaking in? We could just cruise over there and maybe peek in a window or something. You'll have to loan me some clothes, though. I can't go snooping around in my funeral outfit."

"What if she catches us? What if a nosy neighbor sees us? What if Ed finds out? He was not happy when I told him we'd been stalking Melody."

"If she's home, we'll leave. We won't get caught. I swear. And since when do you have to ask for your husband's permission to do something? Geez, Parrish, talk about growing a set!"

Melody Zimmerman's cottage was a modest seventies-era, single-story redwood cottage, in an enclave of half a dozen homes from the same era, each nestled into its own thicket of live oaks, palmettos, and bay laurels.

"Nice and private," Riley said approvingly, as Parrish steered the cart down the cul-de-sac. She pointed to a small green fenced-off public space with a sign designating it as a dog park. "Park over there."

"This is crazy," Parrish muttered as they tried to act nonchalant, walking through the steady drizzle toward Melody Zimmerman's cottage. "We can't see anything here," Parrish said, pointing at two large picture windows covered with closed plantation shutters. "She's probably got the same thing on every window."

"Quit being such a pessimist," Riley said. "Let's check in back."

As they turned the corner they noted what looked like a set of double windows, covered again with closed plantation shutters.

Next, the two women darted around to the rear of the house. A set of sliding glass doors led onto a small brick-paved patio. "See, no more plantation shutters," Riley said.

The two women plastered their faces to the sliders, which were partially obscured by a set of sheer curtains. "Ugh. Total granny city," Parrish said. They were looking at a combined living/dining area. The living room featured a fussy faux French furniture suite with brocade sofa and two matching tufted armchairs. There was a dining room with a crystal chandelier centered over a reproduction Early American maple dining room table and chairs.

"Melody certainly has way better taste in clothes than in furniture," Parrish said.

"Didn't you say the house actually belongs to a relative?" Riley asked. She pointed to a window to the right. It was located halfway up the wall, above an air-conditioning condenser, just high enough that they couldn't see in. Not to be deterred, Riley jumped onto the condenser and pressed her face to the glass.

"See anything?" Parrish asked.

"Wow, talk about stuck in the eighties," Riley reported. "It's just a normal kitchen. For a home-wrecking slut, our Melody is a tidy little soul. Not even a coffee mug on the countertop."

"Okay, let's go," Parrish said anxiously.

"Oh, hello!" Riley said. "There's a doggie door over there, on the side of the house." She clambered down from the condenser.

"Which means there's probably a dog," Parrish said. "Now we really gotta go."

"Don't be such a fraidy-cat," Riley chided. "If there was a dog, it would have barked by now."

She hurried around to the side of the house and stood looking at the dog door, a rectangular opening approximately eighteen inches high by fourteen inches wide. Riley dropped down onto her knees and looked up excitedly at Parrish. "I bet I could crawl through this, don't you?"

"Have you lost your mind? That's a big-ass doggie door. Which means there is a big-ass doggie somewhere inside that house, probably a Rottweiler or a Doberman, just waiting to rip your throat out," Parrish said. "Now let's go."

"I'm just gonna stick my head in and see what's what," Riley said. "If there's a dog, he'll bark, and we'll boogie on down the road. Okay?"

"No! Absolutely not. I did not sign up for illegal entry," Parrish said. But it was too late. Riley poked her head inside the door's outer rubber flap.

"Hellooo. Hellooo. Mr. Doggie, is anybody home? Mr. Doggie?"

She backed out of the door and grinned up at her best friend. "There's no dog in there that I can see. Any self-respecting Dobie would have clawed right through that door if he was home. I'm going in and taking a look around. Cover me, okay?"

"No!" Parrish tried to grab hold of the waist of Riley's shorts, but her friend was too fast. She'd already wriggled all the way through the door.

"I'm in," Riley called, her voice muffled by the door. "Let me know if somebody comes, okay?"

"Get out of there," Parrish said. "If somebody comes I am not making your bail."

Parrish crept along the side of the house, watching to see if anybody approached the house from the cul-de-sac. The rain fell softly, and her sandal-clad feet sank into the sandy soil. Hours passed. Mosquitoes swarmed, and she slapped frantically at her bare legs and arms. She had to pee, and she was terrified.

"Hey!"

Startled, Parrish whirled around to see Riley standing beside her.

"You literally just scared the living piss out of me!" Parrish said. "What took you so long?"

"It was only five minutes," Riley started. "And it was totally worth it..."

"Let's go." Parrish started around the corner of the house but quickly darted backward. "Hide!" she whispered. "Somebody's coming. A cart just pulled up around front."

They backed quickly away from the rear of the house, squatting behind a huge clump of palmettos. They heard keys jingling, and the front door opening. Five minutes passed. "I'm getting eaten alive by mosquitoes," Riley whispered.

"Serves you right," Parrish whispered back.

They heard the sound of the back door sliding open, and then a familiar woman's voice. "Come on Moosey. Come on boy, let's go make poopeys."

Parrish flattened herself to the damp ground, but Riley peered through the palmettos, then did likewise.

Parrish dared to look up. She could see what she knew were Andrea Payne's feet, standing on the patio, holding one end of a leash, while a large golden retriever strained at the other end of the leash, its nose pointing directly at the shrub where they were hiding. She held her breath.

"No, Moosey. We're not chasing squirrels. We're pooping, remember? Come on boy, Auntie Andrea wants to get in out of this rain."

The dog snuffled around, but finally, less than a foot away, Parrish saw it squat.

"Good boy! Good Moosey. Let's go inside and get a treat," Andrea cooed.

They heard the door sliding shut, and then the sound of a lock clicking. They waited five more minutes, and then heard the front door close, and finally, the soft whir of a golf cart rolling away from the house.

They waited another ten minutes before emerging from their hiding place and sprinting through the rain to their cart.

"I thought you said there was no dog," Parrish said, wiping the rain from her arms and legs with a beach towel she kept under the seat. "That looked a lot like a dog taking a dump less than a foot from where we were hiding back there."

"He was in a crate in the laundry room," Riley said. "He must be, like, ninety in dog years. I was walking toward the bedroom and I heard this snuffing sound, and when I looked in the laundry room, there he was. His muzzle was totally white, and it looked to me like he had cataracts, poor baby. He just barely raised his head, looked at me like, 'meh,' and went back to his nap."

She took the towel her friend handed her and started drying herself off. "Anyway, guess what? It looks like Melody is getting ready to move."

"Really?"

"Yeah. The house only has two small bedrooms. She's using the guest room as a closet, and boy, were you right about her being a fashionista. The whole room was full of clothes, shoes, and handbags. She had all these plastic bins, and it looked like she'd started packing the shoes and bags in them. She had a bunch of those cardboard wardrobe moving boxes, and about half of them were packed with clothes. Same thing in her bedroom. Three or four suitcases on the floor, and they were all packed."

"Wonder where she's going?" Parrish said. "And why?"

"I don't know, but I have an idea how we could find out," Riley said. "I bet Melody's best friend, the one who comes over every day to let her dog out for a potty stop, knows. Because, let's face it—Belle Isle Barbie knows everything that happens on this island."

"Nooooo," Parrish said. "Anything but that. You've put me through enough today. I bet I aged twenty years back there when that sliding-glass door opened."

"I can't ask her, because I recently told her to fuck off," Riley said, hugging her friend. "Pleaaase? Pretty please?"

Two hours later, Parrish was back.

"You owe me," she announced when she walked into the library at Shutters, where Riley was reading something on the Internet.

"You did it!" Riley beamed. "But how'd you manage it this fast?"

"I just got lucky," Parrish admitted. "I was going to the Mercantile to find something quick for dinner tonight, and as I passed the nail salon I spotted Andrea in there, getting a pedicure. I walked in, but the girl said there was an hour wait. So I just found a magazine and sat there. And you know our Andrea. She just loooooves to chat. Of course, the main topic she wanted to discuss was you and Nate Milas."

"Of course."

"She doesn't really think he's your kind of people," Parrish said. "She wanted to know where the two of you are going to be living. Surely not that horrible shack he bought."

Riley smiled. "The question is, what did you get out of her?"

"She's devastated that Melody is moving, but totally understands. New management at the bank doesn't really appreciate Melody, and not only that, Melody's elderly aunt, the one who lets her use the house here, has been moved to a nursing home in Wilmington. So Melody has bought a condo at Wrightsville Beach, and she's moving, right after Labor Day, to be closer to her aunt."

"She volunteered all that?"

"I'm a pretty skillful interrogator when I want to be," Parrish said, preening a little. "I just primed the pump a little. Told her you'd gotten a new job in Raleigh, and how much I was going to miss you for the rest of the summer. Stuff like that."

"So she's quit her job at the bank, and bought a condo at Wrightsville," Riley said thoughtfully. "Wonder if the sheriff would be interested in that?"

57

Riley stood in front of the minuscule closet in her bedroom, trying to decide what to wear. Nate was due on the 6:15 ferry, and they were going to have dinner at his place. He'd promised to pick up groceries in town. Now she just needed to come up with a devastatingly adorable outfit.

She really did need to clean out the closet. It was still packed with decades' worth of her old clothes, along with her current clothes, all of them crammed in so closely together it was hard to discern the good from the bad from the ugly.

The problem was, she decided, everything in this closet reminded her of her old life. She dug around, selecting and rejecting, until she found a bathing suit cover-up she'd forgotten about. It was a vaguely ethnic black-and-white geometric cotton print, with long bell sleeves and a drawstring neck. The price tag still hung from the sleeve.

She pulled it off the wire hanger and slipped it over her head, then stepped in front of the mirror on the back of the closet door. Not bad, she thought. It was a little too skimpy as a dress, so she pulled on a pair of white calf-length leggings beneath it.

The bedroom door opened and Maggy came in and flopped down on her bed.

"Chantelle wants to know if you can bring me over for my sleepover tonight, and then stay and have sushi with us. Micki is going to be there, too. She said it would be cool to meet you, since me and Annabelle are so tight."

"I agree, and I enjoyed talking to her this week, but I'm just going to ask Chantelle for a rain check," Riley said, putting on a pair of beaded tassel earrings.

"What's a rain check?"

"It means I'll ask her if we can have sushi another night, because I already have plans for this evening," Riley said.

"Oh." Maggy's face twisted into her all-too-familiar scowl. "I guess you're getting all fixed up for your boyfriend."

"I'm seeing Nate tonight," Riley said carefully. She sat down at the dressing table and smoothed moisturizer over her cheeks and forehead. "Parrish and I are riding to the ferry together, but I'm sure we can drop you off at Annabelle's first."

"Never mind," Maggy said. "I'll just ride my bike over there, since you're way too busy worrying about your love life."

"I said I'd take you," Riley said.

"Don't even bother pretending that you care about me, Mom. I know you only care about yourself. And you know what? I wish Dad was alive and you were the dead person."

Riley jumped up from the stool. Maggy had been surly all week, even more so since Wendell's service, but it dawned on her that this kind of unusually outrageous behavior could be a symptom that her blood sugar was out of whack.

She touched the back of her hand to her daughter's cheek.

"Maggy, when did you last eat? Did you take your insulin?"

"Did you take your birth control?" Maggy asked in a singsongy voice.

Riley sat down on the bed. "This isn't funny," she said sternly, grabbing her daughter's wrist. "Tell me what time you ate, what you had, and when you last tested your blood sugar. Or else you won't be spending the night at Annabelle's. Tonight or ever."

"I had a sandwich and some carrots at two. And I took my insulin. And I had my snack and some apple juice a little while ago and checked my blood sugar." She yanked away from her mother. "As if you care."

Riley stared down at this strange creature who'd taken over her sweet, fun-loving daughter's body. "When did you turn into such a mean, hateful girl?"

"Right around the same time you turned into a bitchy, slutty mom," Maggy countered, hopping off the bed and heading for the bedroom door.

"Nothing you can say to me is going to change the way I feel about Nate," Riley said. "Where's your backpack? Before you go to Annabelle's, I want to make sure you've packed your kit and your juice boxes and cheese crackers."

She followed Maggy into her bedroom and her daughter flung the bag directly at her face. "Here!"

She opened the backpack. Riley saw the purple nylon case holding Maggy's supplies. She unzipped it and checked the cold pack, the insulin, the blood-testing supplies and syringes. She closed the case and replaced it in the bag, noting that along with her daughter's clothes and iPod, there was a plastic bag packed with juice boxes and packages of cheese crackers.

"Satisfied?" Maggy asked, snatching the bag out of Riley's hands.

"Margaret, don't push your luck with me," Riley said. "Or you might never leave this house for the rest of the summer."

"Whatever."

She found Evelyn in the kitchen, warming up a plate of leftovers in the microwave. "Maggy just left to spend the night at Annabelle's," she reported. "I did talk to the mother this week. She sounds very nice. She knows all about Maggy's diabetes. I checked Maggy's bag, and she has her kit and everything she needs. I'm having dinner with Nate, and I don't know what time I'll be home."

Evelyn shrugged and turned back to the microwave.

"Good night, Mama," she said. She was standing on the porch waiting when Parrish pulled around on the golf cart.

"You look cute," her friend said.

"I don't feel cute," Riley reported. "I'm exhausted from fighting with Maggy and getting the silent treatment from Mama. Earlier, I was so excited about the prospect of seeing Nate, I felt like a teenager getting ready for the prom but, right now, I honestly don't know if I have the energy for all this drama."

"Hang in there, Riles," Parrish said. "You can't let those two wear you down. That's what they want."

"I know, but . . ."

"Stop right there," Parrish commanded. "No more buts. And here's a word of parenting advice. I know everybody thinks David was a saint, but I still remember what he was like as a middle-schooler. Let me tell you, as a mother, it was the *worst* time of my life. People think two-year-olds are bad? And teenagers are toxic? No. Tweens are absolutely the worst. And girl tweens are the worst of the worst. All you can do is try to stay sane and wait 'em out. In another year or so, we'll have our dear sweet Maggy back again."

"God, I hope so," Riley said. "But all this angsting has me wondering if I'm cut out for this single-mom dating thing."

"Don't think of it as dating," Parrish advised. "Think of it as sampling."

She stood just outside the arrivals area trying not to look as nervous and apprehensive as she felt. Parrish squeezed her hand. "Butterflies?"

"Huge butterflies," Riley said. "My pulse is racing. I feel like I might throw up."

"Must be love," Parrish said.

"It's so strange to be standing here, waiting for somebody who isn't Wendell to get off the ferry," Riley confided. "I must have stood right in this spot a couple hundred times, waiting for him to get here on Friday nights or Saturday mornings, and I can't ever remember feeling this jumpy. Do you ever feel this way, waiting for Ed to arrive?"

"Not in a while," Parrish admitted. "But maybe it's because I've been with Ed for so long, I know what to expect. I know he'll kiss me, and no matter how I look, he'll tell me I'm gorgeous."

"Wendell hadn't told me anything like that in a long time," Riley said sadly.

"Then he'll ask me how my week was, and tell me he missed me," Parrish said.

"Wendell just wanted to know what was for dinner and if I'd remembered to make his tee time at the club," Riley said.

Parrish pointed toward the horizon. The *Carolina Queen* was chugging toward them. "Don't look now, but here comes your date." She gave Riley a gentle shove. "Go on up and meet him at the gate. Give him a thrill."

Nate was one of the first ones off the ferry. Maybe that was a perk of ownership, Riley told herself. But then she saw the broad smile on his face as he adjusted the strap of his carry-on bag and walked directly toward where she was standing, a few yards apart from the rest of the islanders waiting for their arrivals.

"Hey, you!" Nate said. He dropped his bag to the ground and enveloped her in his arms, kissing her breathless. "God, I missed you," he said when he finally released her.

"I missed you, too," she said simply.

He tugged her by the hand. "Let's get out of here."

"Don't you have groceries to collect?" she asked.

"Oh, yeah," Nate said. "Won't be much of a dinner without that." He dug in his pocket and brought out a key chain. "The cart's parked over beside the Mercantile. Why don't you bring it around here, and by that time the deckhands will have unloaded my cooler and stuff."

On the way to his cabin, he filled her in on the progress he'd made during his business trip. "The UNC board of visitors had called a meeting and approved all the plans for the research center. I met with the architects and showed them some photos of similar centers run by the University of Florida at Cedar Key, and the University of Georgia at Skidaway Island. They're gonna work up some sketches for me. The bankers are down with what I want to do, and it looks like I've got all the financing in place."

"That's great," Riley said. "What about the hotel people?"

"I met with some folks in New York who recently left the Westin and started their own boutique brand. They do small luxury hotels in offbeat destinations. They were intrigued with the idea of putting one on Belle Isle, especially since the only access is by ferry. Each of their concepts is designed for the setting, with its own unique name, design, and branding. I'd be their first franchisee in the South."

"You'd own the hotel?" Riley asked, surprised.

"It's the only way I can completely control what happens with that site," Nate said. "Every other chain requires a certain number of rooms, parking, all of that. Their big thing is uniformity. But I don't want that for Pirate's Point."

"Do you know anything about running a hotel?" she asked.

"Not one damn thing," he said cheerfully. "But they do. And they're really good at it. I stayed in their property in Brooklyn, which is in a converted shoe factory, and in a couple of weeks, I want you to go out to San Francisco with me, so we can check out their property there. It's in an old municipal bus barn."

"That sounds like fun," Riley said, hesitating. She hadn't told him about her job offer yet, reasoning it would be better to wait until they were alone.

He glanced over at her and pulled her closer to him. "Did I remember to tell you how beautiful you look? And how crazy I've been, wondering if you'd really be waiting for me when the ferry docked tonight?"

"I was pretty nervous myself," Riley admitted.

"I forgot to ask you what you wanted to cook tonight," he said, making the sharp turn onto the narrow path leading to Sandy Point. "I didn't know if you'd like fish or meat or what, so I covered all my bets with some mahi steaks and a couple of little filets. I had Mom bring some stuff over from the Mercantile to stock the fridge, too."

"Does your mom know about us?" Riley asked shyly.

"Of course." He paused. "Wait. Was I not supposed to let Annie know?"

"No, that's fine," Riley said. "Actually a lot of people on the island know about us now. Including Maggy and Evelyn."

"Oh yeah?" He pulled the cart up in front of the cabin. It was still daylight, but the front porch light was on.

"Let's unload your groceries and pour a drink," Riley said grimly. "And then I'll tell you what happened."

They found a Mason jar full of sunflowers on the kitchen table and a chilled bottle of champagne in the refrigerator, along with a cheese and pâté plate and a baguette of French bread.

Nate opened the wine and poured a glass for Riley and opened a beer for himself, then led her by the hand to the sofa.

She sat down beside him, and he pulled her into his arms. "I've thought about this every night while I was gone," he said, running his hands through her hair and nibbling on her earlobes. "You wanna know how nutty I am about you? I pulled up some of your old video clips on YouTube and watched them at night, when I couldn't sleep."

Riley laughed. "Now, that's just weird."

"It gets weirder," he chuckled. "It got so I got a hard-on every time I heard that stupid theme music for your *Wake Up, Carolina* show."

She stood up and pulled him to his feet. "Okay, I know how to fix that."

Nate grinned. "Should I put the coals on first?"

"Later," Riley said, slipping out of her sandals. "We've got all night." He had her undressed before they made it to the bed. "I want you," he said, stripping off her panties and bra. "Stand right there and just let me look at you," he said, his voice hoarse. He stood behind her and wrapped his arms around her waist, kissing her ears and shoulder blades. He lifted her hair and kissed the nape of her neck and she shivered with delight. He ran his hands lightly up her belly and cupped a breast in each hand, and sitting on the edge of the bed, he slowly kissed his way down her spine, pausing at each vertebrae. He slid his hands downward, then pulled her onto his lap, teasing her with his fingertips, entering her and stroking her until she was mindless with pleasure.

Riley turned and pushed him backward onto the bed. She pulled his shirt over his head and fumbled with his zipper while he watched, his head propped up on the pillows, while she tugged and struggled until she had him naked.

She ran her hands lightly down his chest, then stroked and fondled and kissed him until he could stand it no longer. He raised himself above her and smiled down at her.

"You're doing it again," Riley whispered.

"What?"

"Smiling," she said, touching a finger to his lips. "Having fun."

"And what about you?" he asked.

She reached up and guided him into her, raising her hips to meet his. "No more talking."

58

Now I wish you had started those coals," she said, hours later. She rolled over on the bed and grabbed her phone to check the time. "It's after nine, and I'm starving."

He nipped at her neck and tried to pull her back to him. "Starved for love?"

"Starved for food," she said firmly. "Dinner now. Love later."

"I'll go start the coals," he said. "You want a shower? There are clean towels in the bathroom."

He went to the dresser, got a pair of shorts, and stepped into them while Riley picked up her discarded clothes and headed for the bathroom.

She'd just stepped out of the shower and was toweling off when she heard her phone ringing in the bedroom. She grabbed it and paused before hitting the connect button. The call was from her mother.

Riley frowned down at the phone. She let the call go to voice mail and got dressed.

By the time she'd walked into the kitchen, Nate was slicing tomatoes for a salad, and smoke was curling from the grill outside the kitchen door. Her phone rang again, and she pulled it from the pocket of her dress, frowning down at it.

Nate gave her a questioning look. "It's Mama. She knows I'm with you. And she's not crazy about the idea."

"You told her?" Nate asked. "That's a pretty bold move for you."

"Unfortunately, I didn't get the chance," Riley said. She poured herself a glass of wine and was telling him about the cell phone photo of their embrace that had gone viral when her phone rang again.

"Don't answer it," Nate said sharply.

She looked down at the caller ID and saw that the call was from Billy.

"It's my brother," she said. "He never calls my cell."

She hit the connect button. "Billy?"

"Riley, I'm at Shutters with Mama. Maggy's locked herself in her bedroom and we can't get her to come to the door. I think she's sick."

"What? She was supposed to be at Annabelle's."

"Look, I'm trying to get the door open. I think you better come. I think something bad has happened."

"I'll be right there," Riley said. "I don't care what you have to do, just get that damn door open. I'm on my way."

"What is it?" Nate asked.

"It's Maggy. I'll tell you what I know on the way," Riley said.

"I don't know why she went home," Riley said, as Nate drove through the darkness. "She was supposed to spend the night at Annabelle's." She looked out at the thick canopy of trees. "Isn't there any kind of shortcut?"

"No," Nate said. "The creek winds all through here. There's only one way in and one way out. I'm going as fast as I can."

"We had another fight before she left," Riley said, on the verge of tears. "Maggy was so angry and irritable, I thought maybe her blood sugar was off. She gets that way when it's too low or too high. But she said she'd eaten and taken her insulin. And I checked her backpack. She had her syringes and her blood-testing kit with her. I don't know what happened."

"What was the fight about?" he asked.

"You," Riley said, glancing over at him. "Maggy's furious that I'm seeing you. She accused me of all kinds of horrible things, called me selfish, said I didn't care about her feelings."

Nate reached for her hand and squeezed it. "Kids say things they don't mean."

She shook her head vehemently. "No. She said she wished Wendell was alive and I was dead. And she meant every word."

"We'll be there in five minutes," Nate said. "What can I do?"

"Drive faster," Riley said. "Please, for God's sake, drive faster."

Lights blazed from every window at Shutters. Riley jumped from the moving golf cart and ran up the stairs. Billy knelt in front of Maggy's door, an ice pick stuck into the lock. He turned helpless eyes to his sister.

"I can't open it," he said. "I've tried kicking it, but this thing is like lead."

Nate came running up the stairs and appraised the situation with one look. "Get me a screwdriver and a hammer," he said.

"In the kitchen, in the drawer by the fridge," Evelyn said, wringing her hands. "Hurry, Billy."

A moment later, Billy was back with tools in hand. Nate grabbed the screwdriver and started working on the hinges.

"Maggy!" Riley called, putting her lips to the door. "Maggy! Can you hear me?"

She thought she heard a faint noise, then nothing.

"Nate, hurry," Riley urged.

"The damn pin is frozen," he said. He took the screwdriver and jammed it into the gap between the pin and the hinge, using it as a wedge, then began striking the screwdriver handle with the hammer, again and again, until slowly the pin moved upward and popped loose. He moved down the door to the next hinge and repeated the same action, until finally, the second pin popped up. "Almost there," Nate muttered. He grasped the door by the knob and middle hinge and yanked it completely off the door frame.

Riley ran past him. Maggy was sprawled backward on the bed, her eyes barely open. An empty Coke can lay on the floor, and the rug was littered with mini Snickers candy wrappers.

"Call nine-one-one," Riley shouted. Evelyn looked on, paralyzed. "Mama, call nine-one-one!" she screamed. "Tell them we've got a twelve-year-old in a diabetic coma. We need to get to the hospital."

"Maggy!" Riley yelled. She knelt beside her daughter and felt that the bed was damp. She touched Maggy's face and sniffed her breath. "Oh, God," she whispered. "She's peed the bed. Where's her kit? Where's the damn kit?"

"Here's her backpack," Billy said, picking it up from the floor.

"The purple zippered case," Riley said. "There's a preloaded syringe. Hurry!"

Billy found the kit and handed the syringe to his sister.

Riley grabbed it and grasped Maggy's leg, plunging the syringe into the outside of her upper thigh.

"Oh, my God," Evelyn whimpered. "Oh, my God." She held the phone in her hand, staring at it.

Billy took the phone and went out into the hallway. They heard his voice echoing in the high-ceilinged room. "Ambulance needed at the Shutters. Bluff Road. My twelve-year-old niece is in a diabetic coma. Please hurry!"

"What should I do?" Nate asked.

"Get her downstairs. We've got to get her to the hospital in town."

Nate bent over the girl, wrapped the edges of the bedspread around her limp form, and cradled her in his arms. Riley picked up her daughter's kit and followed him down the stairs.

He carried her out onto the porch and paused beside the golf cart. "The hell with it," he said. "We'll take her in the cart." Just then they heard the wail of a siren. Moments later they saw the flashing red lights as the Belle Isle ambulance came speeding down the sandy drive.

Two EMTs, a young woman and a chubby tech who looked to be barely out of his teens, jumped out of the vehicle and loaded Maggy onto a gurney. "We called for the Life Flight helicopter from Baldwin Memorial," the woman told Riley. "They'll land on the village green to pick us up." She gestured to Riley. "You can ride in the back with your daughter, but we've gotta go right now."

Riley ducked into the ambulance and turned to look at Nate. She pointed toward the porch, where Evelyn stood, silhouetted in the doorway. "Tell Mama I'll call her as soon as we get to the hospital."

"I'll meet you there," he called. But the ambulance was pulling away.

Nate met Evelyn and Billy at the edge of the porch. Billy had a protective arm wrapped around his mother's shoulders. She stared at Nate with empty eyes. "They're going to Life Flight Maggy to the hospital in Southpoint," he said. "I'm going to take my boat over. Would you two like to ride with me?"

"Your boat?" Evelyn looked confused. "Not the ferry?"

"No, my boat can make it across in half the time it'd take the ferry," Nate explained. "I'll be happy to take you with me. My car is parked at the ferry dock."

"N-n-n-no," Evelyn stuttered. "Not the ferry?"

Billy took a step forward. "She's terrified of small boats," he said, his voice low.

"How about you?" he asked.

"I'll stay here with her," Billy said. "Will you tell Riley to call us? As soon as they know something?"

"I'll call you myself," Nate said.

The next hour was a blur. Riley crouched on a bench-type seat in the helicopter, her eyes glued to Maggy. The techs had started an IV line, and a tiny bit of color had returned to her cheeks. She was wrapped up to her chin in a shiny silver thermal blanket that made her look like a burrito. Her eyes were closed, and her hand, which Riley had not stopped clutching, was still clammy to the touch.

The crossing to the hospital was mercifully quick, and in less than fifteen minutes they were landing on the hospital's rooftop helipad. The door opened and two sets of hands reached in to extract the gurney holding Maggy Griggs.

Riley sat across from a nurse at the admitting desk, giving Maggy's detailed medical history.

"She was diagnosed with type 1 juvenile diabetes a little over a year ago," she told the nurse. "Maggy will be thirteen in October."

"Is her diabetes well-controlled?" the nurse asked.

"Usually, yes. After she was diagnosed, they kept her at WakeMed in Raleigh for three days, while they stabilized her blood sugar and educated both of us on the disease. Maggy's very bright, and picked up all the diet restrictions and blood testing really quickly."

"And is she usually compliant?"

"Usually, she's very diligent," Riley said. "We haven't had a single incident in months and months. But she's had a rough summer. Her father was killed in May, and they were very close."

"That poor kid," the nurse said, shaking her head. "And what happened tonight?"

"We'd had a fight earlier in the day, and she was very upset. She was supposed to spend the night with a friend, and for some reason I don't understand, she left her friend's house around eight o'clock. When Maggy got home, she went directly to her bedroom and locked the door. I wasn't home." Riley felt her gut wrench with guilt and shame. "Around nine o'clock, my mother got concerned and knocked on her door, but Maggy didn't answer. She called me, and I got home, and we managed to get the door off the hinges."

Riley chewed a bit of dried cuticle on her thumbnail. "We found an empty Coke can and several candy wrappers on the floor by her bed, and she was already unconscious, on her way to a diabetic coma. I managed to give her an injection, immediately, and then we called nine-one-one and got her here as fast as we could."

"Okay," the nurse said. "I'm going to go in the back and see how she's doing. Why don't you take a seat and I'll come out and let you know what's what."

"Thank you," Riley said. She collapsed into a chair and covered her face with her hands. Even when she closed her eyes she could still see Maggy's ghostly face, smell the urine on her clothes and the smeared chocolate candy on her fingertips.

Maggy hadn't accidentally gorged herself on a sugary soda and candy bars. Her daughter knew exactly how many grams of protein, sugar, and complex carbohydrates she could safely consume in one day. She knew how to rescue herself with a quick hit of juice and cheese crackers if her blood sugar dropped, and how to inject herself with insulin when it was needed.

No, Maggy knew exactly what she was doing tonight.

"Mrs. Griggs?" The nurse was smiling down at her. "Maggy's going to be fine. They're giving her fluids, and she's resting."

"Can I see her?" Riley asked.

"Just for a minute. Once we get her into a room, you can settle in and stay with her."

Riley followed the nurse to a curtained-off treatment area. She stood by the bed and gingerly touched her sleeping daughter's face. Her color had improved, and her skin was faintly warm to the touch. There was an IV tube attached to the crook of her right elbow, and another to the back of her left hand, and she wore an oxygen mask.

"See? She's perking right back up, like a little hothouse flower," the nurse said cheerfully. She put a gentle hand on Riley's arm. "Come on, Mama. Don't be so scared. Kids this age like to live dangerously. They don't want their friends to know they have a disease. They're embarrassed to have somebody see them pricking their finger to test their blood, or giving themselves a shot. We see this kind of thing all the time. I promise, twenty-four hours from now, you won't even know she got sick."

"I doubt that I will ever forget this night," Riley said. "But I hope you're right about her recovery."

Somehow, she managed to doze off in the hard molded-plastic chair. She felt a gentle kiss on her cheek and opened her eyes to see Nate sitting beside her, holding a Styrofoam cup of coffee.

"Hey," he said softly. "Sorry to wake you up."

"I wasn't really sleeping," Riley said, trying to sit up straight.

"I talked to the nurse a minute ago," Nate said. "I might have let her think I was your husband."

"Oh." Riley frowned.

"I didn't actually tell her I was. She just assumed it," he said. "Anyway, she said they're going to move Maggy into her room in about fifteen minutes because her condition has stabilized."

"Good." Riley yawned widely. "What time is it?"

"A little after two a.m. I texted Billy to tell him I'd gotten here, and that the nurse said Maggy was doing okay."

"Oh geez," Riley said. "I totally forgot to call them. Thanks for doing that."

"I don't want to upset Maggy, so I'll just stay out here in the waiting room," Nate said. "Unless you want me to go back to the island and pick up some clothes and stuff for you? I could stop and bring you some breakfast too, if you want."

"No, Nate," Riley said, biting her lip.

"No, you don't need clothes, or no breakfast?"

"Neither. Both. What I mean is, I don't want you to stay."

"I don't mind," he said. "I can't leave you here by yourself. Really. I got this."

Riley blinked back the tears welling up in her eyes. "I want you to go. Please? It's over. I can't see you anymore."

He recoiled as though she'd punched him in the gut. "Why?"

"Maggy didn't just slip up and forget to take care of herself tonight. She deliberately put herself in a diabetic coma—because she was angry at me. She could have died. I can't risk that again. She's my child, Nate. I can't put her health at risk."

He was shaking his head. "She's pushing your buttons, Riley. Punishing you to get what she wants. All kids do that kind of stuff."

"All kids don't have insulin-dependent diabetes," Riley said. "All kids haven't stood in a hospital morgue and seen their father stretched out in a refrigerated drawer."

"No, Riley," he said urgently. "This isn't fair. Not to you or me. We didn't kill Wendell. We deserve some happiness, don't we? Okay, we can cool it for a while, until Maggy gets used to the idea. But don't tell me it's over."

"I'm sorry, Nate," Riley said. "You have to go. Please?"

She was leaning over the hospital bed, listening to her daughter's steady in-and-out breathing. She stroked Maggy's hair, smiling at the now-faded pink streaks. She turned her head for only a moment, and when she looked back, Maggy's long eyelashes fluttered open.

"Hi," Riley said softly. "You're back."

Maggy nodded. "What time is it?"

"It's almost ten in the morning. You had kind of a rough night, kiddo."

Maggy turned her head and looked at the monitors and the IV pole and then back at her mother. "Is this the hospital? How did we get here?"

"Baldwin Memorial. They sent a helicopter to pick us up on the island."

"I rode in a helicopter, and I didn't even know it?"

"You were pretty sick." Riley squeezed her daughter's hand. "You scared us, baby."

A tear trickled from Maggy's eye, and Riley dabbed at it with a tissue. "I'm sorry, Mommy. I was so dumb. I didn't mean that stuff I said."

"It's okay. We both said some stuff we didn't mean. Do you feel like telling me what happened last night? Why did you leave Annabelle's?"

"We had a fight." Maggy turned her face to the wall. "She said Dad was a crook, and he stole money and the FBI was after him."

"Oh, honey." Riley bit the inside of her cheek until she tasted blood, wishing she could draw blood from Annabelle, and anybody who was ever, ever cruel to her child.

"Then she said I was stupid and ugly and it was gross that I have to stick myself and test my blood and get shots. So I came home. I hate her."

"Is that why you ate candy and made yourself sick?"

"Yes," Maggy said, in the tiniest, barely audible voice possible. "I was mad at you and Annabelle, and I wanted to make you feel as bad as I feel. But I'm sorry now. I won't do it again."

"You better not," Riley said.

"When can we go home?" Maggy asked plaintively.

"Maybe today. Mimi called. Mr. Banks is missing you."

"No, I mean home to Raleigh. To our new house. The kids on Belle Isle are jerks."

"We'll see," Riley said. She kissed the tip of her finger and touched it to her child's cheek. "Get some rest now."

59

Are you sure you want to do this?" Parrish asked. They were on the ferry, bound for Southpoint, and then Raleigh.

"I don't want to, I have to," Riley said. They were on a bench on the upper observation deck. Maggy sat nearby, with Mr. Banks clutched tightly in her arms. "My job starts tomorrow and Maggy's school starts, too."

"You don't need to stay in a hotel, for God's sake. Just stay at our house until your new place is ready. I don't mind staying in town for a week or so, in case you need something, and you and Maggy won't be stuck in some dreary room where you can't even cook."

"It's not dreary. It's a very nice all-suite hotel right across the street from Woodlawn, her new school, so Maggy can just walk there after dismissal. There's a kitchenette so we can cook if we need to, but I don't expect to have much time this first week, so we'll probably do a lot of takeout. We'll be fine," Riley said.

"You won't let anybody help, will you?" Parrish said, shaking her head in exasperation.

"This is our new normal. I love and appreciate you more than I can say, Parrish, but Maggy and I have to figure out how to do this by ourselves. It's enough that you're helping me get some of our stuff out of the storage unit and moved into the hotel, and sticking around to go to orientation with her tomorrow."

"It's not enough, but since you won't let me do anything else, what choice do I have? And let me just say—I think it's super shitty that this boss of yours won't even give you a couple hours to go to orientation with your kid at her new school."

"Yeah," Riley said uneasily. "I guess you can't expect a single twenty-six-year-old to get how important this is, but I kinda agree with you. I'm trying to be optimistic about everything, for Maggy's sake, but I'm afraid this isn't going to be the most family-friendly job I've ever had."

"And she's a woman! There's no excuse for that."

"I just have to educate her," Riley said.

Parrish took a sip from her water bottle. "Did you see who got on the ferry at the last minute?"

Riley shot her an annoyed look. "You know I did."

"Have you spoken to him?"

"No. The whole thing is impossible. If you'd seen Maggy that night, in her room, in a self-induced diabetic coma, lying in a puddle of her own vomit and urine, you'd understand. Now, can we please drop it?"

"I'm not letting you off the hook that easily, Riles. I'm a mom too, you know, and I've raised a child. And no, David didn't have a serious disease, but that's not the issue. Kids that age are manipulative little bastards, and Maggy, bless her heart, is clever enough that she knows exactly how to push your buttons and how far to push you to get what she wants."

"I don't think it's unreasonable of her to expect the only parent she has to put her needs first," Riley said. "That's what parents do, and it's a sacrifice I'm willing to make."

"You're missing the point," Parrish insisted. "Needs aren't the same as wants. You give Maggy everything she needs—in spades. Attention, both physical and medical, affection, education, all of it. But she wants more. She wants to dictate how you live, who you love. That's not fair. And it's not good for her or you. Keep this up and she'll end up a spoiled, self-involved brat and ten years from now you'll be a lonely empty nester who wakes up one day to discover you forgot to have a life for yourself."

"Anything else, Dr. Freud?" Riley asked.

"Yeah," Parrish said, looking up. "I just saw him standing at the window up there in the pilothouse. If you'd seen the way he was looking down at you—the longing, the despair, all of it . . ."

"It wouldn't change anything," Riley said. "What's done is done."

"Come on, Mags. Parrish is here. Let's see how you look in the uniform," Riley called. It was seven thirty Monday morning, Maggy had been in the bathroom for forty minutes, and Riley needed to leave for work.

"No!"

Riley looked at Parrish and shrugged.

"I got this," Parrish said. She pounded on the bathroom door.

"Margaret Evelyn Griggs, get your tail out here. RIGHT THIS MINUTE."

The bathroom door opened a crack and light spilled out into the hotel room. "I am NOT wearing this," Maggy announced, walking out. "I look like that girl from Harry Potter."

She stalked out of the bathroom, the hard soles of her saddle oxfords clattering on the tile floor. The sleeves of the boxy blue blazer stuck out from her narrow wrists by an inch, and the hem of the pleated skirt hit an unacceptable five inches short of her bony kneecaps.

"I think you look nice," Riley said. "Now, unroll the waistband of that kilt and pull up the knee socks." She handed Maggy her backpack. "Your kit is in there, and I packed extra juice boxes and crackers and snacks. You'll get a hot lunch in the cafeteria, but in case you don't like it . . ."

"Mom! I know all that. We've been over it, like, a million times." Maggy sped toward the door.

"You've got the number at the station, just in case, right?" Riley called. "And the key to the room? I should be back here no later than four."

Parrish followed Maggy out the door. "Does she remind you of Julie from *The Love Boat* in that getup?"

"Don't you dare tell her that," Riley said. "I should be off the air at two. Call me and tell me how it went."

Riley looked at herself in the full-length mirror of the communal dressing room at WDHM and recoiled in horror. "I am *not* wearing this," she muttered.

The sleeveless top was made of a clingy reptile-print fabric with a high stovepipe collar and a diagonal mesh-covered cutout across her breasts to her waist, which was accented by a three-inch-wide black leather belt. The skintight leggings were made of black pleather, and a shoebox on the counter held a pair of gold peep-toe suede booties with a four-inch acrylic stacked heel.

Her ensemble had been hanging in her cubicle at the station when she'd arrived—thirty minutes late. The commute from North Hills to Durham had taken much longer than she'd expected.

Jacy, her producer, had made a big show of looking at the huge clock in the newsroom, and then back at Riley. "Your outfit is right there. A six, right? Our sponsor, Floozys, wants you to mention on air that viewers can go to our Web site and click the link to order it."

"Uh, I'm actually an eight," Riley said. "Floozys? That's really the name of the shop?"

"Cute, right?" Jacy said. "Why don't you get dressed and made up, then we'll do a quick run-through on the set."

Riley did a slow turn in front of the mirror and wanted to weep. The combination of the too-small cinched belt and clingy fabric made her butt look huge, and she'd never been a fan of reptile prints. To make matters worse, the booties were nearly impossible to walk in. As she tottered out of the dressing room, she looked and felt like an overage stripper.

The set had been built in the far corner of the cavernous studio, and featured a mod-looking neon-orange sofa and a cobalt-blue swivel "host's chair." The backdrop was a blown-up color photo of the Durham skyline.

"Adorbs, right?" Jacy said, showing her where to sit.

Riley collapsed into the chair, and Jacy handed her a sheaf of notes.

"Okay, here's today's lineup. First, you'll have Bob the Bugman from Triangle Pest Terminators. You're gonna talk about powderpost beetles, Formosan termites, German cockroaches, and um . . ." She looked over Riley's shoulder at the printout. "Oh yeah, voles."

"What's a vole?" Riley asked.

"Something disgusting," Jacy said. "Like a guinea pig, I think, but they live in basements. Whatever. Bob's an old pro at this. All you do is say that our community is, um, infested with pests. Just read what's on the teleprompter."

"Got it," Riley said.

"This part is very important. Crucial. You mention the link on our Web site at the beginning of the spot and at the end for their viewers' special coupon. It's important, because if they don't get a minimum number of clicks on that coupon, we don't get paid."

"We get paid for clicks?"

"Of course. Right? Next you've got Dr. Armand Amonghadang from Better You Cosmetic Surgery."

Riley studied the script. "How do you pronounce that name again? Can they give me a phonetic spelling on the teleprompter so I don't mess it up?"

Jacy rolled her eyes. "Ah. Mong. Ha. Dang. We usually just call him Dr. Dang. He's pretty cool. You'll lead in to him with this new study that shows young teens' self-esteem can be radically improved with properly done breast augmentation. He'll take it from there. His clinic is offering a back-to-school special. Again, you'll promo the link on our Web site."

Riley scanned her notes. "Jacy, are you telling me I'm supposed to say it's a good idea for young teens to have breast augmentation? That there's an actual clinical study making that claim? Who did the study?"

"Who cares?" Jacy studied Riley. "Your job is to make your viewers believe they need whatever you're talking about. To make them want to shop where you shop and wear what you wear and do what you say. Right?"

"I don't know," Riley said uneasily. "Pest-control coupons are one thing, but I'm not really comfortable advocating boob jobs for young girls. It seems unethical."

"How is that unethical? My mom got me a boob job when I was sixteen, and it was, like, life changing. So don't judge, okay? Also? I don't know if your agent mentioned it, but this is not *Sixty Minutes* here."

"But . . ."

"Okay, the last spot is our community calendar thing. It's National Honey Bee Awareness Day on the twentieth, so Seth, the bee guy, will demonstrate how you smoke a hive, and he's bringing a bee helmet for you, too. This demographic loves it when the hosts participate. Then you'll mention that you'll be at the mall Thursday night, judging the North Carolina Beekeeper's Association's honey competition. And one lucky viewer who clicks the link on our Web site will get to have dinner with you before. Right?"

"What? Bees? No, Jacy. I can't wrangle bees. I'm terrified of stinging insects. Literally. I break out in hives."

"Hives! That's adorbs, right? Use that in the intro. They didn't tell me you were funny." The producer checked her watch. "Okay, I need to go make some phone calls and then we've got a meeting with the sales staff—"

"Jacy! Did you just hear what I said? I am not getting anywhere near bees. And while we're on the subject, nobody said anything to me about an event on Thursday night. I can't be at the mall. It's back-to-school night at my daughter's school."

Jacy stood with her hands on her hips, her lips pursed. "You know, Riley, we were a little, um, hesitant when your name came up in our talent search. But our focus groups showed us that our demographic wants a host with some maturity and a high believability factor. Plus, your people told us you were a pro. A real team player. So I don't think it's good for you to go all prima donna right off the bat on your first day, do you?"

"This is not being a prima donna," Riley said quietly. "I'm happy to interview the beekeeper, and he can smoke the hive all by himself while I stand well off-camera. But the Thursday night thing is not happening."

"You know you get paid a hundred bucks for a personal appearance, right?"

"Still not happening," Riley said. She turned and hobbled back to her cubicle to wait for her first guest to arrive.

It was nearly five o'clock by the time Riley made it back to the hotel. She found Maggy sitting on the pullout sofa in their suite, watching television. The room smelled like scorched microwave popcorn.

"Hey, Mom," Maggy said, not looking up.

"Hi!" Riley had been giving herself a nonstop pep talk during the hour-and-a-half-long commute from Durham. So her first day hadn't gone well. Okay, it was the worst first day ever. So she hated the job, and the pay was crap, and her boss was a nitwit, and her show was doomed to be a ratings bomb. She and Maggy had each other, and tomorrow would be better. It *had* to be better, because she really didn't see how it could be worse.

"How was your day?" Riley asked. "Do you like the new school?"

"It's okay." Maggy shoved a handful of popcorn in her mouth.

"Are the teachers nice?"

"They're okay."

"Do you have any homework?"

Maggy aimed the remote at the television and turned up the volume. "*Mom*. I'm trying to watch this."

Riley took off her shoes and sank down onto the bed. She couldn't ever remember feeling as tired and defeated as she did right now.

"What would you like for dinner tonight?" she asked.

"Pizza!"

"Pizza and salad," Riley said firmly. She reached across the bed, found the notebook with all the takeout menus of nearby restaurants, and placed her order.

"Dinner by six," Riley said, yawning. Then she promptly dozed off.

By eight, they'd eaten, and Maggy had taken her insulin, and Riley started to pull out the sofabed.

"Can I just sleep with you tonight?" Maggy asked, curling up on the side of the queen-size bed.

"Sure," Riley said, trying not to act surprised. She pulled down the covers and plumped the pillow next to hers. Maggy climbed in bed, and Riley clicked off the light.

"Mom?"

"Yes, baby."

"You never said how your day was."

"It was . . . okay."

"Was your new boss nice?"

"She was okay."

"Do you have any homework?"

Riley chuckled and gave her daughter's fanny a whack. "Very cute."

"Seriously, Mom. Tell me the truth. I'm not a little kid."

"Umm, it really isn't very okay. It kinda sucks. Nothing is like I thought it would be."

"Wow," Maggy said. Riley felt her daughter's slight frame mold up against her side, and her thin arm snaked around her waist. She felt Maggy's warm breath on the back of her neck.

"You know what?"

"What?" Riley said.

"My day wasn't that hot either."

"Do you want to tell me about it? Maybe there's something I can do to help."

"No," Maggy said. "It'll be okay."

60

The Woodlawn School's Sanford W. Mangrum Performing Arts Center was a far cry from the school auditorium at Edenton Elementary School, where Riley had spent her formative years.

The biggest difference was that this space did not double as the school cafeteria, and thus did not carry the unforgettable scent of steam table chili-roni and soured milk. No. This space was a state-of-the-art masterpiece, with tiered stadium seating, plush upholstered seating, and surround-sound acoustics.

The lights were already flickering as Riley hurried to her seat at back-to-school night, tardy again, because no matter what time of day she left the Durham studio she always got stuck in traffic on Interstate 40.

She drew annoyed glares as she bumped knees and elbows trying to get to a mid-row vacant seat. "Sorry," she whispered.

The headmistress, Dr. Ksionzyk, was a pleasant, freckle-faced woman with a tangle of silver hair and just the slightest hint of an upstate New York accent. She gave a warm welcome to new and old parents of middle school students . . . and that was the last thing Riley was aware of, because she dozed off shortly after the lights were dimmed, awakening only when the parents applauded and the lights went back up, signaling a stampede of parents rushing to beat the fifteen-minute warning bell.

Thankfully, Maggy had delivered a folder to her mother with explicit instructions for back-to-school night. Riley knew she was to report to room twelve at the Dunstan Building at 6:45 p.m. to meet Miss Barlow, Maggy's homeroom teacher.

She found the room and the desk with Maggy's name masking-taped to it, but before she could sit, the teacher approached with barely concealed excitement. "You're Riley from Raleigh! My gosh! What are you doing here?"

"My daughter is in your homeroom. This is where she sits. Maggy Griggs?"

Blank look.

"She has medium brown hair, wears it in a braid? Blue-gray eyes? Thin build? She sits in this chair?" Riley gestured to the desk she was about to sit in.

"Oh, Maggy," the teacher said, deliberately vague. "Yes, such a sweet girl. I'm looking forward to getting to know her as the school year progresses."

The teacher stood at the front of the room and delivered a well-rehearsed spiel on school rules, expectations, and what she called "fun facts about the Woodlawn Woodchucks," which turned out to be the school mascot. Riley surveyed the room as she spoke, counting the desks and the number of parents occupying them. Fourteen desks with fourteen parents. And this teacher had no idea who Maggy was?

After five minutes, the parents were invited to look around and meet the parents of their children's classmates.

Riley felt a tap on her shoulder and turned around. "Excuse me. Did I hear you say you're Maggy's mom?" The speaker was a tall woman with a curtain of waist-length frizzy red hair. "We meet at last! I'm Chantelle Roberts."

Now it was Riley's turn to look blank.

"Annabelle's mom? From Belle Isle?"

"Oh, yes," Riley said. She'd wondered if the woman would ever bother to call to explain why she'd allowed Maggy to ride her bike home in the dark, alone. "I didn't know Annabelle was enrolled here."

Now she wondered why Maggy hadn't mentioned that her sworn frenemy not only went to her new school, but sat in front of her in homeroom.

"Yes," Chantelle was saying. "It was a very last-minute thing. Micki started a new job in Raleigh, so here we are." She paused and lowered her voice. "Listen. About that night on the island. I am so sorry about what happened with Maggy. And I feel terrible that they're still feuding. I've spoken to Annabelle about being mean, but you know how girls are at this age . . ."

The bell rang. Riley nodded curtly and joined the mad rush in the hallway to make it to Maggy's first-period class.

An hour later, Riley dragged herself to the last stop of the evening, the Woodlawn School's Susan B. Foster Dining Pavilion. Here, she knew, parents were supposed to visit booths staffed by club advisors and sports coaches, in order to encourage their children to participate in extracurricular events.

What she really longed to do was go back to her sad hotel room and hug her sad child and forget about her day, about the endless arguments with Jacy about the truly awful Floozys outfits she was expected to wear on-air, about the shameless pay-for-play guests she was supposed to "interview," and about her adamant refusal to participate in after-hours personal appearances.

Part of her weariness tonight, Riley knew, was her nagging, uneasy impression that the Woodchuck Nation was largely indifferent to the existence of Maggy Griggs.

Still, she dutifully strolled around the room, pausing to chat for a moment with the tennis coach, who stood behind a table blazing with trophies, plaques, and awards testifying to the school's reputation as a tennis powerhouse.

The coach was a deeply tanned twentysomething whose name tag said COACH CHASE.

"Hi!" the coach said as she approached. "Do you have a tennis player in the family?"

"I do," Riley said. "She's played mixed doubles at our club, and she's a pretty good singles player, too."

"What's her ranking?" Coach Chase asked.

Riley smiled. "She's only twelve. I mean, she's ranked number one with her family . . ."

"Oh. That's nice. That is, nice that she's a recreational player. But my Woodchuck girls' team has taken the state title for the past four consecutive years. Two of my recent grads are sitting out their senior year of high school because they've gone pro."

"Do you hold tryouts for the team?" Riley asked.

"Oh, sure," the coach said. "And she's welcome to come out. But it's only fair to warn you that I've got my team pretty well set for this year. But, hey, tell her to come see Coach Chase. We can always use somebody to hit around with."

Riley clenched and unclenched her fists to keep herself from hitting the coach's head.

Maggy was already in bed with the lights off. Riley climbed out of her work clothes and under the covers. She felt something squirming on the pillow next to her head.

"Is that Banksy?"

"Yes," Maggy said.

"Can't he sleep in his crate?"

"No. He misses me when I'm gone at school all day."

"Me, too," Riley said. "Okay. Just this once, he can stay. But not on my pillow." She scooted the dog gently onto the mattress between them.

"I met some of your teachers at back-to-school night," Riley said.

"That's cool."

"Hey, Maggy? How come you didn't tell me Annabelle goes to your school? And she's in your homeroom, and sits right in front of you."

No answer.

Riley switched on the bedside lamp, and Maggy pulled the covers over her head. "*Mom.* I'm trying to sleep."

"Talk to me, Margaret. Why didn't you say something?"

"Dad always says nobody likes a whiner."

Yes, Riley thought, he always did say that, but he almost always used it when he was accusing a woman of voicing dissatisfaction.

"It's not necessarily whining to let your mother know you have a difficult situation in your life," Riley said.

"What good would it do? Anyway, it's fine. She acts like I'm not even there."

"Has Annabelle been mean to you again? Said anything about your dad, or the diabetes, or the shots, or anything like that? Tell me the truth, Mags."

"It's fine. I don't care. I don't care about anybody at that school."

Riley propped herself up on one elbow. "It's not fine. You're sad about school, and I'm sad about my job."

"You are? Still?"

"Yeah," Riley said. "I know I said it would get better, but I don't think it will. My boss doesn't like me very much, and the feeling is mutual."

"Are you gonna quit?"

"I'm not sure what I'm going to do," Riley said truthfully. "But I don't think I can keep doing a job that takes away my sense of self-respect."

"Hey! I've got a great idea. If you quit your job, you can homeschool me. It would be awesome. You know, we could live on the island, and go to the beach every day. . . ."

"Whoa!" Riley laughed. "That's a pretty fantasy. But one, I have to work. And two, I'd be a lousy homeschool mother. I can't do math, and I don't know squat about chemistry or biology. And three, even homeschooled kids don't get to go to the beach all day. They have to sit in a classroom, and do homework, and, you know, actually take tests and learn. And, anyway, I thought you said all the kids on the island are stupid jerks."

"I meant mostly Annabelle," Maggy said. "Can I ask you something and you won't get mad?"

"You can ask, but I can't promise not to get mad," Riley said. "I warn you, I've had a pretty crappy day."

"Do you ever miss Dad?"

Riley had to think about that. Did she miss Wendell? Had her anger dissipated enough to allow her to be honest about her feelings for him?

"That's still complicated for me, Maggy," she admitted. "I know you miss him terribly. I guess I miss some things. I miss the pancakes he'd make sometimes on Sunday nights. And I miss seeing you with him, and knowing how proud he was of you. I miss the three of us, piled in bed, watching movies, and drinking Diet Coke, and having burp contests."

"Yeah, the burp contests were awesome," Maggy said. "Dad could really belch, couldn't he?"

"If they had Olympic burping, he'd have been a gold medal contender," Riley agreed. She rubbed her daughter's back. "Go to sleep now, baby. We'll figure it out somehow. Your PopPop used to say everything always looks better in the morning."

But on Friday, things did not look rosy. The day started with a call from her real estate broker. She was sitting in her cubicle at the station, going over her notes for that day's show, whose guests included a Latin dance instructor, an author who'd self-published a book about colon cleansing, and the owner of a vinyl siding company.

"Riley," her broker said. "I've been watching your new show. And I love your wardrobe. So eclectic and youthful!"

Riley looked down at that day's outfit, a purple silk dress with cascading tiers of gathered fabric that made her look like a human dust ruffle. "Thanks, Brenda. I've been meaning to call. You know, Monday is the closing. I've got my movers lined up, but I was wondering when I can do a walk-through of the house. Have you talked to the sellers lately?"

"We've had a little hitch, Riley. The thing is, the sellers have changed their minds. His new job fell through, and it turns out they hate the climate in South Florida. So they'd really like to give you your money back and void the contract."

"No! They can't do that, Brenda. We have a contract. Just tell them no."

"Hear me out, okay? They're proposing to return your down payment, plus an extra five thousand for inconveniencing you. How does that sound?"

"It sounds terrible. Maggy and I have been camped out in a hotel for a week, and we're sick of it. I've started my job, and I don't have any time to go house hunting. Just tell them no, Brenda."

"I tried. I really did, but they just won't budge. I've never had this happen before."

"But it's my house now. I signed a good-faith contract way back in May. You go back to them and tell them I'll sue if they don't get out of that house by Monday."

"I'll tell them, but I don't think it'll make any difference. They clearly don't intend to move."

"This is crazy!"

"Riley?" Jacy stood just outside her cubicle. "May I speak with you?"

"I have to go, Brenda. Monday. I want my house Monday."

Riley threw her phone onto her desk. "What is it now, Jacy?"

"We've had a little scheduling snafu. The dance instructor injured his foot last night, so your tango lesson with him is off, and we have a five-minute slot to fill, and we don't have a backup guest. Instead, we thought we'd try something really radical. An on-air colon cleanse. Totes adorbs! Right?"

Riley held her breath until she thought she might black out. Then she exhaled deeply. "No. And by that, I mean hell, no." She stood up, unzipped the purple dust ruffle dress, and let it fall to the floor. She was standing in the middle of the newsroom in her panties and bra, rediscovering the liberating sensation of knowing that once again her give-a-shit had got up and gone. She pulled a promotional WDHM T-shirt over her head and stepped into her own jeans.

Jacy gaped. "What are you doing?"

"I'm quitting. Right? Cleanse your own damn colon."

The midmorning traffic on I-40 was light, and she made it to the Woodlawn School by eleven fifteen. She went directly to the Alexandra Winzeler Administration Building, filled out the necessary paperwork, secured a visitor's pass, and walked to the Susan B. Foster Dining Pavilion where she found a sad little girl with a long braid and blue-gray eyes sitting at a lunch table by herself.

"Mama! What are you doing here?"

Riley grabbed Maggy's backpack. "I'm busting you out of here, kid. Let's go."

61

Maggy peered out the car window. “Where are we going?”

Riley smiled. She felt amazingly lighthearted. “What do you say we go back to the hotel, get Banksy, pack up our stuff, and blow this pop stand?”

“Are we moving into the new house now?”

For a moment, Riley’s mood threatened to collapse. “It doesn’t look like our new house is going to be our new house after all. The owners decided they want to keep it. And since I no longer have a job, I couldn’t afford that house anyway.”

“Okay.”

“Okay? You’re not upset about not moving into the new house?”

Maggy turned and studied her mother’s face. “Are you?”

“I was, but now, I sort of don’t care. It’s, like, maybe it wasn’t supposed to happen.”

“Yeah.” Maggy nodded her head. “I think that, too. You know what I wish? I wish we could go backward. I wish we could move back into our old house, and I could go to my old school. And, you know. Everything.”

"You know that's not really possible, Maggy. But I'll tell you what, we could go to lunch and maybe ride past the old house and check it out."

"Sweet! Can we go to Snoopy's?"

Snoopy's was an old-style hot dog stand near the St. Mary's house. It had been Maggy's favorite dining spot since toddler days.

"Why not? It's lunchtime. You check your blood and take your shot, and I'll swing past the hotel and get Banksy."

Riley slowed the car as they passed the old house on St. Mary's Street, and Maggy hung out the car window so she could get a look. "Look, Mr. Banks. There's our house." She held the puppy up to the window.

"They painted it." Maggy sounded stunned.

Sure enough, the blue-green spruce color the house had been for the past decade during the Griggs's ownership was now a bright goldenrod shade.

"Eeew. It looks like mustard," Maggy said. "And look! They cut down my tree. And the swing is gone from the front porch. It looks terrible. Like it's naked or something."

"It's their house now, sweetie," Riley pointed out.

"Maybe I don't want to move back there after all."

Maggy ordered the Snoopy's special—hot dog with chili, mustard, and onions, crinkle fries, and a Diet Coke. Riley had her usual, the chicken salad sandwich. They sat at one of the picnic tables and ate and burped, and Maggy snuck fries to Mr. Banks when she thought her mother wasn't looking. The late summer sun beat down on their heads, but Riley didn't care. She was savoring this illicit-feeling moment.

Maggy gave her mother a pleading look. "Do I have to go back to school now?"

"No. You're not going back to Woodlawn School, and I'm not going back to WDHM."

"You mean, like, ever?"

"That's right."

"Sweet!" Maggy's face was wreathed in the kind of smile that had been missing from her repertoire for months. She tapped the puppy's smushed nose. "High-five for no school, Banksy!"

"Hold on, missy. I didn't say you weren't going back to school at all. Just not that particular school."

"Then, what are we going to do?"

"This is going to sound crazy, but I have absolutely no idea."

"Where will we live? And where will I go to school? And you said you have to work, so where will you get a job?"

"The only thing I'm sure of is this: I'm done with television. The truth is, television has been done with me for a while, it just took me until this morning to figure that out."

Maggy sucked loudly on her drink and waited.

One tiny idea had been floating around in Riley's imagination all day. The seed had been planted the night before, when Maggy shared her fantasy about moving back to the island and being homeschooled on the beach. Or maybe the idea had been there all along. Maybe it had germinated when Nate Milas asked her if she'd ever considered working in the family business.

She'd told him that had never been an option for her. But maybe, now that she'd slammed the door on being Riley from Raleigh, a new window was opening in her life. All she had to do was find the courage to crawl through it.

It took longer than Riley anticipated to reinvent herself.

She'd shared her scheme with only one other person—Parrish—strictly out of necessity, since it involved moving into her guest room with a daughter and dog in tow, for the duration.

"It's brilliant," Parrish said, as they sat around in their pajamas in the den of her house in Country Club Estates.

It was, they agreed, just like old times living together at Chapel Hill. Except for a couple of fairly major exceptions.

"Except I don't have to worry about walking in on you and your squeeze du jour," Riley said.

"And I don't have to get pissed about you borrowing my car, my clothes, or my Dooney and Bourke shoulder bag," Parrish countered.

Riley had enlisted Parrish to expedite the refund of her down payment on the new house, plus an extra eight thousand she'd squeezed out of the sellers in return for Riley's signature on a "hold harmless" document.

"Not that I don't love having you and Maggy here," Parrish said, late one night after a dinner of Red Dragon takeout, "but I still don't understand why you can't just go to Evelyn and tell her what you want to do."

"It's simple. I want to have everything in place when I step off that ferry, because I don't want to run the risk of having Mama steamroll me into submission. And I can't live under her roof again."

"Good thinking. So, where will you live?"

"I'll rent something near the village short-term. The season will be over after Labor Day, which is this coming weekend, so prices will be down, and availability should be up."

"What about school for Maggy? Are you sure you won't have second thoughts about pulling her out of one of the top-ranked prep schools in the state?"

"I'm positive," Riley said. "Woodlawn is probably great for lots of kids, but not for Maggy. She was miserable there. I've checked out the Baldwin County public schools, and they look surprisingly good. Their test scores are decent, and the class size is even smaller than it was at Woodlawn. And I've been e-mailing with the principal at the middle school. She seems like she's really on the ball. And, anyway, the schools I went to growing up in Edenton were small and rural, and I did okay."

Parrish dipped her egg roll into the last of the duck sauce. "It sounds like you've got everything figured out. But what about the missing piece in all of this?"

Riley's face clouded over. "You mean Nate? That's a nonissue. This is going to be a big adjustment for Maggy. And for me. Getting us settled into our new lives is my priority. I don't need any distractions."

"How's it gonna be, living and working on the same island with him?"

"It'll be fine," Riley said. "I'll make it work. Somehow."

62

Evelyn called bright and early on Wednesday. "Listen, honey, I hope you're planning on coming back this weekend. I want to start getting the house ready to close up for the season, and your brother is no help at all these days."

"I don't know, Mama," Riley said, trying to stall.

"Don't tell me you weren't planning on coming at all?" Evelyn said. "You never miss Labor Day weekend. I hope they're not planning on asking you to work at your new job, are they?"

"No, I'm not working," Riley said.

"And Maggy will be off school, right?"

"Um, yes, she'll be off."

"Then there's no reason you shouldn't come. In fact, I'd feel a lot better if you didn't wait until Friday. Just come tomorrow, will you?"

Riley had been exchanging e-mails with the owner of a small cottage just off the village green, but they'd yet to agree on a price for a long-term rental. She'd been planning on leaving for Belle Isle on Friday, but if she could get the rental agreement today, it could mean getting a jump on traffic heading out of town toward the coast. The last weekend of the summer always meant traffic would be twice as bad.

"All right, I'll come tomorrow," she said. "I'll call and let you know what ferry I'll be on."

"Good," Evelyn said. "Tell Maggy that Roo and Ollie and I have been missing her. We can't wait to hear all about her new school. And your new job, too."

"See you tomorrow," Riley said, shutting down that topic as quickly as possible.

"We're leaving now?" Maggy asked, when Riley woke her up at seven the next morning.

"I packed your suitcase while you were sleeping," Riley said. "Hurry up and get ready. I want to hit the road before traffic gets crazy. You can eat your breakfast and do your meds in the car."

Riley pulled to the curb at the ferry loading zone in Southpoint and shook her daughter awake. "Hey," she said softly. "We're here. We've only got fifteen minutes before it's time to board. I'll unload our stuff now, and you go walk Banksy while I park. Okay?"

Maggy nodded sleepily and collected the dog and his leash.

The ferry was just starting to unload arriving passengers when Riley and Maggy began lining up to board. Families and couples streamed off the ferry, weighted down with carry-on baggage, kids, and pets. She was a little surprised at the number of islanders leaving today. After all, this was supposed to be summer's last hurrah, a three-day weekend.

The horn blew the five-minute warning, and the crowd of departing passengers streamed forward onto the boat. With an eye on high banks of clouds in the sky, Riley herded Maggy into the main-deck cabin.

As the boat lurched away from the landing, Riley clicked the weather app on her phone. The latest bulletin was about what could be expected for this time of year on the southeastern coast.

The National Weather Service is reporting that the second named storm of the season, Tropical Storm Brody, has formed over the eastern Caribbean, as the area experiences winds up to 60 m.p.h., heavy rain, and seas swelling an estimated 15 to 20 feet. Storm projected to track in northwesterly direction over next 24 to 48 hours.

Riley gazed anxiously up at the sky, and then relaxed. Every other Labor Day weekend, it seemed, the National Weather Service issued dire-sounding storm and hurricane warnings, sending newcomers to the coast scurrying for higher ground. But as far back as she could remember, the last hurricane to make landfall anywhere near Belle Isle had been Hurricane Floyd. What year had that been? She Googled it, and the answer was reassuring. It had been 1999.

Maggy sat up on the bench, took out her iPod earbuds, and set Mr. Banks on the floor. "Mom? Is it okay if I go get something at the concession stand?"

"I packed snacks in your bag," Riley said, looking up from her online search of hurricane statistics.

"I mean something good, like a barbecue sandwich maybe. Okay?"

Riley took a five-dollar bill from her pocketbook and handed it over. "Okay, but I want you to . . ."

"Mooom! I know what to do? Okay? I'm not gonna screw up and get sick again. I promise. So, will you quit telling me what to do? I'll test my blood. I'll take my insulin. And you don't have to remind me. Every. Single. Time."

"Sorry," Riley said. "I'll try not to be such a helicopter mom."

She clipped the leash to the puppy's collar and walked out to the observation deck. Leaning over the rail, Riley could just spot the silhouette of Big Belle on the horizon. She glanced upward, toward the pilothouse, but the sun's glare obscured her view. Not that she cared, she told herself.

Maggy was back, happily licking barbecue sauce from her fingers as Riley reclaimed her seat. "I spotted the lighthouse before you did," Riley said gleefully. "I win."

"And I spotted your boyfriend," Maggy said. "He was going up the stairs to the pilothouse."

"He's not my boyfriend," Riley said quickly, feeling heat seeping into her cheeks.

Maggy gave her an appraising look. "What if I said maybe he's not as bad as I thought?"

"Really? What made you change your mind?"

"When we were in Raleigh, seeing how depressed you were, it made me sad. And I remembered how happy you were, when you were with him, before I got sick. Remember how you asked me if I didn't want to see you happy again? I think now, maybe if Nate makes you happy, that's a good thing."

Riley gave her daughter a light kiss on the cheek. "That's very sweet, Mags. Unfortunately, it's too late. He's a nice man, but the timing is all wrong."

She called Billy but there was no answer. A minute later, he called back. "Are you coming this weekend? Mama's all worked up about closing the house for the season."

"I'm on the ferry, about to dock now. Can you come pick us up?"

"Now? I was kind of in the middle of something. Can't you call Mama? Or just take the shuttle?"

"I could, but I really need to talk to you about something pretty important. So, can you come?"

They waited at the curb at the loading area for ten minutes before Billy Nolan zoomed up in his cart. He jumped out and hugged Maggy. "We've missed you!" he exclaimed. "How's the new school?"

"That's kind of a long story," Riley said, as they loaded their luggage onto the cart. As they pulled away from the ferry dock he took a sip from his insulated tumbler, and Riley looked away, annoyed. She had a very good idea of what he'd been busy with when she called.

"What's so important that you needed to talk to me about?" he asked.

"Guess what, Bebo? I quit my school," Maggy said, temporarily removing her earbuds. "And Mom quit her job. And I'm going to school in Southpoint."

"Whaaaat?"

"It's true," Riley said. "That's what I wanted to talk to you about." She told him, in the broadest strokes, about the plan she'd drawn up for their future.

Billy listened, but looked skeptical. "It sounds fine, theoretically, but do you really think you're up for something like this? I mean, your background is journalism, not real estate. And what's Mama going to say?"

"I can do this, Billy. I know I can," she said. "For the past few weeks, I've been doing a lot of soul-searching. And research. I've read up on small family-owned resort businesses like ours, and I've even talked to some people in the business. And who better to do it than me? I've loved this island my whole life, and I've watched Dad, and then Wendell running it."

"What do you want from me?"

"I need your help."

"You think Mama is going to listen to me? Really? Hasn't she bent your ear about how irresponsible and selfish I am?"

"I do think she'll listen to you. You're a part of this family, and you have a vote in how the business is run. Don't you think I can do it?"

"I don't know why you'd want to," he said, sounding irritated. "The company is on the skids, if you haven't noticed. Wendell gambled everything and lost big, and we've got all kinds of vacancies in the village. Cut your losses, Riley. Let somebody else deal with all the headaches."

"There *is* nobody else," she said heatedly. "Nobody else is going to have as much invested in Belle Isle's future as we do. Please, Bebo? Back me up on this?"

He took another sip of his drink, jiggling the ice cubes absentmindedly. "Okay," he said finally. "I'll try. Even though Mama stays on my last nerve."

"About what?"

He jiggled the ice cubes again. "You know."

Riley glanced at the backseat, but Maggy had her earbuds in again. "I hate to agree with her, but Mama's got a point. I'm worried about you, Bebo."

"Jesus!" he exploded. "First Scott, then Mama, now you. I wish all of y'all would just lighten up and leave me alone."

"I don't want to fight with you. When is Scott getting here?"

"Tomorrow, I guess."

She decided not to pursue the matter. "Will you do me one more favor? Take Maggy and Mr. Banks back to the firehouse with you, and let me borrow this cart? I'm supposed to walk through a house today at two, and if it checks out, I'll get the keys and we can start moving in right away."

"You mean, this weekend? What about your furniture?"

"It's fully furnished, with everything we need. I'll leave most of my stuff in storage in Raleigh until I figure out our next move."

"You got it," he said.

At three, Riley pulled Billy's cart up to the front steps at the Shutters. She found Evelyn in the kitchen, putting a bowl of chicken salad in the refrigerator.

"Riley!" she said, hugging her daughter. "When did you get in? Why didn't you call?"

"I got in a little while ago. Billy was in the village, so he picked me up."

"Where's Maggy?"

"She's with him."

"Was he drinking?"

Her mother's directness took Riley aback. She couldn't ever remember her mother even vaguely mentioning Billy's drinking before. But then, denial was Evelyn's middle name. It had only been since W.R.'s death that Evelyn had publicly acknowledged that her son was gay and that Scott was something other than "a dear friend."

"He had that plastic tumbler. I assume it wasn't water," Riley admitted.

"I'm so worried about that boy, I don't know what to do," her mother said, sinking down into a kitchen chair. "I think he might have a problem."

Riley sat down at the table and took both of Evelyn's hands in hers. She looked her mother directly in the eyes. "Mama, Billy is an alcoholic. We all know it. He knows it, but he won't admit it. We have got to see that he gets help. But nagging at him or giving him the silent treatment won't work."

Evelyn nodded and bit her lip. "He's been working again, you know. He played at a doctors' convention in Charlotte, and a wedding in Charleston.

Your brother has a real, God-given gift, Riley. He just needs to keep busy, that's all."

Riley took a deep breath. "Speaking of keeping busy, there's something I want to talk to you about."

The kitchen door flew open and Roo walked in, holding up what looked like a small portable transistor radio.

"Evelyn!" she said excitedly. "I just got an alert on my weather radio. Brody is on the move. It's over the Turks and Caicos right now, and they've got flooding and huge tides."

"Mary Roosevelt Nolan, I have no idea what you are talking about."

"Tropical Storm Brody," Roo said. "It was just spinning away out there in the eastern Caribbean, but now Jim Cantore says the winds have shifted, and he says we've got a good chance of Brody being upgraded to a hurricane. Isn't that exciting?"

"And just who is this Jim Cantore?"

"He's the Weather Channel storm chaser, Mama," Riley said. "Roo, does the radio say which direction the storm is headed now?"

"Oh, pooh," Evelyn said. "Hurricanes. That always happens this time of year. Some silly low-pressure system dumps a lot of rain over one of those islands out in the middle of nowhere, and everybody starts to panic. Those things always peter out over Cuba or the Dominican Republic. And in the meantime, everybody on the coast gets all hot and bothered. For what? A little wind and rain? If you ask me, it's all a ratings ploy for these television people."

"Right now, he says it's projected to head out to sea," Roo said, sounding disappointed.

"See?" Evelyn said. "A lot of fuss over nothing." She pointed out the kitchen window. "Look at that beautiful sky. Roo, I was just fixing to call you. If we leave right now, we can get in nine holes before dinner."

"All right," Roo said. "My bag is still on your cart. Let's do it."

"You're playing golf? Right now?" Riley asked.

"It's a holiday weekend, and we might not be able to get another tee time. Anyway, with all I've got to do this weekend, this could be my last chance to play." Evelyn patted her daughter on the shoulder. "We can talk at dinner tonight. All right?"

Just as well, Riley thought, watching her mother and aunt head out for the golf course. The size and location of the cottage she'd just leased was perfect, but the long-term tenants who'd recently vacated had left it a filthy wreck. There was no way she and Maggy could stay there while it was in that condition.

She went into the laundry room and helped herself to the cleaning supplies she'd need—broom, mop, scrub bucket, trash bags, rubber gloves, Pine-Sol, and bleach.

Maggy stood in the doorway of the cottage and wrinkled her nose in distaste.

The living room was small, with white-painted pine paneling, a fireplace, and two picture windows that looked out at a tiny fenced garden overrun with weeds and discarded plastic beach toys. The slipcovered flowered sofa was stained and worn looking, and the area rug was strewn with trash and coated with sand. The room smelled like essence of wet dog.

"Gross!" She turned to look at her mother. "I'm glad we left Banksy with Bebo. He might get fleas. This place is nasty. Why can't we get Delores to clean it before we move in?"

Delores was Evelyn's longtime housekeeper at Shutters.

"Because Delores costs money, and we're officially on a budget," Riley said. "Now, let's get busy. I want to take this rug outside and air it out before the rain gets here."

Although the sky outside was still blue, gray-tinged clouds had started to gather on the horizon. They might have a couple more hours of sunshine. Riley went from room to room opening windows to let in fresh air. "Let's do this!" she declared.

Shortly before six, she heard the distant rumble of thunder and saw the first raindrops spattering against the bedroom window she'd been cleaning. "Maggy! Come help me get the rug inside."

They managed to drag the heavy rug back to the living room just as the heavens opened up. "Dang," Maggy said, standing at the window. "Do you think it'll rain tomorrow? I was gonna meet the kids at the beach in the morning."

Riley took her phone out of her purse and tapped the weather app to check on the storm's progress.

NO SIGNAL appeared on the screen.

"Looks like this house doesn't have wireless," Riley said. "I guess I should have asked the owner about that."

"*Mom*! Are you kidding me? There's no Wi-Fi?"

"I'll call the phone company and see about it next week," Riley said. "Uh-oh. Looks like I missed a call from Mimi."

Riley tried twice to return her mother's call, but each time got a CALL FAILED notice. Her phone had zero bars. Fortunately, Evelyn had left a message.

"Riley? Roo and I are at the club because our last couple of holes got rained out. I think we're just going to have dinner here in the grill with a couple of the other girls. You and Maggy could join us here, or you can just have the chicken salad I fixed."

Riley looked over at Maggy, who was still staring out the window. "Are you hungry, Mags? When was the last time you . . ."

"Stop!" Maggy exclaimed. "I had a juice box and some crackers a little while ago."

"Okay, but what about dinner?" Riley asked. "We could go over to the club. Mimi and Roo are having dinner in the grill. Or we could go back to Shutters and get dinner there."

"Bebo's cart doesn't have any plastic sides on it," Maggy pointed out. "We'll get soaked. Anyway, I'm not even hungry. Let's just get this place finished so we can leave. It's kind of depressing here, you know?"

"I'm not really hungry either. And I've got plenty of snacks in the cooler I brought. Okay, yeah, let's keep working." She put an arm around her daughter's shoulders. "I know it looks kind of grungy right now, but we can fix that. The owner said it's okay if we paint, as long as we don't do anything too outrageous, so maybe next week we'll go to town, and you can pick out a color for your bedroom."

"Can I do purple?"

"Pale purple," Riley said. "If you're sure you want to keep going, I'll tackle the bathroom and the kitchen while you finish up your room."

At eight o'clock, with her energy flagging, Riley dragged the last of the trash bags to the living room, adding them to the pile by the front door. She poked her head in the doorway of the bedroom and found her daughter curled up in the middle of the bed, fast asleep with her head on a pile of freshly laundered sheets and towels. For a moment, she panicked.

Maggy opened her eyes and smiled. "Relax, Mom. I'm tired. Not sick. I tested my blood, ate, took my meds. I'm fine. Is it time to go?"

"Yeah," Riley said. "Good job, kiddo. Let's go get some sleep. Tomorrow's moving day."

63

Roo was pouring herself a mug of coffee when Riley walked into the kitchen Friday morning. Riley peered out the window. The rain seemed to be slacking off, but the sky was an odd chromium color. Fallen leaves littered the grass, and the surface of the bay, below the bluff, was gray, with a light chop.

"What's the status of the storm, Roo?" Riley asked.

"Do not encourage her, Riley," Evelyn said as she buttered an English muffin. "She hasn't stopped looking at that silly satellite map since yesterday. She's like a child with a shiny new toy."

"It stalled overnight over Puerto Rico," Roo said, ignoring her sister-in-law. "Jim Cantore is predicting that it's going to head out to sea by noon, but there's this renegade weather blogger I follow—he calls himself StormKing007, and he says he sees a lot of similarities between Brody and Hurricane Fran."

"Roo!" Evelyn said sharply. "I want you to stop talking like an alarmist old fool. You forget, we were all here for Fran in ninety-six, and this is nothing like that. It's just some rain and wind, and that's all."

She turned to Riley. "I went to bed early last night, so I didn't even hear you come in. Where were you and Maggy last night?"

"We were at Billy's," Riley said, deciding to leave it at that. "Scott got in around eight thirty, so Billy fixed us a late dinner. Then we came back here and went to bed. Has Maggy come downstairs yet?"

"About thirty minutes ago," Evelyn said. "She had some cereal and juice, and then she was going to ride her bike over to the club to meet her friends."

Riley shook her head. "I don't like her being out on her bike when it's been storming like this."

"That's what I told her," Evelyn said. "But she just laughed me off and said she wouldn't melt if a little rain fell on her."

"Did you notice if she took her backpack?" Riley asked.

"Oh, yes. She had it, and I made her show me her kit before she left," Evelyn said.

Roo's radio gave off a shrill beep. She picked it up, and a computer-generated male voice floated into the room.

"The National Weather Service has issued a hurricane watch for the eastern seaboard of the United States ranging from Jacksonville, Florida, to Norfolk, Virginia. Latest tracking information generated by storm-tracking flights indicates that Tropical Storm Brody has been upgraded to hurricane status, with heavy rain and intensifying winds up to ninety miles an hour. Residents of these affected areas are encouraged to monitor the situation on an hourly basis, and residents of coastal and low-lying areas should begin emergency preparations, in the event that evacuation becomes necessary."

"Who's an alarmist old fool now?" Roo said smugly.

"It's just a watch, not a warning," Evelyn said, but a note of uncertainty had crept into her voice. "But I guess we'd better start getting the storm shutters out, just in case."

Riley picked up her phone to reach Maggy, but the call went directly to voice mail. "She's not answering her phone," she said, trying to sound calmer than she felt. "I'm going to take the golf cart and go look for her. In the meantime, Mama, don't you think we need to see about getting off the island before things get worse?"

"Now, look," Evelyn said. "I have lived on this island all my life. Every year during hurricane season we get these alerts. And nothing ever pans out. We'll do the smart thing. I'll call my handyman and get him to come over and put up the storm shutters. I've got plenty of bottled water and flashlights and batteries and candles, and enough food in our freezer to feed most of this island. You just go get Maggy and get her back here."

"And I'll have my weather radio right here," Roo said, patting it like a beloved pet.

When she got to the club Riley walked quickly around the pool. The lifeguards were scurrying around, taking down umbrellas and removing anything from the pool deck that could take sail in strong winds. She waved down the head lifeguard, Rachel, a cheerful college senior who'd worked at the club every summer since her early teens.

"Rachel, have you seen Maggy or any of those kids she hangs around with today?"

"Yeah, they were here a little while ago, but they left when they saw that the snack bar wasn't open and I told them the pool was closing." She pointed past the pool deck. "I saw them riding their bikes toward the village. I bet they went to the Mercantile to get something to eat."

It was only a five-minute ride from the club to the Mercantile in the village, but during that time the rain had started up again, and now the wind was blowing. It might not be a hurricane yet, but this was definitely not just a passing summer storm. She glanced in the direction of the ferry landing and noticed that the ferry was just departing for the thirty-minute trip across the sound.

The smell of fresh-ground coffee beans and bakery goods wafted through the air in the Mercantile. It was busy, with every seat taken in the café, and dozens of people wandering the aisles, picking up gourmet groceries and staples. But none of the customers included Maggy or any other young teens.

She spotted Annie Milas at the cash register in the café.

"Hi, Annie. I'm looking for Maggy. Did you happen to see her or the Billingsley kids this morning?"

"They came in and bought some cupcakes and Cokes about twenty minutes ago," Annie said. "I heard them say they were taking everything down to the beach for a hurricane party."

"Good Lord," Riley said.

"Yeah," Annie said. "Only a bunch of kids who've never lived through an actual hurricane would think it's an occasion for a party."

"Are y'all gonna stay open?" Riley asked. "I was just at the club, they've closed the pool, and I saw a sign on the door that the grill is closed, too."

"We'll stay open at least until the end of the day, or the food runs out, whichever comes first," Annie said. "We've had a big run on the prepared stuff from the deli and bakery this morning, so I think a lot of folks are thinking they'll ride out the storm. What about you folks? I bet your mama isn't scared of a hurricane."

"Evelyn still thinks it's just a false alarm," Riley admitted. "But I have to say, it makes me nervous. Has there been a rush of folks taking the ferry back to the mainland today?"

"Way more than we'd expect for the Friday of Labor Day weekend," Annie said. "But you know, a lot of people are still arriving. I guess they've made plans for the weekend, and they don't intend to let a hurricane watch run 'em off."

"Speaking of hurricanes, I guess I better go round up my daughter."

"How's Maggy doing now?" Annie asked. "I know you had a bad scare about six weeks ago."

Had Nate told her the details of their breakup? Annie's face was neutral.

"She's much better. Thanks for asking. And I hope that's the last time I ever have to take a helicopter off this island."

"Me, too," Annie said. "Y'all stay safe."

She decided to try Maggy's phone one more time.

"Hey, Mom," her daughter said. She sounded out of breath.

"Did you see I've been trying to call you?" Riley said, trying to dial down her anxiety level.

"Sorry. I left my phone in the basket of my bike. I'm down at the beach with the kids. We're having a hurricane party."

"They'll have to have it without you," Riley said.

"Mom," Maggy protested. "I'm fine. I've got my kit, and I've taken my insulin. . . ."

"This is not about diabetes," Riley said. "And don't you dare accuse me of being a helicopter mom. There's a hurricane warning out, and I want you at home in case we have to evacuate."

"You mean leave? And miss the storm?"

"That's exactly what I mean," Riley said. "I'll wait for you in the parking lot at the Mercantile. If you're not here in ten minutes you'll be on restriction for the rest of the weekend. Possibly the rest of your life."

"Where are we going?" Maggy asked, after they'd strapped her bike to the back of Evelyn's golf cart.

"To the new house," Riley said. "I want to make sure I remembered to close all the windows last night and see if there's anything outside that might go flying if this storm hits."

They walked through the house, closing the windows she'd left open in the bathroom and Maggy's bedroom, and walked around the front- and backyard, picking up anything that might take flight and stashing it in a tool shed at the back of the house.

"Are we going to spend the night here tonight?" Maggy asked. "It doesn't smell nearly as bad now. And it looks kind of pretty inside, now that it's clean."

Riley looked around the living room. With the rug cleaned and vacuumed, the walls washed down, and the slipcovers washed and smoothed out, the room had a certain shabby cottage charm that it hadn't possessed initially.

"Hmm. We'll see. Like I said, if this storm gets worse, we won't stay on the island at all."

"You're no fun," Maggy said. "Mimi said this morning she doesn't care what happens. She's not leaving Shutters."

"Mimi seems to have forgotten what it was like to live through Hurricane Fran."

"Were you here then?"

"I was," Riley said, her voice grim. "We had a direct hit on Belle Isle. Winds of a hundred and fifteen miles an hour, and there was a storm surge of about ten feet. It was terrifying, looking out the windows and seeing that wall of water crashing over the seawall below. Huge old oak trees that were here for over a hundred years were ripped out of the ground. The porch roof came all the way off. When the winds got really bad, the whole house shook. Bebo and I got in the bathtub and put sofa cushions over our heads in case the roof caved in. I have never been so scared in my life."

Maggy shivered. "Do you think it'll get that bad this time?"

"I don't know. And I don't plan to be here if it does."

64

The rain slashed at the hood of Riley's yellow rain slicker as she dragged the last of the Adirondack chairs into the garden shed at Shutters, stacking it alongside the other seven chairs.

Her shoulders ached, her jeans were soaked all the way to her knees, and she was chilled to the bone. She locked the shed door and trudged back to the house. The wind whistled in the tops of the live oaks, and palm fronds and clumps of Spanish moss went flying past her head as she crossed the lawn.

She left her rubber boots on the porch and went inside, where she found Evelyn assembling her stockpile of flashlights, candles, and battery-operated lanterns.

"The chairs are locked up," she reported. "What next?"

"Did Henry finish with the storm shutters?"

"He did, and you need to pay him double for climbing that ladder to put up the ones on the second story. I was so scared I could hardly watch."

"Have you talked to your brother?"

"Yes. He said he's almost finished boarding up his windows, so he and Scott should be here in about an hour."

"Good." Evelyn nodded. "Now, could you go over to the carriage house and check on your aunt? There's no telling what kind of craziness she's gotten up to. That old fool thinks this storm is better than a circus sideshow."

Just then, the front door opened and Roo walked in with Maggy, water streaming off their boots and rain slickers. Maggy's dark hair was plastered to her head, her face pink, and her eyes electric with excitement. Roo took off her red vinyl rain hat and tossed it onto the hall coatrack. The old woman shook her gray hair like a dog, splashing raindrops everywhere.

"Oh my word! What have you two been up to?" Evelyn demanded.

"I took Maggy down to the beach so she could experience a real hurricane," Roo said.

"Mom! It was so awesome," Maggy enthused. "Me and Roo had our own hurricane party. The seagulls were, like, flying backward. And the clouds are so thick, you can't even see Big Belle. Roo said it was almost as good as Hurricane Floyd. You know, that was the most people ever killed in a hurricane in North Carolina."

"I didn't even know you'd gone out," Riley said. "Roo, I wouldn't have said yes if you'd asked if you could take her down there. It's not safe!"

"I knew you'd say no, so that's why I didn't ask," her aunt said. "And don't worry, she checked her blood, and I gave her a snack, and she's fine. The waves were magnificent," Roo added. "I haven't seen surf running that high since Floyd, in ninety-nine."

"I should have known," Evelyn muttered.

Roo looked around the hallway. "Have you been listening to the radio? Have there been any more updates from the Weather Service?"

"No, I haven't been listening. I've been too busy getting this house ready to weather a storm," Evelyn said. "Check it yourself if you want."

"It's in the kitchen," Riley said. She turned stern eyes on her daughter. "Margaret Evelyn, you need to go right upstairs and get out of those wet clothes and take a hot shower."

"I think I'll go back to the carriage house and change into dry clothes, too," Roo said. "What time are we eating? All this excitement has really given me an appetite."

Riley looked at her watch. "Mama, it's nearly six now. I think I'll go see about starting dinner. I think we ought to eat early, in case the power goes off."

"Good idea. I took the last of the shrimp out of the freezer to thaw, and I picked up a couple of quarts of Brunswick stew and some coleslaw at the Mercantile yesterday. And let's use up the last of the salad stuff, too. Did you call Parrish and Ed and tell them to come over and help us eat up some of these groceries?"

"I did, but Ed's plane was late getting into RDU today, and with the weather and traffic, he's not going to make it down until tomorrow. Parrish said she was going to heat up some soup and hunker down right there. She promised she'd check in with us later tonight if the weather gets worse."

The lights flickered off and then on again, just as she was draining the shrimp in the kitchen sink. Riley hurried into the living room and lit the candles she'd clustered around the mahogany table. The mellow old silver shone brightly, and she put place mats and heavy ironstone plates at each setting, then set the bowls of steaming shrimp and Brunswick stew on trivets in the middle of the table.

The front door flew open, and Billy and Scott walked in and slammed it shut. "Damn!" Billy called. "It's getting ugly out there. I almost turned around and went back to the firehouse."

"Except I threw out the rest of his vodka, so he knew he wouldn't get a drink unless he came over here," Scott said.

"That's right," Billy said. He walked to the sideboard, found the crystal decanter of vodka, and filled a double old-fashioned tumbler nearly to the brim. He took a swallow and grimaced. "Ugh. I think Mama must have cut this stuff with Sterno."

"You notice he's drinking it anyway," Scott said to Riley.

Evelyn came in carrying water glasses and a large wooden salad bowl, followed by Roo, who had a platter of corn bread.

"You two quit fussing or you'll ruin our appetites," Evelyn said. "Riley, would you please ask your daughter to grace us with her presence?"

Riley stood at the bottom of the staircase, lifted her chin, and hollered, "Maggy! Dinner!"

Maggy stared down at the plate her grandmother had just set in front of her and turned pleading eyes toward her mother. "Mom? Would it be okay if I just had a sandwich or something? I'm not really into stuff that's all mixed together like this."

"Now, Maggy," Evelyn started.

"Mama, this once it's all right," Riley said. "Go ahead and get your sandwich. Just make sure you're getting all your exchanges. . . ."

"And take my insulin," Maggy said. "And after that, can I go upstairs and watch a movie on my iPad?"

"I guess so," Riley said.

Riley took a deep breath. "Mama, there's something I want to talk to you about."

Evelyn placed her fork on the side of her plate. "I hope this is not about that Nate Milas."

"No. It's not about Nate. It's about me. I've made some pretty big changes in my life recently. And some of them directly affect you. And the rest of this family."

"I can't wait to hear," Evelyn said.

"First off, I quit my job at WDHM."

"My goodness," Evelyn said. "What brought that on?"

"A lot of things. The pay was crap. My boss was an idiot. And the final straw was that she wanted me to demonstrate a colon cleanse. On the air."

Billy sniggered. "Talk about a shitty assignment."

Evelyn turned to her son with a withering stare. "No more vodka, Billy."

"So I walked out. And, well, I've been thinking about this for a while now. Ever since Wendell died, actually. I don't want another job in television. I want to run Belle Isle Enterprises."

"You?" Evelyn stared. "Sweetheart, you don't know anything about running a business like ours."

"Neither did Wendell, until Daddy gave him his job," Riley said. "And Granddad hired Daddy after the two of you got married. But I've grown up in the business. On this island."

"But, honey," Evelyn said. "Wendell and W.R. had somebody to train them before they took over."

"You mean, *they* were qualified because *they* were men," Billy said. "Mama, for God's sake, quit being such a sexist. Riley is twice as smart as Wendell ever was. And even if she wasn't, there's no way she could screw things up as badly as he did."

"I just don't know," Evelyn sputtered. "This is just so out of the blue. . . ."

"I think Riley would do a wonderful job running the company," Roo said. "You know I loved my little brother, but W.R. could be blind about some things. I don't think he ever thought women were good for much beyond having babies and running a house."

"I'm not saying we shouldn't consider it," Evelyn said, seeing that she was outgunned. "But think of the logistics. Wendell spent more than half his time on the island or traveling. How could you do that and live in Raleigh and take care of Maggy, as a single mother?"

"I've already thought of that. I withdrew Maggy from the Woodlawn School. She'll start seventh grade at Baldwin Middle School on Tuesday. And I've rented a little cottage for us in the village."

"When did all this take place?" Evelyn asked indignantly. "I can't believe you'd take Maggy out of one of the top-ranked prep schools in the state and put her in some little country schoolhouse in Southpoint. And what about your new house in Raleigh? Weren't you supposed to move in there this week?"

"Things happened so fast, there really wasn't time to let you know," Riley said. "I was miserable in my job and Maggy was miserable at Woodlawn. Her homeroom teacher didn't even know who she was. And then, when the folks who sold me the house decided not to move and backed out of the sale at the last minute, I decided it was a sign from the universe."

"A good sign," Roo said, beaming at her niece.

"Roo, please!" Evelyn said sharply.

The weather radio Roo had placed on the floor beside her chair gave out another unearthly blare, and the same disembodied voice filled the high-ceilinged dining room.

"Due to intensifying conditions associated with Hurricane Brody, at seven fifteen p.m. Eastern Standard Time on Friday, the National Weather Service has upgraded a hurricane watch to a hurricane warning for the area from Hilton Head, South Carolina, to Norfolk, Virginia. Residents of coastal and low-lying areas should begin immediate emergency storm preparations including evacuation to higher ground, away from areas susceptible to high winds and storm surge. Hurricane Brody is now a category-two storm and forecasters now predict a direct strike of potentially catastrophic forces to these areas. Stay tuned to this frequency for further updates."

"Only a cat two?" Roo said, underwhelmed. "That's hardly anything. Now Hazel, back in fifty-four, was a cat four. That's what I call a storm."

"Evacuation?" Evelyn said, looking around the table. "Is that really necessary? After all, we managed to ride out Fran."

"And I never want to live through something like that again," Riley snapped. She turned to her brother for help. "Billy, would you please tell her she's crazy to consider staying on the island for this storm?"

Billy took a gulp of his cocktail. "Mama, you're crazy. We need to go."

As if on cue, Riley's cell phone dinged an alert of a text message, and her phone screen lit up while another anonymous voice issued another ominous threat:

"At seven forty-five p.m. the Baldwin County Emergency Management Agency received notice of a category-two hurricane expected to make landfall in this area by nine a.m. Saturday. The agency has now issued a mandatory evacuation order for low-lying areas including Southpoint, Beach Haven, Fiddler's Sound, and Belle Isle. Residents are instructed to take cover or evacuate immediately to higher ground."

Scott gave his mother-in-law a pleading look. "Now, Evelyn, that sounds pretty serious. The county is saying evacuation is mandatory."

"They just say that," Roo said. "In case of lawsuits. But they can't make us leave. Right, Evvy?"

"That's it," Riley said. "I am calling the ferry right now and getting us off before this storm blows us off."

She picked up her phone and tapped the connect button to call the ferry office, but got disconnected almost immediately. "The number's busy," she reported. "Probably because every sane person left on the island is doing the same thing I am."

Oooowwwhoooooo.

"That's Banksy," Riley said, standing up and heading for the stairway. "He must hear something outside."

She stood at the door, and now they all heard the siren, and saw headlights and flashing red lights heading down the drive straight for the house. Riley opened the door and peered outside. The din from the driving rain obscured most of the message, but one phrase emanating from the vehicle's roof-mounted loudspeaker was audible: "MANDATORY EVACUATION ORDER."

"That's the sheriff's car," Riley reported. And as she watched, Sheriff Schumann, in a safety-yellow rain slicker with LAW ENFORCEMENT emblazoned across the front, dashed up onto the porch.

"Come on in," Riley said.

The sheriff looked at the family members assembled around the table. "I'm assuming y'all have gotten the texts and alerts about the hurricane?"

"We have," Riley assured him. "And I'm just getting ready to book our seats on the ferry."

"Better hurry," he said. Then, turning away from the family, he placed his lips near Riley's ear. "Uh, listen, can I speak to you in private? It's about your husband."

"Whatever it is, you can tell me now," Riley said impatiently. "This is my family."

"We followed up on that tip you gave us. About Melody Zimmerman? Now, I don't know how you got your information, but it turns out you were right about her. We checked the real estate records, and sure enough, we found out that last month she bought an oceanfront condo in Wrightsville Beach for eight hundred thousand dollars, but she only took out a four-hundred-thousand-dollar loan. Which got us to wondering how somebody affords that on an assistant bank manager's salary. We took a look at that aunt of hers, whose house she'd been living in here on the island, and it turns out she'd been embezzling money from the old lady's trust account."

"I'll be damned," Evelyn said. "That sweet little thing at the bank was an embezzler?"

"That's not all," the sheriff said, looking chagrined. "After she was charged with embezzlement, she wanted to make a deal, so she admitted that she helped your husband set up those dummy corporations to defraud Coastal Carolina Bank. She forged your name on the mortgage documents for your house. And she pocketed hundreds of thousands of dollars in commissions from the bank for generating all those loans the bank later had to write off."

Riley nodded. "Did she admit to killing Wendell?"

"She admits she was having an affair with him, and to cooking up the loan schemes, but she insists she didn't kill him."

"I don't believe her," Riley said. "She's been lying about her involvement all along. Who else would have a reason to kill him?"

"That's what we intend to find out," the sheriff said. "Her story is that they were together that Thursday night, at your house on Sand Dollar Lane. He came over on his own boat, because he didn't want anybody to know he was meeting her there. Your husband changed the locks on the house, she told us, because of the foreclosure. She says they, uh, had relations there, and afterward, he told her that the real estate deals were falling apart, and he was afraid if you went ahead with the divorce, you'd find out about his financial misdeeds. He told Melody that when he met you at the ferry that next day he was going to beg you to take him back."

"So that's why she killed him," Riley said.

"She says not. Says they had a big fight because she had committed multiple crimes and put her job on the line for him. He shook her off and said he was leaving, so she went back inside your house and packed up her things and then went home to her own place. She insists that was the last time she saw him, and he was very much alive."

"She's a liar," Riley said flatly.

"Maybe not," the sheriff said. "She claims that after she went inside, she heard Wendell arguing with somebody. A man." He glanced over toward the table. "I intend to find out the truth, and charge that person with murder."

"You won't find the killer here," Evelyn Nolan called.

"Not tonight, no," he said. "But the real reason I stopped in here was to make sure you all understand that this evacuation order is mandatory. I'm keeping track of everybody who is on this island, and we will be counting heads tonight, so we don't have to count bodies tomorrow, after that storm hits. Understand?"

"Perfectly," Riley said.

65

Scott stood in the doorway, watching the police cruiser's taillights recede into the distance through a curtain of rain. They heard the words "mandatory evacuation" again just before he closed the door.

He sat down at the dining room table and looked at Riley. "The voice Melody heard that night at the house was mine."

"Yours?" Billy said. "What were you doing there?"

"I'd just gotten the news from the hotel people that they were pulling out of the Pirate's Point deal. Wendell already knew. He'd known for some time. I'd sunk my own money into that project—because he assured me if I didn't sweeten the pot, the deal was doomed. I think he probably knew it was doomed from the start. I got over to the island that afternoon, determined to confront him, and I saw him with that woman, Melody. It was obvious that they were together, literally. I followed them to Sand Dollar Lane, and when I walked around to the back of the house, they were out on the balcony outside your bedroom, Riley. You know how voices carry in the night? I heard almost every word of what they were fighting about."

"In my bedroom," Riley said quietly.

"I waited until he came out of the house again. I was furious. He'd screwed me, screwed her, screwed you, Riley. I grabbed him by the arm and told him I knew about everything, including the affair. I threatened to tell you about Melody, about all of it."

"Why didn't you?" Riley asked.

Scott shook his head and looked away.

"I think I know," Billy said. "He told you about how I killed Cal, didn't he?"

"Who's Cal?" Evelyn asked. "Billy, you never killed anybody. What's he talking about?"

"Cal. He was my AA sponsor, Mama. Cal got me sober, saved my life, and then to repay him, I killed him, drunk driving. Drove my old Delta eighty-eight off the road with him in the passenger seat and wrapped it around a tree."

Billy's hand clutched the tumbler of vodka. He stared down at the clear liquid, then suddenly pushed it away. "Cal was killed instantly. I didn't know what else to do, so I called Wendell. He came out and saw what happened. I was so drunk I could hardly stand up. But Wendell knew what to do. He cleaned up my mess and made it all go away."

"For a price," Scott said.

"He never said a word for the longest time. Then, he came to me last year, told me he had a great 'investment opportunity.' He called it a loan, but we both knew what it was. I gave him everything I had, all the money in my trust fund."

"He blackmailed you?" Riley said.

"Both of us," Scott corrected her. "That night at your house, when I threatened to tell you about the affair with Melody, he said if I told anybody, he'd go to the police with what he knew about Billy. He had proof. Cell phone pictures of Billy, passed out behind the wheel of the Delta eighty-eight, and pictures of Cal, who'd been thrown clear of the car."

Riley's eyes met Scott's. His were a pale blue, red-rimmed with worry and fatigue. "Did you kill Wendell?"

"No," Scott said. "I wanted to. I could have, but I didn't."

"Oh, my God." Billy clutched Scott's hand. "I was sure it was you. I was terrified it was you."

"And I thought you'd killed him," Scott said sadly. "Your drinking was totally out of control."

"I don't understand any of this," Evelyn said. "If Billy didn't kill Wendell, and Scott didn't kill him, who did?" She turned to Riley. "You'd never."

"No," Riley said. "It wasn't me. And I know it wasn't you, Mama. You loved Wendell in spite of everything."

"That bastard!" Evelyn said. "He tried to ruin my family. And he nearly succeeded."

"I still think it was Melody," Riley said. "Who else?"

"Helloooo!" Roo said, pounding the table with her heavy water glass. "Why does everybody always act like I'm not here? I killed Wendell, and I'm not sorry. You can send me to hell or to prison, but I'd do it again in a heartbeat."

"Oh, Roo," Evelyn said. "Don't be so dramatic."

"What? You think I couldn't do it? Think I'm too old?"

"Roo?" Riley said.

"He bulldozed the wildlife sanctuary," Roo explained. "All those birds in the rookery, their nests, their eggs, all of it. He didn't give a goddamn about anybody but himself, the selfish bastard."

Lightning crackled outside, and they heard the wind whipping tree branches, the rusty crackle of palm fronds beating against the side of the old house, and the low rumble of thunder.

"I was going to take Maggy over there, Memorial Day weekend, show her the nests," Roo said. "But half of it was gone! I knew right away that it was Wendell. I tried to call him, but he wouldn't answer his phone. That night, I'd borrowed Evelyn's golf cart. One of my birding friends told me there was an endangered wood stork nesting in a live oak on the beach side of your property, Riley, and I took my telephoto lens because I wanted to get a picture of it. I didn't even know Wendell was on the island. I couldn't find the wood stork, but as I was walking up from the beach, I heard a commotion, and I looked up and saw people on that balcony at your house. They were having a huge fight, and that girl was screaming and carrying on and threatening to kill herself. When I looked through my telephoto, I saw it was Wendell, with that girl from the bank in town. They were both about half naked. I was so shocked, I didn't know what to do!"

"Why didn't you just leave and mind your own business?" Evelyn asked.

"I intended to," Roo shot back. "I kind of snuck back to where I'd parked the golf cart, and that's when I saw Scott. He and Wendell were having it out. I heard Wendell tell Scott about Billy killing that man. And then he said he'd go to the police and tell them about Billy if Scott didn't shut up about his affair with the girl.

"I watched you leave," Roo told Scott. "And then I saw Wendell go into the house. He came out a few minutes later and got in the golf cart and left. I followed him. He never even saw me. Nobody ever notices an old woman like me. He parked in the ferry lot, but walked over to the marina. I rode Evelyn's cart right up behind him, and he still didn't see me. His boat was tied up there, and he was fiddling with the lines."

Another jagged streak of lighting lit up the sky outside the dining room windows, followed by the sickening crack of a tree limb, and a loud thud as it struck the ground close by. The overhead lights flickered, then went out.

"There goes the electricity," Evelyn murmured. "Riley, I think maybe you're right. Maybe we should think about getting out."

"Could you please let me finish my story?" Roo said peevishly.

"By all means," Evelyn said.

"I rode up right behind him and got out of that cart, and I was just so mad, I couldn't see straight. I told him I knew he'd bulldozed half the wildlife sanctuary and I was going to call the Department of Natural Resources and report him.

"He just laughed and called me an old bag and said I should go ahead, because nobody cared, and it was the family's land, and he could do what he wanted with it. So, then, I told him I knew all about his girlfriend, and how he'd borrowed money from everybody in the family. I said I was going to go to Riley and tell her everything. He thought that was the funniest thing he'd ever heard. He laughed and laughed! And then he said everybody knew I was senile."

Roo turned to Riley. "It was the last straw. He was still laughing when I grabbed the first thing handy." She gave Evelyn an apologetic shrug. "It was your seven iron. I grabbed it and I swung it, and I bashed Wendell as hard as I could in the back of his head."

She lifted her water glass and took a sip, then patted her lips with a napkin. "He looked so surprised! Then he was laying there on the seawall, and I was afraid somebody would see him. Lord knows I couldn't lift him, or try to hide the body, so I just sort of rolled him over toward the boat. Then I got the anchor line and tied it around his waist, as best I could, and rolled him off the seawall into the water."

"Oh, my God, Roo," Evelyn said, her eyes round with shock. "You really did it? You killed Wendell?"

"With your seven iron," Roo admitted. "I didn't plan anything. It just happened. After that, I parked Evelyn's golf cart in the ferry lot and drove Wendell's cart back to the house. That girl was gone by then. I used the garage door opener that was in the cart to park it there, then I let myself out. I took Wendell's cell phone, and I walked down to the beach and pitched the phone out into the water. Then I walked back to the marina, and got in Evelyn's cart and drove home, and went to bed and acted like nothing had happened."

She turned to her sister-in-law. "I'm sorry about your seven iron, Evvy. I buried it out behind the garden shed, under that big Nikko Blue hydrangea." And then she looked at Riley. "But I'm really not sorry about Wendell. You and Maggy are better off with him gone. He was evil, honey. Pure evil."

66

Ooowwwww. This time Mr. Banks ran down the stairs and to the front door, howling a protest at the shrill siren screaming through the din of the storm. "Looks like the sheriff's back," Billy said, half standing. All heads turned toward the glass storm door and the red lights flashing atop the police cruiser.

"I guess I'll just go on and surrender right now," Roo said.

"Everybody stay right where you are," Evelyn said. "This is my home, and I'll handle this. You just keep quiet, Roo. You hear?"

But before she could get to the door, they heard the loudspeaker again. "This is Sheriff Schumann. You folks need to get off the island. Now." As they watched, the cruiser did a three-point turn and sped back in the direction it had come from.

Riley reached for her phone but hesitated. "Everybody go get whatever you want to take to Southpoint. I'm calling the ferry and praying it's not too late. Mama, could you go see about helping Maggy get ready? Make sure she has her kit and enough meds for two or three days? Billy, can you and Scott—after you run home to get your stuff—can you meet us back here to make sure we've got everything ready to go? And could you run by Parrish's house and tell her we're all bugging out?"

Billy nodded and he and Scott rushed for the front door. Evelyn began clearing the table. "Mama! Just leave the food. We need to get out of here," Riley called. "Roo, no more arguments, you hear? We are all getting out tonight."

Nate had been waiting all evening for her call. He'd checked all the earlier manifests and knew that she and Maggy were still on the island, and he'd been struggling with how late he would let things go before he drove over to Shutters and forcibly dragged her off the island.

"*Carolina Queen,*" he said, answering the phone.

Riley hesitated a beat. "Nate? Is that you?"

"It's me."

"Is there another ferry tonight? I've finally persuaded everybody we have to evacuate."

He looked out the office window and saw the lights of the *Carolina Queen* riding the chop across the bay. "We just boarded the last passenger and she's pulling away from the dock, Riley. But hang on a minute."

Annie had been working the phones all night, booking passengers and answering panicked questions about whether or not the ferry would keep running. She put her hand over the receiver and turned to her son.

"I've got the sheriff on the line. He said he's rounded up another couple of dozen stragglers who've finally agreed to evacuate. Wants to know if we'll have room to take them."

"Tell him yeah, but this is last call."

Nate checked the NOAA satellite map he'd pulled up on his computer and went back to his own phone. "Riley? I'm looking at the radar, and they're still projecting the storm will make landfall just north of us by nine a.m., which means we can expect tropical storm–force winds in the next four to five hours. If you can get everybody loaded up and waiting by the time the boat gets back here—say nine o'clock, we'll make one more crossing. After that, it won't be safe."

"We'll be there," Riley said. "And Nate? Thanks."

They made a ragtag crew, exhausted, rain-soaked, and shell-shocked, huddled together under the cover of the loading area. Parrish joined them, with her two cats in a carrying case. Mr. Banks, on his retractable leash, and Evelyn's pug, Ollie, spooked by the lightning and thunder, raced around in circles, barking and snarling at each other and the other dogs gathered, ready to evacuate the island.

It was a much larger crowd than Riley had expected, more than a hundred people, which was at least as many as would be arriving on the island on a normal summer holiday weekend. But this, she knew, was the furthest thing from a normal summer, or a normal holiday, than she'd ever experienced before.

Evelyn cradled a large hand-tooled leather case under one arm and leaned against a large black rolling suitcase, which she directed Billy to keep by his side, refusing to allow the deckhands to stow it with the rest of the luggage being loaded into baggage bins.

"Mama, I realize you'd want to pack up all your good jewelry, but did you really need to pack Daddy's old bowling ball in this thing?" he asked, dragging it toward the loading area.

"Hush," she whispered. "It's my silver. And all the baby pictures." She opened her pocketbook, took out a tiny mother-of-pearl case, and popped a tablet in her mouth before extending it to him. "Dramamine?"

"No, thanks," Billy said. "I try never to mix alcohol and drugs."

At nine o'clock, Nate joined them on the loading ramp. "Everybody," he called, raising his voice to be heard above the howling wind, "We'll board in five minutes. Now, it's gonna be a pretty rough ride across the sound, because we've got seas at six to eight feet, and the wind is blowing thirty-five to forty knots with the tide running against us, so I'm afraid there's gonna be a lot of rockin' and rollin', and not the fun kind. And yes, it's going to be crowded because, for safety reasons, I'll ask everybody to stay together in the main cabin. Nobody will be allowed on the upper or observation decks. The deckhands are going to hand out life jackets, and we'll ask you to put them on, not because we expect to sink, but because that's the way my dad always did it when we had a bad storm like this one. Now we won't have the concession stand open for obvious reasons, but my mom, Annie Milas—I think you all know her—rounded up whatever cookies and doughnuts were left at the end of the day at the Mercantile, and she'll be handing those out to anybody who's hungry, once we're under way. Everybody good? Then let's board!"

Riley decided it was the longest crossing of her life. They were all jammed together in the cabin, overheated with the orange life vests strapped around their shoulders, and miserable with crying babies, boisterous toddlers, ill-tempered islanders, and weekenders with ruined holiday expectations.

True to Nate's prediction, the *Carolina Queen* pitched and rolled, and with each roller-coaster descent, Riley's stomach protested violently. She clung to Maggy, who clung to her with each wave that crashed over the bow. She'd never experienced seasickness before, but this time she found herself dashing for the head three different times. When Annie Milas approached, halfway through the crossing, oatmeal cookie in hand, Riley almost didn't make it a fourth time.

Finally, after a lifetime, the five-minute whistle blew, and Nate emerged into the cabin from the pilothouse and called for their attention again. "Docking is not gonna be smooth," he warned. "Captain Wayne is the best there is at this but, again, the wind and the tide are working against us. We'll ask everybody to be patient, and once we're tied up, the deckhands will do their best to help everybody safely disembark. Make sure you have all your carry-on baggage with you, please, because after our passengers are unloaded, the crew and I will be heading out to find a safe place to sleep tonight, and we will not be back on board the *Carolina Queen* until the Weather Service and the Coast Guard give us the all-clear to do so."

Riley turned to ask her mother if she had everything, but was amused to find Evelyn asleep, snoring softly with her mouth open, her head lolling on Billy's shoulder. She gave her a gentle shake. "Come on, Mama. Wake up. We're here."

Evelyn sat up. "I wasn't sleeping. I was just resting my eyes." She looked around and saw Maggy, with Mr. Banks squirming in her arms, and saw Scott and Billy talking quietly, their heads close together. She saw her own dog, Ollie, dozing at her feet. She glanced around the cabin again and blinked, puzzled by what she didn't see.

"Where's Roo?"

Riley looked around, too. "Billy, have you seen Roo?"

"No. Maybe she's in the head?"

"I'll go check," Maggy volunteered. Five minutes later she was back. "She's not in the bathroom."

"You're sure?" Evelyn asked. "Maybe in the men's room? She's bad like that, just goes into the men's room if the ladies' is occupied."

"I know. I checked there, too," Maggy said.

"Oh, my God," Evelyn said in a choked voice. "Roo."

Riley found Annie Milas standing near the cabin door, counting heads. "Annie," she said softly. "We can't find my aunt Roo. Is there any chance she would have gone on the upper deck?"

"None," Annie said. "Nate chained up the gangway. You're sure she's not in the main cabin? Or the head?"

"We looked. She's not there."

"Come to think of it, I don't recall seeing your aunt tonight, Riley. Are you sure she boarded?"

Riley turned back to the rest of the family without answering. "Everybody, think. Did anybody see Roo actually getting on the ferry?"

"Mimi sent me over to bring her back to the big house," Maggy said. "But she said she'd wait and get a ride with Bebo."

Billy shook his head. "I went over to the carriage house to fetch her when we got back from our place, but she told me she was going to ride with Parrish."

"But I didn't even come to Shutters," Parrish said. "I went straight to the ferry from my place."

"She never left," Riley said, as the realization washed over her. "She scammed every one of us. She's still on that damned island."

The ferry's diesel engines shuddered to a sudden halt, slamming so hard against the pier that the impact sent people sprawling onto the water-slicked floor. There was more churning, as the pilot reversed course, and then another, lesser impact. Bells rang, signaling their arrival, and then the engines shut down.

All around them, passengers sprang to life, gathering their belongings and herding toward the exit. Everybody but Evelyn Nolan and her family, who gathered in a small, bewildered knot around their matriarch.

Evelyn clutched Riley's arm. "Roo is back there. Alone. We have to go back. Riley, you have to talk to Nate."

"Talk to me about what?" Nate's face was creased with weariness. He hadn't shaved, and his jeans and windbreaker were damp and salt-crusted.

"It's Roo. My sister-in-law. She's still back on the island. You have to go back and get her. She's nearly eighty. She can't ride out that storm by herself. She wanted to stay, and so did I, but Riley made us see it wasn't safe." Evelyn was babbling, wild-eyed with anxiety.

"Is that true?" Nate asked.

The other passengers streamed around them, bumping and jostling in their haste to be back on solid land again.

"I'm afraid so," Riley said. She looked down and saw Maggy, staring up at her, holding Banksy so tightly the dog gave a sharp yip of protest.

"Mama, why don't you and the others get our stuff and wait for me on the dock," Riley said. "Maggy, you go with Mimi and Billy."

"Come on, Mags," Billy said, touching her arm. "Let's go get in the car."

Maggy stayed planted where she was. She looked up solemnly at Nate. Her blue-gray eyes were beseeching. "Will you do it? Will you go back for Roo?"

"I'll bring her along, Bebo," Riley told her brother.

"Ask him, Mama," Maggy implored. "He'll do it if you ask."

"It's not safe," Riley said, shaking her head. Even now, the heavy boat rocked violently with the break of each wave as the wind buffeted it against its mooring. "I can't ask you to take the ferry back there, Nate. It's too dangerous."

"But she's all alone," Maggy cried. "Something bad will happen to her, I know it will. It's a cat-two storm. They're not as bad as a three or a four, but people die in cat-two hurricanes. Roo told me eight people died in Hurricane Donna."

Nate looked from the little girl to her mother. "I can't ask Wayne to pilot the ferry back to Belle Isle. We've only got enough fuel for a one-way trip. But I'll go back myself. If you want me to."

"Please, Mama? Let him save Roo. He wants to." Maggy wrapped her arms around Riley's waist the same way she had as a preschooler.

Riley stroked her daughter's hair. She'd shot up this summer, almost as tall as Riley now. In the space of three short months she'd grown up more than any twelve-year-old should have had to. And now there was one more hard lesson.

"No, Maggy. I can't ask Nate to risk his life and go back to the island for Roo. I know you love her. We all do. But Roo knew what she wanted. She wanted to ride out one more hurricane. So that's what she's doing. She doesn't want to be saved."

Nate placed his hand on top of Riley's and squeezed it gently, before releasing it. He leaned over until his face was level with the child's. "I'll go back tomorrow, as soon as it's safe. And I'll find Roo. I promise."

Maggy nodded. "Okay."

"Where will you go tonight?" Nate asked Riley. "There's a Red Cross shelter set up at the National Guard Armory."

Riley laughed. "Can you see Evelyn Nolan sleeping on a cot in a gym? Me neither. We'll probably just drive inland until we see a hotel with a vacancy. What about you?"

"We've got family in Fayetteville. They're expecting us."

"Will you call me?" Riley asked.

"You call me," Nate said. "When you're ready."

Epilogue

Riley leaned over the rail of the observation deck, closed her eyes, and breathed in everything: the sunshine, the salt air, even the sharp tang of the *Carolina Queen*'s diesel engines. This was a new sensation, the letting go and letting in. When she opened her eyes and looked down, she saw a pod of dolphins, splashing along joyfully in the ferry's wake, dipping in and out of the waves of the sound. She was by herself this trip but, out of habit, she scanned the horizon, searching for the first glimpse of Big Belle.

The lighthouse had withstood the storm, but the changed topography of the island was something that would take a long time to get used to.

Hurricane Brody had weakened hours before making landfall just north of the island, but the powerful winds and storm surge had done millions and millions of dollars' worth of damage. Hundred-year-old oaks had been downed, homes destroyed or badly damaged.

Half a dozen oak trees had fallen at the Shutters, which had sustained only mild wind damage, but the carriage house that had been Aunt Roo's home had been flattened. Riley's own small rental cottage near the village had roof damage where a tree limb pierced it, but the supposedly impregnable concrete hulk of her former home on Sand Dollar Lane had borne the brunt of the storm surge and sustained such serious flood damage that she'd heard talk that the new owners were considering it a total loss.

Riley found herself curiously indifferent to the fate of that house. Whatever memories she had of her life there, good or bad, would suffice. These days her work took her to every corner of the island, and when she passed the turnoff for Sand Dollar Lane, she no longer had to avert her eyes to the wreckage.

It was her past, and it was real, but she'd made the decision to move on.

Now it was Columbus Day weekend, and she was coming home. There was still so much to be done, sometimes her stomach still knotted up, sometimes she woke up in the middle of the night, making lists, doing Internet searches, reading everything she could to educate herself in her new job. But this weekend, she vowed, she would be on vacation, a weekender again.

When the five-minute whistle blew, she gathered her bag and moved anxiously to the lower deck, lining up with the rest of the passengers eager for the holiday weekend to begin.

Out of the corner of her eye, Riley spotted her old nemesis, Andrea Payne, who spotted her at the same moment, and deliberately looked away. She'd heard through the islander grapevine that Andrea blamed Riley—and Parrish—for her best friend's arrest and incarceration. Having Belle Isle Barbie snub her, Riley decided, was the only good outcome from Melody Zimmerman's predicament.

She allowed herself to merge into the stream of passengers disembarking the ferry, and once she was on the landing, moved quickly toward the parking lot.

He was standing off to the side, away from the crush of arriving and departing passengers, and she was still shocked at her reaction to the sight of Nate Milas. She felt lighter, younger, newer, happier. Nate Milas was not responsible for all of this. But he was definitely one of the better byproducts of her reinvention.

She picked up the pace, walking toward him. And then he did it. He opened his arms and she walked right into them.

"Hey!" he said, holding her closely, kissing her, stirring up a passion she'd forgotten she was capable of. "I missed you."

"I missed you, too," she said. "Like, for the past twenty years or so."

"Is that all?" They laughed together, he rubbed his cheek against the side of her face, and she reached up and rubbed the stubble there, although she'd only been gone four days. "Getting kind of gray here, aren't you, mister?"

"There's nobody else I'd rather go gray with," he said.

They walked arm in arm to the golf cart, loaded her bag, and then they were off.

"How did everything go?" he asked.

"Pretty well. The bankers I talked to in Wilmington seemed fairly open-minded. They want to see architect's renderings for the new shops, but the fact that I have tenants already signed up seemed to go a long way."

"What did Parrish think about the plans for her shop?"

"Parrish is Parrish. She made some tweaks to the drawings, which I'll admit were genius, and then she signed off. I think she's really excited about Parrish Interior Concepts. No more lawyering!"

"I saw Billy this week," Nate said.

"You did? I thought he wasn't allowed to have visitors yet."

A week after the hurricane struck, Billy Nolan and his lawyer, Ed Godchaux, paid a visit to the Baldwin County District Attorney. Billy offered a detailed confession about the real circumstances surrounding the death of his AA sponsor Calvin Peebles, and in return he was given a two-year sentence in a low-security residential diversion center in Southpoint. One condition of his sentence was to enter treatment for alcoholism, another was to perform two hundred hours of community service.

"I didn't visit him at the center," Nate said. "I saw him on the island, with a public works crew, clearing storm debris from the east beach."

"How did he look?" Riley asked. "Did you get to talk to him?"

"He looked good," Nate said. "He's grown a full beard, put on a little weight now that he's not drinking, but I gather he's working out. He was excited because he's going to start giving piano lessons to kids in the after-school program at the youth center."

"Did he say he's heard anything from Scott?"

"I didn't ask, but I don't see how he could have, since he's not allowed visitors or phone privileges for two more months," Nate said. "How about you? Did you see Evelyn?"

Riley nodded. "I stopped in Edenton and stayed with her last night. I thought maybe I could convince her to come back with me for the weekend, but she's just not ready yet. Losing Roo was a bigger blow than any of us realized. She wasn't just Mama's sister-in-law. She was her sister, really. Her best friend, her sparring partner. All of that. Life on Belle Isle is not going to be the same without Roo. For any of us."

"I ran into Sheriff Shoe at Onnalee's this week," Nate said. "We had a cup of coffee together. He told me they were finally able to get a crew over to the Shutters, after the last of the oak trees downed in the hurricane were cleared away. The golf club was right where Roo said it would be. They were going to send it off for fingerprints, but he said there wasn't much question that she was telling the truth."

"No," Riley said. "She was pretty definite about what she'd done. And very definite about why. I can't help but wonder if she started putting an exit plan together as soon as she saw the first hurricane warnings."

"The sheriff said that with the storm surge and the winds, he thinks it's unlikely her body will ever turn up. But the fact that they found the golf cart, parked there near the wildlife sanctuary, by Pirate's Point, with her fingerprints all over the steering wheel, leaves very little doubt, in his mind, anyway."

"It would be nice to have some closure," Riley said, "at least for Maggy's sake."

"Will you ever tell her that Roo confessed to killing Wendell?"

"I think she's already guessed," Riley said. "And maybe she's forgiven Roo. She doesn't talk about her dad as much, but she's still grieving. I think being here on the island, where she feels close to both of them, helps a little."

"Annie's loved having Maggy around the Mercantile after school this week," Nate said.

"Your mom is a doll to step in and help out with Maggy," Riley said.

"She's been dropping pretty big hints that this could be her only shot at having a grandchild," Nate said.

Riley smiled and looked away, and then back at him. "You said you'd give me a year, remember?"

"When did I say that?"

"Last month. Right after the hurricane when I called to ask for a do-over. You said you'd give me a year to be single before pressing me for an answer."

"But it was retroactive to May, right? From when you technically became single."

Riley nodded. "Okay, May. I'll give you my answer then."

"And then we wait a decent interval to get married. I'm thinking at least a day," Nate said.

"Some people would say it's pretty presumptuous of you to think you know what my answer will be," Riley warned.

"A lot of people would say that," Nate agreed. "A lot of people would say you're way out of my class. I know Evelyn would."

"She's coming around to the idea of us, I think. The fact that Maggy changed her mind has a lot to do with that."

"But she's never going to feel about me the way she felt about Wendell," Nate said matter-of-factly.

"It's so complicated with Mama. She's always believed my daddy was infallible—if he picked Wendell for his only daughter, then Wendell was the one. Even when she was presented with the truth of who he really was, she was still in denial. And then there's the fact that you're now the majority owner of most of the available real estate on the island her family developed. That's still a hard fact for her to swallow. Even when I point out that it was all Wendell's doing, she still can't quite accept it."

"She's never forgiven me for that deb-ball fiasco," Nate said ruefully. "Hell, I can't forgive myself. It was the absolute low point of my college career."

"I've been meaning to ask. Not that it matters anymore, but why did you get so drunk that night?"

"I was pre-gaming with my frat brothers, and the more I thought about facing your mother, and all her fancy country club friends, the more intimidated I got, and the drunker I got," Nate said.

"What's important is that I've forgiven you," Riley said. For the first time since they'd left the ferry dock, she looked around at the passing landscape. They'd already passed the village and the road that led to her cottage. "Hey, where are you taking me? Much as I'd love to indulge in a little afternoon delight with you at your cabin, I really do need to pick Maggy up at the Mercantile and take her home. We've got some catching up to do."

"She's fine," Nate assured Riley. "I stopped by to check up on her. She was helping Annie decorate cookies for the full-moon party. She got a ninety-six on her geography test, and she wanted to know if Kristin can spend the night tonight."

"You still haven't told me where you're taking me," Riley said. "Bluff Road? We're going to Shutters? Mama wanted me to take some pictures of the progress on the porch repairs."

"Maybe later," Nate said. He drove past the drive to her family's home, and in another quarter mile, turned down a similar driveway.

The house was the same vintage as Shutters, 1920s, and it was cedar shingle, with wide porches and a spacious green lawn with spreading oaks, but it was not nearly as big or grand as the other house. A FOR SALE sign was stuck in the grass, near a live oak with a rope-hung swinging bench.

Riley got out of the cart and walked up to the sign. "You're thinking of buying it? I've always loved this house. In fact, I tried to talk Wendell into buying it years ago. He thought it was old and ugly, with drafty windows, and he really hated the fact that there was only one shower in the whole house. Not exactly the statement he thought appropriate for the president of Belle Isle Enterprises."

Nate reached into his pocket and pulled out what looked like a bumper sticker. He peeled off the backing and slapped it on the sign. SOLD.

"I happen to think this house makes the perfect statement for the president of Belle Isle Enterprises," he said.

"You bought this? You bought me a house?" Riley stared at him in disbelief.

"I was thinking it could be a wedding gift," Nate said. "You know, like this coming May."

He reached into his other pocket and held out a blue velvet ring box. She opened the box and sighed. It was a slender white-gold band with a circlet of sparkling diamond stones. There was no beginning to this circle, and no end. No giant solitaires; no engraved, empty promises. It was perfect. She slid it on the naked ring finger of her left hand and held it out for him to admire. Nate took the hand she offered and kissed it.

"So? What do you think?"

"I think we might need to move up the date a little," she admitted. "I don't know if I can wait until May."

1. Did you have any guesses as to who killed Wendell? Did they change as you continued reading? Were you surprised when the truth was revealed?
2. Belle Isle represents many things to the different people who go there: home, vacation, the feeling of summer and all that goes along with it. Do you have a place like Belle Isle in your life?
3. On page 131, Parrish refuses to help Riley search Wendell's office for his business papers, but she comes through for Riley in the end. Did you agree with Parrish's decision? How far would you go to help your best friend?
4. On page 143, after Nate finds Maggy out on a boat and gives her a ride home, he says to Riley, "Maybe she needs to have a responsible parent monitor her behavior." How did you react to their argument? Did you think Nate was out of line, or did you agree with him?
5. On page 187, we see Annie Milas ask Nate if he's told Riley yet, and he responds that every time he tries to something comes up. What secret did you think Nate was keeping from Riley? What was your opinion when his plans for the island were revealed?
6. What was your response when Evelyn told Riley that she shouldn't be dating "out of respect for Wendell" and that Nate Milas wasn't "suitable" for her?
7. What did you think of Riley's decision to stop seeing Nate after Maggy ended up in the hospital? What would you have done in Riley's position?

St. Martin's Griffin

8. As readers we watch different family dynamics play out among the characters on Belle Isle. How is Nate's dynamic with his mother different from or similar to Riley's and Billy's dynamics with Evelyn?

9. Many secrets held by different characters are revealed as the story unfolds. Which secrets were you most surprised by? Were there any that you suspected before they were revealed?

10. What do you imagine the future to hold for Riley, Nate, and Belle Isle? What about for Billy, Scott, Evelyn, and Maggy?